Fall down seven times, get up eight
—Japanese Proverb

To all those who get knocked down and who get up
and keep fighting, even when it's hard.
We all have our personal demons, and I remain in awe
of all of us who take what life dishes out
and find a way to keep going.

ARCTIC SUN

———

Annabeth Albert

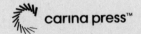

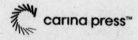 carina press™

Recycling programs
for this product may
not exist in your area.

ISBN-13: 978-1-335-00688-2

Arctic Sun

Copyright © 2019 by Annabeth Albert

www.CarinaPress.com

Printed in U.S.A.

Author's Note

This book deals with some difficult subjects, including sobriety and eating disorders. My heart goes out to all those dealing with their own issues around these topics, whether your own or someone you love. If you need help, samhsa.gov is a good resource as is SAMHSA's National Helpline, also known as the Treatment Referral Routing Service: 1-800-662-HELP (4357), or TTY, 1-800-487-4889. For individuals and family members facing mental and/or substance use disorders, this is a government-run, confidential, free, 24-hour-a-day, 365-day-a-year information service, in English and Spanish. AA also has resources worldwide: aa.org. For eating disorder help, the National Eating Disorders Association is one of several nonprofits doing good work: nationaleatingdisorders.org or helpline at 1-800-931-2237. And they also have text/chat-based help, as well.

In my location research, I tried hard to be as accurate as possible with Alaska-set details in particular. However, minor liberties were taken for the sake of story arc, and any liberties or inaccuracies are entirely my own. If you're inspired by this series and want to take a journey of your own, there are several tourism companies like the one Griffin's family operates, and I'm so grateful to them for sharing their wisdom. Our national and state parks, especially in this region, are true treasures. Finally, I appreciate all our veterans so much, especially those who candidly shared their stories and struggles while I researched details surrounding Griffin's status as an air force vet.

ARCTIC SUN

Chapter One

"You need me to do *what?*" Griffin gave a slow blink. He wasn't used to feeling about as off-kilter as a broken tailwheel, but something about his mother's tone had him bracing for a rough landing. No way was her appearance at the hangar a good thing.

"You're our best hope, Griff." His mother leaned against an out-of-commission de Havilland plane that had seen better decades. Worry lines creased her usually smooth face and made her look older, more fragile.

"You sound like a bad action movie," he chided, if only to make her smile.

"I'm serious. The doctors say no way can Uncle Roger make this trip. His knee surgery is scheduled for Tuesday in Anchorage, and they don't want him to make the injury worse by delaying. I'd do the trip myself, but this is our busiest time of year…"

"And you're needed here. I get it." He could already see where this was going. His mother ran the business side of his family's tourism and transport company, and while a capable pilot and driver in her own right, she was way more comfortable with her account software and customer service lines. "But what about Toby? He would *love* this opportunity."

He put far more enthusiasm than usual into his voice. Their freewheeling pilot and guide was incredibly popular with everyone other than Griffin, who simply didn't trust happy people. However, he wasn't lying. Toby would love the chance to spend the next ten days ferrying tourists around to the national parks, helping them find great vistas to photograph and ensuring they got their money's worth.

"Toby's already booked." His mother flipped her long, silver-flecked braid impatiently. "Trust me, I checked with him first. And I thought we had Clancy to cover, but his wife's due in two weeks, and he decided today that he's not willing to risk missing it. I knew you'd say no."

"I'm not saying no." He wasn't saying *yes* either, but he didn't add that. They both knew that unlike Toby, who was apparently in high demand, Griffin was only booked for some local transports and cargo runs in the next week. He seldom needed to deal with the tourists, and that was exactly how he liked it. He'd been planning to spend a lot of quality time with this Cessna engine he was tinkering with, but he could already see those plans slipping away like rocks into Tustumena Lake. "But why not reschedule the tour? They're coming to see Uncle Roger after all."

His uncle was a celebrated wildlife photographer whose personal tours were exceptionally popular among the eco-tourism crowd willing to pay top dollar to spend time trekking around the backcountry with him. At least Toby would have been charming enough to make up for his uncle's absence. And even Clancy, another of their pilots, was more personable than Griffin, who had zero desire to entertain outsiders, no matter how well-paying.

"You sell yourself short." His mother shook her head. "You're a fine photographer, excellent guide, and this group is mainly newbies—they'll be happy for any assistance. We were able to reschedule four of the participants who'd rather wait for Uncle Roger, but that leaves five still coming. It's *today*. We can't afford to issue refunds and deal with their ill will at being canceled at the last second."

"Of course not." He wiped his hands on a rag. That last bit was a low blow. Griffin knew exactly why funds were tight for his mother and the business. And while she steadfastly refused his efforts to repay her, no way was he going to make matters worse for her by leaving her with a new set of debts.

"It's over ten thousand a head. And Roger said to tell you that he'll give you his entire cut from it. That should make a nice dent in the cabin fund, right?" She smiled encouragingly. Because, of course, not only would the confounding woman not take Griffin's money, she was also cheering on his plans to buy himself a little land of his own.

Ever since he'd returned to Alaska, he'd set the goal of having a place of his own. Not that he minded so much living at home in the small cabin his grandparents had once occupied, but after his stint in the military, he really valued his alone time and privacy. And she wasn't wrong—Roger's cut would go a long way to supplementing his down payment fund.

"Guess I better start packing." He sighed because he'd known this was going to be the outcome from the moment she'd walked in and made the request. One simply did not say no to Annie Barrett. "Is this one of those friend groups or a family at least?"

Those were always easier—a group of people who already knew each other and didn't require Griffin to break the ice. Hell, he could barely pull off his own socializing, let alone be facilitating it for others.

"Uh. No." His mother scratched her temple, and dread gathered in the pit of his stomach. Whatever was coming next, he wasn't going to like it. "Two married couples, not friends. One couple's from Europe. Netherlands, I think. And then there's the supermodel." She mumbled the last bit, and Griffin had to strain to hear her.

"Supermodel? Really?" Oh, Jesus, the last thing he needed was some simpering miss in high heels scared of bears and missing the big city nightlife. "I thought those girls usually travel in packs. What's she doing traveling alone?"

"He," his mother corrected. "Male supermodel. That guy, you know, who wrote the book? *Professional Nomad*? They're making a movie of it. He's a sensation."

"I just bet he is." This got worse and worse. A male supermodel might not wear high heels, but he still wouldn't be prepared for the elements or for roughing it, of that Griffin was sure. And he had only a vague recollection of the book—probably caught mention of it on one of the talk shows his sisters liked—but he already knew he wasn't going to like its author. Those woo-woo spiritual finding-yourself memoirs did absolutely nothing for Griffin. He'd found himself alright. Right here where he'd always belonged. He didn't need some grand rich boy quest to show him what he'd always known—that this, right here, was his place in the world.

"Be nice." His mother touched his arm, her touch gentle but firm. "He's paying. I'm sure he's very…*interesting* at least."

"I said I'd do it. But I don't have to like it." Griffin resisted the urge to shake off her touch. She meant well, and he loved her, but no way was he enjoying this supermodel's company. "How long till we head to Anchorage?"

"Three hours. Uncle Roger is going to come—that way he can meet the guests, introduce you, and then stay on in Anchorage for the surgery. I've booked you both rooms."

"You were that sure I'd say yes, weren't you?" He looked around, made sure he wasn't leaving things too much a mess. This engine would just have to wait.

"Maybe." A little smile teased at the corners of her mouth. She looked younger again and rather self-satisfied to boot. "Might have already laid out a bag for you on my couch too."

"*Mom.*"

"And don't forget your walking stick—last thing we need is you too getting injured out there."

"I'll grab it." No sense in arguing with her when he knew perfectly well that his bum foot would need the cane at some point in the next ten days. Ten. Freaking. Days. Good Lord, what had he gotten himself into?

He was still wondering that a few hours later when he made his way into the lobby of the downtown Anchorage hotel where they often met tourist groups. The flight in from their tiny town on the Kenai Peninsula had been an uneventful forty-five minutes—he did the

flight so often, he was pretty sure that he could land
at Lake Hood Seaplane Base blindfolded. He'd spent
the flight quizzing his uncle about the trip details. His
mother had printed off ample documentation for him,
and this was hardly Griffin's first roundup with tourists, but it never hurt to be prepared. They'd picked up
the rental van that Griffin would be using for much
of the trip and then narrowly made it to the hotel in
time to meet the customers. Oh, his mom called them
guests, but really, it helped Griffin to think of them as
what they were—big dollar signs that could make the
difference for him and the rest of his family.

The company liked using this modern, high-rise
hotel to start and end trips because customers always
seemed surprised to find such luxury in Alaska, and
it made a nice contrast to the more spartan accommodations that would follow. The huge multistory atrium
lobby was tastefully appointed in greens and browns
and was about as far from Griff's vision of a perfect
little cabin in the middle of nowhere as one could get.
All the high ceilings and metal artwork made his eye
twitch.

A concierge who knew Uncle Roger on sight from
all their repeat business helped them to set up a welcome table with a sign with their company logo. Almost immediately two middle-aged women came over
to check in, and in Dutch accents, they fussed over
Uncle Roger's crutches and his injury. Griffin immediately gathered that they were a couple—the matching
red sweaters were his first clue as were their hyphen-
ated last names. But his attention was quickly diverted
by a...*creature* unfolding itself from one of the over-
sized leather chairs in the middle of the lobby.

It took a moment before he placed the gender as most likely male, distracted as he was by a pair of the longest legs he'd ever seen encased in dark purple, skintight jeans. Bright blue hair topped a surprisingly angelic and youthful face, with an equally unexpected square jaw with the barest hint of stubble. A leather jacket that probably cost more than the engine Griffin had been working on earlier topped a T-shirt that advertised some band that he'd never heard of. *Please, don't let this be...*

Griffin didn't even get the prayer out before the elegant person sauntered toward their table.

"River Vale," a melodic voice announced. Hint of New York to it, with just enough of the sort of lilt that always did something to Griffin's insides. He wasn't sure why he'd always been so attracted to musical voices, and this was an incredibly bad time for the libido he'd put in deep freeze to remind him about what he liked. His turn-ons were irrelevant here—he needed to be focusing on how completely unsuited for their ten-day trek this River person was.

Designer clothes. Thin frame. Delicate leather shoes better suited for a night of clubbing than any outdoor activity. High maintenance hair. Rich, floral smelling aftershave. Pants so tight Griffin seriously worried about circulation on a long van ride. Everything about River screamed trouble, the sort of trouble Griffin absolutely did not need.

The mountain man scowled at River. The older guy next to him was the one splashed all over the website—well-known photographer Roger Barrett—with the sort of craggy features that suggested a long life lived in the sun. *He* smiled at River, shaking his hand, and telling him what a fan his sister-in-law and nieces were of his book. But it wasn't the old guy who held River's attention at all. No, that was all reserved for Mr. Tall, Dark, and Cranky, who clearly didn't share Roger's good opinion of River, but good heavens, the man certainly made all those rumors about mountains and fresh air resulting in larger-than-average humans seem true.

He totally looked the mountain man part too—shaggy brown hair, the sort of tan that River's friends would pay good money to emulate, hazel eyes that reminded River of the greenish brown stone of a mosque he'd visited in Istanbul. And muscles for *days*. Big, broad shoulders stretching the fabric of a denim shirt, thighs like tree trunks, and that scowl. This was a guy who would be at home playing the sheriff in some old west drama. Or maybe a gunslinger...

"Yes?"

It took River a second to realize that Roger had asked him a question while he'd been busy riding off into the sunset with Sheriff Cranky. Probably he'd asked more than once, judging by the deepening of the lines around his eyes.

"Um. Sorry. Jet lag." River gave a wave of his hand, but neither of the men smiled.

"I asked if you'd eaten. Typically, the group dines together here at the hotel restaurant. A chance to get to know each other before departing in the morning."

"Food sounds good," River lied. The alarm on his phone earlier had said it was time to eat, so he would, and the group setting would be nice. He always loved getting to know new people.

"Excellent. My nephew Griffin Barrett here has some waivers for you to sign before we get started."

Griffin. The name totally suited the man, all masculine and larger-than-life and a little rough around the edges… And there River went into fanciful territory again. He'd been in Milan most recently and wasn't kidding on the jet lag—he'd been traveling over twenty-four hours now with only some catnaps on the flights. He knew the tour website recommended coming a few days early to acclimate to the time change, but River had had to make an appearance at a friend's fashion collection unveiling in Milan and hadn't had that kind of time to spare.

But Griffin's glare made him wish he'd complied with the recommendation—both so that he had the mental capacity to deal with the paperwork and because this was the sort of guy one did not like to disappoint. He dealt with the paperwork quickly—he'd been on enough tours to guess at the wording. Risk of death, not responsible, blah blah blah. River's corporate lawyer father would shudder at the speed with which River signed all liability away, but his father wasn't here to glower at River.

No, that privilege was all Griffin's, who managed to make River feel like an annoying bug. Which was weird because usually people *loved* River. He got along with everyone. It was a huge part of what made his travels so successful—he knew how to make friends just about anywhere.

"Tell me you brought better shoes than those." Even Griffin's voice was hypermasculine, all rich and deep with the sort of slowness and deliberate pauses that River associated with western states.

"I brought suitable clothes." River narrowly avoided rolling his eyes at the guy. This might be his first time to Alaska, but he'd survived traveling all over the globe. A little tundra wasn't about to do him in. "I just like to look glam when flying. Better service, you know?"

Griffin's raised eyebrow said that he most certainly did *not* know, and River had to sigh. Mountain Man had probably never been upgraded to first class before. Although one look at those thighs, and River would have moved him to the head of the line pronto.

Another couple joined the women from the Netherlands, who had been at the table when River walked up. The man and woman were both doctors from Kansas City celebrating their retirements. They were the sort of earnest, overeager Americans that River had met all over the world, the sort you could spot as tourists a mile away, but whose niceness made up for the embarrassing gaffes. They had to get a picture with Roger and hear all about his upcoming surgery as the group slowly made their way from the welcome table to the hotel restaurant.

River had received the emails about Roger's fall and the tour company's subsequent efforts to find a replacement guide. They'd offered to put him on a different tour, but River was under something of a time crunch. He needed his North American outdoor adventures done so he could write those chapters before the whirlwind of movie release activities in the fall. Because so much of his first book focused on Middle East and Asian travel, his publisher wanted the follow-up to focus more on this hemisphere, on finding himself closer to home this time.

Which was a little hysterical as River didn't have

a home, didn't want a home, and wasn't going to get a home. He had a small storage unit for off-season clothes, valuables at his dad's place, and an endless string of friends to crash with when he got lonely. But he trusted his editor about what would sell—and the movie rights for this book had already sold at auction, so he darn well better finish the thing. Besides all his social media followers were expecting pictures of bears and such. He wasn't going to disappoint. And if this Griffin was the replacement guide, then he was *far* from disappointed as at least he could guarantee quality scenery even if it rained every day of their tour.

It would be easier, of course, if Griffin didn't seem so determined to dislike River.

"Is that all you're eating?" Griffin looked at River's tomato soup with the sort of disapproval River usually reserved for a stain on a T-shirt. He'd ended up next to River, and River hadn't missed his look of distaste when he'd taken his seat.

"Yup." He'd learned a long time ago to not make apologies for what he ate. Besides soup was great after flying—hot, hydrating, and filling. Didn't matter if Griffin and the rest of the table were chowing down on steak and burgers and various forms of potatoes. A few years ago, the proximity to all those carbs would have ruined whatever appetite he'd managed to summon for the soup. But now, it was just a minor irritation, one easily ignored, right along with Griffin's ire.

"Are you vegan? My mom's paperwork didn't specify any dietary restrictions." Griffin kept right on frowning at River.

"I don't have any dietary restrictions." It wasn't *technically* a lie. In the movie, his character was a

major foodie, which River found ironic in the worst
sort of way. No one traveled as much as he did without sampling the local cuisine, but it wasn't something
that came easily to him, that was for sure. Food was
calories and occasionally nice Instagram fodder, but
celebrating it was hardly River's idea of fun.

"Good." Griffin nodded, then lowered his voice.
"Listen, my mom offered you a reschedule, right?"

"Yup. Not taking it. I need this trip." River could be
every bit as firm as Mountain Man if he wanted to be.

"You need to be prepared for very rustic accommodations—"

"I have literally been to Siberia. And Tibet. And a
bunch of places you've probably never heard of." River
wasn't usually that snappy, but the jet lag was messing
with his head. "I've camped. I've sweated. I've hiked.
Bring. It. On."

"If you're sure." Griffin didn't so much as flinch
from River's bad mood. "I just don't want you hurt.
Or disappointed."

That last bit would almost have been sweet, had
Griffin not looked like ten days with River might be
worse than being sat on by an elephant.

"I won't be." And because he really didn't want to
be antagonistic the whole trip, he added a smile. The
sort of smile that usually got people on his side, joking and making friends. But all it did was make Griffin look away fast.

Hell. It was going to be a *long* ten days. Even with
the Griffin eye candy and the prospect of natural wonders, River was already counting down the hours until
his next adventure.

Chapter Two

Griffin was not going to be done in by a simple smile. He just wasn't. He was thirty-six years old, not sixteen. And it didn't matter that River's floodlight-bright grin revealed gleaming white teeth and two shallow dimples on either side of a full, lush mouth that had to be a big part of what had made him such a hit modeling. Griffin looked away because he wasn't going to get pulled under River's spell. He had a job to do, and he was going to do it, but he wasn't going to make the mistake of liking it.

"Let's get to know each other." His uncle's voice echoed from the other end of the table. Griffin suppressed a groan. He'd known icebreakers were a part of the evening's agenda, and he got why, but as with River's smile, he didn't have to like it. But he nodded as his uncle tapped his water glass to get the attention of the Dutch women, who were deep in conversation. "How about a friendly game of three truths and a lie?"

"Oh, how fun!" The female doctor, who was named Melanie, patted her husband on the arm. She'd apparently been a pediatrician while her husband was a urologist. Griffin had already picked up on enough of their life story because the chatty Melanie couldn't seem to help herself from spilling.

"Good, good." Uncle Roger rubbed his hands together. "How about you start us off?"

"Let me see..." Melanie licked her pale lips. Griffin supposed he needed to be thinking of his own set of answers, but he was too busy imagining what outrageous things River might be about to share when it was his turn. Finally, Melanie smiled. "I've got four children, I hate corn, I've spoken in front of the state legislature, and I just bought my first camera in fifteen years."

"Hmm." One of the Dutch women was first to speak. "The lie is the camera, yes?"

"Nope." Melanie grinned. "New life, new things to try, right?" She looked specifically at River. "Isn't that what you say in the book, Mr. Vale?"

Great. River had *fans*. Griffin held back a sigh.

"River, please." River's laugh was just as melodic as his voice. "And yes, we can all use a reboot. Go you, trying something new. DSLR camera?"

"Yes. A Nikon." Melanie smiled proudly. "Who else has a guess?"

"You don't have four kids." River winked at her. "No way. Not enough worry lines and you haven't shown me grandkid pictures yet."

Oh, he *was* a charmer, and Griffin needed to remember that his easy smiles were probably honed over a decade or more in front of the camera.

"You're right. I've got three. And here's our first grandson." Melanie produced a picture on her phone that the whole table oohed and aahed over. "Now how about our mysterious replacement guide?"

Griffin had hoped to have more lead time, and he shot his uncle a pointed look, but all Uncle Roger did was give him an encouraging smile, not unlike the one his mother had given him earlier. The two of them really were too similar. And too good at dragging Griffin into things.

He took a deep breath as he thought fast. *Keep it light.* These people weren't paying to know any deep truths about him. "I love moose meat, I love haircuts, I found out a few hours ago I'd be traveling with all of you." That got a laugh, as he'd expected it to, and hopefully it also served to lower expectations. "And I served in the air force."

The air force bit got a few murmurs from the table, the sort of thanks for his service that Griffin never knew how to deal with. Melanie's husband, Dan, apparently had a brother in the service, so he guessed that that one was a truth. Then, the other Dutch woman whose name Griffin really needed to learn, made her guess, looking him over critically.

"You do not love the haircuts," she proclaimed.

"You got me." Griffin gave what he hoped passed for a smile. "Someone else's turn?"

"I'll go." River offered another of those supernova smiles. "I've ridden an elephant, I once had to wear a live cactus on my head, I've got six piercings, and I love my unicorn tattoo."

"No way on the tattoo," Griffin growled, forgetting to let one of the customers go first. "Pretty sure that's not allowed in modeling, right?"

"I'm a rebel." River waggled his eyebrows at him. Judging by their shade, his natural hair color was brown, a bit lighter than Griffin's own hair, in keeping with River's pale coloring.

"Live cactus?" Dan snorted. "That sounds painful."

"It was." River gave another of those musical laughs.

"Then it must be the piercings. I remember the elephant riding from your book." Melanie beamed at River like a kid expecting a good grade.

"Yup. Only got four." River looked right at Griffin as he delivered this bit of news. Griffin tightened his jaw. Now he was going to wonder about the location of those piercings and that tattoo all night, and he had a feeling that might have been River's goal. His ears were the obvious choice for two piercings, but where else? Nipples? Tongue? He did *not* need to let his thoughts wander down this path.

But his mind ignored him, continuing to mull over River's revelations as the game passed to the first Dutch woman, whose name turned out to be Fenna and her wife was Lieke. Fenna was a fan of knitting, speed skating, and disliked flying, while Lieke liked sketching, had brought watercolors, and was allergic to cats. Griffin laughed at the right intervals as they took their turns. Meanwhile, he tried not to think too much about where exactly one got a unicorn tattoo and *why*. Had to mean he was bi, right? And if so, was he trying to make sure Griffin knew that fact?

God, he was going to drive himself crazy with all this wondering when none of it mattered—wasn't like he needed to know which way River swung and wasn't like Griffin was going to attempt flirting with him to find out. Toby, he was not. He wasn't a total monk, but he made a point of never picking up customers.

Melanie's husband had no tattoos, loved steak, and

had a namesake in his grandson. Yet another baby picture was produced, and Griffin made the appropriate noises even though most little kids looked identical to him.

Uncle Roger called for a toast and wished them all well on the journey and then stuck around for any questions the group might have for him. Griffin could see him fading fast—the subtle grimace to his mouth and the way he kept shifting his weight in his chair—so he stayed close as the dinner party broke up. Melanie had all sorts of questions for Uncle Roger about her brand-new camera, because of course she did.

The Dutch women were more concerned about the fifty-pound weight limit on luggage and how warmly to dress in the morning, easy questions Griffin could handle.

"It's July. This is our warmest season, but we still shouldn't see temperatures above seventy on the coastal parts of our trip." He did some fast math in his head for them. "That's probably around twenty Celsius. It'll be warmer farther inland, but cooler at night in the mountains."

"And you are a good driver?" Fenna's eyes narrowed. Probably a decade or two older than him, she was tall with striking Nordic features and severely cut blond hair.

"I've driven Alaskan roads since I got my license twenty years ago," Griffin reassured her. "In all sorts of weather and road conditions. I'm not worried."

"I wouldn't send him if I didn't think he was up to the task." Finished with Melanie, Uncle Roger turned to clap him on the shoulder. He wished he shared his uncle's certainty. And it wasn't the drive that worried him. It was all the interaction necessary to make this thing a success—he simply wasn't that good with people, and a certain blue-haired whirlwind was throwing him off his limited game.

Said whirlwind was holding court with Lieke and Melanie, who'd moved from camera questions to fawning over River, asking him about Oprah and Ellen and other celebrities. Predictably, River had phone pics and a seemingly endless supply of stories.

"Think we can make our escape?" his uncle asked in a low whisper. The tension in his voice indicated he was hurting, and Griffin hated himself a little for being so relieved at having an excuse.

"Sure. You want me to see if the front desk has a wheelchair?" He eyed how heavily Uncle Roger was leaning on his crutches, mentally calculating whether having him lean on Griffin might be a better option.

"No, no. We'll just go slow." His uncle gave him a pained smile

Griffin reminded the group that he'd see them at breakfast for an early departure, and then led his uncle to the bank of elevators in the lobby. Uncle Roger settled himself on a convenient bench to wait, and Griffin let himself really look at the man for the first time in a long time. When had his hair gone completely silver? His shoulders so stooped? The brackets around his eyes and mouth so deep? Had he aged so much while Griffin was gone with the military? Or was it more recent, the effects of a particularly hard winter plagued with knee issues culminating in the most recent fall?

In his mind, his mother and Uncle Roger were still in their forties, trapped in his memories as the vibrant adults his younger self had looked up to. It was more than a little startling to realize that they were both past sixty-five now, and now *he* was the adult, the one helping Uncle Roger to bed. He fussed over him, getting ice from the machine for a makeshift ice pack, and settling him back against the pillows, making sure he had the remote for watching one of his favorite crime dramas.

As if he could sense the direction of Griffin's thoughts, Uncle Roger grabbed his hand. "You know, I can't keep doing this forever."

"What do you mean?" Griffin knew only too well when playing dumb was the best option.

"Gonna need you for more than cargo flights. This will be good for you, get you out with the guests. If it goes well, maybe—"

"How about we get through this one first?" Griffin kept his voice light. "You might not want me doing more tours if I get awful reviews."

"Don't joke. The family needs you." His uncle seemed determined to be serious. "It's time you took more of a role in the business. Can't spend the rest of your days on the fringes of life."

Watch me. Griffin shrugged.

"I mean it, Griff. You've got too much talent to waste, and this business is my legacy to you."

"Don't be dramatic. You're going to come through surgery good as new." Griffin's voice came out too thick. "You've got a lot more years taking one week wonders out in you. It's you they come to see."

"Could be you. If you ever let me show your work—"

"Not this again." Griffin shut down this line of attack with a firm look. He knew his uncle was hurting but this was an old argument, one he wasn't going to revisit. "Listen, I'll do you this favor, but that's it. We'll see afterward what you and Mom need. Holly can help her more in the office, and I'll get on Toby and Clancy to take more of your burden."

He was deflecting, but really, he wasn't ready to take on the family business, and his uncle should know that better than just about anyone. Why he thought he could trust Griffin when Griffin couldn't even trust himself was beyond him. No, Griffin knew what he was, knew his limitations, and knew his uncle was wrong on all fronts. He just needed to get through this trip, then he could get back to his plans. The last thing he needed was this guilt trip and pressure. Getting through the next ten days was going to be hard enough without the future of the business hanging over him.

River liked watching Griffin walk away with his uncle—not only was the rear view spectacular, but also seeing the surprisingly tender side to the big man did something squishy to River's insides. It made it hard to concentrate on the women's questions and underscored how exhausted he really was.

As soon as he escaped the group, River headed up to his room. He'd taught himself to sleep just about anywhere, but he never stayed asleep long, unless he'd been up a few days first. And after a week with limited sleep and now going on thirty hours without more than a nap, he was more than ready for some serious pillow time. Stripping down to his briefs, he sprawled on the big bed, much too tired to take in the room's decor or even shower.

He was still recovering from Milan and all his well-meaning friends there. He'd be thirty soon, and he just couldn't keep up with these crazy hours as easily.

The old crowd didn't get him anymore anyway, didn't understand why he'd left the fashion world to travel, why he felt more at home in a yurt in Siberia than on a runway with them in Milan. They'd never get that the further away from his former reality he went, the better he felt. That was why he'd signed up for this particular tour—they had special permits to get deep into the Denali National Park and Chugach National Forest, much more remote areas than he could get to traveling solo and sticking to the public areas.

The other reason he often went for tours like this was that as much as he liked traveling alone, he liked being around other people, especially when there wasn't any obligation involved. He was still a people person, still the same River deep down—something others often seemed to lose sight of. And before he could get all emo about that, he fell asleep, dreaming about a big strapping sheriff with a bad attitude roving the suburb of New York City he'd grown up in, him trying to take a history test while getting distracted by the sheriff's...six-gun.

And so much for not sleeping long. He had to race through showering, barely remembering Griffin's commentary on appropriate footwear in time to lace up his hiking boots, which he paired with looser, older jeans and a T-shirt advertising the new perfume brand his friend Francesca was the face for. Making sure he had a hoodie accessible in case it was colder than he was expecting on the drive south toward Seward, he readied the rest of his luggage and headed down to meet the others for breakfast.

Griffin was already in the restaurant, along with the women from the Netherlands. Melanie and Dan, the doctors, were right behind River, but he focused on Griffin because he was determined to start things off on a better foot than they'd been last night. To that end, he took the open chair near Griffin, letting Melanie and Dan sit together. And remembering how Griffin had scoffed at his dinner, he ordered scrambled eggs and toast instead of the coffee he usually subsisted on until his midmorning alarm went off.

Naturally, Griffin had one of those big farmer-type platters with eggs, a slab of some sort of meat, biscuits, and potatoes. And if he noticed River's breakfast or his attire, he didn't show it.

"No Roger this morning?" River asked, keeping his voice bright.

"Too stiff to make it down." Griffin's forehead creased. "I hate leaving him like this. His surgery's Tuesday, but I'm having Mom come in today to keep an eye on him, make sure he eats and takes his pain pills."

"That's too bad. He seems like a great guy." River turned a sympathetic eye toward Griffin while waiting for his own food to arrive. "I see why you'd be worried. You guys close?"

Griffin shrugged. "He pretty much raised us along with my mom after my dad died. He's the best man I know." Then, almost like he regretted sharing something so personal, his face shuttered, and he changed topics, raising his voice to address the group as a whole. "Everyone excited for today? It's a Monday, so the traffic heading south shouldn't be too bad. The drive to Seward would usually take us two and a half hours, but we're going to be making plenty of stops for pictures, so make sure you've got your cameras handy. We've got nice, clear skies predicted, so we should be able to find you some impressive vistas."

"So exciting. And lunch is in Seward?" Melanie leaned forward.

River never understood people who made lunch plans while they were still waiting on breakfast. And he'd looked at the itinerary on the website, but otherwise, with tours like this, he generally preferred to be surprised. Take things as they came.

"Right. After lunch, those who choose to can explore Seward and I'll take the rest down to Lowell Point. It's probably one of my favorite drives in the state." Again, Griffin seemed sheepish to be sharing something more than just the schedule. River found his discomfort adorable. Big gruff mountain man had a mushy streak, and River wanted to see more of it.

He also wouldn't mind seeing more of the muscles Griffin displayed as he loaded the van after they were all done eating, expertly stowing luggage in the rear and roof storage compartments, turning down all offers of help.

"Usually, we've got a twelve-passenger Transit Wagon, but with only six of us, they booked us in this smaller van. Hope everyone's got space to get comfortable."

River quickly surveyed the two rows of seating and weighed the possibility of sitting between one of the couples against seeming too eager for Griffin's company.

"I'll take shotgun," he offered, trying to make it sound like more of a gesture of goodwill than a bid for Griffin's conversation.

"You're so nice." Melanie patted his arm and gave

him a grateful smile, one Griffin didn't echo as he scowled.

"Later, you will sit with us. Lieke wants to show you her sketches." Fenna had a firm voice, and River dug her and Lieke's accents. He'd had some excellent times in Amsterdam.

"Sure thing." He made sure he had his camera, his small laptop, and a water bottle before climbing into the front seat.

"There's no Wi-Fi," Griffin warned. "Can't even guarantee the lodge in Seward will have it."

"I'm prepared. Even got an emergency charger. I just like to be able to jot a few notes if the spirit moves me."

Griffin made a noncommittal sound before he started the van. And honestly, River was glad for the laptop as they navigated Anchorage traffic because Griffin did not seem inclined to talk at all. The chatter in the back of the van was hard to hear over the road noise, so River lost himself in reviewing what he'd written about Utah and biking in Moab, searching for the right turn of phrase that would get a laugh about him trying a bicycle for the first time in ten years but also inspire his readers to try it for themselves.

It wasn't far until their first stop at a day use area and scenic park just outside Anchorage. They had a gorgeous view of the Turnagain Arm of the Cook Inlet and mountains beyond with a possibility of seeing some beluga whales if they were lucky. The mountains were brown tinged with green, and reminded him more of Griffin's eyes than they should have.

They took a short walk to a wooden bridge over a fast-moving creek, and Melanie insisted on getting a group photo at the bridge. River had a feeling he'd be on her social media by bedtime, but that was okay. She and her husband were nice, and she tried hard to make sure everyone felt included, which was more than he could say for their reticent guide, who spent most of the stop silent. Maybe he forgot that he was supposed to provide some commentary for their experience.

"You ever do any of the longer trails here?" he prodded on their way back toward the van.

"Some. Been years." Griffin grimaced, and for the first time, River noticed that he walked with a hint of a limp. Hell. He hadn't meant to be insensitive with his question. Before he could apologize, Griffin turned to the group. "Everyone ready to head on to the next stop?"

At the murmurs of agreement, they headed on toward a lesser-known vantage point of the Turnagain Arm, and Griffin masterfully handled the narrow roads off the Seward Highway that led to the viewing point. River himself was a public transit kind of guy—he'd never owned a car and had no plans to change that, but he did appreciate a good driver.

"What do you drive at home? Pickup?" River was having fun imagining him on horseback, but he had a feeling pickup was more likely.

"You mean when I'm not flying?" Griffin gave him another of those not-quite-smiles that he seemed rather practiced at. "I pretty much drive what the company needs—SUV, van, truck, whatever—I've got a class-C license, so I can drive even big loads."

I just bet you can. River bit back the flirty retort. "I meant what do you personally own?"

"Older F350. Bought it off a friend's mother a few

years back." Griffin's voice had a wistfulness to it River hadn't heard yet.

"Nice." He nodded like he knew how to translate the letter and numbers into truck-speak.

Griffin parked at the viewpoint and was slightly chattier at this stop, telling them about the nearby waterfalls as they admired the vista of towering glacier-topped mountains.

"Who needs coffee?" Griffin asked, consulting his ever-present clipboard. River totally suspected that his mother or uncle had put reminders to smile and be friendly on there. "There's a nice place for a quick cup before we get back on the highway."

He took them into a tiny town with lots of touristy shops and mining memorabilia, and they all got drinks to go. The pretty young barista with a nose ring flirted rather shamelessly with all of them, but Griffin especially, who seemed to have no clue what to do with the attention. That was sort of refreshing because in River's experience, most men who looked like Griffin were accomplished charmers. Griffin got a cinnamon roll latte, and River couldn't help himself from teasing.

"You don't look like the type to drink sweet things. Figured you for a day-old-black-coffee kind of guy."

"Hey, I can be plenty sweet." Griffin sounded a little offended, which River found funny, considering how standoffish the guy seemed determined to be.

"Barista certainly thought so." River settled back into the passenger seat. "You should get her number."

Griffin's entire face shut down. "I don't date."

"Now isn't that a darn shame." River really wanted to ask a follow-up or ten, but Griffin's expression didn't invite further inquiry. But that didn't stop River from trying to lighten the mood. "Thought I saw a sign back there for Virgin Creek…"

Griffin totally didn't take the bait, didn't even crack a smile as he navigated back toward the highway. River forced himself to focus on the scenery. Hell. One would think *River* was the one belonging at Virgin Creek the way he was all twisted up over his cranky guide. And the *I don't date* comment had just made more questions buzz around in River's brain. Like did he not date ever? Or not date women and didn't want to put it like that? Or he was more of a hookup guy going between one-night stands? Or he'd taken some bizarre vow of chastity? Whatever his reasons, River dearly wanted to know them. And if there was one thing River was good at, it was finding out people's stories. Griffin didn't stand a chance.

Chapter Three

As a general rule, Griffin liked driving. In addition to the flying, he did what the company needed on a given day, such as taking a load from the plane to a customer. But it was alone in the air where he felt most comfortable, had all his life practically. Driving involved different muscles, different sorts of concentration, and different distractions. Flying, he almost never got distracted by a passenger, but as he drove the tour group to their next stop on the Seward Highway, he really had to fight to keep his mind on the road and not on the blue-haired devil next to him.

Didn't help that River seemed determined to be nice today, trying to make conversation and joking around with him, not knowing that Griffin didn't really do jokes. Never had. Even Hank had always gotten on him for being too serious, too stuck in his own head. After Griffin shut down River's attempt at discussing the flirty barista, River got absorbed in his laptop again. But the little sighs he kept giving were a hell of a distraction, and when River laughed to himself, Griffin had finally had enough.

"What?" he demanded. "What's so funny?"

"Oh sorry." A quick glance revealed a sheepish expression on River's face, a faint pink tinge on his perfect high cheekbones. "I was just rereading something I wrote about my experiences in Moab. Was remembering this cute guy…" River gave a little knowing laugh. "Anyway, you know how it is. Fond memories and all that."

Griffin wasn't sure how to respond to that. More than other people, he did know the power of memories, fond and otherwise, but he wasn't sure he wanted to go down that conversational path with River. So he stayed quiet, but apparently River misread his silence as hostility.

"Shouldn't I have mentioned the cute guy?" River's voice was light and tinkly, not accusing. "Sorry. I'm pan. It's going to creep out when I speak. I promise it's not catching."

This would be a perfect time for Griffin to say *Me too.* And then they could both laugh, and Griffin would say how he usually used bi in his own head, not pan, but that he had no issues with cute-guy talk. Except for the part where he never really talked about cute *anyone* with other people. And maybe he'd express his immense frustration at how there wasn't really an exact word that described him neatly because "obsessed with my best friend for twenty years" wasn't a sexual identity category, and maybe River would express sympathy and they would laugh some more.

Or maybe Griffin would stay silent.

Which he did, and River let out a weary sigh and dropped his voice further. "If you're homophobic, this is going to be a long week. Just saying."

"I'm not." Griffin's voice came out terser than he'd planned. At least he managed to avoid tacking on some lame-sounding *I have plenty of friends...* That would only make him sound like either a clueless idiot or a closet case. Which he wasn't. Well, maybe he was the clueless idiot part. Especially since he felt a weird pang over the missed opportunity.

Whatever. He wasn't going to beat himself up about it—he was what he was. So instead, he focused on the road ahead and his uncle's typical stop at the Alaska Wildlife Conservation Center, which was a short distance from their coffee break stop. Since so much of the next ten days were all about trying to capture wildlife on camera, Uncle Roger liked to stop in at the center, visit some old friends, and do some demonstrating of camera angles and lighting while talking about the sorts of animals they were hoping to encounter later on. It was all very chummy, designed to warm up the group, and Griffin had been along more than a time or two, so he knew the drill, but hell if he was looking forward to the delivery.

"Oh my God! It's a moose!" Melanie exclaimed before they even exited the vehicle.

"See, what you don't want to do, honey, is startle the animals." Her husband tried to settle her, and Griffin wondered if he could let them run the tour for him, just kind of trail along in their wake.

"What sort of moose are these?" Fenna turned a critical eye toward him as they made their way down the path to the enclosure with the moose.

Darn. He was going to be required to speak, wasn't he? So, in a much more halting delivery than Uncle Roger's, he explained about these particular moose and how the center helped wounded and endangered animals. He helped the overexcited Melanie get her camera shutter speed optimized for pictures of the moose, which were currently moving from a covered structure to come closer to the high wire fencing.

And he wasn't feeling half bad about his efforts until River said, "Guess a lot of kids' school groups come here, right?"

He didn't say it mean, more simply bored, but Griffin felt the diss nonetheless. River was paying big bucks to be impressed, and so far he wasn't. And that was on Griffin.

And he had to admit, he had been rather passive. He'd be frustrated with his tour guide skills too if he were River. So he forced his voice to be more cheerful and dug deep for the take-charge attitude that had come so naturally during his years in the military.

"Here's what we're going to do. I'm going to let you guys wander for fifteen minutes, and I want you to take your best shot at some animal photos. Then we're going to show them off back at the visitor center, and I'll pick the most promising one. Winner gets their choice of beverage at lunch, on me."

Meals were included in the price of the trip, but beverages were extra. It was a little risky, basically inviting the group to drink at lunch. He much preferred the remote lodge stops where there was no question of alcohol. But he liked to think he could handle forking over a few bills for someone's beer without issue. Besides, no one would expect their driver to drink. And a little friendly competition was exactly what the group needed, as evidenced by how everyone perked up, River included.

He got his laptop out of the van while the group wandered. River wasn't the only one to travel with technology, but Griffin preferred to save his gadgets for emergency purposes. Like now when he desperately needed to prove that he could handle the responsibility of the group. Snagging a table at the cheerful log-cabin-style visitor center, he set up so he was ready to display photos as the group reassembled.

The center spanned many flat acres, dotted with enclosures and small structures designed to both protect the animals and let visitors watch them. He lost sight of his group members until they reappeared at the visitor center. Each produced a memory card or cable for him to grab pictures to display. Fenna had captured an artfully framed shot of two bison in the distance, while Lieke had gone more fanciful, finding a playful-if-blurry reindeer. Melanie and Dan went for shots that attempted to show herds of animals. And River got a close-up of a grinning musk ox. The whole group burst out laughing.

"It's going on my social media as soon as we get a better signal." River didn't do humble bragging well—his twinkling pale blue eyes and puffed-up chest said he knew he had this in the bag. "Climbing the fence was—"

"You did what?" Griffin knew he sounded way too parental, but he couldn't help it. "That's exactly what I was talking about earlier—no crazy risks just to get a good shot."

"Eh. It was a calculated gamble." River gave a shrug of his elegant shoulders. "And other people were climbing too."

Griffin bit back a lecture about going along with stupid people. He had a hard time placing River's age—he looked young with that baby face, especially clean shaved like he was that morning, but seemed so worldly in certain moments before pulling crazy stunts like this.

"You're lucky most of these animals are herbivores. Don't you dare try goading bears when we're in Denali."

"Yes, *Dad.*" River rolled his eyes. "And some of us like bears."

Griffin wasn't so clueless that he missed the double meaning on *bears.* He needed control back of this conversation, fast.

"Fenna, you win. You just let me know what you want at lunch."

Fenna gave a rare smile. "I guess I could have a glass of wine. Thank you."

They headed back to the van, most of the group more cheerful than they'd been prior to Griffin's big idea, but River's stooped shoulders and heavy sighs said he was sulking. Fine. He'd just have to deal. Griffin had a dual responsibility to show him a good time but also keep him alive. Before he got in the van, River took a long drink from his water bottle, and Griffin didn't look away fast enough, instead finding himself mesmerized by the long line of River's neck. Forget the wildlife. Griffin wanted a picture of *that,* those full lips wrapped around the bottle's spout, head tipped back, eyes half shut…

Shaking his head, he forced himself to walk around to the driver's side. He could not let himself get caught up in River's spell for so many reasons including that the guy clearly wanted to court disaster. There was no sense in getting wrapped up in wanting someone who was a walking danger sign. Griffin had had enough risk and danger to last a lifetime. Wasn't going there again.

The drive to Seward turned more mountainous as they navigated two passes lush with spruce trees and made several stops for pictures, including a few side roads off the main tourist trek. River liked those best, even if the bouncier roads made typing challenging and had him putting the laptop away. The natural vistas were too good to miss anyway. And the people-watching was almost as good as the scenery. It was funny how Griffin seemed to relax more whenever he approached a favorite spot—those real, genuine moments of pleasure were fast becoming an obsession for River.

He loved how Griffin inhaled, almost like he was drinking in the stillness of a particular small lake or vista. River got more than one sneaky photo of Griffin at Upper Trail Lake, looking for all the world like a genuine mountain man with his plaid shirt rolled up past his meaty forearms, surveying his domain, mountains behind him, pristine blue-gray waters in front. A seaplane swooped in for a landing off on the distant side of the lake, and Griffin's longing was almost palpable.

It must be nice to be that in love with a place one lived, to be able to still be amazed by the scenery. River envied that sense of belonging because he'd never had it. Sure, he loved traveling, loved seeing new places, but he didn't have strong emotions for any one place, not like Griffin seemed to. He embodied Alaska in the same way that some of the monks whom River had met embodied everything he liked about Tibet.

But Griffin's ease at being outdoors quickly faded

back to his grumpy self when they finally arrived in Seward for a late lunch. The mountains had turned sharper and rockier again, skies more gray than blue, the missing sun taking with it Griffin's mood. They checked in to their accommodations—adorable tiny log cabins set near a pond, away from the main roads. He and Griffin had teeny one-room affairs that would be right at home on *Tiny House Hunters* or some such show, while the couples each got larger accommodations.

They made their way from the cabins into downtown Seward, right on the waterfront, where Griffin had reservations waiting for them at an upscale seafood place that overlooked the marina. Their waitress was somewhere between River and Griffin's ages, and like the barista, looked like she'd like to make a daily special out of Griffin. She led them to a waiting table in the back of the space, right next to a picture window. The place had a refined nautical theme—dark wood floors and chairs, gray walls, wood-paneled ceiling, pictures of ships on the walls.

For his part, Griffin seemed to go out of his way to sit at the opposite end of the oval table from River. Fenna and Lieke both ordered white wine, and Melanie got the same, to be "festive," as she put it. Dan ordered a local microbrew beer, and then when it was Griffin's turn, he took forever looking at his menu, brow as tightly knit as the sock Fenna was working on until finally he mumbled a request for a lemon-lime soda brand River hadn't had since he was a kid.

River had been thinking of joining the women in getting some wine—it would make him likely to eat more, which he supposed was a good thing, and it was the social thing to do. But Griffin's discomfort did something to River's chest, made it tight and hot and made him firmly say, "I'll have a diet soda."

Griffin gave him an unreadable expression—a toss-up between gratitude and exasperation. Well, tough. He'd just have to live with River trying to be nice. And honestly, River was as surprised at his empathy as Griffin undoubtedly was. He ordered a broiled piece of salmon and some broccoli, while several of the others and Griffin ordered a sandwich the place was apparently famous for. Crab salad, fried fish, fried onion rings, and bacon all on a buttered house-made roll with a side of steak fries. River got nauseated at the picture of it on the menu, his ever-present mental math making anxiety bubble up in his gut at the thought of how many meals' worth of calories that sandwich was.

During the wait for their food, he wasn't the only one who took advantage of the good signal to check phone messages. Francesca was having a predictable post-Milan meltdown and was already jonesing for the next big event.

I'm going to turn thirty ALONE next month. Someone give me something to DO!

Uninvited, a memory tried to take hold. Twenty-one. Alone. Mom so sick. Everyone forgetting. But using years of practice, he shut it down, even as he softened toward Francesca. She was always so sweet to him and didn't deserve to have her special day forgotten. He clicked around on his calendar app, trying to make something happen for her.

I'll be in British Columbia that week, pretty sure, he typed. Want to meet me in Vancouver? We can see who else wants to join us, find some fun.

He half expected her to turn it down as Vancouver was awesome, but no LA or NYC when it came to nightlife. However, her reply was fast. That sounds amazing!!!! We can do Davie Street!!!

Like almost all his female friends, Francesca saw him as her ticket to every gay clubbing district in the world. Which was fine. Wasn't as though River didn't like Davie Street himself or wouldn't be happy to see Francesca, keep her from being alone on her birthday.

And plans were good. He liked finding a balance between time stretching in front of him, wide open and inviting, and the reassurance of knowing where he'd be moving on to and when. Because he always moved on. This year North America. Next year...who knew? He was toying with the idea of the South Pacific. Islands sounded fun.

And maybe he had islands on the brain because Griffin had reminded them all about the boat tour tomorrow, asked if anyone needed a stop at a store for nausea meds or waterproof shoes.

"I think we might need the medication, but we were thinking we'd wander the waterfront after lunch, so we can pick up what we need before dinner." Dan patted Melanie on the knee. "We've never been on a boat before."

"It's fun," River reassured them. He gave some thought to whether he too wanted to explore Seward or continue on to Lowell Point. A break from his weird obsession with Griffin might be a good thing. But then Lieke talked Griffin into driving up into the hills before coming back for dinner.

"There is this one spot I know..." Griffin rubbed his jaw. "Might be a nice vantage point for a sketch."

A prickle raced up River's spine, strange anticipation making him want to see Griffin's secret spot.

"You will come, River?" Fenna made it sound more like a command. "Lieke will sit with you, show you her work. She's very good. Several shows in Amsterdam."

Her pride in her wife was more than a little cute and River found himself nodding. "Sure. I can come."

Griffin's jaw hardened at the news, but River pretended not to notice, and he kept things light as he settled into the middle seat next to Lieke and let Fenna take the passenger seat.

Lieke's paintings and sketches were indeed lovely, as was the coastline on the drive to Lowell Point. The gravel beaches gave way to more dense vegetation as Griffin drove up into the hills surrounding the point. As before, Griffin's tension seemed to recede the farther they got from town and he was almost gleeful when he announced, "We're going to have a short hike to get to this spot, but I promise it's worth it."

The hike took them over a long wooden bridge away from the road until River felt the familiar thrill he got when hiking away from civilization—all the obligations and expectations that rattled around his head faded until it was only him and this spot on the planet, the rush of being privileged to get to see all this abundance of beauty. Perspective. That's what his well-meaning therapist had called it. River supposed she was right, but it went deeper for him, like he finally achieved the optimal amount of oxygen for his body or like sacks of cement left his shoulders. And he almost forgot that he was not alone until he caught Griffin looking at him strangely, like River had just morphed into some species of bird.

"What?" he demanded.

"Nothing." Griffin blinked. "Just...you like hiking, don't you?"

"I guess." River really didn't feel like examining his psyche with Griffin, not when he'd turned down all River's other friendly overtures. Instead, he sped up to catch Lieke. "You need help setting up your easel?"

"You are very sweet." She arranged herself with a good view of the river, the bay, and the mountains beyond. But as she got occupied with her watercolors and Fenna retrieved her sock knitting, River found his eyes drifting back to Griffin, who'd settled himself on a log a short distance away from the three of them. Surprisingly, Griffin's attention seemed to be on them, not the view, and their gazes caught in a weird, electric moment.

He'd had this crackle of awareness before, and it never failed to give him a thrill. He felt noticed in some primal way, and he wasn't going to be the one to look away first.

I don't know what this is, but I'm not scared of it, he told Griffin with his eyes. *You don't scare me, Mountain Man.*

It was the sort of look that with someone else might lead to a breakthrough, a change toward friendship or flirting or simply more meaningful conversation. But with Griffin all it led to was Griffin frowning, a hardness coming over his features that remained all the way back down the trail, and left River with even more questions than answers.

Chapter Four

Griffin's feet dragged as he made his way from the van toward the tiny cabin that was his room for the night. After they returned from a salmon bake dinner, he'd needed to check the locks and retrieve his laptop and backpack. By the time he walked up the path, he was greeted by River's musical laugh echoing down from the fire pit, where some of the group had gathered along with a few other occupants of the rentals that surrounded the pond.

God, that laugh. The things it did to his insides. Made him slow further. Pulled him in, sure as a towrope. But going over there would be foolhardy. In addition to the laughter, the clink of beer bottles cut through the otherwise still night. Someone had brought a guitar, and the whole evening had the vibe of an impromptu party. What would happen if he went over there, took the empty Adirondack chair next to River? Let himself laugh too, joke and…

Nope. Not for him. He set his shoulders and forced himself to keep walking down the path. Too risky to go forgetting who—*what*—he was. And what he wasn't. He wasn't social, never had been without that cold bottle in his hand, easing the way, making him more talk-ative and relaxed. Funny how temptation worked—the drink ordering at the restaurant had been more awkward than truly tempting. Wine had never been his thing, but this, happy people getting happier and looser around a fire, brought back so many memories of teen parties, back when everything had been simpler and a beer had been a beer, before one became one too many became a pattern became the present where a beer was anything but simple. It wasn't so much that he craved the taste even, but more that every now and then, he missed who he'd been back then, the kind of guy who could go and have a conversation and relax around someone intriguing.

But that wasn't going to happen, not tonight. River had plenty of groupies. He didn't need Griffin. And more to the point, Griffin didn't need him. Didn't matter that there had been this *moment* while hiking, when River's face had been filled with so much joy, eyes glowing, face tipped heavenward, almost like he was having some sort of spiritual awakening. It had taken all Griffin's self-restraint not to touch him, try to capture some of that magic for himself.

Then that had been followed by the strangeness when they'd paused at the overlook. He wasn't such a hermit that he missed the clear intent in River's eyes or the energy buzzing between them. But none of that mattered. He had a job to do here, and that job most certainly did not include nighttime partying. So instead of lingering on his little porch watching the group, he did the only sensible thing and decisively turned on his heel, went inside where the bed that barely qualified as a double waited for him. The cheerful moose dancing across the red and brown quilt seemed to mock him as he flopped on the bed. Tomorrow he'd be more resolved. More in-charge. Less vulnerable to River's charm. Less adrift.

But that resolve was tested the moment he exited his cabin in the morning to find River sitting on the porch of his own tiny cabin, lacing up waterproof hiking boots.

"These okay?" River called.

"They should work." Griffin did a fast scan of the rest of River's wardrobe—jeans, sweatshirt with a narwhal on it that declared *I believe in unicorns*, and a windbreaker tied around his waist. He did look appropriate for a day on the boat tour, and if a part of Griffin missed the designer persona he'd first presented, he quashed those thoughts fast. And if the unicorn line on the T-shirt reminded him of River's tattoo, he stomped on any lingering questions about where the tat could be. Not his business.

River's quirked mouth said he might have more to say, but the rest of the group came walking up the path, and it was time for Griffin to slip back into leader mode, away from…whatever bumbling fool he turned into around River.

After making sure everyone was loaded, he navigated back to the waterfront marina from where the boat tour would depart. One of the highlights of the trip, the tour was run by a friend of Uncle Roger's, Ted Unger, who would take them farther into the Northwestern Fjord and through less-traveled routes than any of the other commercial day trips available. And unlike the big cruises, which were packed with tourists, Ted limited his trips to a max of twenty passengers on his luxury yacht.

The boat had an impressive viewing deck, and Ted's steward had already laid out a light breakfast of scones and fruit to greet them as they came aboard. The nine-hour trip would take them deep into the Kenai Fjords National Park, an area Griffin flew over when they had a load going from someplace like Homer to Seward, but he hadn't explored up close on a boat like this in well over a decade or more.

Predictably, the affable Ted greeted him like a long-lost nephew.

"Damn. You went and got old, Griffin." Ted clapped him on the back. A white captain's hat covered his bald head. He had an actual captain to pilot the boat, a young woman Griffin hadn't met before, but Ted always did like to look the part when he hosted the tours. "Guess that makes me old as the glaciers, huh?"

"Uncle Roger said to tell you hello. Says only surgery could keep him away."

"Oh, I know. And how's that pretty mother of yours?" Ted's blue eyes twinkled.

"Not bad." Griffin had had about enough small talk. "How's the weather for us today?"

"Couldn't ask for better." Ted gestured at the calm waters. The gray skies of the previous day had given way to a clear blue canopy draped over the bay as they departed Seward. Ted gave a "welcome aboard" talk while the passengers ate their food.

Griffin snagged two scones and some coffee. As usual, River wasn't eating enough to keep a sandpiper alive, what with the small plate of fruit balanced on his lap.

"Here." Griffin offered him one of his scones. "You need to eat more."

"No, I don't." The good humor he'd come to expect from River was gone, replaced by a snappish tone.

Griffin shrugged. Pissy River was actually easier to deal with than the friendly version. "Suit yourself."

He moved away from River, making sure that Lieke had all the art supplies she'd need for the journey and that the married doctors had taken their anti-nausea meds.

Eagle-eyed Fenna spotted the first whale as they made their way down the coast, and everyone rushed to take pictures. Leaning against the rail, Griffin reminded them what he'd said yesterday about shutter speed for fast-moving animals.

"Sorry I bit your head off." River left his deck chair to come stand next to Griffin, the sea breeze ruffling his hair, which almost matched the turquoise color of the water. "I'm…weird about food. Sorry."

"No problem." Despite his resolve to stay distant, Griffin was curious. "Is it a modeling thing? Thought I read that all of you are supposed to be super picky eaters."

"Something like that." River's tone was cryptic, and he looked away. Griffin had the strangest urge to find out what River did like to eat and procure it for him, wanting to see his expression if he actually enjoyed his food.

"Anything we could do different for you? I can call ahead to the Denali lodge, make sure they've got fruit for you, if that's your preferred breakfast." He told himself he'd make the offer to any customer.

"Thank you." River's angelic smile was worth any effort it cost Griffin to be nice. "That would be lovely."

Lovely. Lovely was River's ice-blue eyes and the

hint of pink on his high cheekbones. If Griffin were a poetic guy, and he most certainly was *not*, he'd write an ode to the guy's bone structure and his ability to make even the most picturesque of surroundings recede.

"No problem." Griffin tried to return his focus to the coastline, all the rocky outcroppings and tiny islands that made this area so popular. And he succeeded for a time, standing there next to River, hyperaware of his presence but not conversing. He liked that River wasn't a chatterer—he didn't automatically seek to fill the silence Griffin was so prone to, and that was nice.

"Oh, man." A look of pure pleasure crossed River's face as he pointed to a group of mini-islands. "They look almost like faces. And the trees are the hair. Big, medium, little, all lined up."

Griffin squinted. He wasn't used to such fanciful description, but he had to admit River wasn't wrong. "Cute."

"Do you get used to it, living here year-round? All the mountains and stuff, I mean?"

"Hmm." Griffin had to consider the question. "Maybe a little. Especially when I was a kid, I'm sure I took it for granted, but then I was gone...what? About twelve years with the air force. Served a good chunk of it in the Midwest. Flat as a pancake. Tried to appreciate Alaska more once I came home."

"Never thought about settling down elsewhere?"

Sort of. No way was River getting his full story, so he shook his head. "No. I always knew I'd come back here. Family needs me."

That reminded him of Uncle Roger's talk the night before they left, and his chest pinched. He wasn't doing enough for the family that had done everything for him.

Uncle Roger was right, it was time for him to step up. Maybe not by doing more of these blasted tours, but he could man up, take on more of his mother's and uncle's burdens. He'd been coasting far too long.

"Must be nice, being so close to them." River's expression was wistful enough that Griffin was going to ask a follow-up question when he heard his name being shouted.

"Griffin! Something's wrong with Dan." Melanie gestured wildly from where she and Dan were standing by the bow. Sure enough, her husband did look green around the gills and his legs were wobbling. Griffin rushed over, River right behind him. Right as they got there, Dan slumped into Melanie, pushing her against the rail and—

"Whoa." With lightning-fast reflexes, River prevented Melanie from tumbling overboard, dragging her away from the edge as Griffin caught Dan.

"Dan? Can you hear me?" Melanie called anxiously as she righted herself in River's arms.

Dan blinked slowly and grunted. He was conscious at least, and that was a very good thing.

"Can we get him to one of the deck chairs?" Griffin was prepared to haul the large man back to the seating area himself, but to his surprise, River was right there, taking Dan's other arm, and the three of them made their way to the closest chair. They got Dan settled, and Griffin knelt in front of him.

"Is it your stomach?"

"Yeah." Dan grimaced. "Head too. Dizzy. No balance."

It sounded like classic seasickness, but he wanted

to rule out anything that might necessitate a medical emergency. "No chest pain? Shortness of breath?"

"No, no." Dan waved the questions away. "Not my heart. Just...sick. And I took the medication."

"Doesn't always work." Griffin sighed.

"Here." River pulled something off his wrist. "Try this. It's an acupressure band. I use it for flying and boats both."

Dan looked at the stretchy band like River was offering witchcraft.

"It can't hurt," Melanie urged. "Try it. And can we get him some water?"

"Of course." Griffin fetched him a glass from the food table and hurried back. When he returned, River was managing to make Dan smile with some story of his first time on a boat, someplace in Turkey.

"I was so much sicker than this," River assured him. "It'll get better, I promise."

"Thanks." Dan gave him a grateful smile, touching the band on his wrist. "Hope this helps. But don't you need it?"

"I'll be fine. It was just a precaution." River's voice was airy. He really did have a gift for putting people at ease, and Griffin had to admit he was impressed by how River had helped in this situation.

"I'm going to talk to Ted. I'm sure he's got some of the wristbands too." Griffin didn't want River suffering silently, some strange protective urge driving him to search out Ted, who was on the other side of the boat, chatting with Fenna and Lieke.

Sure enough, Ted did have more wristbands, and soon everyone was outfitted. Dan seemed to be improving, and disaster averted, they headed on into the glacier field.

When River left Dan and Melanie to get a drink of his own, Griffin stopped him near the table. "Thanks. For your help, I mean."

"It was nothing." Even River's shrugs were elegant, lithe rolls of his narrow shoulders. "What? Were you expecting me to faint too?"

Actually, yes, he had. But River had busted through his expectations, leaving Griffin more than a little bit impressed. "Well…"

"I told you. I'm up to this trip." River's chin took on a defiant tilt. Hell, Griffin wished he had his certainty. His easy confidence was just so damn appealing that Griffin had taken a step forward before the surprise in River's eyes alerted him to what he'd done. Then River's eyes darkened, taking on an almost feral glint as he lowered his voice. "Up to you too."

"No one's asking you to be." Griffin managed to sound firm and commanding even though his insides were trembling from a force he really didn't want to name.

"You know, this trip could be a lot more fun for both of us…" River's voice was even more melodic than usual, sending little bolts of lust racing down Griffin's spine.

"Nope. Sorry. Don't mess with customers." Griffin clung to that principle like a piece of driftwood.

"Darn." River didn't sound the least bit put out. Or deterred, eyes still hot and mouth all soft and inviting.

"I better check on the others." Griffin finally stepped away.

"You do that." River laughed, clearly enjoying Griffin's discomfort. He tried to walk away slowly, not like River had spooked him, but wasn't sure he succeeded. When it came to River, he felt every bit as unsteady as poor Dan had been. Why couldn't there be some sort of magic bracelet for getting rid of unwanted attraction? He needed a cure and fast, because he had a strong feeling River wasn't going to give up easily.

The Kenai Fjords were everything River had hoped for—majestic, almost mythical beauty, with the sort of contrasts he loved. Sharp mountains. Smooth glaciers. Dark rocks. Blue water. Towering cliffs. Tiny birds. He had a thing for juxtaposition—it was part of what had made him a good high-fashion model. He knew when to show his sharp edges in something soft and floaty and when to go pouty in something severe. And his thing with contrasts explained his obsession with Griffin as the man was a whole glacier's worth of contradictions. Kind but gruff. Confident leader but adorably uncertain at odd moments. Distant, colder than crisp sea air, but hot, needy eyes.

River knew damn well what the look Griffin had given him meant. There was attraction there, and River was going to exploit it. He was used to getting what he wanted, and right now, what he wanted was his gruff guide, wanted to see what other contrasts Griffin might have for him to uncover. To that end, he stalked Griffin with his eyes as Griffin checked on Dan and Melanie then sought Fenna and Lieke on the opposite side of the boat. He gave a wide berth to River, going the long way around to reach the women.

Cute. River let him have the illusion of control and space, biding his time. Instead, he used the provided binoculars to watch the sea otters Ted pointed out. With his bare eyes, he saw a group of three large whales. The sun glistened overhead, making the coastline even more inviting. There was no shortage of things to hold his attention, and yet, his body seemed attuned to exactly where Griffin was at all times.

And when Griffin disappeared from the deck, River went exploring. The yacht was a luxury boat, lushly appointed for longer-term adventures than their day trip. Quilted leather couches and a stately bar dominated the main cabin. A narrow wood-paneled hallway led to a marble-appointed bath that while small had nothing in common with airline facilities. On his way back from the bath, he passed a cracked door that led to a bedroom decorated in rich reds and dark woods.

"That's Ted's personal room." Griffin appeared out of nowhere to reach around River and firmly shut the door. "Not a guest space."

"Sorry. Was just investigating the yacht." River didn't step away from Griffin, instead luxuriating in the nearness. "Does Ted live on the boat?"

"No." Griffin laughed, a deep sound that washed over River, sweet and warm like melted chocolate. "He's got places in Seward and Anchorage both. The yacht's more like a hobby for him. He mainly uses it for entertaining."

"So he doesn't make a living doing the day trips?" River tried to keep the conversation going, if only to bask in Griffin's closeness longer.

"No. Retired from the banking industry. The trips are mainly just a favor to Uncle Roger. He enjoys playing host, and they go way back. He owns a number

of Uncle Roger's prints and has hosted receptions for
him before."

"Sweet. And they're not..." He made a vague gesture with his hand, confident that Griffin would know
what he meant.

"No." Griffin's eyes sprang wide. "Why would you
think that?"

"No wedding rings. And confirmed bachelors of a
certain age... Not implying anything. Just curious."

"Well, not the case here. Roger's dated some over
the years, just never settled down. And Ted's widowed.
If anything, Ted's got a thing for my mom. Always
flirting with her, but she's oblivious, I think."

"Sweet." It hadn't escaped River's notice that Griffin hadn't moved away, and if anything, seemed to have
relaxed against the wall. "And you?"

"And me, what?"

"Bachelor? Ever married? Got someone back
home?"

Griffin's face hardened. "Never married. Told you.
I don't date."

"I heard." River kept his voice light. "I just want
to know why. I won't blab, I promise. You not out?"

He was taking a chance, but he hadn't been imagining those looks. There was *something* there. And Griffin's weighty sigh confirmed it, even before he spoke.
"It's not like that..."

"And how is it?" River wasn't letting this go.

"I hooked up some when I was in the military. And
after. But it was...complicated. And I'm not closeted.
Not about to lead a parade..." His eyes dipped to River's sweatshirt, and he gave a little shake of his head.
River smiled. He did love his unicorn references. "But

my mom and uncle know I've dated different genders. Beyond that, it's not really anyone's business unless I'm looking for action. Which I am not."

"So you say." River stretched out his hand, trailing a finger down Griffin's shirt. "And yet, you told me. This doesn't have to be one of those complications. I'm not asking you to wave a flag or ride a float. Just to have a little fun."

"I don't do fun." Griffin's face was still stony, but there was a hunger in his eyes that hadn't been there a few moments ago.

"I do." River closed the narrow gap between them. Despite Griffin's breadth, the height difference wasn't that much, and River didn't have to stretch far to bring his face level with Griffin's. "Come on. What's the harm?"

"Plenty." Instead of leaning in as River had hoped, Griffin pushed him away, right as footsteps sounded in the hall. Fenna headed for the restroom, sparing the two of them a skeptical glance.

"They are putting out the lunch," she announced.

"Excellent. I'll be right there." Griffin's voice sounded fake to River's ears. Too hearty. But Fenna must have bought it as she continued on her way down the hall.

"We're not done," River said in a low voice as soon as the bathroom door shut.

"*We* are getting lunch." Griffin's voice was firm and commanding as he steered River back down the hall, and it did delicious things to River's insides. Yes, indeed they were not done, not by a long shot, and Griffin might not want to admit it—yet—but this was going to be fun. Frosty glaciers. Hot mountain man. This trip was looking up already.

Chapter Five

Griffin hadn't lied to River. He didn't do fun. Had learned the hard way that what looked like a harmless hookup never was as guilt-free as promised. Besides, even if he was tempted by River's come-on, he honestly wasn't sure how his libido functioned sober, couldn't remember how a man tasted without whiskey on his breath. And since getting smashed with River wasn't happening, he really didn't want to use him as some sort of test case and wind up disappointing them both. No, better for both of them that they keep it in their pants.

To that end, he kept his distance from River at lunch, which was gourmet sandwiches and salads. The boat went deeper into the northwestern fjords, and Griffin kept himself busy discussing how to cope with the light bouncing off the glaciers to ensure decent pictures. Handling Melanie's camera, his breath slowed, restlessness receding as he played with her settings for her.

"Here." He took a few snaps. "See what you think of these."

Melanie thumbed through the pictures on the viewing screen. "Wow. These are amazing. Are you sure you're not a professional?"

"I'm sure." Griffin tuned out the memory of Uncle Roger and his mother trying to argue otherwise. "Now you try."

She took some decent pictures of the blue-tinged ice that seemed to make her happy, so he chalked the interaction up as a win. On the other side of the deck, Lieke was happily sketching, Fenna standing guard over her like she alone could control the weather and lighting. A weird twinge raced through Griffin. What would it be like to have a connection like that? To know what someone else needed and be able to provide it? To be that invested in someone else's happiness and have it run both ways?

He'd probably never know, a fact that didn't usually bother him, but today made him uncomfortably wistful. He wasn't supposed to get all emotional like this. Feelings were dangerous. Being as cold and stoic as the glaciers, that was easier. Safer.

It had been years, but the majesty of the towering glaciers impressed his adult self every bit as much as they had last time he'd been here, a younger, freer man. He knew a moment of envy for the family of otters they passed on their way back up the fjords—they didn't seem fazed by the passage of the boat at all. They had their place in the world, and nothing was going to disturb them.

Unlike Griffin, whose body seemed attuned to River's every movement—he spent a fair amount of time at the rail, taking pictures, but also retreated to a deck chair with that slim laptop of his, typing away. And no, Griffin was not curious about his writing. And definitely not wondering whether he'd shown up in the day's recounting yet.

"Is the nature walk at Fox Island before or after dinner?" As if aware of Griffin's thoughts, River closed the laptop, tucked it away in his bag, and sauntered over. "I'm hoping before. I need to stretch my legs before I can think of even smelling food."

"Boat getting to you?" Despite himself, Griffin knew a moment of sympathy. "The walk is before. It's a late dinner. Do you want me to chase down some meds for you? Water?"

"Nah." River gave an elegant shrug. "Just tight muscles. I'm used to more...*activity.*"

And how River managed to make that word sound dirty, Griffin had no idea. But he did, sending little sparks of lust racing down Griffin's spine.

"We'll get you your walk." Griffin's voice came out harsher than he'd intended. But damn if he wanted River—or him—visualizing other, more fun forms of exercise.

"All right." River's arch tone said he knew exactly where Griffin's mind had gone. But he didn't press the issue, instead drifting away when Griffin didn't engage him in more small talk.

When they arrived at Fox Island, River wasn't the only one who looked ready for a break. The lodge at Fox Island had a nice buffet for them and a few other cruises with salmon, prime rib, and crab among the offerings. But first, they explored the island with the help of one of the lodge's guides, who explained the island's unique ecology. The jagged cliffs and pebble beaches were a big hit with Griffin's group, and he busied himself with making sure they got good pictures in the evening's lower light.

"Oh, hey, look at all the heart-shaped stones!" River

made a delighted sound that went right to Griffin's gut. Crouching, he arranged several of the flat stones, which did indeed look like hearts. "My followers are going to love this." Frowning, he tried several camera angles before motioning Griffin over. "I keep getting shadows. You have advice?"

Fuck. Griffin had no choice but to crouch next to him, lean in much too close to see his camera's viewing screen. Despite the long time on the boat, River managed to still smell fresh and luxurious, a lush, expensive scent that got to Griffin every bit as much as that melodic voice of his.

"I think the worst of the shadows are coming from you," Griffin advised, trying to tamp down his body's reaction to River's nearness. "Let's try rotating the stones and coming at it from the other side."

It was an easy fix, one River undoubtedly could have come up with on his own. Had he asked for Griffin's help merely to get him close? Griffin's back tensed. Both frustrated and flattered, he gave River some more advice about camera settings, making sure to keep more distance between them.

"There it is." River's happy noise when he got the picture he'd wanted had Griffin wondering what he sounded like when...

Nope. Not going there. Instead, he focused on rounding everyone up for dinner. As they went through the buffet line, River looked like the mashed potatoes had personally offended him but did take a small portion of the salmon and vegetables. At the table, Griffin pulled out his phone, used the lodge's Wi-Fi to send a fast email to his Denali contact asking for more fruits and vegetables. He wasn't going to have River going hungry on his watch.

They were treated to a spectacular sunset on the way back to Seward, which elicited another of those near-pornographic sighs from River, making Griffin need to look away fast. Even though Ted's cabin staff had provided blankets for those remaining on the deck in the dropping temperatures, Griffin still busied himself making sure everyone was comfortable. And he'd be lying if he said he wasn't relieved when Dan ended up taking the passenger seat on the ride back to the cabins. He could still hear River's sleepy-sounding chatter with the women, but at least he wasn't right there for Griffin to smell, *feel.*

And it wasn't too much longer before he was kicking off his boots, firmly shutting the door on overheard conversations about fire pits and beers to share and collapsing on the silly moose quilt in his little cabin, finally alone. Except aloneness lasted precisely five minutes before a knock sounded at the door—not nearly enough time for his mind to quiet, not even enough time for him to get around to taking off his clothes. Which was actually a good thing, as he didn't have to scramble into his pants on his way to the door, praying the whole way that it wasn't River.

As usual, though, the Almighty had no use for Griffin's feeble requests, and it *was* River, standing there, looking somewhat sheepish in the glow from the little porch light. The unexpected reluctance to River's expression was the only reason Griffin moderated his tone as he opened the door.

"Can I help you?"

"Yeah, actually." River offered a small smile. "I need a favor."

"Like?" Griffin's tone came out intentionally skeptical. If the favor was sex, Griffin was going to turn him down flat, march him back to his own cabin, customer satisfaction be damned.

"I need a bandage." River held up his right index finger wrapped in a tissue. "I cut myself on the edge of the mirror in my bathroom. I don't want to trek all the way back to the main cabin if I don't have to."

"I've got some." Griffin had no choice but to usher him in. And he tried hard not to let his exasperation show. River might be angling for some alone time with him, but he didn't think the guy would go so far as to intentionally hurt himself to get it. Which meant he probably really was hurt, and Griffin needed to do his freaking job and take care of him. Damn it.

"Thanks. I figured you would. I usually travel with a small first aid kit myself, but somehow my conditioner leaked all over it. Now I'm going to have to suffer major color fade on top of needing to beg bandages." River made himself at home in the wooden rocking chair in the corner of the small space.

"Can't have that. I'll swing by that pharmacy on the way out of town. You can pick up what you need." Somehow River's chatty tone cut through Griffin's cranky mood, made him want to make things better for him, an impulse he didn't fully understand. And he was rewarded with a full-wattage River smile, one that lifted his pristine blue eyes and brought color to his perfect cheekbones.

"You're the best."

"It's nothing," Griffin mumbled, not sure what to

do with the praise. He searched through his bag for the first aid kit. It was one of those deluxe ones, complete with carefully labeled compartments in a nylon case. Given how red the tissue around River's finger was, he snagged a pair of gloves first thing. "Now what exactly are we dealing with?"

"I get tested on the regular. Nothing to alarm you if you're worried. And I've had a tetanus shot." River held out the wounded finger as Griffin crouched in front of him.

"I'd grab the gloves even if it was one of the doctors bleeding," Griffin assured him as he unwrapped the tissue to reveal a nasty gash. Yeah, River definitely hadn't done this for attention, and Griffin felt a little bad that the thought had even crossed his mind. "Okay, I don't think you need stitches, but this is deeper than a scratch for sure. We better clean it out well first, which is probably going to sting. Sorry."

"I can take it." River offered up a brave smile that Griffin couldn't help but return. "Want me to do it? If you just give me the stuff—"

"Nothing doing. You're not getting an infection on my watch. Besides it's awkward to do one handed." After blotting away more of the blood, Griffin opened two alcohol wipes. "This is probably the unfun part."

"Aaaah." River gave a pained gasp but otherwise held still as Griffin scrubbed the wound. "Leave some skin, will you?"

"Sorry. All done with that part. I want to put some ointment on it and then we'll bandage it. Maybe we should use a gauze pad for extra cushioning? I know how much you type. Which, honestly, you might want to lay off tonight. Put some pressure on this, but don't try to use it until it has a chance to start to heal."

"Wow. That might be the longest speech I've heard from you yet." River gave him another easy grin. "And I'm touched by your concern for my typing."

"No problem." Griffin's neck heated as he bandaged the wound, discarding both the wipes and his gloves into the trash. "There you go."

"Thanks." Holding up his finger to the light, River shifted in the rocking chair, which put him way too close to Griffin. Right when Griffin was going to move back, River reached out, patted Griffin's shoulder. "I mean it. You did a good job. And I really didn't mean to disturb your evening. It was a long day. I'm sure you're exhausted."

"I'm okay," Griffin said even though he was weary down to his socks, but a lot of his tiredness had to do with having been hyperaware of River all day, and no way was he admitting that.

"This is hard for you, isn't it?" River apparently had no intention of letting this drop. "All this people-ing and interaction? Something tells me you're much more used to working alone."

"I like my space," Griffin admitted, not sure what it was about River that made him want to open up. "I've talked more in two days than I usually do in a week. But I'm all right. I don't have an issue or anything." That last bit was a little lie, and it came out more defensive than he would have liked.

"I didn't say you had issues." River's voice was patient. "Just that I appreciate you…stepping outside your comfort zone for us."

"Thanks." Griffin realized with a start that he was

staring right into River's blue eyes and that he'd unconsciously leaned into River's grip on his shoulder, moving way closer than was advisable, especially since River had bent forward, bringing their faces almost level.

"You know..." River's tone switched to more teasing, and the skin on Griffin's neck prickled. "If I can't type tonight and I'm not tired..."

"Not happening," Griffin said weakly, licking his lips.

"No?" One of River's perfect eyebrows arched. "You're not even a little curious?"

"About what?"

"This." River closed the gap between them, brushing his mouth over Griffin's. He'd loosened his grip, and Griffin could have easily pulled away. But he didn't. Because damn it, he *was* curious. Curious about what River tasted like. Sounded like. Curious about whether this weird pull between them was a mirage. He'd seen those in the desert when deployed—shimmering visions that disappeared as soon as one got closer. But that wasn't the case here, River getting more solid and overwhelmingly *real* as their mouths met.

And yup, just as he'd feared, the pull intensified as River continued the soft kiss—little brushes of his mouth, not seeking entry or trying to deepen things. More like he too was curious, trying to feel out Griffin and giving him plenty of time to object. Which Griffin really should, but somehow, that was him groaning, him reaching to tug River closer, one hand on his jaw, the other sweeping down River's slim back. And that was him being the one to take the exploration a step further, tongue coming out to trace River's full lips.

Soft. So soft. And sweet. Probably due to something boring like lip balm, but a rarely used fanciful part of Griffin liked the idea that it was River himself, an innate sweetness to his skin and his person.

River's lips parted on a gasp, a welcoming sound inviting further discovery. And hell if Griffin could resist, tongue delving into River's mouth. More sweetness. Minty. Not even a trace of alcohol. And it turned out that even if Griffin's mind was still making sense of this, his body knew what to do, what it liked, tongue slipping over River's. Tasting. Playing. Figuring out what got more gasps and happy noises from River. And far from being passive, River met him eagerly, chasing Griffin's tongue back into his own mouth, then relaxing when Griffin paused to sample at his lips with little nips.

The kiss went on and on, first River leading, then him, then River again, back and forth, an easy, addictive rhythm that kept Griffin rooted to the spot. River's uninjured hand moved from Griffin's shoulder to tangle in his hair, and Griffin welcomed the touch, the little tugs that made him feel even more alive. Without waiting for permission from his brain, Griffin's hand slipped under River's T-shirt, finding his flesh warm and supple, lean muscles and soft-as-silk skin.

"Bed." River pulled away with a low groan, and all Griffin's doubts and objections came rushing back.

"No." He finally succeeded in forcing his legs to work, scooting back before standing and pacing away.

River followed, easily unfolding from the rocking chair to stride over to Griffin and wrap his arms around Griffin's neck. "The reluctant thing is kind of sexy, but we both know you want this. And I'm not a jerk.

No means no unless it's a kink for you, in which case, please, speak up now."

"It's not a kink." He managed to find the strength to gently free himself from River's embrace.

"So, why not simply say yes then? You can help me take my mind off my throbbing finger, and I can take your mind off...whatever makes you so damn serious. Just have a little fun, Griff."

He was only Griff to close family and friends and wasn't sure what to make of the nickname coming from River. Made him both warm and more resolved at the same time. He didn't *want* to be Griff to River, didn't want to soften to him further, let him in. And fuck it all, but he hated having to make a choice. This was infinitely easier with a buzz on, letting the other person lead him to bed, doing what River said and having a little fun, shutting off his brain.

But now, sober as a saint, he couldn't stop his brain from racing ahead, considering practicalities like whether or not he could perform without a buzz to loosen him up or thinking how awkward the morning would be regardless of how things went. And hell, he did not want River to be seen leaving his cabin in the morning. Practicality. The ultimate dick-wilter.

"Told you. Not interested in fun." He steered River toward the door, keeping his touch light but firm.

"Liar." River shook his head. "But, fine. Suit yourself. Talking people into bed isn't my kink. The offer will still stand, though, if you change your mind."

"I won't." Even to his own ears, the words sounded weak, the barest of protest. It wouldn't take much for River to get him to reconsider, another kiss or two, a well-placed touch and Griffin would undoubtedly be putty again. But River wanted him to choose, and that he couldn't do, couldn't let himself consciously decide to have this, couldn't divorce himself from all the good reasons why giving in would be stupid.

And River didn't kiss him again, didn't touch, only let himself out. "Night, Griff. Sleep well. Dream of me."

Ha. He'd be lucky to sleep at all. And as for dreaming of River? That much was probably a given. Damn it. Tomorrow he'd be stronger. Firmer. No more kisses. No more letting River under his skin.

Chapter Six

River didn't do regrets. Or recrimination. At least, he tried hard not to. God knew, he'd done enough of that in the past. Beating himself up only led to bad, dark places. So the morning after his kiss with Griffin, River woke up resolved, not regretful. He dressed quickly because the morning was chilly and because he wasn't aiming to impress Griffin with his choice of clothes.

Oh, he was going to get Griffin in bed before the end of the trip, and that was just a fact. But when he did, Griff would come willingly, and it wouldn't be because River had made a pest of himself. Pushy wasn't part of River's MO. He did like the thrill of the hunt so to speak, but he'd give Griff plenty of space to sort himself out. *Griff.* The softer nickname really did suit Griffin. Gruff, but vulnerable, approachable.

It was probably that vulnerability that drew River to him, another of those fascinating contrasts in the man. So competent. So commanding. But in his unguarded moments, so sensitive that River wanted to wrap him up, show him a space where it was safe to feel, to let out all the emotions River could sense simmering below the surface, especially when they kissed. And man, could Griff kiss. If River regretted anything, it was that he'd pressed for moving to the bed too quickly. He could have easily endured the awkward position longer if it meant more of those kisses.

He laced up his hiking boots, trying to work around his injured finger, smiling to himself because Griff was undoubtedly the type of guy more likely to be turned on by boots and flannel than club wear. On that note, he threw a plaid shirt on over his tee and paused for a last look in the dresser mirror. Okay, okay, maybe he was out to impress Griff, make him think twice about saying no. But he was resolute about not being too pushy, and with that in mind, he gave Griff a wide berth when the whole tour group gathered by the fire pit. Breakfast was a bagel buffet set up under the picnic shelter, but River hung back, only helping himself to a coffee.

"We're going to hit the road, but when we pass through Anchorage, we're going to stop at a store so you can get any snacks or supplies you may need for the next few days." Griff addressed the group as a whole, but his eyes found River's and he subtly nodded at River's finger. He went on to give other morning announcements about their drive to the Knik River area, including a weather advisory that could impact their planned helicopter ride over a glacier-filled lake.

"Thanks for the store side trip," River said in a low voice as they made their way to the van.

"No problem. Figured you might have more luck finding hair stuff you like in Anchorage." Griff looked at the gravel path, not River. "How's the finger?"

"Fine. Your bandage held up well." River followed his lead and didn't allude to the kiss, not that he would have brought it up with the rest of the group as an audience.

"Bandage?" Melanie swiveled around. "Do you need me to take a look? You should have come to me."

"It's fine, and I didn't want to bother you," River said smoothly. While the finger had been a total accident, he could admit to himself that his choice of going to Griff rather than one of the doctors or the main lodge was deliberate. Melanie would have fussed over him too much, made him feel silly for the injury. Even without the prospect of sex, Griff had been the easier choice with his more matter-of-fact handling of the cut.

"It's no bother. Let me see it later when you change the bandage." She settled in next to Dan, leaving River the passenger seat again.

"I will," he promised even though he had little intention of seeking her out. He could take care of himself. However, the finger was painful enough checking messages on his phone that he didn't bother pulling his laptop out. No typing that morning.

Instead, he tried to focus on the scenery as they got back on the Seward Highway, retracing their route from the day before yesterday. But the morning was hazy and overcast, and he quickly lost interest in the gray skies and endless forests.

"So the helicopter ride might get canceled?" he asked Griff, mainly to make conversation. He was used to changes of plans when traveling and didn't have his heart set on the sightseeing trip.

"Probably not, but we have to see what this storm front moving in does. I'll call the pilot while we're stopped in Anchorage, find out what his thoughts are."

"You won't be the one doing the flying?"

That got a laugh from Griff, which had been River's entire purpose in playing ignorant. "No. Helicopter is a whole different set of skills. We've been using this pilot for years—his whole business is doing scenic trips around the Knik River area."

"Why not just use one of your planes? I wouldn't mind a chance to see you fly." Because the back of the van seemed deep in conversation, he was able to make his voice a tad more flirty.

"The bigger tour groups would require a larger plane than we usually use, and a helicopter can get in and out of tight spaces so much easier. Plus the views are a lot better this way. The whole point is to get you guys the best pictures possible. Besides, Brand's a family friend, like Ted. And a vet. We're happy to give him business."

"Oh? You knew him when you were in the service?" River was curious about Griff's past, who he'd been before, who he was now as a result. He loved getting people's stories, and he had a feeling that Griff's would be worth waiting for.

"Nah. Brand was army, and he's older than me. His parents ran the business first, and they were friendly with Uncle Roger for years." Griff kept his eyes on the road, more of the scenery they'd enjoyed the day before passing by, but River's focus was all on Griff and keeping him talking.

"How long did you serve?"

"Twelve years. Four years at the academy in Colorado, then eight as a pilot."

"Why'd you get out?"

That question brought a grimace to Griff's features, and he took a long time to answer. "Got pretty banged

up in a training accident. Took a medical discharge."
His low sigh said there was plenty more to that story.

"Your leg, right?" River had noticed his uneven gait
a couple of times on the trip.

"Among other things." Griff's tone didn't invite further questions. "Why'd you get out of modeling?"

It was a clear bid to change the topic away from himself, to make River uncomfortable, but River wasn't
going to let himself get ruffled.

"You should read my book," he said lightly. "I go
all into the dirty deets."

"I'm not much of a memoir reader. How about you
give me the condensed version?"

"I burned out." If Griff could be cryptic, then so
could he. "Traveling's more fun."

"Fun." Griff made it sound like a curse word.

"Yeah, some of us actually enjoy that. And life's too
short to be too serious. Fun isn't so terrible of a goal."
Damn it, now River was defensive again, which he
did not want to be. But hell if he was going to explain
to Griff that traveling was a deep-down need to keep
moving, one he didn't always understand himself. "You
should try it sometime."

"Been there. Wasn't worth it." Griff's tone was firm,
but an underlying pain there burrowed under River's
skin, made him want to change Griff's mind, make
him laugh, make him let go.

"Maybe you just need to try a different angle," he
said lightly, stopping short of volunteering himself for
the job.

"Too old to be chasing a good time." Griff radiated
tension, so River decided to let it go. But, seriously, the
guy was mid-thirties, not eighty. He needed to lighten

up. And he might not realize it yet, but a few nights with River would serve him well in that regard. And when they finally did get there, River was going to do his damnedest to make it fun, to wipe some of that darkness away, even if only for a few hours.

The rain, cold and unrelenting, pelted Griffin as he brought the luggage into the lodge at Knik River where they had reservations. Four unhappy faces greeted him as he entered the building. Both couples were understandably sad about the helicopter ride being canceled due to the weather. In contrast, River had been indifferent, simply shrugging and digging out his laptop despite the way he kept wincing while typing. Part of Griffin wanted to offer to re-bandage the finger, try to cushion it more, but not with the group around, and not when either of the doctors could undoubtedly do far better than him.

"We'll try again first thing in the morning," he promised the group. "Brand assures me the skies should be clearer then. It'll put us behind for getting to Denali, but the views will be worth it."

"Yup." Right then, Brand himself strode into the lodge. Unlike Griffin, he still wore his hair military short and he walked with the bearing of a staff sergeant. "We're sorry, folks. But the lodge here has excellent food, movies, and a huge supply of board games to keep you busy indoors until the weather clears."

Griffin made introductions to his group, and Brand shook hands all around, lingering more than was necessary with River, appraisal clear in his eyes. *Fuck my life.* He'd never known Brand to swing that way, but River's lips and fine-boned features could probably sway even a straight, celibate monk let alone Brand, who shared Toby's freewheeling approach to seasonal hookups. And speaking of hookups, Griffin wasn't the jealous type. Really. But no way was Brand fucking around with River right under his nose.

"See you in the morning?" he said to Brand, not inviting him to hang out with them as he might have with another group.

"Sure." Brand gave him a curious look but nodded anyway. "I'll be here bright and early. You guys need anything before then, you just send someone to my office—it's the cabin next to the helicopter pad, can't miss it. Or Griff has my number."

"Will do." Griffin watched him walk away, then turned back to his group. Taking a deep breath, he tried his best to channel Uncle Roger, who would not leave them at loose ends until dinner, especially not after effectively dismissing Brand. "So, who's up for a movie in the lounge after you put your things in your cabin? Or maybe a board game sounds fun? We can watch the storm roll in from the big windows there."

After some discussion and time to put their bags away, the group settled on Fenna and Lieke watching a movie on the plush couches in the media space off the large open room dominating the front of the lodge, while the rest of them gathered around a circular wooden table with a board game that Melanie picked out.

With TV service often spotty, Griffin had plenty of experience playing games with his sisters and other family members growing up, but it had been years since he'd indulged himself in more than the odd game of chess. Melanie's first choice was a classic detective game, and she declared it perfect for four players, so he had no chance to gracefully get out of playing a round.

Or two as it turned out. And once again, he was acutely aware of River next to him, and his melodic laugh as they played kept making the hair on Griffin's arms crackle. Outside it was damp and cold, rain continuing to pour down, but next to River, his skin felt like he'd spent a day in the desert. River didn't know the rules, having apparently never played this one, and he was endearing in his mistakes and miscues. After River lost spectacularly, Melanie insisted on a second round to give him another chance.

"We should do teams!" Melanie declared, tone leaving little room for objection. "That will help poor River. You can show him strategy, Griffin."

"Yeah, that sounds fun," River said before Griffin had the chance to come up with some plausible reason why he couldn't lean closer to River, why he couldn't converse in hushed tones with him, sharing cards, fingers brushing as they passed each other cards and tokens. Each turn was a fresh exercise in torture. He was probably the first person to ever get a boner over what was essentially a kids' game and over little more than just accidental touches with River. And it was no wonder that they lost, due more to his own distraction than River's inexperience.

"Why don't you guys pick a different game?" Dan suggested as Melanie packed away the game. "We're up for anything."

"Sounds good. I'm going to see if they have any word-based games. I'm always good at vocab stuff." River collected the game and stood, but crooked a finger at Griffin, who would have been happy to let him go on his own. River's tone was light, almost but not quite flirty. "Come on, Mountain Man. Let's see which game would make you less grumpy. Maybe they have a board game version of log toss? Glower-and-guess?"

"Funny." Griffin followed him to the narrow hall that housed the cupboards with the games, which was out of sight of the rest of the room. He waited until they were out of earshot from Melanie and Dan to speak further. "Listen, I'm not sure I'm up for another game. I should probably check on dinner."

"Poor Griff." River turned toward him, much, much too close. "All the people. Do you want me to make an excuse for you?"

"Would you?" Griffin hated asking, but he really did need a break.

"Of course." River was still much too close. "Did you notice that our cabins are right next to each other? And mine has a king-size bed…"

"You can sprawl out. Alone." Griffin kept his tone nice and firm.

"Oh, I don't know about that. Might go see what the weather report is for tomorrow. Bug your pilot friend."

"Pretty sure he's straight." A muscle twitched in Griffin's jaw as he tensed up.

"Pretty sure you're wrong." River laughed again. "Besides I'm just talking about a little conversation. Harmless."

"I'll get the weather report for you," Griffin ground out.

"You're freaking adorable when you're jealous." River rested a hand on Griffin's shoulder. "Gonna offer me a better distraction?"

"Not jealous." Despite his irritation, he couldn't

bring himself to remove River's hand, which felt too damn good. And as if he sensed Griffin's weakness, River started a light massage of the tight muscles between Griffin's neck and shoulder. It took all he had to not groan aloud at the contact, especially when River's other hand got involved too.

"Come over tonight. Let me give you a back rub, if nothing else."

Griffin had to snort at that. "We both know it wouldn't be just a massage."

"See? We're in perfect agreement then. You, me, some oil. What could go wrong?"

So many things. Griffin's head hurt just thinking of them. But his dick kept trying to drown out the negative thoughts, insisting on the one way that things could go very, very right. And looking into River's eyes while his hands worked magic on Griffin's muscles, he couldn't summon the energy to shut the flirting down.

And when River tugged him closer, he went willingly. They were going to kiss again, and he was strangely okay with that. Needed it even. Their torsos brushed, and his skin sizzled, even under his clothing. A little closer and—

But then River was stepping away fast, right before Fenna came down the hall. And unlike Griffin, he recovered lightning fast. "So, that sounds fine. You go check on dinner, and I'll play another game with the doctors until you come back."

"Thanks," Griffin managed to mumble, meaning more than just him relaying the message to Melanie and Dan. River had sensed that Griffin wouldn't want to be caught in a clinch, and he wasn't wrong. Griffin appreciated his quick reflexes, even as his body mourned the loss of contact.

Fenna continued on past them, and River's eyes sparkled as he whispered, "Tonight."

"No," Griffin said, even as he wasn't sure he'd be able to stick to his resolution to stay away. But he had proven before that he could say no to temptation. River was simply one more desire to tamp down and ignore as best he could.

Chapter Seven

After dinner, River settled in with his laptop in the center of the big bed, mountain of pillows behind him, trying to ignore the throb of his healing finger. Also ignoring? The bottle of massage oil he'd picked up along with his color-preserving conditioner in Anchorage. Ever since their near kiss in the hall, Griff had gone out of his way to not be alone with River, which would have been comical had it not been so obvious. He'd seated himself between the two couples at dinner and hadn't returned for more board gaming. After dinner, he'd said he needed to check the weather for the next day and disappeared again.

River supposed he could use the weather pretext himself to go search out the hunky helicopter pilot, but didn't have much enthusiasm for the idea. Goading Griff into jealousy had been fun, though. After the couples had decided to watch a recent rom com, he'd claimed that he needed to write. Which he did. But the tiny cabins were close enough that he'd heard Griff's footsteps on the small porch sometime after he'd settled in, heard the door shut, and spent way too long distracting himself with visions of what Griff might be doing.

Was he pacing, debating coming over? Showering?

Exercising? He had to do something to have all those muscles, and somehow, River couldn't see him kicking back with his phone or laptop. River liked to think of Griff distracted, tempted, arguing with himself until he finally gave in...

Except he didn't. River finished the chapter he was editing, started a new one, and still no knock. And no, he wasn't going to go search him out. He wasn't going to stop flirting and offering, but he also wasn't going to cross the line from available to needy. Besides, he needed to find the narrative thread of this book, the concept that would take it from collection of travel essays to cohesive book with a clear hook. The first book had more or less poured out of him, the need to share the deep personal transformation he'd experienced while traveling keeping him up at night until it was done. And he could fully admit he'd lucked out with an agent who was a friend of a modeling world friend. But this second book...

Man, this one was harder for reasons he couldn't quite pin down. However, he wasn't going to be defeated by this draft. He needed writing the same way he needed travel, needed it to process and make sense of who and where he was now. And maybe that was the entire damn problem—these days he simply wasn't sure who he was, who he needed to be, what direction would yield the same sort of peace that travel had originally afforded him.

Much later, resigned, he fell into a light sleep and was up far too early in the morning, unable to stay asleep. Knowing his body well, he didn't force it, instead packing his things, dressing warmly in anticipation of the helicopter trip, and heading up to the main lodge in search of coffee.

He found a full carafe in the lounge area and a surprisingly alert-looking Griff on one of the couches checking his phone. Figured that he was a morning person.

"You're up early," Griff observed as River helped himself to a large black coffee. "But good news. The helicopter ride is on. We'll leave after the others are up. There's breakfast in the restaurant area if you're hungry."

"I'll eat something later," River said lightly. And he would. Later. But hell if he was going to search out something instead of taking advantage of the quiet moment with Griff. The room was empty other than them, but that didn't stop River from taking his coffee and sitting right next to Griff, putting the coffee on a coaster on the coffee table. "If I say I'm nervous about flying, will you hold my hand?"

That got a rare laugh from Griff. "I'd say you're a bad liar. You're what? The king of adventure travel? Surely you've been up in a helicopter before?"

"I have," River admitted, keeping his tone casual and teasing as he made a grab for Griff's free hand. No one was around, so they could play a little. "But maybe I'd just like to hold your hand. After all, I didn't get to give you that massage last night."

"I'm not the holding-hands type," Griff said even as he made no effort to pull away from River, who took advantage and started caressing Griff's bigger, tougher hand. River traveled with several different moisturizers, but Griff's skin probably never saw lotion and his calluses were rough against River's exploring fingers. Contrasts. Sexy as hell.

"I think you are. Maybe it's simply been so long you forgot? Got a dry spell I could help you end?" He was blatantly fishing, but his curiosity about Griff continued to percolate. Outside the picture windows, the sky started to lighten, dawn starting, casting a pale glow over the vast green landscape.

"Holding hands?" Griff snorted. "Early high school maybe. Sweet girl who probably deserved better. After that… I didn't have much room for sweet. Can't remember holding hands as part of a hookup."

"Oh, so you admit we're going to hook up?" He waggled his eyebrows at Griff. "And that's all you've ever had? Hookups? No longer relationships?"

"I'm not admitting anything." Griff still didn't pull his hand away. "And I told you, I don't date. I'm not going to pretend to have always been celibate, but I was too…never mind."

"Too what?" River prodded, massaging all the tense spots in Griff's hand.

"There was someone, okay? A…crush I guess you could say. And that occupied me for… God. Years. I didn't want more with anyone else. And then…" His gaze retreated far away and pain crossed his rugged features. "And then it was too late. H—they were gone, but I still wasn't looking to date. Too late for all that."

There was a world of hurt in that *gone,* and River also picked up on the fact that the crush had probably been a guy, despite Griff being vague on gender.

"Despite your pretending, you're not that old. At all. Way too young to declare yourself over relationships. But, luckily for you, I'm not asking you to change your stance. And I know unrequited crushes. I had this huge crush on one of my modeling mentors. And he was super straight and super not interested. I swore my poor teenage heart was breaking when he turned me down flat."

"Yeah." Griff let out a heavy sigh, one that made his whole body sag. "Life's not porn. No flipping the straight guy. I'm not sure I'd call it a broken heart, though. We were too good of friends for me to ever even try anything seriously, you know? And I had the friendship for...fuck, nearly thirty years. Wasn't going to write it off just because of my...whatever. And I have no clue why I'm telling you all this."

"I'm a good listener," River said without ego. "And maybe you need that. Also, for what it's worth, I think you can totally have a broken heart even if you never tried it on. Especially if that person isn't around anymore. A loss is a loss, Griff. You're allowed to grieve."

Griff's face shuttered, and he finally did pull his hand away. "It's been six years. I should be...maybe not *over* it, but better, right? Moving on."

River had a vision of a cold day in November, dirt hitting a casket, the ache settling in his chest that had yet to leave. "Nope. I wish I could say yes, but nope. Some things you don't get past. Rather, they become a part of you."

"That some of your New Age self-help babble?" Griff sounded skeptical.

It would have been easy to say yes, but Griff had offered up a little chunk of himself, so River could do the same. "No. Experience. My mom died when I was twenty-one. It would be nice if I had some pretty words about healing, but I don't. Loss fucking sucks."

Hell, some days he still wasn't sure whether he was running or effectively channeling his energy. And no matter what he did, the hole in his heart remained. So he got where Griff was coming from. He really did. And with anyone else, he would fall into his self-help speak, not be so honest. Because honest was hard and left him feeling raw, but something about Griff made it difficult to keep his usual persona in place.

"I'm really sorry about your mom." Unexpectedly, Griff grabbed his hand back, squeezed it. "I can't imagine losing mine. Losing my dad was bad enough, but I was so little that I don't remember much. But Mom… she's my rock. Man, that bites for you."

"Yeah." River squeezed back, sitting there simply absorbing the contact. Voices sounded from the door area, and he reluctantly untangled their fingers. And this was where usually he'd make some sort of flirty overture, but somehow the words didn't come, the conversation having created a closeness that felt very new and fragile. The sort of thing a single joke or wrong word could undo. So he stayed silent as the others filtered in, moving away and occupying himself with his coffee, which was now lukewarm at best.

After a breakfast where he managed to find an apple and yogurt while the others had biscuits and gravy, they headed for the helicopter pad. The hot military dude, who said to call him Brand, let his eyes linger an extra beat on River again, but River still wasn't in a flirty mood, so he simply nodded. The flight would take them out over a glacier-filled river, where they'd actually land, explore briefly, and then return to the lodge.

River was glad that he'd worn layers and thick hiking socks as the already chilly air cooled further when the helicopter took them out over the river and lake. Even though he'd ended up next to Griff, the chopper was too loud for much talking, so he tried to focus on the scenery and not on how good Griff smelled.

Below them, a craggy black landscape was interspersed with glacier flows. This gave way to water that was so aquamarine as to be almost unnatural—a color even his favorite salon would struggle to replicate. The glacier-filled water absolutely warranted several pictures as did the black mountains in the background. They flew close to towering, gleaming white glaciers with ice that appeared slightly bluish in his pictures.

When they landed on a glacier, Brand and Griff helped everyone down, and despite Brand's welcoming grin, River chose Griff's solid hands. And yeah, he probably could have kept his own balance, but hell if he was turning down another electric touch with this confounding man.

He took some impressive panorama shots from the glacier while Griff helped Melanie with her camera. Lieke sketched rapidly while Fenna took pictures of both Lieke and the scenery. They weren't allowed to go far of course, and Brand and Griff had both issued stern warnings about the danger of crevasses, but simply knowing they were standing on a literal mountain of ice was pretty damn cool.

Wandering away from the group for a few moments, his chest expanded, the same glorious sensation he got while hiking. Here, he was part of something so much bigger than himself, and it grounded him like little else could. *This* was what he'd come for. Not grumpy mountain men. This sweeping vista, this novel experience, this centering of his chaotic brain.

As the flight finished, a calmness descended over him, which made him both sleepy and energized at the same time. It was entirely possible that he might end up dozing part of the way to Denali. River had been waiting all trip for this experience—only a few lodges were this remote inside Denali and the next few days promised not only great pictures, but also more of that wide-open feeling he'd had on the glacier. Somehow the more rustic the accommodations, the more at peace he felt, far removed from the glitz and glam. Which he did also enjoy, but he was honestly looking forward to the limited electricity, plumbing, and cell service at the isolated site.

But not so much looking forward to more glowering from Griff, who was on a phone call and had reverted to distant and gruff. And as he ended his call and strode back over to the group by the van, he looked positively murderous.

"What's wrong?" He put himself in position to take the brunt of his anger.

"Nothing." Griff scrubbed at his shaggy hair. "Just that when my mom called to adjust our Denali reservation because of the cancellations due to Uncle Roger not making the trip, she told them the wrong number. Or something."

"Which means?"

"You and I are sharing a cabin. We will, of course, refund a portion of your—"

"Don't be ridiculous." It was all River could do not to bounce on the balls of his feet like a little kid. "This is going to be *fun*."

Griff mumbled something that sounded an awful lot like "That's what I'm afraid of."

They had hours of travel ahead of them, plenty of scenery between them and nightfall, but suddenly, River couldn't wait for bed.

Griffin's dread for the coming night increased with every mile closer to the remote Denali lodge. But it was a long trek for his group, and Griffin had to focus on the logistics enough to distract him from the gnawing in his gut. First, he drove from the Knik River to the park entrance at Denali—a trip that took several hours, especially with breaks for pictures and lunch. At the visitor center for the park, they were met by employees from the lodge. Griffin checked his phone one final time while they had something resembling service and assured himself that Uncle Roger was recovering nicely after his surgery. His mother had wanted an update on the trip, and the best Griffin had managed was "fine." They were fine. No one injured. No one demanding a refund. No arguments. Fine. She didn't need to know all the ways that Griffin was twisted up over the rooming arrangements for the days ahead. That was on him.

The park was strict about what vehicles were allowed beyond the first fifteen miles of Park Road, so they would travel in the lodge's small bus, which had the necessary permits, for the remaining hours to the lodge and camp located deep within the park, off the main road. It was a long drive of many hours on barely maintained roads, one that reminded Griffin how much he preferred being the driver to being a passenger.

"If you try to brake again, you're going to hurt something," River teased.

Griffin would have loved to ride shotgun, next to the driver, but the young female driver had an equally fresh-faced male guide with her who took that seat. So he'd ended up next to River, who'd been in a surprisingly chipper mood all day, taking pictures and joking.

"You really should have let me message my mom about a partial refund while we still had cell service," Griffin said during a lull when the scenery shifted to seemingly endless scrubby meadow without a great view of the mountains. "I'm sure you were expecting a single."

"Quit apologizing. You're the one put out, not me." River offered a grin, one that seemed authentic, not the practiced smile he used with others. "This is going to be fun. Like summer camp or something. We can…" He paused, eyes sparkling as if he knew exactly where Griffin's mind was going. "Roast marshmallows. Tell ghost stories."

"Don't know any," Griffin half lied. The scariest tales he knew of loss and haunting weren't exactly campfire classics.

"Luckily for you, I do. I have many ways to keep us occupied. I went to summer camp up in the Catskills growing up. I can tell you all about this haunted well." His seemingly endless supply of good cheer continued and something odd happened to Griffin. Some of his tension gave way without him even consciously exhaling. Just melted off him until he was laughing along with River.

"Okay, you win. You can tell me the story later."

"Later." River made the word sound like a chocolate he was savoring. "Hey, look! There's a moose!"

Distracted, River dug out his camera and left Grif-

fin to stew in his thoughts until they stopped for a picnic dinner at a rustic grouping of picnic tables near a
trailhead. The two guides set out a cold dinner of fried
chicken, potato salad, and other classic sides.

"Which of your people is the special dietary request?" asked the male guide, who'd introduced himself as Daryl and had a dark braid even longer than the
one Griffin's mother usually sported. "We had a message about more vegetables?"

"Yup." Griffin pointed at River, a weird fondness
filling his chest. "This is my picky eater. What do you
have for him?"

"A hummus wrap with a side of fruit salad." Daryl
held out a clear plastic box.

"Thanks." River accepted the food with one of those
practiced smiles. "Looks great."

And indeed, he managed to eat more than Griffin
had seen from him at other meals.

"You didn't have to go to any trouble for me," River
said between delicate bites. "I could make do."

"Yeah, but we want your five-star review." Griffin
winked at him, not really sure who this laughing, joking self was. And he continued to wonder that as they
passed an impressive lake before proceeding on min-
imally maintained roads off Park Road. The late-day
sunlight highlighted the expansive vistas until well
after dinnertime with sunset not scheduled until ten.
Eighteen hours or so of sunlight in July made up for
the dreary short winter days, but he could still sense
the group starting to flag as they neared the lodge.

He…well, *liked* was a bit strong of a word, but he
didn't hate who he was around River. The joking. The
laughing. The lightness in his chest. The warmth in his

muscles when River looked his way. The way River's delight at the views felt personal, each exclamation a fresh rush of something close to pleasure.

They finally arrived at the lodge and cabins with the clock saying bedtime even as the Arctic sun continued to blaze, only just now starting to shift with full darkness still a ways off. Despite the hours of daylight remaining, it had been a long day of travel for Griffin's group, and he wasn't surprised that everyone wanted to head straight to their cabins, save exploring camp for the morning. The guides showed each couple to their cabin, making sure to point out the location of the water spigot and private outhouse for each small unit. Griffin and River's cabin was last, set back from the others and farthest from the main lodge. Humble, it had two narrow twin beds made with fluffy sleeping bags, a sink basin, a single lantern, and a propane-powered hotplate.

He expected some pushback from River about the outhouse and spartan accommodations, but yet again, River surprised him, sighing contently as he tossed his bag on one of the beds after the guides left. He turned, giving Griff a smile far brighter than the weak light of the lantern.

"This really does remind me of summer camp. You in your bunk, me in mine. Wind whistling outside…"

"It's likely to get cold tonight," Griffin warned. "Might want to sleep in your clothes."

Please. It was more of a plea than a suggestion, but as usual, the universe thumbed its nose at Griffin.

"I brought some sweats to sleep in. Do you mind if I change here?" River all but batted his eyes at Griffin, clearly enjoying his discomfort too much.

Yes. Griffin was a hair's breadth from sending him up to the shower house to change, but manners took over. "No problem."

He'd seen other men change thousands of times— sports, military academy, barracks, and camping trips. And it had never once made him this odd combination of queasy and excited. Trying not to stare, he opened his own bag and pulled out the flannel pants and sweat-shirt he slept in when heat was in short supply. His travel alarm clock was on top of the clothes, so he set that on the shelf by the bed. Maybe if he also changed, it wouldn't be so awkward. And he'd be too busy to gawk.

Except as it turned out, he was an excellent multi-tasker. And it was absolutely possible to undress and sneak glances at River at the same time. He was slim, as Griffin already knew. Narrow shoulders and waist and miles of pale, creamy skin without even a hint of tan on a surprisingly long torso. No tattoos. No pierc-ings either, at least that he could see.

"It's on my hip," River said with a knowing smirk as he caught Griffin's eyes. "And my piercings aren't in right now."

"I…uh…good to know," Griffin stammered as he shuffled his feet. Damn River and his unerring ability to know what Griffin was thinking.

"Wanna see?" Without further warning, River dropped his jeans and pulled at the waistband of expensive-looking black briefs.

"No. I'm good." Looking away fast, Griffin busied himself with putting on his clothes, hoping that River wasn't scrutinizing his body. He was way hairier than River, that much was for sure, and River was sure to notice the surgery scars on his leg and burn scars on his back and shoulders.

"Liar." Fabric rustled before River spoke again. "I'm decent now. And crawling into my own sleeping bag. All the way over here. Your virtue is safe."

"Not worried about my virtue." Honestly, he was way more concerned with losing his mind over this man, but of course he wasn't going to share that. He flipped off the lantern, throwing the room into darkness thanks to the blackout shade covering the cabin's lone window, the sort of complete stillness only really possible far off the grid. He felt his way to his own bunk, but rather than slipping into the sleeping bag, he lay on top of it, too overheated for that yet.

"Maybe you should be worried," River teased, melodic voice cutting through the still night, apparently far from rolling over and going to sleep. "Lying here like this, I keep thinking of the hundreds of summer camp fantasies I've had over the years."

Griffin was going to hate himself for this later, but he couldn't stop the words from coming out. "Yeah? Like what?"

Chapter Eight

Griffin's pulse sped up, the anticipation of waiting for River's reply almost doing him in. He had no business asking the question, let alone being excited about the reply.

"Oh? You want to know?" River didn't pause long enough for Griffin to reconsider his question. "There's something so sexy about the dark and the quiet. A lot of my fantasies center around other tents or campers being close by and needing to stay super, super quiet so no one knows what we're up to."

As a general rule, Griffin didn't usually consider quiet sexy, but there was something magical about River's voice, about his words, about the picture he was painting. All Griffin could manage in response was a barely audible "Yeah."

"I know you and your assumptions, and you're probably thinking the fantasies get kinky fast, but they really don't. I don't know what it is, but I love the energy of first times. Discovery. Kissing and making out for endless hours. Sneaking around. Finding convenient dark corners. Furtive touches. All that."

A groan escaped Griffin's mouth before he could swallow it back. He'd never really had any of that, and suddenly, he wanted that with the same fierceness he usually reserved for longing for the sun in January and February.

"What else?" he asked, voice rougher than the rocky path leading to their cabin.

"Getting into this?" There was an almost palpable smirk in River's voice. "Okay, so imagine this. It's late at night at camp, and we've been flirting and teasing on the down low all day. I sneak over to you…"

"Go on," Griffin commanded, dick swelling from nothing more than River's words.

"And we have to be quiet. So quiet. But we just can't help ourselves. We can't wait to get our hands all over each other. I squeeze into your bunk—"

"No way," Griffin said even as River's tale turned him on so hard he ached with need. "We wouldn't fit. Sorry."

"I beg to differ," River said archly. "Want me to show you? I'll tell you what happens next if you let me come over there…"

This was the ideal place to shut River down for the night. Hell, he could even fake snoring. Anything to get River to be quiet, stop painting such tempting pictures. But this was just too good, leaving his head behind, living in River's fantasy, being that guy, the eager young one, not the jaded, grumpy one he carried around with himself daily. Because yeah, maybe *Griffin* didn't know how to have sober sex, but this other guy, the one River was dreaming of, was carefree and innocent and didn't have any hang-ups. And that guy? He was pretty fun, and Griffin wasn't ready to let him go quite yet.

"You'll probably end up on the floor," he warned,

letting his voice be as light as it wanted. "And I don't think the accident insurance on the trip covers that."

"I signed all those liability waivers. And I'm feeling rather...determined to show you that you're wrong."

"Well, then, don't let me stop you."

A zipper sounded, then feet hitting the plank floor, and one...two...three steps and he could *feel* River looming over him, hear his breathing even before he spoke.

"Lay on your side against the wall," River ordered, tone rivaling several commanders Griffin had served under.

"Still not gonna work," Griffin muttered as he shifted over.

"I'm skinnier than I look." Contrary to his words, River's weight made the old bed frame creak alarmingly as he settled himself next to Griffin.

"I take it back. *Both* of us on the floor isn't outside the realm of possibility." His words came out shuddery because River's nearness made it hard to breathe. He smelled good, his rich, almost floral scent mingling with the pine of the cabin. And he was warm, a warmth Griffin had almost forgotten existed, because it had been years since he'd had someone this close. He was acutely aware of every one of those years, awkwardness descending as this got more real than he could easily handle.

"Hush. Now where was I? Oh yeah. I sneak over to your bunk and it's chilly, so we have to huddle extra close." River scooted even closer until they were chest to chest, leg to leg, and there was no way he'd miss that Griffin was turned on. But he didn't remark on it as he wound himself around Griffin, holding on as if

Griffin were his new body pillow. The shiver he gave felt real, not an affectation, so Griffin reached down and tugged the bristly camp blanket from the foot of the bed over them both.

"Better?"

"Much." River was so near that each word was a warm brush against Griffin's skin. "Now, in my fantasy, we've been teasing a lot, maybe some little touches, but we haven't actually kissed yet."

"No?" Some of Griffin's unease fled as he slipped into the role again, happy to be a pawn in River's fantasyland.

"No. So when we do…" River grazed Griffin's cheek with his lips. "When we do, it's *electric*. But slow. So slow."

"Yeah." Griffin could barely inhale from all the anticipation coursing through him. But River seemed determined to draw this out. Little kisses on his jaw and neck. Tiny nibbles. Then right when Griffin was about to have to do something or risk crawling out of his skin with need, River's mouth found his in the softest, sweetest kiss Griffin had ever known. So light at first, it was almost like they weren't touching, then slightly more pressure. Darting his tongue out, River traced Griffin's lips with a reverence that made his breath catch.

Little samples. Like Griffin was a box of one-of-a-kind truffles, not to be rushed. And even though they'd kissed once before, Griffin lost himself to the fantasy that this was the first time. First kiss ever maybe. Which was a lovely, fanciful thought as Griffin wasn't sure he entirely remembered his actual first kiss. He let River lead, followed his cues to go at a glacial pace, kisses staying shallow and fleeting.

"Mmm," River made a happy noise. "Exactly like that. We kiss more and more. But remember, *quiet.*"

Griffin found complying with that order increasingly difficult as River finally deepened the kiss, exploring the inside of Griffin's mouth with the same deft touch he'd shown his lips. The rub of their tongues made Griffin's hips shift restlessly, and he had to stifle several moans as River became friskier, nibbling and sucking. It seemed like River fed off his struggles to stay silent, getting more determined and aggressive each time the smallest sound escaped Griffin's throat. Even his shushing noises were sexy as fuck, added to the fantasy that they were getting away with something forbidden.

"This is torture," he gasped when River let him up to breathe.

"Best ever." River's soft laugh made Griffin's skin heat further, warmth spreading to his lower back and feet even. "Of course, eventually our hands start to roam…"

"Do they?" Taking the suggestion, Griffin ran his hands under River's sweatshirt, caressing his back with broad strokes of his palms.

"Mine too," River whispered before his agile fingers found the bare skin along Griffin's waistband, making him need to suck in a breath. For a second, he thought River was going to go for his ass, but he went higher, mimicking Griffin's exploration.

"Fuck, that feels good." Griffin forgot for a second that he was supposed to be quiet, which earned him a stern warning noise from River. "Sorry."

"Too chilly to lose the shirts." River swept his fingers up and down Griffin's spine, tone regretful, but Griffin couldn't tell whether it was part of the fantasy or the reality of the dropping temperatures.

"I'll keep you warm." Griffin pushed River's shirt up, giving himself more to explore. Slim sides. Delicate collarbones and ribs.

Their mouths found each other again in the dark, a much needier kiss this time, one that left him panting. River cuddled into him more, as if he really were using Griffin for warmth, and there was something sexy about knowing he could do that for him, that he had something River needed. So, he pulled River even closer, focused on trying to warm him up, with both kisses and his touch. With not even enough space for a sticky note between their bodies, there was no question that they were both turned on.

River's tongue dragged against Griffin's, making him be the one to shiver. Fuck. It was so good. Their cocks pressed against each other through their pants, and without waiting for permission from his brain, Griffin's hips started a subtle rhythm of pressing into River.

"Mmm. Keep that up and I'm going to get off," River whispered, words tickling Griffin's mouth.

"Shh." Griffin was a little too into this fantasy now, but he couldn't deny how right this all felt. "Gonna have to stay quiet."

"Yeah." River shuddered against him. "Quiet. Don't want to make a mess, but damn you feel amazing."

"Here." Griffin wiggled around, shoving both their pants down and rucking up his own shirt. "Make a mess on me. I clean up easier than your pants."

The skin-on-skin contact had them both groaning, fantasy temporarily forgotten as Griffin reveled in the feel of River's smooth skin, the drag of his patch of hair against Griffin's flesh, the prodding of his hard cock, all of it. Even though it would spoil the fantasy, he needed light, wanting to see and explore River properly.

But River was right—there was something super sexy about not seeing, about having to guess, rely on touch and sound instead of visual cues. And all signs pointed to River being on edge—his breathy moans, the way he clutched at Griffin, how he met each movement of Griffin's hips with thrusts of his own, the dampness on his cockhead, and the desperate way he kissed. The darkness also fed the fantasy that this was the first time either of them had done this, first time a cock had touched his, first time he'd felt the relentless high of arousal. Swallowing down River's little noises had Griffin moving faster, determined to get River there.

"Griff," River panted. And damn that was sexy too, knowing he wasn't entirely a fantasy actor to River, that it being him here with River mattered. "Harder."

That Griffin could do, grabbing River's high, tight ass and pulling him even more snugly in, increasing the friction. With his other hand, he cradled River's head and neck, kissing him harder. Far more pliant now, River let him fuck his mouth with his tongue, sucking on Griffin's questing tongue. River started shuddering, whole body shaking as he moved faster against Griffin, moans muffled by the kiss.

"That's it," Griffin urged.

"Yeah. Griff. Oh God. It's…" River drifted off in a

series of whimpers right before warmth hit Griffin's belly. He held River through it, making encouraging noises, and stroking his back. "Oh fuck. That was... damn. Best role-play ever."

"Yeah." No way was Griffin admitting that this was the only one he'd ever attempted.

He stretched like a pleased cat before giving Griffin another kiss, this one soft and slow. "Your turn."

"I'm good." Griff meant it too. Feeling River go had been better than any solo orgasm he'd mustered up in the past few years, and he felt warm and content in a way he hadn't in ages. Giving that experience to River had freed some essential place deep inside of him. Coming himself felt like an afterthought to all that, not something he needed.

"No, you're not." River seemed determined, wrapping a hand around Griffin's cock right as he nibbled the tender skin of Griffin's neck. And suddenly, Griffin wasn't quite so noble and disinterested.

"Do that again. Bite my neck," a voice he scarcely recognized as his own demanded.

"Yeah? That gonna get you off?" River licked Griffin's neck, tongue dipping down to where his shoulder and neck met, a spot that would be hidden by his collar and a place where he'd always been supremely sensitive. And when his teeth met the flesh, Griffin moaned, noise be damned.

The strokes were different than what Griffin was used to—lighter touch, softer fingers, faster rhythm—but the novelty of it contributed to his rising arousal. Then River did a twisting motion on the upstroke, and his body went from not needing to come to gotta come now.

"Fuck." His eyes squeezed shut as all he could focus

on was the pleasure, how damn good this felt, how unexpected this was.

And when River bit him again, a sexy openmouthed
kiss on his shoulder, Griffin's body heaved, thrusting
almost hard enough to send River to the floor. He had
just enough presence of mind to hold River to him,
keep them both on the bed as he spurted all over his
own stomach and River's fist. The climax was a lot
like his first real shower after his injuries—cleansing
on a soul-deep level that went beyond mere relief or
pleasure. And like then, he let himself simply luxuri-
ate in the sensations, holding River, breathing slowly,
no rush to rejoin reality.

And River seemed to understand, moving so that
his head rested on Griffin's shoulder, both of them
in a heap now with River more or less on top of him.
Griffin welcomed the weight, let it ground him in this
moment. Later, he'd have plenty of time for regrets
and resolutions, but right now, all he had room for
in his chest and brain was…happiness. Unexpected.
Rare. Fleeting. Worth savoring, the way River did with
kisses. And so he did, pressing kisses to River's head
and listening as their ragged breaths evened out, stillness blanketing them.

River wasn't usually a big post-sex cuddler. He liked
sex, liked having it and dreaming about it and antici-
pating it, but afterward he liked his space too. But
something about the way Griff held him after he came
made River want to stick around, made him want to
pay attention, not simply drift off.

And it wasn't like Griff was sleeping either—his
breathing said he was awake, but it was sort of like

he'd descended into a meditative state, and frankly, River envied him that peace. Not that he hadn't also found peace—the role-play had gone from something fun and a way to get Griff in bed to something he desperately needed, quenching a thirst for sweetness he didn't usually let himself acknowledge. And when he'd come, he'd almost felt like laughing because it felt like he'd shed a hundred-pound pack and taken a potent hit off a bong at the same time.

"There. That wasn't so hard, was it?" he said at last, if only to break the quiet. And maybe to reassure himself too that he hadn't strong-armed Griff into more than he'd wanted to do.

"No." Griff's chuckle rumbled through River's body, warm as the blanket he'd pulled back around them. "Damn easy actually. I've never..."

"Never what?" River prompted. Now, cuddling he could take or leave, but he did love pillow talk, the confessions people were only willing to share after getting off together. When sex was good, that was, and when his partners weren't twats who ghosted the second they came. River had known plenty of those too. "Never role-played?"

"That too." Griff's tone was adorably sheepish, but there was something else there, something that made River want to dig deeper.

"Well, you were excellent at it. A plus, and next time we'll do a scenario that gets you off since you indulged me. But, never what? Never before with a guy?"

"No..." Griff struggled to sit, an awkward endeavor that ended up with River taking the hint and climbing off him.

He felt his way to the towel rack he'd spied by the

basin. He sponged off his hand and stomach, then brought the towel over to Griff. "What then?"

Griff's sigh as he cleaned up could have sliced through concrete. "There have been guys, okay. But I'm not...not used to having my full head about me getting off with any gender, okay?"

River took a moment to unpack that statement. "You don't usually have sex sober?"

"Something like that, yeah." Griff flopped back down, not leaving any room for River, who went back to his own bunk and sleeping bag, but he didn't drop the conversation.

"That's too bad. I've had my share of sex high or drunk, and it almost always sucks. I usually regret it, and I always seem to choose losers when I'm high. Or they choose me. Something. Anyway, lousy drunken sex bites." That was an understatement, but no way was he telling Griff specifics about how awful he always felt afterward, so vulnerable and raw. "You need more sex without tying one on."

That got a rattly laugh from Griff. "Not like I've got much choice in that matter. But, anyway. Thanks. I wasn't sure...never mind. Doesn't matter now. But thank you."

"Oooh." A lot of things made sense all of a sudden. "You're in recovery?"

"Something like that." Griff kept up the cryptic routine.

"Hey, you don't have to feel bad around me, man. You really do need to read my book. The whole first part is about deciding to leave partying and certain... behaviors behind that were killing me slowly." He'd kept the book light, of course, glossing over his mother's death and the mess with his dad and Marisa and his downward spiral. But it would be a hell of a lot easier for Griff to read that version than for River to share the real one with him.

"Liking to do E at pretty-people parties isn't the same as a long-term drinking problem, sorry."

"Hey, I take offense at that." River's voice came out as wounded as he felt. "If you must know, I almost died from an eating disorder. And no one around me really got what I was going through. So, no, I wasn't an alcoholic. But there were plenty of days when vodka and diet soda and laxatives were the only things that passed my lips."

"Oh. Sorry—" Griff made a surprised noise, but River plowed ahead.

"It wasn't some teen rebellion that I was leaving behind. It was a lifestyle that was slowly killing me. And I know travel is a bit of an unorthodox sort of rehab, but that doesn't make my issues any less real."

"I'm sorry. I was dismissive." Griff at least sounded sincere. "I don't mean to be a jerk. It's more... I don't usually talk about this shit. With anyone."

"No one?" River blinked into the darkness. "I've got a therapist I see for Skype chats. She's great."

"I don't need a therapist." Griff's tone was so firm that River could almost see the hard set to his jaw.

"Everyone needs therapy of some kind. I've got travel and then Jennifer on standby. Works for me. I mean surely you've got coping strategies?"

"I did rehab." Griff's voice was so soft that River had to strain to hear him. "Spent my time talking, thanks. And now, I just... Routine, you know? Avoid temptation. Keep to my routine. I know what works for me."

"Routine is good, but you can't be a prisoner to it." River knew of what he lectured—he'd had so many little routines in place back when the eating disorder had been in full flare. This many sugar-free mints. That many sit-ups. Routine could save, but it could also shackle.

"Come back to me when you've got a degree under your belt," Griff scoffed, then gentled his tone. "I mean, I know the no-plan, no-home thing is working for you. And I'm not wanting to be a dick about your choices. Or problems. But I'm a guy who needs roots. Grounding. Traveling like you do… I just couldn't do that."

"I know." An unexpected sadness settled over River. He knew this was simply another vacation fling, not something that was ever going to be serious. So Griff not liking travel wasn't something to take personally. But tell that to his suddenly tense back and fisted hands. Apparently his body wanted more than the universe was willing to give. But really, he should know better than to go goofy over Griff. He did *not* want a relationship with anyone, and he tried to use mindfulness to relax his muscles.

"I'm…" Griff trailed off again.

"What?" River hated leaving things unsaid, and for all that he was good with people, he was a crappy guesser where Griff was concerned.

"I'm tired. That's all." Griff was lying, of that River was sure, but before he could call him on it, Griff added, "Night, River."

"Night." River lay awake, listening to the wind outside the cabin as he burrowed deeper into the sleeping bag. Griff's breathing went from probably-faking-sleep to definite soft snores. Maybe tomorrow night they could push the bunks together…

And there he was, getting goofy again. He needed to remember that getting Griff in bed again was supposed to be a fun endeavor, not some emo quest. He needed to be dreaming up new role-play scenarios, not longing for the cuddling afterward. He'd never had a problem sleeping alone, and he wasn't about to start now, no matter how much his enigmatic mountain man got under his skin.

Chapter Nine

Griffin knew even before he opened his eyes that River was in a good mood and would undoubtedly be angling for a repeat of the previous night. The good mood was obvious because he'd beaten Griffin's alarm, already awake when Griffin hit the off button, and was humming softly, some pop tune, as he heated water on the hot plate. Griffin stretched and took in the sight of a shirtless River shimmying as he sponged off his chest and arms.

"Morning, Griff." River gave him an overly familiar smile. Yup, he was totally under the impression that they'd started something the night before. "Sleep good? I saved some warm water for you if you want to clean off before we're supposed to be up at the main lodge."

"Slept okay," Griffin lied, not wanting to let on that he'd slept better than he had in months, whole body still humming from the sex, a pleasant sensation that drowned out any regrets. But now it was a chilly morning, despite the sun from an early dawn, and those regrets kept hollering at Griffin, reminding him that he'd made a mistake. And not just the sex, but in letting River in, telling him some of his truth. He hated telling people about his drinking problem, hated the way it changed how they looked at him, how it colored every interaction from that point onward.

Trying not to blush like a kid, he pulled off his sweatshirt and grabbed a washcloth. River had the right idea—no need to show up at breakfast smelling of spunk, and the shower house was a good five-minute trek away. He cleaned up best as he could and got dressed warmly for that morning's crack-of-dawn photography hike. The plan was to take advantage of the lighting conditions and high probability of wildlife so that the group could get some unique photos. They'd bring sack lunches along then return to the lodge for a hopefully hearty dinner. At the lodge, coffee and breakfast awaited them, and he told himself it was hunger and cold, not wanting distance from River, that made his feet speed up on the gravel path.

But he was a bad liar these days, even to himself. It was more that if they didn't *talk* about the previous night then he could pretend it had all been a pleasant dream, not have to deal with the changed reality. And it really had changed—he was more aware of River than ever, more attuned to his responses. Caring when River rubbed his hands together on the walk, pulling his jacket around him tighter. The urge to wrap him up, pull him close, was almost overwhelming.

Only the knowledge that the others would be coming along soon kept him with his own hands in his pockets. And, of course, River didn't pick up on Griffin's please-don't-talk vibes.

"Is it wrong that I'm already thinking of fun things we could do tonight?" River's voice was light and low, pitched so that even if others were behind them, they were unlikely to hear.

"Yes," Griffin said firmly. "Listen, I think—"

"Last night was a mistake, we can't go there again, must be professional. Yeah, yeah. I knew you'd be stuffed with regrets this morning. But I don't have any."

"Good for you," Griffin ground out, even if a part of him was relieved. Only thing worse than him having morning-after thoughts would be River regretting what they'd done as well. Griffin was ready to be done with this conversation, but there was no relief in sight. The gravel path to the main lodge meandered through scrubby pine trees and seemed to be getting longer, not shorter.

"And I don't see any reason why we can't simply enjoy ourselves while we're rooming together. You're single. I'm single. We've got wicked chemistry. No reason to deny ourselves."

"We're more than our hormones." He barely suppressed a groan. River made it sound so simple. See attractive man, fuck attractive man, move on. And maybe in his universe that was how it worked, but Griffin was already having feelings he didn't want to have, caring more than he should. A repeat wasn't advisable for all sorts of reasons, even if part of him wanted to agree, longed to see what River could dream up for them that night…

No. He could be adult here, put some distance between them. And when River's chance to reply was cut off by Fenna and Lieke coming up the path, Griffin did just that, moving to the other side of the women and trying to strike up a conversation about the day ahead.

The unfamiliar caring urges kept up at breakfast when he watched closely to make sure River ate something. What he'd said about having an eating disorder had given Griff pause. He was ashamed to admit that he'd always seen eating disorders as something belonging to super rich young women, but there had been no mistaking the pain in River's voice. He knew that kind of hurt, what it meant to have done battle with habits threatening to do a person in, what it meant to resist temptations to backslide, and how coping really was an individual thing. Who was he to judge if River coped by traveling? And if he felt a pang that three trips from now River would likely forget him and their time together, well that was on him, being too sentimental.

"Thanks for making sure they had fruit," River said in a low voice as they boarded the bus that would take them to the starting point for their trek. Each day the bus would take them to different interesting sites the lodge had exclusive access to.

"No problem." Griffin looked away, afraid of giving away too much if their eyes met. "You ate more than fruit, though, right? We're going to be hiking a number of hours today at different stops."

"Oh, I'll have energy." There was just enough innuendo in River's voice to make Griffin's neck heat. As a result, he carefully found a seat close to Melanie and Dan and tried to focus on giving wildlife and morning light photography tips.

The bus took them to a verdant valley with a view of the mountains as well as the rivers meandering through the lower elevations. Because the maintained sections of trail were few and far between, he had to trust that their young guide knew what she was doing as she led them along a creek bank, taking advantage of the flat pebbled terrain.

The group was delighted when they spotted a lone

wolf not five minutes into their hike. They stopped frequently to take pictures, which meant a slow pace, but Griffin was grateful for all questions and distractions as otherwise he would have used the whole time observing River and the way he utterly bloomed the farther they trekked. Griffin had known plenty of dedicated hikers but none who seemed so joyous in the endeavor.

And because Griffin was enjoying that joy so much, he noticed immediately when it seemed to disappear during a stop at a particularly scenic vista. Below them green hills rippled like gentle ocean waves until they gave way to mighty snow-topped granite peaks. Above them, a pristine blue morning sky created the perfect backdrop for the mountains. But River wasn't looking at the view at all, instead scowling down at his camera.

"Hell." River's mouth twisted as he flipped different dials on the camera. "I've never had this issue before, but it's not letting me adjust the zoom."

"Let me see?" Griffin stepped closer, away from the others who were clumped together around some boulders, trying for the best shot.

"Sure." River handed it over. It was a nice camera— pro quality but not so snazzy as to stand out and probably several years old. From what he'd seen, River was equally likely to use his phone to snap pictures, but he'd heard him explaining to Melanie that he used the digital camera for pictures that might make it into the book. And the faint scratches on the body spoke of it being well used, which Griffin always liked seeing. Cameras were meant to see real work.

Griffin was intimately familiar with this manufacturer as he owned two as well as it being Uncle Roger's go-to brand. After finding out that River was right and the camera appeared locked up, he dug in his backpack for his emergency repair pack. He'd learned from Uncle Roger that it paid to be prepared for the tourists. Extra batteries. Cleaning cloths. Small screwdrivers. Cleaning kit including bulb syringe. Plenty of amateurs relied on compressed air for cleaning, but Griffin had learned the hard way that that method led to blurry pictures and expensive repairs. So he carefully cleaned River's camera and lens with the bulb syringe and a tiny brush before doing a hard reboot.

Looking over Griffin's shoulder, River let out a happy sound. "Problem solved!"

"Yeah, it was probably a speck of dirt or dust. I've had it happen with sand before. You got lucky—sometimes it gets in there and even a good kit like this one won't save you."

"Take a few pictures for me," River requested when Griffin moved to hand the camera back. "I was struggling with getting a good shot even before it stopped cooperating. I want to see what you see."

Griffin had been giving pointers all morning, but this felt different, more intimate somehow. Still, though, he couldn't exactly gracefully decline.

"Okay." He stepped away from River, breathing deeply, really letting himself see the vista, try to get a feel for what he wanted to capture for River. He crouched low, changing his perspective. Tiny yellow flowers dotted the slope down from their vantage point, and Griffin used the newly working zoom to focus on those, framing a group of three with the vast landscape beyond them. Rising, he took another shot that captured the river carving its way through the valley, try-

ing to showcase its gentle S-curve. And then, because
he could, he took one of River, hair bluer than the sky,
expensive sunglasses, lush mouth with a hint of a smile
for Griffin. He had a brief twinge in his chest, wishing
he could get a copy of that one. It would be nice to…

No. Not going there.

"Here." He handed the camera back to River, who
immediately pulled up the pictures on the screen.

"Wow." River whistled. "You're good. Like really
good."

"Nah." Griffin shrugged. "I play around here and
there, but that's all. No formal training other than listening to Uncle Roger a lot."

"Well, whatever training, it worked. Especially the
one of me. I'm picky about photographs of myself." He
sounded genuinely surprised.

"Really? But you must have been in thousands of
pictures back in your modeling days."

"Yeah, but not minding being in front of the camera isn't the same as enjoying dissecting shots of me.
Easier to simply not see the finished products."

"I can get that." Why it made Griffin's chest hurt
that River couldn't look at himself, couldn't see his innate beauty, he couldn't say.

"Anyway, you've got a knack for balancing people
and background." River offered him a warm smile that
made Griffin's cheeks heat. Damn this man and his ef-
fect on him. "I should be jealous."

"Oh?"

"Not only do you take better pictures than me, and
I've had several workshop trips like this one, but I bet
my…camera's going to prefer your touch now. You've
ruined it for me."

Griffin had to laugh at that because he knew damn well they were actually talking about sex. "I think you'll live."

"Yeah, but what's the fun in merely living?" River tossed back before he stowed the camera in his pack and sauntered back to the group.

What indeed. Griffin stewed on that question as they moved on to the next stop. Ahead of him, River moved with a fluid grace, navigating the uneven terrain far better than Griffin could have predicted a few days ago. He'd vowed to not repeat last night's moment of weakness, but watching River, he wasn't sure he trusted himself to stick to his resolution.

This. This was why he stuck to his planes, his town, his dream of a cabin in the hills. Wishing for more was a fool's journey, and he'd left his fool days behind. He knew himself. Knew he was weak in the face of temptation. And even knowing that, his pulse still thrummed at the thought of bedtime, at what River might try to entice him into doing.

After a long day hiking, eating came much easier to River, and dinner was a pleasant affair with lots of chatting while dining on grilled halibut burgers and vegetable kabobs. After, they all retreated to a cozy fire pit area for a bonfire and more conversation. And s'mores. Because of course. All fires needed marshmallows, at least according to River's inner eleven-year-old, even if his current self had things to say about eating again so soon after dinner, years of inner lectures distancing him from the sweet tooth that had ruled his younger years.

"They do them upscale here. Homemade cookies,

good-quality dark chocolate, jumbo marshmallows."
Well, look at that. Mr. Mountain Man himself had actually sought River out, settling in the chair next to
him. And even if it was only to urge him to eat, River
still saw it as a win that Griff wasn't actively avoiding
him. "You should try one."

"Maybe a taste," River allowed. "Split one with
me?"

Griff's laugh at that was a warm, welcome chuckle.
"No way, I want my own. They're not that big. Here.
I'll get us some ingredients."

Without waiting for River to agree, Griff approached
one of the guides, and got a stick and the makings for
the s'mores on a plate. He returned to River, handing
him the plate before crouching in front of the fire.

"I'll roast yours for you, if you want."

"Will you now?" No way was River missing the
chance to flirt. "I like mine done. Very gooey. *Messy.*
But not burnt."

Griff turned a shade of red at the mention of *messy*
that probably had little to do with the fire. Good.

"I've got you," he said without meeting River's eyes.

"Excellent." Calories be damned. This was fabulous
banter that warmed him even more than the fire, and
he wasn't going to ruin it by obsessing over whether
or not to eat Griff's creation. Griff expertly got the
marshmallows on his stick brown but not black and
transferred them to two cookies with chocolate bar
chunks on them.

"Here. Try this." The smile Griff offered was even
more enticing than the treat. Remembering the con-
sequences of too-fast gobbling when he was a kid at

camp, River waited a few seconds for the s'more to cool before taking a small bite, Griff's eyes still on him.

"Wow." The slight bitterness of the chocolate. The sweet of the marshmallow. The crisp edges of the cookie. Griff's intense gaze. It was all so good that he took a second, bigger bite. And the memories of his childhood didn't compare to this moment right here, this man watching him like River's enjoyment was all he needed or wanted.

"Good." Griff nodded at him. "Thought you'd like it."

"Oh, I do." River tried to tell him with his eyes that they were *so* getting it on as soon as they were alone, Griff's misguided nobility and all. Chemistry this good wasn't meant to be resisted.

And watching Griff eat his own dessert was like bizarre foreplay, the way his tongue came out to lick at a stray drip of chocolate, the way he sighed after a big bite, the small smile as he finished and grabbed the stick to make himself a second. River wanted to be savored like that. Enjoyed. Appreciated. He'd enjoyed last night's make-out session more than just about any other encounter he'd had, the way Griff was so present, so into it, so patient and letting River lead, trying to give him his fantasy, not pushing for more. By the time talk around the fire died down, his body vibrated with low-level arousal. He'd used the shower house after their hike, before dinner, and he was *ready* for bed even if not sleepy in the slightest.

"I'm going to turn in," he said to the group, not letting his eyes linger on Griff, but hoping he'd take the hint and follow.

After a chorus of goodnights, he made his way back

to the cabin. Anticipation buzzing, he changed into sleeping clothes. He didn't bother with his sleeping bag, stretching out on top of it with one of his notebooks, a pretext of doing work and insurance that he wouldn't pounce on Griff as soon as he came in.

Which wasn't too long. Stamping feet sounded on the small porch, then Griff came into the cabin quietly, holding his boots, almost as if he'd expected River to be asleep. Silly man. He sat up because it was easier to talk to Griff that way.

"Writing up the day?" Griff asked, faint flush on his cheeks as he pulled out his bag and dug around for the same flannel pants he'd worn the night before.

"Day, yes. Not last night if you're worried. I don't usually kiss and tell, promise."

"Good to know." Griff changed with brisk movements, but River still appreciated the view—fuzzy, well-muscled chest, strapping shoulders, broad back with a faint smattering of freckles. Tight, meaty ass that he only got a quick peek at before Griff was pulling up his pants. "Okay to turn off the lantern?"

"Sure." River stowed his notebook away. "Come over here."

That got a long groan from Griff as he turned off the lantern, casting the room into darkness thanks to the already drawn shade. "Bad idea."

That wasn't a no, so River laughed. "Best idea. Come here and tell me one of your fantasies."

"Think you're the creative one, not me. You've got quite the imagination."

Still not a no. "Thank you. You want to hear another of mine?"

Long pause. Shuffling sound. Griff was closer now,

but made no move to join him on the narrow bunk. "I should say no."

"But you won't," River said confidently.

Another low groan, this one almost pained. "Tell me," Griff whispered.

There was a rustling sound as he crouched next to River's bed, almost, but not quite, close enough to touch. River took a moment to consider which of his vast collection of fantasies was most likely to appeal to Griff. He wanted to turn him on enough to saw through those reservations, maybe finally get him past guilt and doubts to enjoy the rest of their time together without more flip-flopping between avoidance and arousal.

"Cabins like this always make me think of being snowed in."

Griff snorted at that. "Come up here for a winter, and I guarantee you'll be cured of those fantasies by spring."

"Hey now, no judging. I'm picturing a well-stocked cabin, no imminent danger of death, but super chilly. And we're near strangers, but we need to huddle for warmth." He'd chosen this fantasy because Griff had seemed to get off on warming him up the night before. Also, it was close enough to reality that he could toss in details that made it more personal. "We're shy around each other, but there's this crazy chemistry. And it keeps getting colder and colder. So we're sitting by a fireplace, and gradually we move closer and closer…"

"You really do like the first-time thing, don't you?" Griff's voice was soft.

"Yeah. Wasn't kidding about that." River's skin cooled, making him shiver. Admitting this truth stripped him bare—he might have fooled around with role-play before, but he didn't usually reveal his most private of desires.

"I can work with it." Griff's tone was contemplative, as if he were getting into this despite himself. "So me keeping you warm, it's a survival thing?"

"Partly. Like I said, I'm not thinking fuck-or-die, but more like…comfort. Like we *need* each other. And the storm just makes it worse."

"Yeah." Blowing out a breath, Griff seemed to let go of some of his tension.

"Come sit up here by me. It really is getting chillier. Not a blizzard, but we can pretend."

There was a long pause where River started to resign himself to Griff gluing himself to the plank floor, but then he hefted himself up, coming to sit next to River. Not touching, but close enough that River could smell his woodsy scent, feel his warmth already. He tapped Griff's leg with his foot simply because he could.

"We've got a fire, but it's still cold. Wind whistling, even louder than this. And even though we're strangers, we scoot closer…"

This time Griff moved quicker, sliding over so that they were hip-to-hip, shoulder-to-shoulder. And miracle of miracles, his arm came around River. "Better?"

"Oh, much." River burrowed into his side, getting comfortable in the embrace. "Now for the fun part. Both of us want to kiss, but neither of us wants to make the first move. The tension is absolutely delicious."

"You get off on the waiting?" Griff's laugh felt as good as his arm holding River close.

"The moment that 'will we or won't we' changes into 'when will we' is just the best. Like the air almost crackles. And yeah, it gets me hard. Even before our lips meet."

"Yeah." Griff made the closest thing to a happy noise that River had heard from him.

"And the beautiful thing is that we simply keep moving closer and closer and neither of us has to make the first move. It happens, almost spontaneously. Without us forcing it."

"That easy, huh?"

"Yup." River let his lips graze Griff's collar, then shifted so that they were almost cheek-to-cheek, close enough to feel Griff's breath, but true to his word, he didn't close the gap, didn't force it. Instead, he breathed slowly, cultivating patience.

The payoff was more than worth it, as after several long moments, Griffin's lips brushed his cheek. Then his nose and chin. Little featherlight kisses almost as if Griffin couldn't believe he was letting himself do this. Then their mouths met, soft and slow, Griffin showing that he remembered how River liked it. But unlike the night before when he'd let River do most of the leading, Griffin allowed himself to explore, little sips and tastes that had River squirming.

When their tongues finally met, it felt like coming home, an almost alien sensation for River, the rightness of this, the way his whole body relaxed into the kiss, let Griff have his way with him. And far from taking advantage like a lot of people would, Griff kept things painstakingly slow. It was like he had a direct line to River's brain, knew exactly how he liked things to go. Their tongues slid together, making him tremble with each contact.

"Still cold?" Griff asked, voice so caring that River almost forgot about the fantasy for a moment.

"Yeah," River said, mainly because he was curious what Griff would do.

"Here." Griff hauled River into his lap, a show of strength that made River gasp. Mountain man indeed. "Let me warm you up."

With that, he slid his hands under River's shirt, stroking his back while finding his mouth again for a searching kiss. River purred and gripped Griff's thick shoulders, leaning into the contact.

"Definitely heating up." He licked at Griff's neck, the way that had driven him nuts the night before. And it worked, Griff moaning low and firmly palming River's ass, encouraging him to grind. "I think eventually the fire and you would do the trick, and we'd need to lose a few clothes…"

"That so?" Griff didn't sound opposed to the idea.

"Yeah. No messy clothes, remember?" He laughed because damn this was fun, unraveling Griff like this, taking him from grumpy guide to willing playmate.

"Mmm, yeah, don't want that." Griff gently set River on his feet. They both scrambled out of their clothes, and River grabbed the sleeping bag and blanket before pushing Griff back on the bed.

"Now where were we?" He straddled Griff's waist, luxuriating in being skin-to-skin, Griff's hard cock against his own. He draped the sleeping bag and blanket over them. "See, our own cozy nest."

Growling low, Griff pulled him in for a kiss. His mouth was more demanding now, sucking and biting and driving River out of his head. Damn but he loved making out, grinding together. Give him this over fucking any day. And luckily, Griff seemed on the same wavelength, encouraging River to rock against him.

"Yeah. Like that." Griff's head fell back, opening himself up for River to attack his neck and bare shoulders. He adored the drag of Griff's chest hair against his own, much more sparsely populated torso. Using his lips and tongue, he discovered all the places that made Griff moan and that made his hips thrust up to meet River's motions.

"Damn. You have the most sensitive neck. Love it. Can you get off this way?" River asked right before he nibbled a path down one strong collarbone.

"Supposed…to be…warming you." Griff's voice was stretched taut, each word an effort, and fuck, River loved having pushed him to that place.

"Oh, I'm plenty hot." River laughed. The covers pooled around his legs, but he was beyond caring about their warmth. He and Griff had more than enough heat between them.

"Yeah, you are." Griff worked a hand between them, wrapped it around both their cocks. Griff was only a little longer but impressively wide, and his cock was warm and hard against River's. Griff started a slow stroke that matched River's languid assault on his neck. His grip was tighter than River's own, but it was the noises that Griff made that really made River's blood hum. "God. So good. More."

River obliged him with a kiss on the lips, this one more aggressive and dirtier, fucking his way into Griff's mouth. That earned him a low moan from Griff, one River felt all the way to his balls. Griff sped up his strokes, which made River tempted to stop things to find something slick, but Griff's harsh breath said he was on the edge, and no way was River missing out on that.

"Close?" He moved to nibble at Griff's shoulder again, sucking up a bite that would undoubtedly leave a mark under Griff's shirt tomorrow. He liked that, liked marking this big, strong man, knowing that he could make him writhe and beg for it.

"Oh fuck. Like that. Wanna come."

"Do it."

"Want you to come too. Please." God, Griff's begging was almost enough to get River there, from nothing more than the needy tone of his voice.

"Get there. I will too, promise. I wanna use your come as lube."

"Fuck. So hot." Griff's body started to shudder under River. "Need it."

Reading his reactions, River timed his next bite for when Griff's grip tightened and wasn't surprised when Griff bucked and cursed.

"Fuck. Fuck. River. Right there." Warm, slick fluid seeped between them and was exactly the slickness River had been waiting for. He rocked into Griff's hand as he shook with the aftershocks, riding each moan to get closer and closer. Griff made an encouraging noise and kept up the stroke even as he kept twitching and gasping. Reducing Griff to this fucked-out pile of goo was the biggest turn-on in the world, and it wasn't long before River too was moaning and shooting all over Griff's stomach.

"Damn." Griff cradled River to him. "That was…"

"Enough to burn the cabin down?" River laughed. "And better than my best blizzard fantasy. Hell, I'll be using this to get off for months."

Griff was quiet for long moments then whispered, "I like knowing that. That you'll remember this."

"I will. And that's exactly why we need to take advantage of this. Make as many memories as possible while we can."

"I…" Griff trailed off on a heavy sigh. "Wish it was that easy."

"It can be. Tell me you don't need a few sexy memories of your own to use when winter comes and you're back to your I-don't-date ways."

"Yeah." Griff surprised him by agreeing. "That might be nice. Didn't know I could want this again. It's like the spring thaw for my sex drive. I want you all the time, but I hate that I want you, if that makes any sense at all."

"I get it. And Griff, I don't want to hurt you. Promise. I just want to give us both a good time. I don't want to upset your life or be drama. It's okay to want this." God, he wanted to be a safe place for Griff, a space where he could let himself want and feel again, wanted that so bad his muscles tensed waiting for Griff's reply.

"I'll try."

Somehow that answer was more satisfying than a ready yes from Griff. He'd try. Try to let River in. Try to enjoy himself. And that would be enough. River would make sure it was enough by showing Griff over and over that this thing between them was good and safe and worth exploring.

Chapter Ten

Griffin's alarm interrupted a very nice dream about River and a big bed where they could sleep next to each other instead of retreating to their separate bunks after sex. Funny that Griffin's dream was more about sleeping and holding River, not more sex.

"It's still night." River made adorable snuffling noises into his pillow.

"It's the morning of our sunrise trip to Wonder Lake. It'll be worth it, trust me." The last few days had flown by, days full of hikes and photography tips, nights full of River. And now it was their last full day in Denali, and he didn't know what he was going to do with himself when they left this place behind.

"Anything that requires a flashlight for getting dressed better be." Shivering, River got out of bed. No fantasy this time—he was genuinely chilled, and Griffin couldn't resist wrapping him up in a big hug from behind.

"Mmm." River's head fell back on Griffin's shoulder. "That's nice. Too bad we don't have time for you to warm me up properly."

Time. It was the one thing they didn't have, an ever-dwindling supply of days and hours until River would leave Griffin's life forever. And the thought should have been enough to have him pushing River away, but instead, he held him tighter, like that mattered, like he alone could stop the march of time.

Fool. But by this point, he'd pretty much accepted that that's what he was around River. Fool for him. Reckless. Incapable of resisting the pull between them. Last night had been homemade ice cream night, real old-fashioned ice churner and all, and he'd been mesmerized watching River sample the wild berry dessert. Turned on, sure, and impatient to get River alone, but there was also this growing tenderness that he had no clue what to do with.

Thus, he simply hugged River, held him close while he had him. Last night they'd rubbed off together, River's kisses tasting like strawberries and only the flimsiest of fantasies driving their bodies. He'd been easy. A few whispered words from River about being cold, and he'd been only too eager to slip into that other self again, the first-time sexy stranger who was fresh and new for River. It was almost too easy to be the guy River wanted for a night or two, and he'd do well to remember that despite his newfound acting chops, the real him wasn't anything River needed or wanted.

"Dress warmly," he ordered, shivering himself in the chill of what was for all intents and purposes the middle of the night. But with the Arctic sunrise around five a.m. this time of year, they had to sacrifice some sleep if they wanted to capture it. "Dawn's still a ways off."

"I know." River still didn't make a move to pull away from Griffin's embrace. "Tell me we get a nap later?"

"It's something of a down day, yes." Griffin laughed. "But stop your plotting right there. I don't nap."

"Ha. Like I was thinking of sleep." River finally did step away, pull out his bag.

"No nooners." God, Griffin loved bantering with River like this, wasn't sure he'd ever had this before. It was as if he'd been dragging around a fifty-pound cement block for years now and River had cut him loose, made him light and disoriented at his new freedom. And hell if he knew how to properly express his gratitude. Or what he'd do when the weight returned, heavier than ever after River left.

"We'll see." River gave him an arch look as he put on layers of clothes as Griffin had suggested.

Griffin completed his own morning routine in short order, then led the way up to the main lodge. They had an unspoken rule that what happened in the cabin stayed in the cabin—no holding hands on the trails, no stolen kisses, no flirting around the others. And Griffin liked that, he really did. Keeping his private life private was important to him, but as River shivered next to him, hands in his pockets, jacket gathered tight, Griffin wanted nothing more than to hold him close again, warm him up, not in their sexy game way, more the way a good boyfriend—

Wait. He was *not* River's boyfriend and could not afford to be thinking like that. River didn't do boyfriends, and Griffin didn't do dating, and this was simply a casual fling. Wanting to take care of River was all well and good, but he couldn't go losing his head. And he tried hard to remember that as they met up with the rest of the group and got fast fuel of coffee and sack breakfasts for later.

Wonder Lake was something of a drive from the lodge, and they bounced over uneven roads in the lodge's small bus, giving him plenty of time to daydream about that nooner. Which he wasn't going to do, but his libido was on overdrive after years of being packed away. But he did manage to flip back into guide mode as they arrived at the lake with the barest hint of light over the horizon.

Griffin had talked to the group last night about low lighting conditions and sunrise, and he repeated some of his tips now, helping Melanie and Fenna get tripods set for potentially catching the reflection of Denali in the lake, a rarity even for regular park goers. For himself, Griffin was more captivated with the curve of the lake, the way it perfectly angled toward the mountains and made the lake look even larger and more epic. Despite carrying a camera in his pack, Griffin had been too busy to take many pictures of his own, but he had to make an exception for the rosy dawn glow hitting the water.

"I want to see your pictures later," River said in a low whisper. "And no, not a come-on. I bet they're far better than mine."

Griffin shrugged. "Everyone sees different things. That's all."

"Isn't that the truth." River gave a small nod. "But I like seeing what you see."

Griffin wasn't sure what to make of that, whether he wanted to be seen in that way, and took advantage of a question from Melanie to step away. They were situated on a hill with the lake below them, enabling them to get the sort of once-in-a-lifetime panoramas they'd come for. But the angle of the hill was tricky, scrubby vegetation sloping down and not enough level ground for them and their equipment.

"Look!" Griffin pitched his voice to get attention, but not startle. "See that moose by the shore? You can frame him in a landscape shot or use your zoom and make him the focus. But act fast before he moves on."

Everyone jockeyed for position to get a good shot, and Griffin had to make a shushing noise to remind them not to make so much noise.

"I want to get closer," River whispered, taking a few steps down the hill. Before Griffin could call out a warning that the decline was far steeper than it looked, he was slipping and tumbling down the hill, bouncing like the rocks falling after him. Griffin's heart lodged itself somewhere around his sinuses, clogging his thinking, filling him with terror.

"River!" he shouted, like that might make a damn bit of difference.

River came to a stop where the land flattened out a little, and Griffin and the lodge's bus driver both hurried after him.

Griffin struggled with going slowly and carefully enough to avoid slipping himself, and the journey to where River had landed was far more painstaking than his clamoring chest liked. He cursed himself for not bringing the walking stick his mother had pushed on him and knew he'd be feeling this sharp descent in his bum foot later. By the time he approached River, he was struggling to sit up.

"I'm okay," he called. "Just my pride that took a fall."

"Stay down until we can check you over," Griffin ordered. Relief made his pulse speed up, sweat gath-

ering at the base of his neck. Thank God, River didn't
seem to be showing signs of a head or spinal injury, but
Griffin wasn't taking any chances. Ignoring the other
guide, he knelt next to River as best he could on the
uneven terrain, taking stock of his injuries—scratched
face and hands, but no big bruises on his head. Even
sized pupils. He obediently wiggled his fingers and
toes for Griffin with a pained laugh.

"Okay, maybe I've got a minor ankle sprain, but I'm
okay, promise." River rolled his shoulders as Griffin
paid extra attention to the ankle. He knew all too well
what broken looked like, and his gut roiled at the memory. "Bruised, but nothing's broken. Even my camera
appears to have survived with only a few scratches.
Can I get up now?"

Griffin was torn between wanting to shake him for
the scare and wanting to hold him close because he was
safe and in one piece, but in the end did neither, merely
holding a hand out to River. "Easy now."

Working with the other guide, they helped River
get back up the steep incline without putting too much
weight on his ankle. The whole time, Griffin's head
continued to reel. God, that moment when he'd been
sure River had been seriously injured…

He wasn't going to get over that any time soon.
Not since Hank had he been so concerned for someone else's welfare and look how that had turned out.
Hank had still died, and Griffin had slid into that dark
place he hoped never to revisit. Caring too much about
another person was dangerous and meant he was des-
tined to lose big.

And even knowing that, he couldn't bring himself
to put distance between him and River when they were

back with the rest of the group. Melanie fussed over River, doing her doctor thing and checking him over, much as Griffin had.

"We'll have to keep an eye on you, make sure there's no latent head injury," she said with a frown. "Luckily, you're not rooming alone, and Griffin can watch for any warning signs."

"Luckily." River glanced at Griffin, their eyes meeting. Funny, how only a few days ago, Griffin had been cursing his poor luck of having to room with River, and now here he was wondering how he'd cope when their time here came to an end.

"I'll take care of him," he promised Melanie, voice rough, eyes still on River, promising him too.

And while it was a given that Griffin would make sure River stayed off the foot as much as possible, part of him yearned to really take care of River. Run him a hot bath. Cook him some filling food. Wrap him up in one of his sister's quilts. Make love to him, sweet and slow. Silly, silly impulses, but hell if he could stop them.

One more night. He'd let himself take care of River best as he could today, but tomorrow they'd leave Denali behind, and he'd have to turn off all these unwelcome feelings and urges, turn back on his real life and real self.

When they loaded the lodge bus for the long drive back to the main Denali visitor center, River was more than a little sad to say goodbye to the little camp. Usually by this point in a planned trip, he'd be already thinking of the next adventure, spinning how he'd summarize this trip on his blog and in his book. But for the first time in a long time, he wished he didn't have an itinerary or book deadline. Bumming around places had been more fun when he'd set his own agenda, extended or cut short trips as his moods dictated. Now he had an editor wanting a draft who wouldn't be amused if the last third of River's book was "and then I stayed at camp in Denali until snow fell."

He was tempted, though. Tempted to stay in this place with Griffin, keep making magic at night and taking head-clearing hikes all day. He couldn't remember the last time he'd been this happy, this at peace. Hell, he was even eating without thinking about it, a minor miracle in itself. That had always been something he'd loved about hiking—the genuine appetite he worked up, the way it tapped into his childhood camping experiences, made it easier to eat without forcing himself or overanalyzing every bite.

However, that last morning, he was back to having a cactus in his stomach, a prickly, angry thing that only allowed a little black coffee. His ankle still smarted some, but he could put weight on it and had been able to wear his regular shoes. Also smarting? His ego because Griff had used vague excuses about not wanting to hurt him and wanting him to rest for why River hadn't managed to wheedle more than a few reluctant kisses out of him when they were alone in their cabin. Their last night together in Denali, and he'd hoped...

Well, that was pointless, wasn't it? All that was left was the long trek back. Lieke and her sketchbooks sat next to him, not Griff, who was sitting silently next to Fenna, both reviewing pictures on their cameras. Being so close yet so far away from Griff was torture, and he had to restrain himself from yelling "shotgun" like an overeager kid when they were back at the visitor center.

Luckily, he had no competition for the passenger seat in their van as they transferred all their luggage over, and he stuck his water bottle there like a place-holder. After a few hours in the lodge bus, they were all ready to stretch their legs, so after stowing their things, they wandered around the visitor center. Or rather, the others wandered, and River rested his ankle on a handy bench near a wildlife exhibit.

"Do you need a painkiller?" Griff came to sit next to him, offering him a cup of coffee. "It's black—that's how you take it, right?"

"Usually." River offered him a smile for remembering that little detail. The coffee tasted not unlike burnt shoe leather, but he wasn't going to complain. "And no, I don't need meds. Just taking it easy. Did I hear something about a hot tub in Talkeetna?"

"Yup." Griff's return smile was a little wary. "But don't go getting any ideas—it's a rustic outdoor one open to all of that lodge's guests. It's not..." He made a vague hand gesture.

"I'm wounded, Griff." River laughed. "I wasn't trying to imply anything other than that my muscles wouldn't mind a soak. But now that you've put the idea into my head..."

"You can take it right back out again." Griff rolled his eyes, an adorable glimpse into what the adolescent Griff must have been like.

"You won't keep me company?" River gave him his best pleading look. "And speaking of, any chance there's a room shortage?"

Griff snorted at that. "Nope, and just FYI, the two

doubles are in the middle of the two singles—I got the room assignments from the lodge when I checked my phone a few minutes ago."

"I can be *very* quiet," River reminded him. "In fact, I like that, remember?"

"River," Griff groaned. "We can't—" He abruptly stopped as Melanie and Dan headed their way. And of course, River knew better than to bring up sleeping arrangements when they were all back in the van. Griff valued discretion, and no way was River ruining his chances of some hotel room fun that night. Besides, he couldn't shake the image of a younger Griff that he'd had earlier. Curious, he tried striking up a conversation once they were back on the highway leading to Talkeetna.

"When was the first time you flew?" he asked. He'd seen the land-bound Griff plenty, but hell if he didn't want to see Griff among the clouds.

"As a passenger?" Griff laughed, a warm, rich sound. "Probably less than a month old. Both my folks flew back then, and the business was still getting started. Not much money for childcare. There's a picture of my mom wearing me in some backpack thing doing a preflight checklist."

"Cute. I want to see that photo. Neither of your folks flies now?"

Griff's mouth twisted. "Mom still does on occasion. Dad passed away from an aneurysm when I was four or so. I don't really remember him much at all. He was Uncle Roger's older brother, and the whole family rallied around Mom after that. We're a close-knit bunch."

"I'm sorry he died." River winced, ashamed that he'd forgotten that detail about Griff's father being deceased. "I still miss my mom, but I'm glad I've got my memories, even when they hurt." That was more than he usually shared, but somehow talking about her with Griff didn't cause the same raw feeling he usually got.

"Memories do tend to do that." Griff's eyes got distant, and River had a strong feeling that he was thinking of his friend, the one who died, not his dad.

River didn't want either of them wallowing in past pain, so he lightened his voice again. "And when did your mom let you fly for real? Bet she was a nervous wreck teaching you."

"Ha." Some of the tension left Griff's features. "You don't know my mom. Nothing ruffles her. Even when I was…" His mouth pursed as he trailed off. "Difficult. When I was difficult, she still never let it show. She's got a steel backbone, that's for sure. And when I was in my teens, she taught me how to fly, but it took a number of years before she'd let me go up without her or another pilot. Eventually the tourism and transport business grew enough that she needed me making runs and she loosened the reins some."

"But then you left for the air force?"

Another heavy sigh alerted River that he'd probably asked the wrong question, but before he could retract it, Griff resumed talking. "That was all Hank, my best friend. He had big dreams. Convinced me to try for the academy with him. I never dreamed we'd both make it in, and hell, I was eighteen. Fighter jets sounded a lot more fun than twin engine Cessnas. Shows what I knew."

"Sometimes we have to try something. Modeling always sounded so glam to me. And when I was scouted,

I was so flattered that I went down that path all giddy and excited. Like you said, teenager and all that."

"You don't miss that life?" Griff's eyes were on the road, but his tone was thoughtful. Outside, the sun bounced off the endless supply of spruce trees.

"Some." River was honest. "I like my friends, and that world…it's a bit addictive. Hanging out. Partying. Being glam. But if I spend too long with it, I get restless. Need a break. Need to keep my batteries charged, I guess. You miss the military?"

"Some." Griff echoed River's reply. "I liked flying. Liked the routine and discipline. I guess I needed the structure. But I missed my family, missed Alaska. I spent a fair amount of time being angry about my discharge, but I've made my peace. This is where I belong."

"Yeah," he said weakly. Griff sounded so firm that River's chest pinged, another reminder of how far apart they were. This was Griff's place in the universe, and River… Well, he didn't exactly have a place. Which was how he liked it. Needed it. Roots meant they could be ripped away, leaving a person reeling, tumbling into awful places. He should know.

He had no business wishing he could be more like Griff. Or *with* Griff. But that didn't seem to stop him from entertaining fantasies where they could part friends. Or okay, friends with benefits. Because hell if he was done with Griff yet. And no matter what Griff said, he refused to accept that Denali had been the end of anything between them.

Chapter Eleven

Griffin liked talking with River way more than he should. Perhaps even more than he liked kissing River, which was really saying something. But it wasn't like they were going to kiss that night. He hadn't been kidding about the room situation being challenging. The large log-built lodge was laid out much like a family house—generous lounge room and restaurant on the ground floor, and guest rooms on the second floor, with a few auxiliary cabins surrounding the main structure. Each room was decorated uniquely with different regional influences, and even if Griffin had been tempted to play with the room assignments, he needed the two couples to have the more elaborate suites with soaring ceilings and views of Denali. And he also did not need to be seen sneaking into River's room at the end of the hall like a guilty teen.

After putting his bags in his room, he walked quickly to the stairwell, not slowing down at River's door. He needed to set up for that evening's photo show in the lounge, and he did not need to be imagining River in the shower or napping or any other position. Over. Done. Moving on.

But tell that to his body, which still lurched when

River appeared downstairs for dinner, hair a little less vibrant blue, but perfectly styled for the first time in days, mouth looking extra pouty. Damn it.

"Melanie said you need me?" He sauntered over to Griffin, wicked smile tugging at his mouth.

"I don't," Griffin said automatically even if that was fast becoming a lie.

"Oh?" River held up a small square. "My pictures for the show?"

"Oh. That. Yeah." Griffin held out a hand, both hating and loving the sizzle when their fingers connected. "Dinner is salmon pot pie. Does that sound like something you can eat?"

River shrugged, but his eyes sparkled. "Depends. What's for dessert?"

"Not *that.*"

"Darn." He sighed dramatically. "But, yeah, I'll try it. Seriously, Griff. Don't worry about me."

Too late. Griffin already did. Even when River wasn't tumbling down a hillside, Griffin worried. Cared, all the lectures to himself be damned. And at the dinner, he watched carefully to make sure that River didn't hate the home-style meal. He'd eaten better at the camp, seemed freer, and Griffin hated if him trying to put up some boundaries was the reason why River seemed tenser tonight.

After dinner, they all gathered in the lounge where Griffin had hooked his laptop up to the big-screen TV. This was always the sort of event Uncle Roger excelled at. He loved his tradition of everyone sharing the best of their Denali pictures, and he always had the right words, the right compliments to put even novice photographers at ease. Griffin tried to channel that energy as each person took turns sharing.

"You really took what I said about lighting," he said to praise Melanie's picture of a sunset.

"Thank you." Melanie's cheeks darkened. "I tried. You really think I improved on the trip?"

"Oh absolutely," River interrupted. "You've grown so much. This is lovely, just lovely."

"It's all because of *you.*"

Griffin had to blink for a second when he realized that she meant him, not River. "Me?"

"You're one of the best teachers I've had." She beamed at him. "You really know your stuff, and you always had a tip right when I needed it."

The others murmured their agreement and Griffin's neck heated. Turned out that the only thing worse than doling out praise was accepting it.

"Just helping Uncle Roger out," he mumbled and went on to the next photo. After they finished with Melanie's pictures, Lieke showed some truly impressive sketches and watercolors.

"Wow. Those are going to fetch a big price back home," River told her.

"I can hope." She smiled at River, then surprised the heck out of Griffin by handing him a sketch. While most of her work was landscape and nature based, this was a sketch of the whole group, the night they'd had s'mores. All six of them around the fire, him and River sitting closer than he'd remembered. "For you."

"Me? No, I couldn't possibly—"

"You'll want to remember this trip." Her eyes danced, and he wondered if perhaps he and River hadn't been as good at secrets as he'd hoped. And she wasn't wrong. He did want to remember this trip, knew he'd rely on some of these memories in the dead of winter. Hell, ten years from now, he'd probably still be getting off to the memory of how River tasted.

"Thank you." That didn't seem adequate for such a personal gift, but it was all he had.

"My turn." River was every bit as eager as Melanie and Lieke, clearly enjoying having an audience at his disposal. He'd chosen to share a number of pictures of the group—whimsical shots of Melanie taking a turn churning ice cream, Fenna and Lieke admiring a family of bears from the safety of the bus, and several from hikes, sweaty but happy people. Griffin was struck by the ones he was in. When was the last time he'd seen pictures of himself smiling? And true, he wasn't smiling much in the Seward pictures that River shared, but by the start of the Wonder Lake hike, he'd seemed to be smiling on the regular.

"Oh, there's the lumberjack!" Melanie laughed as River revealed his next picture, a snap of Griffin in a red plaid shirt on one of the hikes, Denali perfectly framed behind him, stern expression on his face. Probably because he'd told River to stop photographing him.

"Better not end up in your book," he said, voice gruff.

"Of course not." River made an exasperated noise. "These are my just-for-fun snaps. Like this one."

He moved Griffin's mouse to click the next picture, which was another of Griffin, one he hadn't been aware of River taking. He was watching a plane come in for a lake landing, eyes skyward. And he looked… God, Griffin wasn't even sure he had words. Strong. He looked strong and confident, like he hadn't felt in

years. And handsome, weird as that was. River's camera had a kind eye, that was for sure. It was almost like
River saw him as he wanted to see himself, an almost
paralyzing realization.

Made his back sweat, knowing River saw him as
all that, and he was more than a little relieved when
River's turn ended and Fenna took over. She had several tasteful landscape shots, and it wasn't long before
their little viewing party broke up.

"My ankle and I are going to find that hot tub."
River didn't even look Griffin's way, and still he felt
the invitation.

"Good for you. Dan and I picked up a lovely white
wine exploring Talkeetna earlier. You want a glass for
your soak?" Melanie offered.

"Nah." River's tone was airy, but Griffin had a feeling he'd declined on his behalf, and that made a granite
lump form in his gut. He didn't want to be responsible
for River reining himself in, be a burden in that way.

"How about you?" Melanie asked him next. "No
driving until morning. Join us? Or you going to soak
too?"

"Soak." Griffin grasped the word like a lifeline.
It wasn't even that he was that tempted to drink. He
wasn't. His no was a given. It was more that he hated
being on the spot, hated being asked, having to think
up a reply. Hated that what used to be social never
could be again. Hated the bargaining that happened in
his brain—his head trying to tell him that wine wasn't
his thing, that a taste wouldn't be his undoing, not the
way whiskey would, but years of experience reminding him that there were some paths he simply couldn't
head down. And the way the mere thought of whiskey

had memories of the burn and the buzz swamping him told him that tonight was going to be a long one, one where he'd welcome a distraction.

River. And while escaping to the hot tub might mean confronting another temptation, right then it was the out he needed, a good excuse for packing up the laptop quickly while Melanie tracked down glasses for those imbibing.

And technically, he didn't *need* to change into swim trunks once he was back up in his room. He could simply hole up for the rest of the night. No one would probably notice if he never made it back downstairs. But he tried to be a man of his word, and he'd said he'd soak with River, so he dutifully pulled on a pair of shorts and grabbed one of the hotel-provided robes. And if he was honest, it was the twitchy need for a distraction from the churning in his brain, not a need to be honorable, that had him taking the stairs back downstairs. The hot tub was located outside on a deck with an impressive view of the rapidly fading light, night falling in a cascade of soft pastels that made Griffin wish he'd grabbed his camera.

Equally impressive? The view of River shrugging out of his robe, revealing a blue Speedo, looking like some young European aristocrat on vacation. He quickly climbed into the hot tub, which was an older round model with high redwood siding and small steps to assist with getting in.

"Coming?" he made a beckoning gesture at Griffin, leaving him little choice but to join him. However, he carefully angled himself across from River, not next to him, both glad and disconcerted that they were the only two in the hot tub.

"Man, this feels amazing." River made a happy noise as he arranged himself in the tub, almost a purr, and it went straight to Griffin's dick. "Just what I need."

I've got what you need right here. The flirty retort almost slipped out before Griffin swallowed it back. What the hell? He didn't flirt, wasn't good at it, even in his younger days.

"How's the ankle?" he asked, trying to keep his voice normal. "Do you think you should go to urgent care when we're back in Anchorage? I could take you."

"That's sweet of you." River's small smile said he knew perfectly well that the offer meant more time together. Which wasn't why Griffin had made it, but he couldn't deny that he wasn't ready to say goodbye. "But, I think I'm fine. Just a sprain, and it became a little stiff with all the hours traveling today, but this is helping."

"Good." The water was hot and roiling, soothing knots Griffin hadn't known he'd had, and his voice came out more relaxed than usual.

"It would be a better use of our time to have dinner tomorrow night after the group disbands." River's smile this time was wider. "You can take me to whatever red meat haven you like in Anchorage, and it'll be my treat. What do you say, Mountain Man?"

"I need to go see Uncle Roger at the orthopedic rehab place," he hedged. The water temperature seemed to climb twenty degrees as he tried to sort out how he felt about the invite. "He's itching to go home, and Mom says he may be discharged in time for me to bring him back home with me tomorrow."

"It can be a late dinner. Doesn't matter to me." River shrugged, making the water ripple around his elegant shoulders. "Or just come by my hotel room after you're done with your uncle. My flight isn't until late the next day. I'm easy."

"There's a good joke there." Griffin had to laugh despite his reservations. "And we both know it wouldn't be a smart idea to...hang out."

"Hang out?" River's eyes danced. "I mean we *could* watch a movie or something, but I'd rather make your eyes roll back in your head. Repeatedly." His bluntness made Griffin have a coughing fit, like some maiden aunt. "Don't pretend you don't like that idea."

"Not about liking it."

"Then at least think about it. No need to give me an answer right now, okay?"

"Okay." Griffin had to change the subject and fast. "I've been wondering...is there any food that you genuinely like?"

"Why?" River sounded mildly put out by the question. "You want to feed me well on the date you won't agree to? I told you, I'm fine with a steak extravaganza for you."

"Not for me. And not a date thing. Just curious. I know food is...problematic for you. But is there anything that you really enjoy eating?"

River thought for a long moment. "Some soups really work for me. But...like if we're playing the last supper game, I'd go with someone magically recreating my mom's rigatoni recipe and some birthday cake. Which I know is a weird combo..."

"No." Griffin's throat went strangely tight. God, River needed someone to take care of him. Not that Griffin could—or would—volunteer for the job. "Cake is great. And I've never had the other, but you can't go wrong with a good casserole."

"And for you? Last supper?" River kept his voice light, but there was a certain sadness in his eyes that Griffin really wanted to erase.

"Hmm… You've got me wanting cake now, but a chocolate one with chocolate icing. And a steak, because you pegged me right there. A big rib eye maybe. Probably some loaded mashed potatoes as a side. I'm predictable, I guess."

"I like that." River gave him an indulgent look. "Tell me something else about you. Something few people know."

"I already told you that one," Griffin mumbled, neck itching. "I don't exactly advertise that I'm an alcoholic."

"Not that." River's voice was gentle. "I appreciate you sharing that with me, but I meant something that's important to you but that most people would never guess looking at you."

It was River's gentleness that stopped Griffin from blowing him off, that made him stop and think, want to give River a real reply.

"I like to cook," he said at last. "Because my mom and sisters do so much, I don't get a ton of chances and I'm not gourmet, but I entered a chili contest a few years back on a bet with a cousin, and that was surprisingly fun."

"I bet. What else?" River gazed at him expectantly, clearly wanting more.

"Okay, okay. Truly hidden interests… You're going to laugh, but they made me take art therapy in rehab." God, this was hard to talk about. He almost never mentioned rehab, not even with his mom, who had paid for the damn thing. But the memories were fresh in his head from the earlier lecture he'd needed to give himself about choices and what he wouldn't—couldn't—do. "And I got into coloring with fine tip pens. Geometric stuff mostly, not like a kid's picture book or anything too cutesy."

"I love it." River's eyes went wide, but his voice was sincere enough. "You should show me sometime."

"Maybe." Griffin shrugged, knowing sometime was likely to never materialize. "How about you? What's something people wouldn't guess looking at you?"

Mouth twisting, River blew out a breath. "I don't like to bottom. Everyone *always* assumes I must—hello, skinny guy with a pretty-boy face—but it's not usually my thing."

Griffin bit back a choking noise because he hadn't been expecting River to bring up sex. He probably should have figured the conversation would find its way back here, though. And he also had to resist the urge to brag that he could change his mind. Which was a stupid, adolescent urge, and neither helpful nor probably accurate. Sure, they'd had a lot of fun rubbing off together, but Griffin was still trying to figure out who he was in bed these days and wasn't sure he could back up any bragging.

So, instead, he sputtered, "I wasn't assuming…"

"I know you weren't." River's laugh was rich and refreshing. "I like that about you."

"You prefer to top? Or is it all anal you're not crazy about?" Griffin couldn't help his curiosity.

"Bit of both. I'll top if someone asks, but it's not something I absolutely crave."

"I can see that. Suppose I'm similar that way."

That got a loud snort from River. "Ha. You? You're a total top, and don't try to tell me otherwise."

"Now who's making assumptions?" Griffin frowned. "Honestly, I'm not sure what I am. Like you said, people have certain…expectations. Most people I've been with seemed to want me to do the fucking, so I did. A couple of times they asked for the other, and I did that too. But I was generally pretty trashed for all of it, so it's hard to say what's my preference."

"Fair enough. Sorry." River's full mouth quirked, looking appropriately contrite with an apology in his eyes.

"And just for the record, I was more than okay with what we did in Denali—wasn't secretly craving something else." He meant that too. The sex with River had been better than even the hottest of his drunken encounters, and he was going to carry the memories with him a long, long time, along with gratitude to River for giving him this part of his life back.

River's expression turned feral. "Good. All the more reason for you to come see me."

"*River*," he groaned.

"Not tonight, okay? I'll respect that you want to be professional around the others. But the group is disbanding when we're back in Anchorage. No one will know if we get together or share a meal or whatever."

Griffin opened his mouth, intending to object, but what came out was "Maybe."

Beaming like Griffin had handed him gold nuggets, River leaned forward in the water. "I like the sound of that."

Somehow River had drifted closer as they'd been

talking and now he was inches away, and it would be all too easy to kiss him, to change his *maybe* to a *yes please*. But the large picture windows behind them gave Griffin pause, as did his own rattling chest. He was in too deep already, no life raft in sight, and worst of all, he wasn't sure he wanted rescue.

"I don't want this trip to end," Melanie mused as they loaded up the van one final time.

"Me too." River shared her sentiment, something that wasn't usual for him. He was good at goodbyes— something about having already made the hardest, worst goodbye of all made it easier to let go of temporary places and acquaintances. Sure, he had people he kept in contact with, but he seldom got this heaviness in his step, this reluctance in his arms as he hefted his luggage up. And he knew all his weird emotions were tangled up in Griff, who seemed rather oblivious as he drove.

"You're quiet," Griff observed as they stopped at a scenic overlook for pictures about halfway to Anchorage. They'd taken a planned side jaunt to see the famed Hatcher Pass area, a prime spot for some last pictures and a short hike, but River's attention was far more on Griff than the surrounding mountains and little lakes. "You okay? Foot bothering you?"

"Nah, it's okay." It was Griff, not his foot that really troubled him, not that he was going to admit that. They'd crossed some imaginary threshold last night, even if they hadn't so much as kissed. They'd chatted in the hot tub until the stars came out, sharing confidences, like Griff's confession of liking adult coloring books. He didn't know it yet, but River was totally

sending him a souvenir from his next trip—gift stores
always had coloring pages, and he enjoyed the thought
of Griff's reaction. He was one of those rare hard-
to-let-go-of people, and as they headed back to Anchorage, River was determined that this not be a final
goodbye.

What he felt for Griff was too new, too unfamiliar,
too special to let go quite yet. Of course, all good things
came to an end, but River wasn't to that point with
Griff by any means, and it wasn't simply the heaviness in his limbs but also the deep pinch in his chest
that said he wasn't done here.

And even though he'd probably never admit it, he
knew Griff *had* to be feeling the same way. It was
evident in the tight lines around his eyes and mouth,
and in the way he asked, almost shy, "Can I get your
picture here?"

"Why? You wanna capture how badly my hair faded
over the course of the trip?" he teased as Griff dug his
camera out of his pack.

"Maybe." Griff shrugged, expression cryptic with
shuttered eyes and thinned lips. "Or maybe I like how
it blends into the sky today. It's almost the same color
as your eyes now, which is…nice."

"I'll take nice." River smiled for him, not giving him
a modeling pose or practiced look, more offering Griff
a personal memory, not some celebrity snap.

"Oh, let me get one of both of you with your camera?" Melanie asked, coming over to where they stood.

To River's surprise, Griff agreed with a sharp nod,
handing over his camera. "Guess you can."

He moved to stand closer to River, not touching or
leaning in. They might as well be a pair of brothers for

all the distance Griff so carefully put between them, but River wasn't going to embarrass him in front of Melanie, even if he did yearn for a little more...intimate picture. Maybe if Griff ended up seeking him out that evening, he could convince him to take a private selfie with him.

And that thought made his body hum with fresh anticipation. Surely Griff would come, right? Could he really let River go that easily? River simply couldn't believe that Griff wasn't feeling the same conflicting emotions he was battling himself. But damn was the man ever hard to read, even when they were on the road back to Anchorage and River got him talking about flying and other small talk. He was more chatty than other times, but still distant, like he was working overtime to avoid giving River the wrong signals. Or any signals at all. Hell, River would settle for a smile that reached his eyes, a laugh only for him.

The group disbanded back at the same hotel they'd started from. Had it really been only a little over a week? River had had years slide by faster, less eventfully. But here they were, days removed from not even knowing each other, and River profoundly changed by the entire experience. Sincere goodbyes were made all around before Melanie and Dan caught a shuttle to the airport, and Fenna and Lieke retreated to a hotel room to rest up for their early-morning international flight. Leaving only him and Griff. Alone. Staring at anything other than each other.

"You need help with your bags?" Griff asked, not meeting River's eyes.

"If I say yes, are you coming in?" River kept his voice low.

"River...." Griff shuffled his feet, still looking away. "I promised Uncle Roger I'd be there in about thirty minutes."

"Ah. Not nearly enough time. So, tonight then?" He used an airy tone, like them getting together was already a given.

Griff's mouth opened and shut a number of times, as if he was waging some sort of internal war.

"I take it that it's still a maybe?" River wasn't going to let Griff turn him down flat, not yet. Let him bicker with himself a little first, see if he could resist River's pull.

"Yeah." Griff gave him a pained expression, mouth quirking and eyes as hard to read as the rest of him.

"I'm in room 414." River tried to project confidence. "Come see me after you're done with your uncle. We can get food or...whatever."

"Whatever." Griff echoed weakly, scrubbing a hand through his hair, taking it to another level of mountain man wild. "I'll...uh...see."

"You do that." River forced himself to walk away first, not give Griff another chance to come up with a firm no. Once up in his hotel room, he took a long shower, and since he wasn't expecting Griff for a while, he touched up his color, a skill he'd perfected over several years of travel, managing to not turn the hotel bathroom blue. After that, he spent far too much time agonizing over what to put on for if—when—Griff showed up. Shirtless or less seemed a bit...presumptuous, but fully dressed felt equally silly. In the end, he settled for a nice shirt, partially unbuttoned, and upscale jeans, no belt, as if he was available to either take to dinner or bed, Griff's choice.

Then, that taken care of, he tried to turn his attention to work. No sense wearing a hole in the carpet pacing. Either Griff would show or he wouldn't. Of course, River had a strong preference, but he couldn't force Griff to return his eagerness for one more encounter. But as he reviewed his notes and pictures from the trip, he kept coming back to how Griff was at the center of his experiences, the thing he'd remember even more than the iconic scenery he was trying to describe. It felt a bit disingenuous, sharing breezy stories about s'mores and the two couples, and never mentioning Griff. But he'd promised to leave him out of his tales, so he attempted to come up with a narrative thread that didn't include more than passing reference to their guide.

He worked for a couple of hours in frustrating silence. Usually, he'd take his laptop to a coffee shop or someplace with background noise, but he wanted to stick around the room. His "please eat something for dinner" alarm went off, but he ignored it, refusing to give up hope of Griff appearing. Finally, his stomach let out a rare growl, and he was about to capitulate and order something small from room service when a knock sounded at the door.

Showtime. River's heart beat double time as he hurried to the door, zero chill, not even bothering to pretend he wasn't dying for it to be Griff. *Please let it be Griff.*

Chapter Twelve

Relief washed over River the second he opened the door. Sure enough, there was Griff, looking freshly showered himself with damp hair, different clothes, and a lopsided, almost nervous grin.

"You did your hair." Griff licked his lips, making no move to come into the room.

"Yup. You came." River held the door open wider. "You want to come in or you want food first?"

"I… I'm not sure why I'm here." Rubbing the back of his neck, Griff spoke to the carpet.

"I am." River took his hand, tugged him into the room. "You came to see me. Because you're no more ready to say goodbye than I am."

"Maybe." Griff breathed deeply, still not meeting River's eyes. "Or maybe I just didn't want to eat alone tonight."

"I can work with that." River stepped closer, the way he'd yearned to do all damn day. He let his breath brush Griff's newly smooth cheek, almost close enough to kiss. "You want me to order something or…"

"Or." Griff reacted to the nearness the way River had hoped, closing the last millimeters between them and capturing River's mouth in a hungry kiss, full of pent-up energy and all-consuming in its intensity. He kissed like River was appetizer, dinner, and dessert all in one and like he only had minutes to devour it all. All River could do was clutch at his shoulders and hold on for the onslaught.

And fuck, it was glorious. Griff tasted minty and desperate, a man at the breaking point, losing whatever resistance battle he'd been fighting. He nipped at River's mouth, demanding access that River happily gave, welcoming Griff's demanding tongue. Hell, especially once Griff crowded him into the wall, big body rubbing against his own, River was pretty sure he could get off from nothing more than the power of this kiss and Griff's almost palpable hunger.

"Can't get enough of you." Griff sounded surprised, as if he was just now realizing this. He bent his head to attack River's neck next, and while not as supremely sensitive there as Griff, River still shivered from the contact. His knees threatened to buckle from how damn good everything felt.

"You've got me," River groaned. "Whatever you want tonight, it's yours."

"Anything?" Griff's eyes went wide, and River took advantage of his surprise to urge him the few more feet to the bed, pushing him to sit on the edge, then straddling his thighs.

"Anything," River confirmed. He'd confessed his ambivalence about fucking to Griff, but he was turned on enough right then to be willing to go along with whatever would make Griff the happiest. He cupped Griff's face, peering down at him. "We keep coming back to my fantasies, but I want to be one of yours tonight. Tell me."

"Hmm." Griff didn't immediately brush him off like he had back at the cabin, taking a moment to think. "A lot of my fantasies are just flashes of sexy images—not a story like you're able to dream up. You seem to have this thing for beginnings—and that's hot—but I think I'm more about middles."

"Middles?" River wasn't entirely sure he followed.

"You know…" Griff's cheeks turned an adorable shade of pink. "After the awkwardness of the first time and before the bitterness of ending things. The middle. Not that I've ever really had that, but I think about it sometimes, knowing someone so well that they know what I like and vice versa. Fitting together like an old pair of jeans—comfortable."

It was so ridiculously sentimental and perfect that River's breath caught, making it hard to reply. "And that's what you'd like tonight? A middle-type encounter?"

"Yeah." Griff's cheeks further darkened. "Just wanna pretend that this is real. That we don't have to say goodbye in a couple of hours."

"Oh, Griff." Long preserved walls around River's heart tumbled down at Griff's words. "This *is*—" Before he could finish, Griff caught him in a punishing kiss, but River tried again when Griff let him up for air. "I want—"

"No. Not now." Griff's tone left no room for objection. "Pretend, okay? Don't promise. Just pretend with me."

He pulled River down for another kiss, not allowing him to reply. River's whole body buzzed with weird energy—he wanted more than anything to tell Griff that this *was* real, that he wanted to come back, in part as friends or maybe a little more. He wanted to give Griff his fantasy. Hell, he shared the fantasy. Couldn't remember ever having a middle to a relationship so to speak, and now he craved it.

But he wasn't going to waste time arguing when he could show Griff with his kiss and his body how sincere he was. To that end, he softened his mouth, kissing Griff like they had all the time in the world. No more rush to get it all done like a stopwatch was ticking. And he drew on the last week of knowledge about what Griff liked—firm contact, the rasp of teeth, the tug of lips. Rocking his hips, he started a slow grind, not intending to get either of them off, but rather to ramp up the kisses, another point of contact.

"Fuck. Like that." Griff pulled away, breathing hard. "Tell me."

River knew instinctively what Griff wanted—he'd always seemed to like it back at Denali when River spun a story. "So, we're on a trip together. An anniversary of some kind maybe. And we've waited all day to be alone…"

"Yeah." Griff's sigh was as close to happy as River had heard from him.

"And I know what you like…" River smiled down at him, heart so full he could barely stand it. God, he wanted this fantasy for real, wanted to prove to Griff that this *was* real, already. And he was willing to do whatever it took to show Griff that.

"Not *that*." Griff's tone was light even as his eyes were serious. "I want what *you* like too. Show me what our favorite thing for both of us is."

"Our Friday night special?" Beaming at him, River thought fast. He'd been willing to go there with fucking to give Griff what he needed, but with that off the table, he felt freer to dig into his own fantasies and preferences.

"Yeah." Griff bit him lightly on the shoulder, through the fabric of his shirt. "Pretty sure we're wearing less though…"

River could take a hint and immediately started in on the buttons of Griff's simple white shirt. Scooting backward and dipping his head, he let his lips explore the bare skin his fingers uncovered. Not wanting to make Griff beg, he gave him plenty of the bites and deep kisses that Griff always went crazy for on his neck and chest. He kept going until Griff's shirt hung open, and then slid to his knees between Griff's meaty thighs, which gave him plenty more access to lick Griff's flat brown nipples and trace the trail of hair that went to the waistband of his jeans.

Moaning low, Griff's head fell back. "Fuck. I love that."

"I know." River let himself gloat a little as he reached for Griff's fly. "And you're going to love this even more."

He punctuated his declaration with a firm bite right above Griff's belly button, then licked all along his waistband before lowering the fly.

"This is the something for both of us?" Griff sounded wary, which was the last thing River wanted.

So, he went for bald honesty. "There're few things I love more than coming with a cock in my mouth. And I haven't tasted you yet, and that seems like a crime. Trust me, in your fantasy world I do this all the time."

"Well then, by all means." Griff stretched, spreading his legs more, giving River more room to work.

"But feel free to come back up here too. Two can play at that game."

River ignored that in favor of mouthing Griff's bulge through his boxer briefs. Sixty-nine wasn't his jam as he wanted to mainly focus on Griff, have control over the pace. He knew from their late-night explorations that Griff was long and thick, the kind of thick that made his mouth water and his competitive drive perk up, because he did love a good challenge. He started by pulling the cock free and nuzzling up to it, drawing out the anticipation until Griff growled.

Too bad. This was River's show and he intended to enjoy it. He traced circles right at the root with his fingers and tongue, slowly, oh so slowly, working his way north, keeping his fingers on the base as his lips slid up the thick length, exploring the vein meandering up the shaft. But he kept his mouth light, glancing contact, loving how Griff started to pant like a racehorse coming into the homestretch. Griff's hand kept approaching River's head and backing off.

River glanced up at him, thrilling at his hooded eyes and slack mouth. "You can touch my hair. I rinsed all the dye. Not gonna turn you blue."

"Don't wanna hurt you," Griff mumbled.

"You don't remember?" River teased, getting into the fantasy again. "I love it when you touch my head. Play with my hair all you want. Just let me breathe occasionally and we're all good."

"Yeah." Griff moved to tangle his hand in River's hair. "God, your hair is so soft."

"Good conditioner," River replied smugly, right before he teased the underside of Griff's cock with the tip of his tongue. He worked that spot, licking and sucking until Griff was moaning and not-so-subtly rocking his hips. Having a little mercy, River finally gave his cockhead some attention. Not swallowing it yet, but licking around and around, memorizing Griff's taste. He smelled like the same hotel soap River had used, but he tasted a little salty and earthy, the sort of unique flavor that River always loved when he got to play with a cock.

Finally, he couldn't deny himself any longer, and he sucked the cockhead in, starting a slow slide that he mimicked with his fingers at the base of the cock.

"Oh hell, that's good." Griff's voice was a harsh whisper.

"Think that's good? Just wait until I have my tongue piercing in."

"*Fuck.* Can we get to the part where you're coming too?" Griff gasped, strain evident both on his face and in his voice. "Because it's been…a while, and you're damn good at that."

The praise made River extra compliant. Pulling back long enough to unzip himself, he withdrew his cock, which was already aching and leaking. He shifted so that he could do his favorite thing—stroking himself in the same rhythm that he sucked Griff's cock, starting and stopping, edging them both closer and closer. The more turned on he got, the harder he sucked and unlike at the cabin where the "keep quiet" game had been sexy, he let himself moan around Griff's cock, the muffled noises amping him up even further, especially when Griff groaned too.

Eventually, he let go of the base of Griff's cock with his left hand, eager to take Griff as deep as possible. His strokes on his own cock sped up as his senses filled with Griff. His smell. His taste. His silky texture. His low, keening moans. The deeper River went, the more he slipped into that space that he craved, a place where nothing else mattered except him and Griff and what he could do with nothing more than his mouth.

"Close?" Griff said it as a question, not an announcement. "God, I want you to come. Come around my cock, just like that. Fuck. I love your moans."

Preening under the praise, River redoubled his efforts to get Griff off first, going deep and sucking hard. Griff's hand tightened in River's hair, big thighs trembling around him. He was holding himself back, and it was sexy as fuck. But it needed to stop now. Using his free hand, River played with Griff's heavy balls. Feeling them turned him on too, his own orgasm inching closer than he'd like.

"Please. Please come. Need it." Griff's voice broke on the word *need*, and River was powerless to deny him. His hand tightened on his cock, almost without permission from his brain, and he went deep on Griff's cock, letting all the good feelings swamp him. Filled mouth. Filled senses. Filled empty places inside him, everything drifting away until the only thing important was making his orgasm last as long as possible. He rode that sweet edge until it was all too much and he was coming in hard waves, moaning around Griff's cock until even that became impossible and he had to pull off, gasping for air.

"Fuck. So sexy," Griff mumbled as his hand left River's hair to stroke himself, harsh, fast strokes that had Griff coming quickly with a shout. It seemed to go on and on for him—spurt after spurt all over River's face and hair, but he was beyond caring about the mess.

Hell, part of him found it hot as fuck, being marked by Griff, knowing that he'd gotten him off so hard that even now Griff was still shuddering.

"Sorry." Still breathing hard, Griff gave him a sheepish smile. "Didn't mean to get spunk in your eyes or anything. You okay?"

"Fabulous." River swiped an already-messy finger across his cheek before popping it in his mouth, savoring their mingled taste. "Told you I wanted to taste you."

"Couldn't wait." Griff hauled River back up next to him on the bed. "That was the single hottest thing I've ever seen. You're gorgeous when you come. Wish I had a picture. I'd show you."

River paused from pulling off his shirt to shrug. He dabbed at his face. Usually he had a very strict no-sex-tape policy because he'd seen that go bad for friends, but Griff was different, for reasons he wasn't ready to fully examine. Under normal circumstances, he hated the idea of someone watching him that closely, noticing his reactions when he climaxed, but with Griff all he felt was warm. Wanted.

"I'm not into all that, but I trust you. I'd let you photograph me however you want." Looking at said pictures would be a whole different matter—he wasn't always a fan of what the camera saw in him, but he could pose for Griff and shut off his doubts, same as he did on a job. "Speaking of pictures, I want a snap of both of us. A real one this time, not us looking like executives forced to take a trip together."

He grabbed his phone from the nightstand, but Griff stopped him with a raised hand. "Not all covered in spunk maybe?"

"Fine, be no fun." River laughed and put the phone down. "Fast shower, then food? Better keep your strength up. I'm not done with you by any means."

"Guess I'll let you feed me." Griff sounded sleepy and content, a combo that made River's chest go warm and tight.

"Good." He said it lightly, but he meant it. He was even more determined than ever that this not be a permanent goodbye, not yet. There was too much he still wanted to explore together. Griff felt like a brand-new country he'd discovered, new experiences to soak up, and he was far from having his fill.

Griffin had hazy memories of sharing a shower with another person, but he was pretty sure it had never been so fun with lots of silly laughter and slippery flesh. Neither of them seemed in the mood to start sex back up, so the vibe was playful. River wanted cool water so that his hair wouldn't run, but Griffin wanted to not freeze and teased him about his diva ways until they were both laughing. Griffin still had no clue why he'd come to River's room or what he was hoping to accomplish by staying. The sex was done, so the fantasy should have vanished, same as it had back in Denali, but this felt different. Almost like he was still living in that imaginary world where this was an anniversary trip and where they were a couple who did this all the time and where Griffin was a guy who deserved all that good stuff.

"I'm going to bet pizza is a no-go for you?" Griffin enjoyed toweling River off, letting himself memorize the feel of River in his arms. "There's a place I love here that delivers, but I'm open to whatever you want to eat."

River's mouth pursed as he stepped away. "I don't mean to be difficult. Really. It's more that I have… issues with heavy foods. Lighter foods are easier for some reason. Less triggering I guess."

"Hey, it's not a big deal to me." Griffin pulled him back into his arms. If all he got was this night, he wasn't going to squander a single moment. "And it's probably not the same thing, but I kinda know what you mean. I can't eat wings anymore—I associate them too much with late-night drinking. They don't even taste right these days, and I feel gross if I eat even a few."

"Yeah. Kind of like that." River offered him a grateful smile, one that made Griffin glad he'd shared something that he'd never voiced before. "If your pizza place has a salad option, I'll have that and a bread stick or something."

"That works." Griffin refrained from the urge to tell River that he needed more than lettuce as he used an app on his phone to place a fast order for his favorite pizza and a salad with white beans and prosciutto for River as a step up from the side salad River was probably intending. That taken care of, another deeper impulse came out before he could recall the words. "I wish I could cook for you sometime. I bet I could make something you'd like. Not rigatoni maybe, but I can do some soups okay."

River beamed at him. Perhaps they were still in fantasy land, both of them. "I'd love that. Tell me more about where you live."

Naked, River sprawled on the bed, looking up at Griffin expectantly. Figuring he'd need to open the door for the food delivery soon and not nearly so comfortable nude, Griffin pulled on his pants from earlier, but left the shirt on the floor. Still letting his desires rule his brain, he grabbed his phone from where it had landed on the carpet and took a quick shot of River's upper torso and face, him looking very much like a naughty imp come to tempt Griffin.

"Need me to pose?"

"Nah. This is perfect." Griffin set the camera aside so he could sit on the bed next to River.

"It is. Now tell me about your place."

"It's a little town called Wedding Creek on Cook Inlet, part of the Kenai Peninsula, but the other side from where we were at Seward. I grew up there and both my parents grew up there too. Little church, gas station with a diner, motel, hangar for the planes, some houses. School a few small towns over. Not much but it's home."

"Where do you shop?"

Griffin had to laugh because of course River wanted to know that. People always asked that. "Homer's our nearest bigger city for shopping and such. Only about thirty-five minutes or so. It's a good four hours to Anchorage by car, which we do for big stock-up trips."

"But you've got a plane, right?" River's head tilted.

"Yeah, the business owns several, but the planes eat fuel and expenses. And there's the question of room for additional cargo. I'll fly it for paying charters and cargo trips and try to combine trips where I can to save money."

"Do you have a cabin?" River's eyes sparkled, paler than his hair now but no less mesmerizing.

"Someday I'll have a house of my own, up in the

hills outside town maybe or possibly up the inlet some. Right now, I've got a place on my family's piece of land—a tiny old one-room cabin that my grandparents used in their later years. It suits me fine while I save up." True, he'd like more than a two-burner stove, to have a real oven and maybe a deep tub, but he'd get there eventually, and he wasn't going to get into his financial issues with River. A custom-built place with some acreage like he wanted wasn't cheap, even if he hadn't wrecked his credit and burned through all his prior savings with the gambling that had accompanied his drinking.

"Single bed?" River teased, moving so his head lay on Griffin's bare stomach.

"Are you fishing for an invitation?" Petting River's damp hair, Griffin tried to figure out what he was up to.

"Maybe." River propped himself up with an elbow so he could look at Griffin. "Got a place for me to sleep?"

Tilting his head, Griffin studied him carefully. River seemed serious even though his voice was light. Griffin tried to echo that lightness as he answered. "It's a queen and I change the sheets regularly."

"Excellent. You can make me soup and I'll make you scream when you come like you did earlier. It'll be the perfect trade."

Were they still playing out the fantasy? Griffin was no longer so sure. "It's not a tourist destination, really. Won't see it in many Alaska guidebooks."

"I specialize in off-the-beaten-path places." River offered him the same eager expression. "And I'm serious, Griff. I want to see your town. I want to see all the places you don't take the other tourists to. And your bed. Definitely your bed."

"Riv—" A knock at the door interrupted him.

"That was fast." River pulled a comforter over himself. "You've got pants on. Can you get the door? Need cash?"

"I've got it." Griffin found his wallet on the floor and grabbed some cash for the delivery person, a diminutive older woman with dark hair who held out their food. And hopefully didn't peer too far into the room as Griffin tipped her well. Not that he was embarrassed to be with a guy, but old habits of discretion died hard and all that.

After he closed the door, he carried the food toward the small desk on the other side of the bed, but River sat up and pointed at the bed. "Let's have a picnic over here."

"Crumbs." Griffin gave a weak protest even as he placed the food in front of River.

"Are you staying the night? I'll brush the bed off extra thoroughly if so." River looked so damn amused at himself that Griffin couldn't resist giving him a fast kiss as he arranged himself next to him, legs folded under him like a little kid breaking all the rules to eat in the big bed.

"Technically, I've got my own room—"

"*Technically,* you're welcome here. Or we'll go sneak over to your crumb-free bed later. It'll be an adventure."

"Why do I get the impression that everything is with you?"

"You're not wrong." River took a delicate bite of

a puffy breadstick. "Come on, Griff. Have an adventure with me."

Griffin didn't answer right away, instead digging into his pizza for a few bites. "You want an adventure? This is reindeer sausage and sweet onion. Dare you to taste it. Not a whole slice, just a taste."

"I've had yak milk and all sorts of local foods. Little bit of *sausage* doesn't scare me." River's tone was heavy on the innuendo as he plucked a piece of meat off an unclaimed slice. "Spicy. Tastes a little like jerky combined with kielbasa. You want some salad?"

"Sure." Griffin wasn't typically much on arugula, but the Parmesan, white beans, and meat went a long way to balancing the flavors. And there it was, this thing between them feeling real again, like they were a long-standing couple sharing food and inside jokes.

"Maybe I do like...sausage." River snickered as he stole another two pieces of meat and popped them in his mouth.

"I can make you chili with reindeer sausage," Griffin volunteered. "Not too heavy. I've also used it in omelets and stuff."

"Yes, when I visit, you can absolutely make me something with this." River went ahead and took charge of the slice he'd been picking at. "Maybe sex is like hiking. Gives me way more appetite than usual and makes food feel...not so problematic."

Griffin had to laugh at that. "I'm glad to be useful. But you're not visiting."

"Yes, I am. You invited me." River batted his insanely long eyelashes at Griffin.

Griffin almost choked on a bite of crust. "You invited yourself."

"And you want me to come. Admit it."

"You'd be bored." He was deflecting again, his mind a jumble of competing thoughts.

"You in my bed? A new place to explore? Hiking nearby? I don't think so." River used the same smile he'd used when he'd suggested having an adventure, making it clear that was what he thought this was. "And I'm not talking about taking up your time for too many days. But I've got some time in a couple of weeks when I could swing it, between the Seattle and British Columbia stops."

Of course, River didn't mean a long stay. And hell, just the idea of letting him visit at all should be giving Griffin hives. The fact that he was even considering it was proof he was thinking with the wrong head.

"It wouldn't be just us—like I said, I live on my family's land. Both sisters live nearby, and my mom's in the big house, and Uncle Roger's just up the road. Everyone's gonna be up in our business. And they've seen you on some talk show. They'll have questions." He didn't have to fake his shudder.

But River simply shrugged. "Doesn't bother me. I'm good with family. And fans. But if you'd rather take a few days away, meet here in Anchorage or somewhere else, I don't have to disrupt your regular life. I wouldn't want to make things awkward."

This whole damn thing was likely to be awkward as hell. Which was exactly why he should say a firm no thank you. But what came out was, "You wouldn't. Not with the you-being-a-guy thing, I mean. My mom guessed about me years ago, and I told Uncle Roger way back too because I was worried he'd care, but he didn't. Figure my sisters probably wouldn't be shocked—or at least not any more shocked. Me turning up with a guest of any gender would be surprise enough, let alone a celebrity."

"I'm not a celebrity. And this wouldn't be for the book." River patted Griffin's leg. "This would be just for me. A little vacation from getting these last chapters together. And if you've got work of your own, I'll simply hole up and work on edits until you can take me up in that plane of yours."

"You want to fly?" Despite every possible reservation, Griffin was warming to the idea. "It's not like a commercial flight—"

"*I know.* That's what I want. I want you to fly me somewhere you love. I want to see what you see."

"This is madness." He was so damn close to giving in, and River's eager expression said he knew it.

"No, this is *real.*" River said what Griffin most wanted to hear, further softening his resolve. "You can't deny there's something here. Something worth keeping going. Friendship maybe or something a little more. I'm not asking for forever, Griff, but give us another visit at least?"

"Is ten days really enough time to call it a friendship?" His tone was less accusatory, more simply musing, trying to make sense of the mess in his head.

"Dunno." River snagged another piece of meat. "Is it enough time to rule it out? I'm not ready to say goodbye, and I don't think you are either."

Griffin couldn't argue with that, so he polished off another piece of pizza before he spoke again. "There is this place…"

"Yeah?" River leaned forward, all anticipation, like a puppy about to go for a run.

"It's a flight across Kachemak Bay. The state park over there is always gorgeous, but there's a little cove I like. Not a town—more a thinking spot. Good hike."

"I like thinking spots. And hikes."

"I know." Griffin rubbed the back of his neck. He'd lost the battle. Maybe not the war, but he'd lost any chance of turning River down flat. Hell, even now he was thinking ahead to what he might cook River that he'd eat and how to best avoid his family as much as possible. "Only a few days, right? And you get that I'm not always the best company—"

"Yup. I've got your grumpy number." River sighed happily. "And I'm not looking to disrupt your life. I know routine's important to you. I just want to give you an adventure. That's all."

Too late. Griffin was already disrupted, the walls he surrounded himself with in disarray, and hell if he could bring himself to do the necessary repairs quite yet. He could be alone all winter. What was the harm in eking out a little more summer? A few more hot memories. A few more stolen moments he didn't deserve, but hell if he was strong enough to turn down.

Chapter Thirteen

Ping.

 Glancing around the empty hangar, Griffin quickly grabbed a rag and wiped his greasy hands so he could check his phone. His heart stuttered in a way it hadn't since he was a teenager waiting for Hank to call—but unlike his stupid crush on Hank, this wasn't a one-way path to misery. Or at least he hoped not. He clicked open on the message, knowing it didn't matter whether it led to unhappiness or not. He was too deep in this thing now.

From: professional_nomad
To: BarrettG
Subject: Rain, rain, rain

How's my favorite Mountain Man? I'm exploring the Hoh Rainforest this weekend. Me and half of Washington, it feels like. But I've got some great photos, which should make my editor happy, along with a fun story about the hot springs. (Don't worry! I didn't cook any essential parts ;)) Here's one of a bridge that reminded me of the place south of Seward you showed me. I'm staying in a little upscale cabin at a resort. Too many chatty people at the pool and small plates of pretty food—you'd hate it. Tell me again what you're cooking for me next week? Did you get some…sausage? I know you probably don't care, but I haven't been sampling the local meat here so to speak. Oh, and since I hate to come empty-handed, I got your mother some chocolates in Seattle. I hope your family isn't giving you too much trouble about having a visitor! Chat me later?

~River

Griffin grinned about River not going out and getting laid. Not that they were exclusive or anything like that, but Griffin sure as heck wasn't getting any on the side.

He reread the rest of the message, smile fading to a frown. Huh. Of course River would be thoughtful and bring a hostess gift, and he'd obviously put some thought into it, not bringing the typical bottle of wine. Which meant he was thinking of Griffin too and his needs, a thought that should have warmed Griffin instead of making him vaguely itchy. These were all good things, or at least, they would be if Griffin had actually told his family about River's visit. And if his brain could decide whether he was excited or queasy at the thought of seeing River again. What had he been thinking?

Now that he was back in Wedding Creek, their time in the hotel seemed like a dream. A really sexy dream, but unconnected to his real life, as if a different self had lived those hours, had agreed to this visit. He'd been riding high on sex hormones, addled by their picnic in bed, and a second round of orgasms had further killed his brain cells. It was the only reason he could come up with for why he'd lingered in bed with River the next morning, kissing him slow and tender until River had to be at the airport and he had to pick up Uncle Roger, never once rescinding the invite. Never letting reality intrude on their little bubble. And now they had a steady stream of emails—River's chatty, his more painstakingly drafted since he wasn't the writer in this thing—and late-night chats along with texts saying this was more than simply some hormonal lark.

The sound of a clearing throat pulled him back out of his thoughts.

"Griff?" His mother's tone said she'd been trying to get his attention more than once. Somehow, she'd managed to come all the way into the hangar without him realizing, standing in front of him now, forehead creased and eyes wary. "You okay?"

"Yeah. I'm fine." He replaced his phone on the shelf. "Sorry. Just lost in my thoughts I guess."

"That seems to be a theme of yours lately." Her voice was cautious, as if past experience with him slipping too far into his own head had burned her. Which it had, and the same guilt he always got when he worried her swamped him, pushed out any lingering giddiness over River's email.

"Sorry. I'm okay, I promise. Just…keeping in touch with a friend."

"A friend?" Her face brightened. "That's wonderful. You're alone far too much. It's not healthy."

"I do better alone," he said firmly. River getting under his skin hadn't changed that, hadn't changed what he needed for himself, for his family. But he didn't want an argument with his mom, so he softened his tone. "Did you need something?"

"Yeah. I wanted to see how you'd feel about taking another tour? Shorter one—just a long weekend next week. Last-minute booking, but it's good money. I thought I'd offer it to you before I go to Toby or one of the others."

Griffin rubbed the base of his neck. "I can't. I've got…plans next weekend. Sort of. I should have put it on the calendar."

But he hadn't because that would mean questions, the sort apparent in his mother's wide eyes.

"Plans? With your friend?"

"Yeah. But I could try to cancel." Maybe that would be for the best, the excuse he'd needed to shut River down.

"Don't be ridiculous." She touched his arm. "When was the last time you had plans with a friend? You deserve this. I could use your help, sure, but I'll lean on Toby, then put you on the next one. Is it someone from the air force?"

"Uh…no…" Griffin studied the cracked concrete floor. "You remember the tour group I covered for Uncle Roger?"

"Of course." Her head tilted, clearly calculating. "The model? River Vale? *Him*?"

"Yeah. Him," he mumbled. "Just a casual thing—"

"Griff. I'm happy you made a friend. But is this wise? That's a glitzy, glamorous world. Not like it is around here. I worry about you…"

"I'm not joining his world. Not really. He's coming here for a few days. Wants to see more of the state, and I'm going to show him around. We might stay friends awhile, but this isn't me…backsliding or something. I know my limits." Or at least, he hoped he did. And he knew his mom worried. Hell, he worried too. It was why he kept such a strict routine, avoided temptations, stuck close to home. But he wanted to believe he could have this thing with River—a few more stolen days— and not jeopardize all he'd worked hard for.

"I hope you do." His mother shook her head. "I want to be happy for you. But I can't help but think some-one local might be better. Maybe someone you met at a meeting? If you'd ever go to one, that is. You might find…understanding people there."

"Mom. Please." This was an old argument for them. After his last stint at rehab, he'd buried himself in fam-ily and hard work, refusing to think about the therapy the rehab center had recommended or the twelve-step meetings that everyone, his mother especially, seemed to think he needed. He'd gotten sober, one white-knuckled night at a time. That was all that mat-tered. And staying sober was his number one priority, so his mom could back off a little. Also, as much as he loved this area and community, he hadn't had a good friend locally since Hank.

If he was going to meet someone around here who made him feel like River did, it would have happened already. Which was part of why he was doing this— he had long years stretching ahead of himself, and if he could stockpile some good memories while he had this friendship, maybe that would actually make his plans easier. Or so he justified things to himself late at night when he went back and forth about the visit.

"All right." His mother sighed, a long-suffering

sound that made his back muscles tighten. "I just hope you know best."

Me too. But he couldn't say that, could only nod. And even though she had a point, his heart still surged at the thought of seeing River again. Hell, even thinking about chatting with him that night had him on the verge of bouncing on his feet. And he wasn't going to let his mother's advice ruin his tentative…friendship or whatever this was with River. All he knew was that he needed this visit, probably even more than River did.

The Anchorage airport layout was familiar to River on his second arrival, but the flutter in his insides was new, hadn't been there when he'd arrived for the tour group. Before Griff. *Geez.* Was all his life going to be divided this way? Pre- and post-meeting Griff? Was he always going to feel this low thrum of anticipation at the thought of seeing him? He wasn't sure what to hope for—that these feelings would stick around or that he'd get over himself. All he knew was that his feet sped up at the sight of Griff waiting near the baggage claim for River's flight.

God, he looked good. Sleeves rolled up, his green plaid shirt made his hazel eyes greener than usual and stretched across his big chest in a most appealing way. Same face scruff as their first meeting, but it looked more intentionally groomed. Strong forearms poking out of the sleeves, muscles rippling as he insisted on taking River's backpack while they waited for his checked bag. His hair had been cut at some point recently. Still shaggy but not quite so unruly. River tried not to be too obvious checking him out as he figured

Griff wouldn't want anything public like the kiss River was dying to give him.

Still, though, he could flirt in low tones. "You look hot, Mountain Man. Dress up for me?"

"Nah." Griff's neck turned pink and his eyes dipped lower to River's feet. "You came dressed for the climate this time. Proper shoes."

"Got a hiking boot fetish?" River teased as he spotted his bag on the carousel, narrowly nudging Griff out of the way to grab it.

"Got a thing for you not slipping when you get in my plane. These are your only two bags, right?"

"Yup." River barely had time to react when Griff wrested the bag away, easily carrying both large bags as he led the way out of the baggage area, headed to the nearby seaplane complex.

Griff moved fast, like a guy on a time crunch, not a guy desperate to find a dark corner to drag River to, which made uncharacteristic doubts chase River. Had he done the right thing in coming?

"So… I take it the mile-high club is out?" he asked, keeping his voice teasing, trying to not be needy.

Griff gave him a dark look, one River had only seen from him a couple of times, and one that made his toes curl. "I changed my sheets for you and left a slow cooker on for dinner. I'd like to live long enough to get you in my bed."

"That works." Mood considerably brighter, River turned his attention to the area they were navigating.

The Lake Hood seaplane airport was way more fascinating than a regular airport. The largest floatplane base in the world, it was a maze of hangars and airplane storage facilities and planes coming and going across the large lake as well as by land. Pedestrians enjoying the summer sunshine clogged the walking paths, taking in the sights of the busy facility. They passed private planes of various sizes in many different makes in bright, primary colors, some with whimsical names painted on the tail.

Griff made his way toward the designated space his family business leased. They had a tiny shed with access to both the lake via a dock and the roadway via a gravel path.

River had been in helicopters and smaller commercial planes, but this was his first time in a bush-style seaplane. Griff could, of course, fly both land and water landing planes, and he had explained how the tiny airport his family operated from in Wedding Creek had landing areas for both types of crafts.

"We have a number of planes but this de Havilland is one of my favorites."

"It's pretty." River snapped a fast picture of the red-and-white plane with a large exterior door, which Griff popped open to reveal a few spartan seats and a stack of boxes behind a cargo net. Like most of the planes they'd passed, it had both pontoons and wheels—enabling it to land in a variety of situations. At present, though, it was lined up with the wooden dock, and Griff deftly avoided falling in the lake as he showed River various compartments and features.

"Already loaded it up with some requested goods for the return flight. And you can choose whether to ride up in the cockpit next to me or one of the more comfortable seats in the cabin." Griff stowed River's bags near the boxes.

"Next to you." River laughed because it was a no-brainer. No way was he turning down the chance to ride up front.

"You'll want your camera in that case because the views are worth it, but FYI it's super loud—don't expect much conversation." Griff handed him a pair of bulky headphones after he showed him how to climb up into the cockpit.

It was a tiny space, barely enough room for both of them, and their shoulders rubbed as Griff settled in after shutting the back hatches. Most of the instruments and controls were on Griff's side, but there were still some switches in front of River he was going to make triple sure not to touch or bump. Like the seats in back, these were plain, old cracked brown leather affairs with metal floors under their feet.

A pair of sunglasses dangled from the instrument panel, and Griff slipped them on before doing up his seat belt. Damn. Hot mountain man pilot. River was going to have to spin up a fresh set of fantasies just for Griff.

"Now, I'm going to do my checks and talk to the tower for a minute, see what kind of wait we're looking at for a takeoff—this is the not-so-fun part. With so many planes in and out each day here, we could be looking at a wait before we get clearance." Griff put on a headset and started to flip switches as he talked into the headset, a bunch of jargon River didn't quite follow.

They taxied slowly away from the dock, heading closer to the main part of the lake. River studied the other planes taking off and landing from the large lake. It was elegant, the way the planes glided in, soft landings with far less splash than he would have expected. Other planes took off from the long runway behind the lake, swooping overhead on their way to the skies. Griff navigated what River could only describe as a seaplane traffic jam—a line of private planes waiting for their turn to take off. A jaunty neon yellow and green plane was ahead of them, skimming across the water.

Finally it was their turn, and Griff flipped several more switches, more engine power coming on with a huge roar. And unlike a commercial flight, which needed a long takeoff space, this smaller plane was designed to maximize efficiency and take off and land in tight quarters, so it hurtled down the lake, hard charging until they were airborne with a gorgeous view of the lake beneath them and then downtown Anchorage as they turned southeast, skirting around the main airport to avoid interfering with commercial flights.

Griff hadn't been lying—he didn't even try to make more than passing announcements of what they were flying over—but River found he didn't miss conversation one bit nor did he mind the roar of the engines. Instead, he enjoyed the scenery, taking pictures of the water and terrain as they left Anchorage behind, flying first over an inlet, then green land dappled with what seemed to be hundreds of tiny lakes. A serpentine river came into focus before some larger lakes, and next they were back over the inlet. Metaphors kept slipping into his head, turns of phrase that might work to describe the landscape, and he had to remind himself that he'd promised to leave Griff out of the book, a promise that was harder to keep than it sounded as Griff and Alaska burned far brighter in his psyche than any other stop in the past year.

Right when he was finally used to the noise and

turbulence and relaxing into his seat, they swooped low, heading for a far tinier lake than Lake Hood—a puddle really. No way could they land there. But then Griff said something into his headset, and they circled once before dipping lower, making River's stomach plummet too.

Unlike on a runway, where there was always a harsh jolt from the landing gear meeting the tarmac, this was more of a soft *plop-plop* as they touched down and skidded across the water's surface to come to a stop by a dock. Other nearby docks housed planes. Beyond the small body of water was a wide runway and several metal hangar buildings.

"Doing okay?" Griff grinned at him as he started shutting off switches, clearly in his element in a way River hadn't seen him before. Damn. He was ridiculously attractive all cocky and confident like this, and River really hoped that bed of his was close by.

"Fabulous."

"Watch yourself getting out. Let me go first, and I'll help you. It's a little tricky."

Finding his legs were on the rubbery side, River accepted the help and narrowly kept from ending up in the lake.

"Can I help you unload?" he asked, remembering Griff's cargo.

"That's what he's for." Griff jerked his thumb at a guy around River's age who pulled up on an ATV towing a small trailer. "Afternoon, Toby. This is River."

Toby had an appraising stare for River, not unlike Griff's helicopter pilot friend, and his grin was open and flirty as he shook River's hand. He had even longer hair than Griff and dark brown eyes along with a lean, muscular build. He was hot, but River's attention was still riveted to Griff as he and Toby made fast work of loading the cargo onto the trailer. Speeding away, Toby left River and Griff to walk to the hangar area at a more leisurely pace.

Three women emerged from a smaller building and Griff groaned. "My family. My mom and my sisters, Indra and Holly, who work with her in the business office, although Indra can also fly."

River was less concerned with names and more worried about the three matching scowls as they watched them approach.

"I thought you said they were fans," he whispered to Griff.

"They were—are. It's complicated. They're...protective of me. It's not you, promise."

River tried to picture a universe where his father or siblings would have more than a passing care about who he brought along for a weekend but came up short. His dad was far too busy with his new life to give a flip about him. His mom would have, though. She'd been a worrier, and he hadn't realized how much he'd miss her hovering until she was gone. So he pasted his most understanding smile on his face. It was good that Griff had people in his life who cared.

But for once River's charm seemed to fail him as introductions were made and the three women continued to regard him suspiciously.

"You'll come up to the house for dinner tomorrow night," Griff's mother decreed in a tone that suggested more interrogation than hospitality. Tall, like Griff, but willowy where he was broad, she had a long braid of graying hair and an expression that said she tolerated no fools.

"Mom—"

"That's fine." River would win them over eventually, show them he had no intention of hurting Griff.

"You're the one from the tour who was a picky eater, right? Will you eat grilled salmon?" Flashing the same hazel shade as Griff's, her eyes dared him to object.

"That sounds fine. Thank you."

She nodded sharply and gave Griff a long look, some message there that River couldn't decipher.

"I better get back to the office," she said at last, leaving them to walk toward a battered truck parked near the larger hangar.

"I'm thinking this is older than me." River laughed.

"So's the plane." Any humor Griff had had earlier was gone.

"Sorry. I wasn't insulting it." River got in the passenger seat. "It's special to you?"

"Guess you could say that." Griff leaned hard on the steering wheel, not moving to start the truck. "Learned to drive on this old workhorse. Me and Hank. It was his dad's before his. We went all over the peninsula in it before we left for the academy."

"Sounds fun. I learned on a Lexus sedan. Nothing so…special." He tried to offer an encouraging smile, appreciating the rare personal glimpse at Griff.

"Yeah. It was special." Griff released a low breath. "That's one way to put it. Anyway, when I came back after…everything, I had nothing. Drank all my money away one stupid decision after another, letting myself get talked into stupid bets at the card tables, then rehab ate the rest of it plus a huge chunk of mom's savings too. And Hank's mother comes to me, one day when I was working at the hangar. Wasn't even flying again yet. Says Hank would want me to have a ride."

"That was nice." River was almost scared to speak, not wanting to ruin the mood where Griff was really talking for once.

"More than nice. She didn't have to do it. Wouldn't have blamed her if she wanted nothing to do with me. I made her let me pay her installments, but I wasn't gonna turn down a chance to get this old girl back, fix her up proper. Might be old, but she runs better than some new."

"I bet." River reached over, patted Griff's knee. "I think it's…sweet that you've got this as a memory of Hank. It's nice to focus on the good times. I wish I had something like that from my mom, something tangible maybe."

"Nothing you could ask your dad for?" Griff's voice was kind as he finally started the truck.

"Not really. I mean, there were certain pans and dishes I'll always associate with her. But those hardly travel well. Few pieces of jewelry, but my one sister got those. I wanted this old kitchen timer—shaped like a chicken, stupid thing."

"It's not stupid if it meant something to you." Griff headed up a small road, past a cluster of older buildings and gas station that River supposed was the town center so to speak.

"Yeah. Even though she had a nice microwave and stove, she still kept the timer. Used it for everything from eggs to workout intervals to timeouts when we were little. But my dad donated it in a bunch of kitchen stuff before I could make it back to hunt it down. He donated almost everything, sold the house, and moved on with his life."

"That's rough. But maybe it's what he needed?"

"No, what he *needed* was to not knock up one of his paralegals less than six months after Mom died. And what he *needed* was to not get rid of everything, get a new family, a giant do-over." River was surprised at his own venom. He almost never shared his thoughts on his father's hasty remarriage with anyone, even his therapist. "He could have kept something."

"I hear you." Griff reached over, gave River's leg a fast squeeze. "It sucks that he moved on so fast. I was surprised that Hank's mother kept the truck. But that's what people do around here. We keep stuff, long past when we should give up on it."

River had a feeling he was talking about himself, not physical possessions, but he couched his reply in the same metaphor to avoid pissing Griff off and calling an end to this mutual sharing. "But that's good. You never know when something will be needed. When it will surprise you. You don't give up on something just because it's seen a few miles."

Griff shrugged as he turned onto a side road. "Some things are simply damaged goods. But not this truck. She'll see me another decade if I treat her right."

"You're a good man, Griff." River tried to tell him with his tone that he'd never see Griff as damaged goods. He was strong and admirable and more than worth River's friendship.

"We're here." Turning into a short gravel drive, Griff ignored the compliment. A large log house dominated the middle of the clearing with a few smaller outbuildings to the side, then three more medium-size houses beyond it. River supposed one could call it a family neighborhood, or maybe more accurately a compound, but it was homey and welcoming.

"This is nice. You're not tempted to put that cabin of your dreams here? With your family?"

"I've thought about it." Griff got out of the truck and collected River's bags before he was able. "But they can be a bit much. Smothering almost. I need my space. And there's something about land of my own… I dunno. Maybe it's silly."

"It's not silly. You want something that's yours. A quiet place. I get it. It's okay to want something for you."

"Maybe so." Griff led him to a small cabin behind the main house. "But until then, I've got this, and it suits me fine."

His tone dared River to object to the humble building, but far from repulsed, River was charmed. It was a simple square with a small porch where Griff removed his boots. River did the same, then followed Griff inside, where a rich aroma of meat and spices greeted them.

"I like it," he said, taking in the space. To the left of the door was a small kitchenette—diminutive fridge, two-burner stove, narrow stretch of counter with a slow cooker on it, same brand and color as the one River's mom had used, and a two-person table in a corner. An open door beyond that showed what looked like a bathroom. To the right, a small love seat sat in front of a TV stand, with a crowded bookcase on the wall, woodstove in the far corner, and the promised quilt-covered bed in the back of the space.

"You want food, or you want to explore the area a

little? There's a trail I can show you." Tight lines bracketed Griff's mouth.

"Showing me the bed isn't on the agenda yet?" River tried teasing to ease some of Griff's discomfort and was rewarded with a small smile.

"Once I get you in bed, I might forget to feed you. And you came to see more of the state, not for...that."

Draping his arms around Griff's neck, River gave him the firm kiss he'd been waiting on all damn afternoon. "I came for you. Scenery's a bonus."

"I'm not—"

"Yes, you are." River cut him off with another kiss, trying to tell him with his mouth that Griff was worth so much more than he thought he was and how happy River was to be here with him. He didn't need a gorgeous vista or even Griff's dream cabin. All he needed was this man right here, this moment, and River was going to appreciate the hell out of both for as long as he had this.

Chapter Fourteen

Having River in his space was simply flat-out weird.
And, okay, it would be weird to have just about anyone else in his little cabin, seeing as how he hadn't had
a guest beyond family members bringing food to the
door since he'd moved in here. But it was especially
weird having a person he liked here. Cared about even.
And that was precisely his issue—he cared too much
about River already, and now here he was caring about
what he thought of Griffin's space. The cabin seemed
way too inadequate to hold them both plus all this
charged energy between them.

"Let's get you exploring," he said, pulling away before River could steal another kiss.

"I wanna explore you." River cast a longing look
at Griffin's bed.

And Griffin did want sex. Badly. But later. After
he'd acclimated to having River around. Maybe it was
his years of military training or something, but afternoon sex felt like the ultimate indulgence, lazing
around in bed while the rest of the world worked. He
wasn't sure he could allow himself to enjoy that the
way River deserved to be enjoyed.

"You will," he promised. "And maybe it's my turn to do the exploring."

"Maybe." River sounded strangely ambivalent at the prospect. Despite the variety of ways they'd rubbed off together and River blowing him, most of their encounters had been rather focused on Griff. Which was nice and all, but he wouldn't mind getting better acquainted with River's body, especially with the lights on this time. Despite all his reservations about timing, a familiar thrum of arousal started, and he headed for the door before it could take hold.

"Come on. Grab your camera. You ever ride an ATV?"

"I've seen them before." Sighing like Griffin was the meanest guy in the world, withholding sex, River followed him out to the porch and put on his boots before tossing his camera bag on, cross-body style. "And I've been on the back of a motorcycle."

"Good. Same basic principle. Hold on tight and don't distract the driver." He led the way to the shed that housed their ATVs and selected a two-up quad that easily held two riders.

"I don't get to drive one?" Apparently over the lack of sex, River bounced on the balls of his feet.

"Maybe tomorrow. Ride with me this time, get a feel for how they handle, and then we'll see."

"Oh, okay. Holding on to you is hardly a hardship." River accepted the helmet that Griffin offered him, putting it on and nimbly climbing onto the back of the ATV. While plenty of Griffin's friends rode helmet-free, losing two different high school friends to ATV fatalities had made Griffin always insist on them.

Strapping on his own helmet, Griffin took the driver's position, starting up the vehicle.

"I'm going to take you on a tour of the property, then we're headed into the forest. Last part will be on foot, but the view is more than worth it."

"I'm game." River held him closer than strictly necessary, but Griffin wasn't going to complain.

He pointed out the main house and the purpose of the various outbuildings before taking him by the houses where his various relatives lived—Indra and her husband in their contemporary cabin, then Holly's, and the nearby homes for various aunts and cousins. He couldn't exactly say why he was so hell-bent on finding land of his own rather than building here close to the others, but for as long as he could remember he'd craved his idea of a custom-built cabin without neighbors, a yearning that had only become stronger the past few years, an almost palpable drive. He'd needed a goal post-rehab, and somehow his brain had latched on to this one, rebuilding his credit and finances and building his retreat from the world and all its temptations and risks.

He headed down a dirt track past the bubbling creek that bordered his family's property and north into the state forest. He'd ridden these tracks since he was old enough to drive an ATV, and he'd spent many hours back here, racing Hank and his cousins and siblings, but somehow it felt new again, seeing it through River's eyes. The towering trees. The winding creek. The rolling hills. The wind whipping at them. The smell of birch and spruce and damp earth. The nothing around them for miles.

Stopping for a moment, he pointed at a falling-down

collection of logs and moss. "That's where we built a secret hideout back when we were thirteen."

"Cute. I love seeing all this. Thank you." River's sincerity made Griffin's stomach do a strange wobble. He continued down the route, trying to outrace his churning thoughts. Wanting to share with River was a dangerous, unwelcome impulse yet he couldn't seem to stop himself from unloading on him. Telling him about the drinking. About Hank. About his truck. Even about these, his secret places, long-forgotten memories. He wanted to share it all, hurt be damned.

They crossed a gravel road, taking it northwest until they arrived at a seldom-used trailhead that would end in a fabulous view of the inlet, which he hoped River would appreciate, craving that expression River got when he was hiking and truly happy.

"You're not worried about someone stealing the ATV?" River asked as they stowed the helmets.

"Nah. Not how it works around here." He led River past a long-abandoned, rusted-out truck from the thirties and into the forest, trees scrubbier here closer to the coast than the taller ones near their property. The ridge they climbed was steep, but he knew River would be able to keep up. Hell, with it being a while since Griffin had taken this trail without his walking stick, he was more worried about his own ankle and lungs.

"Look down," he said as they neared one of his favorite spots, the sound of rushing water greeting their ascent.

"A waterfall!" River's sound of delight and look of awe warmed long-frozen parts of Griffin's soul, frostbitten places he'd long since forgotten about, feeling returning in almost painful waves. "Oh man. This is so cool."

River took a number of pictures of the waterfall beneath them, feeding the same creek that ran through Griffin's family's property. The steep tree and foliage-lined banks framed the rocks of the waterfall, something Griffin himself had spent countless hours photographing, and he gave River some tips he probably didn't need.

"I want to see more of your photographs while I'm here." River followed him around the bend to an even better vantage point for the waterfall.

"Maybe. They're not that great—"

"So you've said. And I still want to see. That and your coloring work."

"You don't need to see some coloring pages."

"Need, no. Want, yes." River beamed at him. He'd get his way, of course, because that was what River did. But that didn't mean Griffin entirely liked the thought of River seeing his private hobbies. "Wow. This place really is fantastic. I see why you like it here."

"Thanks. Trail forks here—this way to the view at the top of the ridge and that way is a long, slow hike to the pebble beach at the bottom of the cliffs."

"View. Maybe the beach another time." River's grin was so endearing that Griffin couldn't resist tugging him close and giving him a slow kiss.

"First time you brought someone here to make out?" River's tone was light but his eyes were serious, almost as if the answer mattered to him.

"We're not making out," Griffin said sternly. "But yeah, you're the only one I've kissed here."

"No making out?" River fake pouted.

"Save your energy for the climb back down." God, this banter was everything he'd never known he'd needed, and his heart was light as they crested the top of the ridge, the expansive view of the inlet spread out before them, snowcapped mountains across the bay barely visible.

"Wow." River found a nearby boulder to perch on as he took a number of pictures, but then he set the camera aside and patted the spot next to him. "Come sit with me. This is too amazing not to share."

Sharing. Griffin realized with a start that that's what this was. Him sharing with River in yet another way beyond all the talking he'd been doing. And he loved how River seemed to instinctively get the magnitude of the place and the reverence Griffin had for it, sitting in silence with him, not flirting or joking, just sitting there contemplating. Sharing. Griffin reached for his hand, held it tight.

This, even more than the kiss, might be the single most romantic, genuine moment of his life. No fantasies. No role-play. Only the two of them, this place and this moment. Sharing. Weaving a seductive spell until he had to kiss River again, this one long and searching, leaving them both breathless.

"Ready to head back?" Griffin's voice was rough.

"Yeah. But I'd like to come back here sometime." River sounded like he'd surprised even himself with that impulse, so Griffin tried not to put too much stock in it. People like River seldom made return trips, always in search of the new and different.

Instead of dwelling on a future that wasn't going to happen, Griffin focused on the present, on allowing himself the small pleasure of holding on to River's hand on the way back to the ATV and trying to soak up as much of the warm weight of River against his back as he could.

Back at his cabin, he checked on the soup. "This is almost ready. Do you want to shower first?"

"You want to join me?" River waggled his eyebrows, which made Griffin laugh.

"Ha. Go take a look. It's practically coffin size. No way are we both fitting, sorry."

"It's okay. But your dream cabin better have a walk-in shower for two," River said as he grabbed his back-pack.

"It does," Griffin said, almost automatically, even though up until that moment he hadn't thought about a single "for two" feature in all his daydreaming and sketching. But all it took was River's wide grin before that dream shifted, and he too craved a bathroom big enough for both of them, maybe a private hot tub so he could get that kiss he'd been hankering for back in Talkeetna.

"Good. I'll be fast." And River was, emerging a short while later in low-riding sweatpants and that unicorn shirt of his. "What did you make me? It smells good."

"Spinach, white bean, and reindeer sausage soup. I just added the fresh spinach. I know you like green stuff."

"I do." River took a seat at the tiny table, Griffin's first guest in…well, ever, looking totally at home.

"I'll shower after we eat." He dished up the soup along with some crusty whole wheat bread. A big part of why he'd taken River hiking was that River had way more appetite after outdoor time, and while he took pride in his humble cooking, he'd wanted to up the chances of River enjoying the meal.

His ploy seemed to work as River ate with what was for him gusto. "This is really good."

"Thanks. I don't have an oven, but I picked us up some dessert in Anchorage." Griffin's neck started to heat.

"Dessert? I'm intrigued." River set his spoon aside and propped his chin on his hand.

"Eat more soup and I'll show you," Griffin bartered, getting up and retrieving a small cardboard box from his pack, which he set in front of River. He dished himself up a second helping of soup to distract himself from waiting for River's reaction. "I might eat mine after my shower."

"It's from a cupcake shop?" River studied the gold foil label on the box with narrowed eyes.

"Go on, open it. It's not a bomb, promise." Griffin itched behind his ear. Maybe this gesture had been a stupid idea. "It's just two, chocolate maple bacon for me and birthday cake flavor with sprinkles for you. And if you don't feel up to eating or whatever—"

"You remembered." River's tone held a fair amount of wonder.

"Yeah. Not a big deal—"

"It is to me." Leaning over, River brushed a kiss across Griffin's cheek. "It's super sweet. Thank you. But this isn't our last meal together."

"I'd have to come up with rigatoni for that." Griffin tried to shrug off the praise.

"I'm going to save mine for after your shower too. Maybe we can eat them in bed?"

"You and crumbs on the sheets." Griffin groaned

even as his blood started to head south, body way more interested in sex now. "But sure. Let me clean up and shower, then we can have dessert."

"I'm counting on it." River winked at him. "But let me help."

And so they ended up side by side at the sink for the few dishes, him washing and River drying, exactly like they'd done it a hundred times before, hips rubbing, River teasing him until Griffin fled to his shower. He washed with lightning efficiency, and he had to agree that a big walk-in shower, stone maybe, would be perfect, especially if River were in it...

But he couldn't go thinking like that. River was never going to see his cabin, let alone do dishes with him there, share his shower, his life. Not happening. *Focus on the present,* he reminded himself as he toweled off.

He found River already sprawled in the center of his bed, shirt gone, cupcake box on the nightstand, grin as tempting as a fifth of Jack.

"Don't bother with pajamas," River ordered. "And lose the towel too."

"You're awfully bossy," Griffin said even as he complied and stretched out next to River on the bed. "You're not in charge tonight."

"I'm not?" River's forehead creased.

"Nope. I've got your number. All the fantasy stuff, the role-playing, it's all you in control, making something happen for me."

"And you have a problem with that?" River's voice was strangely small. "Pretty sure you got off on those games."

"I did. And I like the role-play, I do. But you're always asking me for a fantasy, and I realized the other day that I've got a new one."

"You do?"

"Yup." Griffin brushed the hair from River's forehead. "It's a really good one too. It's called 'I take my time with River with the lights on' and I've gotten off to it a bunch of times already, just imagining how you taste."

"I like the dark. Like the cabin. That was perfect." River's face was still too serious.

"It was." Griffin gave him a soft kiss. "And this will be too. What's making you nervous? You don't like getting oral? The naked thing? I've seen you naked a few times now. Haven't seen any tentacles or scales."

River didn't laugh. "It's weird. And you're right it's a control thing. Naked is fine, but being…seen, examined makes my skin all itchy."

"Not planning an in-depth medical examination." Griffin cupped his face. "I just want to enjoy you. Maybe blow you? I don't promise to be terrific at it, but I'd like to try."

"Oral feels good, but getting it is…hard. I don't like being the focus of sex. It's partly control—I don't like not having charge of what happens—but it's also wrapped up in my body image stuff and the eating disorder. I have a hard time letting myself have good things."

Tenderness bloomed in Griffin's chest, made his voice as gentle as he'd ever heard it. "I do too. So much. It's not a body image thing for me as much as the memory of everything I've done wrong, everything I screwed up. I have a really hard time letting myself have even this, here with you. Feels like cheating almost, to get something this good."

"It does, doesn't it?" River met his kiss, a meeting of two wounded souls finding each other. Maybe neither of them deserved this thing, but here they were, each wanting to give to the other what he wouldn't take for himself.

"You feel like a present I haven't earned," Griffin admitted. "I almost canceled on this a dozen times."

"Thank you for not." Rolling, River took Griffin with him, settling himself under Griffin and pulling him close for another kiss. "You do deserve this, Griff. I meant what I said earlier. You're a good guy."

"So are you. And you're gorgeous." He paused, considering the impatient sigh River made. "Is that not okay to say? Pretty sure you're the hottest thing I've ever had in my bed, but I don't want to make things worse for you."

"It's a sweet thing to say. And I appreciate it, I do. I'm just…challenging. Years of trying to be as attractive as possible, addressing all possible flaws. It… warped me. Made it hard to take a compliment. But I'm working on it. I'm sorry. I've ruined the mood, haven't I?"

"You haven't." Griffin gave him a firm kiss. "I'm a challenge too. Let me give you what you need tonight, okay?"

"But your fantasy—"

"Can wait until you're more comfortable." Even though he was on top, he tried to let River control the kiss, letting him decide when to take it from a slow slide of lips to something hotter, tongues tangling and moans mingling. Breathing hard, Griffin pulled back.

"Tell me what would make you feel best right now. You in a mood to fuck me? Tie me up? That kind of control? Want one of your first-time fantasies? I'm game for whatever."

River blinked, head tilting. "You really are, aren't you?"

"I never expected to have you here. Now that you're here, I want to give you what you need."

"I don't need the fantasy, not really. Us reuniting after some time apart, desperate to have each other is sexy enough." River's tentative smile turned more seductive.

"Yeah, it is." Griffin growled.

"You'd really be cool with me topping?" River stroked down Griffin's bare back, fingertips digging in, making Griffin shiver. "You like that idea?"

Griffin's skin temperature went up another ten degrees both from the question and the touches. "Yeah. To be honest, it's one of those things I'm curious as to what it feels like sober, see whether I can get off on it."

"Oh, I can get you off on it." Laughing softly, River bit his shoulder. "And now that you've got the idea in my head, yeah, I want that kind of control. Want to drive you crazy."

Griffin fully intended to get his River exploration time eventually when River trusted him enough. He could wait. And he certainly wasn't turning down River's desires in the meantime. River wanted to top? He'd happily push past his own doubts and fears to make that happen.

"Bring it on."

Chapter Fifteen

River hadn't been lying—he generally was fairly ambivalent about fucking for a whole host of reasons. But as Griff rolled off him, flopping onto his back, offering up a crooked grin for him, River found that he really did like the idea. Far more than the thought of letting Griff explore his body. The emotionally heavy conversation had almost killed his earlier desire for sex until Griff showed surprising compassion in letting River have back the control he needed. Maybe someday—maybe even this weekend—he'd be brave enough to let Griff have his way, but right then he craved what he'd had at the cabin and in the hotel room, Griff desperate and needy and letting him lead.

"You have supplies?" he asked. "I've got lube, but I'll have to check the expiration date on my condoms. Been a while."

Griff's smile grew wider. "I kinda like knowing that. Stuff in the nightstand. Pretty sure my condoms are more recent—I use them with uh…" he coughed, so adorable in his flustered state "…personal items."

"You own toys?" River tried to reconcile his image of the big, tough mountain man with one of him playing with his ass. Unexpected, but hot as fuck.

Griff's blush stained his cheeks and neck. "Saw
something online. They called it a massager. Like I
said, I was curious about what worked for me sober.
At first, I had a hard time even jerking off. Body didn't
want to cooperate. Got the toy thing on one of those
late-night larks, you know?"

"Oh, I know how those go." River reached over him,
finding lube and unexpired condoms and a cute orange
medium-size curved plug in the drawer. A little remote
sat under it, and a thrill rushed through River. "Can I
use it on you? I'll use a condom on it, but it would be
hot as fuck to make out with you with it in your ass."

Eyes fluttering shut, Griff nodded. "Yeah. Don't use
the highest setting, but sure, have fun."

God, the amount of trust Griff was showing was
heady stuff, more of a turn-on than even his gorgeous
naked self next to him. Taking a second to lose his
sweatpants and underwear, River scooted so his body
was pressed against Griff's side and claimed his mouth
in an aggressive kiss, one meant to seize control.

Gasping, Griff met him willingly. Eagerly even,
opening for River's questing tongue. He idly rubbed
River's back, but otherwise seemed to relax into whatever River wanted.

And what River wanted was lots of kissing. All the
kissing. Until Griff was panting, pulling away long
enough to gasp, "You had plans for my ass?"

"Uh-huh." Working quickly, he got a condom on
the plug and lubed it up before also getting some lube
on his fingers. The position was slightly awkward, but
he managed to keep kissing Griff while his slick fingers played with Griff's rim, making him gasp and
moan some more.

"Do it. Please." Begging Griff was the best Griff, and River made him wait a few more moments, slicking him up, working him open before he lined up the plug.

"Yeah." Griff let out a low whine from nothing more than the pressure of the toy, making River's balls tingle. This he wanted to see, so he sat up enough to push Griff's legs wide and tease him with the tip of the toy.

"Do I turn it on now or…"

"Stop teasing." Griff rocked his hips up, seeking more contact.

"But it's fun." River turned the toy on its lowest setting, rubbing it all around Griff's rim, mainly to hear the sounds Griff made, but then finally gave in to the urge to push it in, a little at a time. Not wanting to hurt Griff, he grabbed his hand and led it to the base of the plug. "You get the angle of the curve right for you, but I'm keeping the remote."

"Because of course you are." Griff released a strained laugh. Way faster than River would have done, he had the whole plug firmly seated in his ass.

"Now for the super-fun part." Settling himself back along Griff's side, River studied the little remote. It had up and down arrows along with a button for different vibration patterns. While he resumed kissing Griff, he had fun experimenting with the different settings, finding out what made Griff beg.

"Please. More. God. River."

"Like this?" River toyed with increasing the vibration slowly.

"That. That right there. Fuck. Kissing adds…so much. Fuck." Griff's babbles as River moved to kiss his neck and shoulders were adorable. "Wait…not… that. Might come."

"Really?" River was torn between wanting to get Griff off hands-free and wanting to fuck him like they'd planned. "You want that?"

"Want you to fuck me." Turning his head, Griff buried his face in the pillow, but River still heard him add, "Please."

"I suppose you *are* asking nice." River pretended to consider the request. Meanwhile, not waiting for River, Griff reached down and removed the plug.

"Ready. Just go." Griff's breath came in harsh pants.

"Okay, okay." It had been long enough that River fumbled the condom some and probably added way too much lube, but he had a feeling that however long it had been for him, it had been even longer for Griff, and he really didn't want to bungle this. "Is on your back like this good for you?"

"Yeah. My one leg isn't as flexible as the other, but we should be good to go." Griff spread his legs wider, eyes kind, almost as if he could sense that River was a little nervous. "Wasn't that you going on about people's assumptions? Trust me. I want this."

That made River smile, because it was true that he'd marked Griff as a total top who'd probably never made the acquaintance of his prostate, never mind asking to get fucked.

"You're a delight." Kneeling between Griff's thighs, he lined up his cock. "Thank you. For today. For this."

Griff let out a harsh chuckle. "How about you wait to thank me till you get me off? Dying here."

"You're still bossy, even when you let me be in charge."

"Complaints, complaints." Griff arched his back,

rocking up to meet River's first thrust. "Fuck. You feel better than the toy."

"Thought we were waiting on compliments?" River asked breathlessly as he slid all the way in. Griff was slick and stretched from the toy, so there wasn't as much initial resistance as River remembered. If anything, Griff seemed to pull him in, a tight, hot vise meeting each of his tentative thrusts. "I lack the fun curve of your friend the massager. Tell me if I'm close?"

He angled his hips, trying a few different approaches until Griff moaned low. "There. That. Keep doing that."

"This?" More confident now, River started a rhythm in earnest, aiming for that spot that got Griff biting the pillow. Angle set, he arranged himself so that he could lean forward and kiss Griff's neck.

"Hell. Yes. Bite me like you did earlier." God bless bossy Griff and his ability to tell River exactly what he wanted while making River still feel in control, like this was all his idea. River followed the suggestion, biting and sucking along his collarbone while continuing to thrust.

"Faster." Griff worked a hand in between their bodies. Darn. River had been wanting to see if he could get him off without jerking off, but that would have to wait for another time. Both because they were sure as hell doing this again and because River's own orgasm was gathering steam. Everything about this was working for him—Griff's bigger body under his, the hot clench of his ass, the way he moaned every time River hit his gland, the way he seemed to crave River's mark on him. He loved kissing Griff's neck anyway, but the combo of fucking him while dragging more helpless moans out of him from kissing and sucking the tender skin of his shoulders was indescribably good.

And he was good at description, he really was. But right then, words failed him. Hell, thought failed him too, body starting to move by instinct now, hips pistoning faster as Griff had urged. Harder too, but Griff seemed to love that, moaning louder.

"Gonna…" Griff's breath caught for a long moment before he released it in a primal groan. River didn't much need the warning—the warmth seeping between their bodies was clue enough as was how Griff was shuddering and how tight his ass squeezed River's cock. That increase in pressure made River's balls tighten, made him fuck Griff through his orgasm, faster now, thrusts losing his careful rhythm and angle as his body drove him toward his release. He felt like Griff's plane—racing across the lake, lifting off at what seemed to be impossible speed, leaving the ground below in a mighty heave.

"Griff…" He wasn't sure what he was asking for, what he needed, but when Griff's strong arms and legs pulled him closer, tethered him to the earth, he flew, climaxing in harsh waves that left them both shaking. They were a mess of tangled limbs and sweaty, sticky bodies, but River was so far beyond caring.

"Now do I get to thank you?" Laughing, he tried to pull out as gently as he could.

"Ahh…forgot about that pinch." Griff winced. "Yeah, you can thank me all you want. Damn. That was something else."

"I mean it." Mess be damned, River snuggled up to Griff's side. "Today was amazing. The plane ride. The ATV. The view. You feeding me. The sex."

"And we still have cupcakes." Griff kissed him on the forehead. "What do you say we eat them in bed like you wanted before we clean up and I change the sheets? You were a bit…ambitious with the lube."

"Sorry."

"Don't be sorry." Griff kissed him again. "I…I needed that," he mumbled into River's hair. "You give me back things I thought I'd lost forever. Feels like I should be thanking *you*."

River gulped, swelling heart suddenly cutting off his oxygen. Griff needed him. Maybe every bit as much as he needed Griff. And maybe what Griff said earlier was right—perhaps neither of them deserved this gift that was this time together, but he could give Griff what he needed, what he wouldn't allow himself. Even his own demons couldn't stop his desire to give that to Griff.

Soft contact on his shoulders and back slowly roused Griffin. Kisses. Kisses were waking him up. He groaned, pleasure radiating down his spine. He hadn't been lying yesterday—he did not deserve this, a wakeup even sweeter than the cupcakes they'd indulged in while laughing in bed last night. Even washing up and changing the sheets had been fun, joyous and silly. He'd fallen asleep holding River, natural as if they'd been snuggling for years, and dreamed of pancakes and blue skies for their morning. No stress dreams. No too-early wakeup. Only good, pure sleep and now this morning surprise.

"You trying to start something or are you trying to remind me that we've got a date with my plane?" He turned so he could look at River's sleep-creased face.

"Both." River grinned down at him, the vulnerability of last night replaced by his usual good humor. But Griffin wasn't forgetting their talk and the sex afterward anytime soon. He'd always seen River as a bottomless well of confidence, sure of who he was and what he wanted, and learning that he too had insecurities had been…reassuring. Yeah, that was the word. Reassuring. Made him feel so much less alone in this thing. Maybe River was floundering too, feeling his way as much as Griffin was. And maybe he needed Griffin, needed what Griffin could give him, an idea that lifted Griffin up, buoyed him like a rising tide of hopefulness.

Rolling over, Griffin checked the time on his bedside clock. "Fuck. We really should get moving—it's not set in stone, but I put in a flight plan for the day."

"I can be quick." River tugged him back.

"Not sure I can," Griffin admitted. He had some aches he hadn't had in years, but much as they were a pleasant reminder of the night before, he wasn't certain how fast he could get off that morning. "But if you want me to help you…"

"Nah. I'll wait until we can both enjoy it." River met him in a soft kiss, one that made enough promises for later that Griffin almost changed his mind about the quickie.

"What can I feed you for breakfast?" Sitting up, he stretched. Yup. Definitely feeling last night. "And don't say only black coffee. We're going to be gone a number of hours, and you passing out on me isn't part of my agenda."

"Do you have more of the bread from last night? I can do toast."

"And eggs." Griffin searched out clothes from his

small closet and dresser. "I've seen you eat those. And I'm just curious here and trying to understand—is it the feeling of being full that you have trouble with? Or certain foods that cause you more…distress?"

"Both." Looking like a tall blue-haired fairy in the morning light streaming in through the window, River left the bed to dig in his bags, not looking at Griffin as he talked. "I've worked on it a lot in counseling, but truly full still feels gross to me. Lighter foods are simply easier in that regard, but it's not just the mental aspect. I'm cautious about what I eat because certain things amp that gross feeling up, make it more physical—upset stomach, that sort of thing. Not fun."

"That makes sense. Don't want you ill. And it's a control thing too?" Griffin guessed.

"Yeah." River sighed as he pulled on a shirt and jeans. "Old habits like controlling what and when I eat are hard to break, so focusing that energy on making sure the food is healthy stuff helps me some. I don't like feeling out of control, so even when the food choices are sparse like in Denali, my brain still plays games with me, tries to create control for me."

Griffin had never thought of eating disorders as an ongoing thing like this. But as much as he hated the thought of River suffering, he also felt a certain weird sort of kinship with him. "So it's kind of like addiction is for me—not something you're ever going to completely cure, but something you have to manage and live with?"

"Yeah, exactly. I'm not going to say it's the same thing, because it's not, but I usually think of it as being in recovery from the eating disorder. Some days are better than others, and flare-ups still happen. There are times like last night when I can eat with pretty much zero issues, but other days where forcing myself to have anything at all is a struggle."

"I get that." Griffin hadn't talked about this with anyone since rehab, but somehow with River the words simply flowed, long-hidden truths. "Plenty of days I don't think about drinking at all. But other days...yeah, it's a challenge. Those are the times when I really lean on distraction—like I guess travel is for you. For me it's flying and hard work or taking pictures and editing them or doing the coloring thing if it's too late at night for work."

"Show me?" River's question was far gentler than his demand the day before, and Griffin found himself genuinely wanting to share this part of himself too. Holding back seemed impossible around River, something about this connection, this level of understanding that made him want to give River everything he could.

"Here." Walking over to the living area, he pulled a stack of books off the shelf. "You'll see a few of my photos when we go to Mom's for dinner, and maybe I'll boot up the laptop later for you to see others, but here's some of the coloring. You can look while I fix us some food. Try not to laugh too loudly."

"Griff." River stopped him with a hand on his shoulder before Griffin could turn away. "I'm not going to laugh. Promise."

The seriousness in his eyes made Griffin's heart stutter. All that connection Griffin felt was reflected back to him tenfold. Whatever this thing was between them, Griffin wasn't alone in it, and that thought made it easier to leave River to curl up on the loveseat with the books. He made quick work of toast and eggs, making a point of not glancing over at River, trying to trust in his reactions.

"Food's ready," he called as he set plates on his table.

"In a minute." River sounded distracted, not even looking up from the book he was looking at, which was one of Griffin's favorites, a forest-themed collection of highly detailed and stylized trees and foliage, lots of excuses to use greens and browns. But sometimes he got whimsical, like on the picture River was examining, doing pops of unexpected color, having fun with purple trees and yellow leaves and such. Silly little things, but they got him through some tough nights.

"These are amazing. You should frame your favorites." River flipped the page to another one Griffin liked, big towering pine trees and little forest creatures. That one had taken hours, but he'd never thought of removing any of the pictures from the books.

"Nah. They're fun, but not the sort of thing you put on the wall."

"Sure they are. Colorful mats, professional frame jobs—they'd look amazing. Like your photos—I loved the few glimpses you let me see on the tour. Why are you so reluctant to see yourself as an artist?" Setting the books aside, River unfolded himself from the couch, following Griffin to sit at the little dining table.

"Because I'm not." Griffin tore off a piece of toast with more force than the bread deserved. "That's Uncle Roger—he's the artist, the one the tourists pay the big bucks to hang out with."

"Our tour group was plenty happy with you as the photography expert. And your family doesn't have room for two artists?" River blinked, clearly not buying the excuse.

"Nah. It's not them. He and my mom would be happy for me to do more with my photos. It's more…" He sighed, toast turning to ash in his stomach.

"So what is it?" River reached over and squeezed his forearm. Griffin's chest clenched. God, was there nothing he'd keep from this man? Even as he took a deep breath, he knew he'd end up telling the whole damn story.

"It's stupid, but Hank used to tease me about art. Said only girly men took art classes, so I ended up in shop and extra math classes with him. He'd laugh if I pulled out the camera Uncle Roger gave me, tell me that wasn't a hobby that would get me laid and that my stuff was shitty. Told me to focus on flying and what I was good at."

River rolled his eyes, the way Griffin had almost known he would. "Lord save me from toxic masculinity. Seriously? People of all genders love artists. All soulful and stuff."

"Ha."

River's tone shifted from sarcastic to something far gentler. "He never knew, did he?"

"No." Griffin didn't bother playing dumb. River had filled in enough blanks about his past to have a pretty decent picture of how things had been. "I never told him about my crush. If he suspected, he never said a thing, never acted differently. And while he could be a homophobic ass, I never got the impression that he was holding back a secret bi side either—it was simply one of those pointless obsessions, not a love story waiting to happen."

"I'm sorry." River tightened his grip on Griffin's

arm, looking him deep in the eyes. "That sucks. I'm sure keeping quiet was tough on you."

Griffin snort-laughed, making his sinuses burn. "You've got no idea. Hiding it was hard. It's kinda how I started drinking. He was always on me to get laid when we went out to the parties or bars and he wanted to pick up women. I figured out fast that a few drinks made that far easier, got him off my case, kept him from asking questions I wasn't ready to answer back then."

"That's rough. I guess I'm kind of lucky—modeling was toxic in other ways, but it was filled with people of many different sexual identities. I never felt I had to hide. I mainly went with guys, but occasionally a nonbinary person or a female, and no one gave me shit. And half of the modeling community are aspiring artists of one kind or another. Liking to do photography and write were simply cool hobbies to have. I'm sorry you didn't have a more supportive environment."

Griffin opened his mouth to say that it was okay, but what came out was "Me too."

"Not to be blunt, but he's gone now. You shouldn't hold yourself back as an artist just because you hear his voice in your head telling you it's crap. And trust me, I know voices. I have to battle the one every day that tells me that I'm ugly and worthless and don't deserve anything good. So I get it."

"You're not ugly or worthless," Griffin said sternly.

"And neither is your art." River matched him hard stare for hard stare.

"Maybe." Griffin didn't want this to turn into an actual argument. "We should probably head to the airfield."

"Okay. But you're showing me more photographs later." River's tone didn't leave room for objecting, something Griffin kind of liked. Like last night—it was easy to let go and let River have his way, not have to wrestle with decisions on his own. Sure he liked being in charge some too, but River made it easy to not think, and that was a good thing. This way he wouldn't have to spend the day agonizing over whether to show River his laptop later. He would and that was that and he could get on with the business of enjoying their day together.

His skin tingled from all the talking—a raw, itchy sensation, but it was also as if a dam had broken inside him, like he was saying things that had needed saying for years. And once he'd freed the words, he wasn't sure how to stop or how he'd cope when he no longer had River to share with.

Chapter Sixteen

As they finished the breakfast dishes and made their way to the airfield, River wasn't quite sure what to do with this newly chatty Griff, but he liked it. A lot. He'd come to visit Griff for more than sex, of course, but he hadn't expected to enjoy his company this thoroughly or to feel this intense closeness. He had plenty of adult friends, had grown up with siblings, and never had trouble making friends at camp or school, but he couldn't say he'd ever felt this way about another human before. It was big and scary and glorious all at once.

"Got your camera?" Griff asked as they exited the truck.

"Got yours?" River countered, shouldering his backpack. "You're not my tour guide anymore. You get to have fun too."

"I wouldn't have said it a few weeks ago, but being your guide was fun." Griff gave him a rare, wide grin that showed his teeth. "And yeah, I've got my camera. Kachemak is full of great chances for a decent shot. And then there's you."

"Me?" River blinked.

"You did say I could photograph you however I wanted." Griff winked at him.

"I meant like posing nude for an artsy shot or something." Emphasis on *pose,* sexy or otherwise. Modeling was a thing where he could shut off his brain and all the voices and doubts and simply do the job. And not look at the resulting photos unless he absolutely had to. But unguarded photos, like the one Griff had taken of him in Denali, made him nervous. He'd kept that one, looked at it several times, trying to see what Griff saw.

"No skinny dipping, even at the height of summer like this. You'd freeze." Griff laughed. "And I don't really do artsy. I do real."

And that was what River was afraid of. Griff saw all of him, the real him, and it was scary as fuck, being seen like that. He was trying to be brave, trying to be worthy of Griff's attention and gaze, but old doubts kept plaguing him, had him shrinking into his sweatshirt as they made their way to the office so Griff could check in with his mom and check the flight plan log.

Griff's mom seemed marginally less suspicious that morning with her long hair wound into a coil held on top of her head with a clip and a tight smile for both of them. He'd bring the chocolates along that evening, hope that maybe coming with a hostess gift helped smooth things.

"You'll be back for dinner?" She made it sound more like an order than question. "Indra's husband is doing the grilling."

"Sounds lovely." River tried to sound both encouraging and enthusiastic.

"Yeah." Griff's tone was neither of those things, but he gave his mom a kiss on the head, which seemed to mollify her somewhat as she and Griff talked flight jargon for a few minutes before Griff led him down to the lake and to a smaller plane than the one they'd taken the day before.

"This Super Cub is great for the sort of tight landing and short takeoff we'll make today and is a great two-person plane." Griff tossed their backpacks behind the back seat. "You get in and I'll make my final checks on the exterior."

Like the other plane, the fit was tight, and in this one, he'd ride behind Griff because the cockpit was only one person wide. Griff gave him a headset to wear and pointed out some of the workings of the plane as he got in. Always thorough, he did a bunch of other checks on various dials and switches before talking to his mother on the radio, making sure none of the business's other planes were coming in or leaving right then, and getting cleared for takeoff.

If anything the Super Cub was even faster than the other plane, practically skipping down the small lake, getting them airborne almost as fast as a helicopter.

"Whee!" River's inner ten-year-old came out to play as Griff took them higher, giving them a spectacular view of the inlet and the peninsula.

"I'm taking us on the scenic route." Griff's voice sounded in River's ear. "We'll go as far southwest as Port Graham, then northeast to the tip of the fjords before coming back to the bay to land in one of my favorite hidden spots away from the tourist lodges and trails."

The terrain beneath them became more mountainous as they crossed the bay, white-tipped peaks below their plane, making River feel exceptionally tiny in this little plane above the vast land beneath them. Griff used the headset sporadically to point out different attractions beneath them. They flew over a number of teeny towns on the southern part of the Kenai Peninsula. The plane swooped north, closer to the mountains and over the majestic fjords that he'd seen up close in the boat. Back closer to the state park region, many small lakes and rivers broke up the valleys of green land. As they descended, he spotted more wildlife like a huge flock of white birds all over a little island not even big enough for a house.

"It's a bird party," he joked to Griff over the headset.

"Look to the shore—think there's a bear emerging from the water, shaking off his swim." Sure enough a rather skinny brownish-black bear lumbered along a rocky river bank as Griff dipped low enough to spot him.

Griff navigated them over several coves, some populated with boats and colorful kayaks and log-built lodges, others untouched by civilization. Near a gorgeous large natural archway, a collection of yellow kayaks bobbed along, little happy dots beneath their flight.

"Ready to stretch your legs?" Griff circled one of the unpopulated coves, an area tucked between the bay and the mouth of a small river, with towering pine trees on both sides of the gravel shore. Then, soft as a feather falling on a pillow, Griff landed in the water.

"There's no dock?"

Griff's chuckle crackled over the headset. "You'll see."

He taxied close to the shore, then cut the engine and surprised the hell out of River by hopping out, deftly leaping from a pontoon to the bank, and using metal chains on the pontoons to tug the plane up closer to the shore. River saw now why Griff had put on tall boots and thick pants when they were getting dressed.

"Get out carefully," he said. "Don't worry about the packs—I'll get those."

More than a little impressed at Griff's maneuvers, River climbed out. He was wearing his waterproof boots but he still tried to stay clear of the likely frigid water as he disembarked and landed next to Griff on shore.

"Now what?" River shouldered the pack that Griff handed him.

"I secure the plane, then we explore. I want to show you the view from the ridge. Don't worry—we'll have the plane in our sights most of the time. It'll be fine."

Stopping several times for pictures, they made their way from the rocky shore to what River supposed could be optimistically called a trail leading up a steep hill. Griff leaned heavily on a walking stick, and River had to bite back several offers to go slower or cut the hike short. Griff wouldn't take kindly to being babied, and River didn't want to ruin what was turning out to be a near-perfect day. The payoff for the climb was a gorgeous view of the plane beneath them and the towering mountains on the other side of the shore.

"Don't forget to drink," Griff reminded him when they stopped near the summit of the ridge for some panoramic shots. "And I'm having a protein bar. Want one?"

"Half of one?" River could compromise and was rewarded with a deep smile from Griff. "I really like it here. Thank you for bringing me."

"Thanks for giving me an excuse to come." Griff

gave him a tender look as he passed over the protein bar. "We bring tours to the state park all the time—we're licensed operators here, but I haven't come for pleasure in years. Usually I bring groups to populated areas like Halibut Cove."

"I love watching you fly," River confessed after a long swig of water to wash the bar down. "Can I ask something?"

"Sure." Griff stowed their wrappers in his pack.

"Was it hard resuming flying?" He'd been curious about that for a few weeks, more so now that he'd actually seen Griff pilot.

"After my injuries you mean? Or when I got sober?" Tone somber, Griff looked away, out at the mountains across from them.

"Both? You're so good at flying, and it seems like such a big part of your life. I can't imagine you not."

"I never lost my license if that's what you're thinking. Never flew drunk. I was what they used to call a 'functional' alcoholic right up until I wasn't after Hank died, and I took a hard spiral to the bottom of the barrel so to speak. After the accident, I just quit flying. Quit everything really. Hung out in Vegas and Reno with some buddies who were even a worse influence than Hank, gambling and drinking my money away. I wasn't even that good at cards, never liked making bets, but somehow when I was drunk…" He drifted off, studying the water.

"It's okay." River scooted closer, trying to let Griff know how much he appreciated getting these truths, the past that had shaped Griff into the man River knew and appreciated.

"Anyway, I was damn good at making stupid

choices, ones that left me broke and hanging on by a thread when my mom finally got ahold of me, got me to get some help. Didn't even get in a plane until I was coming back from rehab, and that was a commercial flight."

"I know a little about hitting bottom," River admitted. "I'd had my eating disorder for years before my mom died, but then…yeah. It got bad. Dad married Marisa, and it felt like I was the only one who cared, the only one who missed Mom. All my control issues and negative self-talk grew out of control. Took two hospitalizations before I was able to admit I needed help. The first time they didn't even formally diagnose the eating disorder—just called it exhaustion. But then I lost so much more weight and was hospitalized a second time and the right doctor finally saw what I was doing to myself before it was too late. Rock bottom is a terrible place—I still have nightmares about the hospital, especially that second stay when I was so sick."

"And the travel? How did you go from the hospital to traveling the world?"

"My dad gave me my portion of my mom's life insurance and trust—she'd left a little note for each of us to go along with it." River hated how his sinuses burned, and he had to blink repeatedly, even now.

"Hey. It's okay." Griff put an arm around him, holding him close. "You don't have to tell me. I'll read your book like you keep telling me to."

River offered him what was likely a weak smile for the joke. "No, it's okay. Anyway, in my letter, she told me to go somewhere I'd never been. She mentioned always wanting to go to Turkey. I went there first. And it helped, so I just kept moving, kept up with my therapist and doctors long-distance. If it started getting bad again, I just went somewhere else until traveling was… this part of me. I know it doesn't make the most sense."

"It doesn't have to. I'm glad it got you healthy." Griff kissed his temple. "Whatever it took to get you healthy was worth it. But it's okay to slow down too, you know?"

River groaned. "You sound like my therapist. And I get that. It's been on my mind a lot lately, wondering about having a home base so to speak, putting down roots, but…"

"But?" Griff continued to hold him close, which made this conversation far easier.

"It's scary. The idea of not moving. I remember that dark place a little too well, you know?"

"I know." Griff didn't release him, but his voice did get a little sadder. "Been there. Afraid to rock the boat or upset what's working. Hell, right after rehab, I didn't want to do a damn thing other than whatever manual labor Mom or Uncle Roger needed doing. Lifted boxes and engine parts and chopped firewood and kept my head down… Yeah. I get it."

"And how did you start flying again? That must have been hard after so long away from it."

"Took a while before I realized that I missed it, honestly. My mom took me up in the de Havilland a few times before the urge to fly started coming back, little by little. I was afraid to try, frankly." Griff's voice was so tight that River leaned into him, rubbed his thigh, trying to give him the same support he'd given River. "Worried about having people counting on me and letting them down or taking on too much, pushing it."

"I get that."

"But she didn't lose faith in me, kept pestering me to take a few cargo flights, so I started small. Got my wings under me so to speak. Doubt I would have returned to the air if it wasn't for her needing me. Same deal with the tour. The business needed me, but…"

"You worried." River understood that fear, a little too well. "But you did it. You stepped outside your comfort zone, proved something to yourself, maybe?"

"Now you sound like the self-help guru I know and I—like." Griff stuttered just enough over the last word to make River's heart skip its next beat. This thing between them—it wasn't simply *like,* and they both knew it, but naming it… Another big, scary thing. Right up there with the idea of having a place to return to.

But as Griff continued to hold him close, the sweeping vista of the bay spread out before them, he wanted to be brave, wanted to be the kind of person who saw the potential in this thing they were building between them and didn't run the other way from it. Hell, Griff was the sort of man one ran to, headlong, held tight, built something real with. *I only do real,* Griff had said. And right there on that ridge as they sat quietly, River wished for the courage to be exactly that.

"Here's to hoping that hiking did its usual magic on you," Griffin said as they boarded the plane for the flight back to Wedding Creek. "When my mom grills, she makes enough for half the peninsula."

"I could eat." River gave him a lopsided smile. He'd been quieter than usual as they'd hiked and explored the little cove, other than the heavy conversation on the ridge about recovery. And Griffin understood River's retreat all too well—he'd felt it too, chest rattling like he was outside in wet clothes in January, an awful, damp, deadly cold taking hold as he'd confessed things that he never talked about. But holding River, knowing that he understood on some level—that was worth the chill. River was like the fire or hot tub waiting on the other side for Griffin. Opening up with him simply felt right.

And that was strange and new and more than a little frightening, putting so much of himself out there. The way he figured it, River was probably feeling the same sort of jumble of emotions, and Griffin was happy to simply hold his hand, keep him close as they explored, telling him about the area and stories of other trips. Stealing kisses, simply because he could. Guys like him didn't get many perfect days, but this one was pretty damn close.

His nerves returned though as they crossed the bay. God, he hoped his family didn't scare River off. They could be a little much, even for Griffin. But this was River, who unlike Griffin was good with people, and if he was nervous at all, he didn't show it. They made a quick stop at Griffin's cabin for the chocolates River had bought in Seattle, and River cast a longing glance at Griffin's bed.

"We could be fashionably late…"

"We could not." Man, Griffin loved how River could make him laugh. He'd laughed more in the few weeks of knowing River than in the five years prior.

"One of these days, I'm going to introduce you to the idea of the afternoon quickie, and you're going to like it." River draped his arms around Griffin's neck, pulled him down for a slow kiss.

"I'm looking forward to it." It was another fantasy,

the one where they had more time, an endless supply of days and encounters and would get around to both of their wish lists and more. "But ten minutes before my mom's dinner is not that time."

"Such a grumpy bear." River took another lingering kiss before releasing Griffin and gathering up the box of chocolates. "Okay, lead the way to the firing squad."

That got another laugh from him. "I'm hoping it won't be *that* bad. They're simply protective of me, that's all."

"I'm messing with you. It'll be fine. Trust me."

"I do." Griffin's throat went tight at how true that was. He did trust River. With his truth. With his past. With his body. And maybe with his heart too.

Now it was his turn to be the quiet one on the walk up to his mother's house. Rather than go in the front door, he took the steps up to the large back deck where the grill was already going and family members were gathered around. Uncle Roger had been staying with her as he continued his recovery, and he was holding court in a lounge chair, leg propped up with pillows.

"Come tell me about what you saw across the bay," he called to Griffin. "Any good pictures?"

"Some." Griffin's favorite was one he wouldn't be showing anyone, a selfie with River's phone camera that he'd goaded Griffin into doing, saying Griffin had enough pictures of only River but none with the two of them. They were both flushed from hiking, sun beating down, hardly the most photogenic. But they were happy, both grinning at each other, not the camera, and that was why Griffin had made River send him a copy. He'd keep that one close. But it was too private to share, as were most of the candids he'd taken of River while they were exploring.

"Tell him about the second bear," River urged, digging out his camera from its bag. "Here. I'll show you."

"Second bear?" Uncle Roger offered an indulgent smile as River knelt next to his chair.

"Well, third really if you count Griff." River's laugh had Uncle Roger joining in as River thumbed through the pictures on his camera before holding the camera out to Uncle Roger and launching into the story of the first bear, the one they'd seen from the air. They talked wildlife photography for several minutes until Griffin was confident River had control of the situation.

"I'm gonna go see if Mom needs any help," he said, putting a hand on River's shoulder. "I'll take her your chocolates. You okay out here? Need some water or tea?"

"I'm good." River waved him off. "I'll thank her myself for the hospitality later, but I'm getting a free lesson here. I'm not going to turn that down."

"Good." Griffin was still smiling as he entered the house, heading to the open kitchen where his mother was setting out dishes on the island. He set the chocolates River had brought next to the other dessert items. "River got you these. He's talking with Uncle Roger now, but I know he'll want to say thank you later for having him over. He's nice that way."

"Seems so." She looked him over like she was inspecting for cracks. "Someone's happy."

"Yeah. Maybe." He snagged a chip from a bowl on the counter. "He's…fun. Uncle Roger seems to like him."

"He's personable. No one's arguing with that. And

I like seeing you happy." Her eyes were sad and voice weary. "I really do. I just... I worry, okay? We got you back, got this second chance with you. I don't want to lose you again."

"You won't." He gave her an awkward one-armed hug. "I'm not going anywhere. It's a summer thing. He'll move on soon, I'm sure. And I'll be fine."

Even as he said the words, they felt wrong. Cold and empty. While this thing between them might not live to see the fall, it wasn't simply a fling. And he probably wasn't going to be fine. He was in too deep, cared too much. Old voices still told him that he didn't deserve River, but at some point he'd started telling those voices to fuck themselves. He wanted this. Needed it.

"Griff." Shaking her head, his mother leaned into his hug. "I wish you had someone to talk to about these sorts of choices. Make sure you're being healthy. I could look—"

"Mom. I don't need therapy. Or a meeting. Maybe just let me have this?" The words seemed directed at himself as much as her. Why not simply let himself have this? As long as he could? Why not have something good? Especially if it meant helping River at the same time, giving him what he needed. Watching River encounter unfamiliar things was a true, pure joy, and Griffin wasn't going to get sick of giving him new experiences.

"I don't want to fight. Take the fish out?" She pulled away from the hug, tension rolling off her.

Part of Griffin wanted to capitulate, say what she wanted to hear, but the other part of him knew this was a rare time when he couldn't do that. So instead, he only nodded at the request.

"Oh and I'm going to need you to take a tour in two weeks. Roger just isn't healing as fast as we'd hoped. Can you do that or are you too…preoccupied?"

"I'll do it. Last one wasn't so bad." He tried to offer her a smile, but his cheeks were tight, muscles almost creaking with the effort. "Anything else I can do for Uncle Roger?"

"No. I'm flying him into Anchorage myself later this week. I'll handle it. Having him here is…no burden. Just making sure your head is on straight for work."

"It is. My having a friendship or whatever, it doesn't change my priorities. Family first and all that."

"I know." She patted his cheek before handing him the platter of fish steaks. "You and the rest of the family are my biggest blessings. Couldn't ask for more."

But what if I can? Griffin swallowed back the question as he carried the fish outside. He'd always been the odd one out, even before the drinking almost ruined his relationship with the family. The loner. The one dreaming of a cabin somewhere on his own, not part of the family land. The one who went to chase fighter-plane dreams instead of doing the smart thing and staying to help grow the family business. And he'd thought for years now that the family was all he needed, his place here secure. But what if he was wrong?

Chapter Seventeen

River liked Griff's family. Maybe a little too much, given that his mother still seemed to not trust him, but they were a cohesive family unit, something he hadn't been around in too many years. They were boisterous, close-knit, and charming from the loud play of the nieces and nephews to the teasing of the adult siblings and the adorable romance he suspected that Uncle Roger and Griff's mom were carrying on under everyone's noses. They doted on each other, but as soon as anyone glanced their direction, they switched off their private looks—a nifty trick that River would like to learn someday.

As they said their goodbyes for the night, he was hit by memories of his mom's last holiday. Sleepy kids rounded up like this, hugs all around, leftovers shared. This was a *family,* and Griff was so lucky to have them. His chest hurt with trying to outrun the memories, but unlike their usual deep pain, tonight's hurt was more bittersweet. Wistful even. He'd had something magical like this once. Maybe once was all he got.

"You okay?" Griff asked on the walk back to his cabin.

"Yeah." Then, because this was Griff, and he didn't

need to pretend or lie, he added. "Just missing my mom. We all drifted apart after she passed. I need to call my sisters sometime soon."

Even though they were probably still in sight of the main house, Griff threw an arm around him. "I'm sorry. I'd say you could borrow mine, but I know it's not the same thing."

"Don't think your mom would have me." River managed a small laugh.

"Ha. She'll come around, promise. She liked the chocolates."

"Good." River really should correct his assumption that there would be plenty of time for his mother to warm up to River, a future where River was more than just a bystander to this family. However, he simply didn't want to. Maybe this was the night's fantasy—this notion that they could have a real future together, a prolonged middle like Griff craved, a space where this friendship blossomed into its full potential. The big scary words and all.

The big scary words—and feelings—were undoubtedly a big part of why an end date for this thing was suddenly on his mind. The longer they kept going, the deeper he got into unfamiliar waters, and he simply wasn't sure he knew how to swim in this sea of emotions. Ending now would be simpler than opening up to more future hurt. Because eventually this would end. All good things did. And old voices telling him what he deserved kept humming, threatening to roar, making him twitchy.

But even with all that, he tried to relax into Griff's unexpected embrace, cuddling up to his side as they entered the cabin. This was too good to ruin with an awkward conversation.

"I'm going to take the first shower," Griff said as he pulled his laptop off one of the bookcase shelves. "But I'll let you amuse yourself with looking at some of my photos."

"I liked the ones at your mom's place." He'd made Griff show him which pictures on the cluttered walls of his mother's house were his and which were his uncle's. After a few though, he'd been able to spot Griff's distinctive style and way of framing his subjects. He had a knack for focusing on something small while still capturing the epic nature of the background. Mostly landscapes, but some of family and friends, including some super-special candids from one of the sisters' weddings. He had a truly special talent, and it was a pleasure to curl up on the loveseat and page through the hundreds of other edited pictures Griff had in his galleries.

"Your turn." Griff emerged in a towel wrapped around his waist.

"These are truly incredible." River reluctantly set the laptop aside and accepted the clean towel Griff held out for him. "Thank you for sharing with me."

That was an understatement, and one he dwelled on as he showered. There was so much of Griff in his pictures—his passion for this land, his vulnerability, the big emotions he kept beneath a still surface, his gifts and his limitations both. He wasn't precisely sure how to repay the present Griff had given him, but he wanted to do something. Something that would show he appreciated what Griff had been doing the past few days, opening himself up to River.

When he finished in the bathroom, he found Griff stretched out on the bed, laptop next to him. He had a lazy smile for River and patted the bed next to him. "Hey. I'm uploading the pictures from today. I wanna show you this one."

"Okay." River lay down next to him, using the excuse to snuggle into Griff's side. On the laptop screen, Griff had a picture of him, one of several he'd been vaguely aware of Griff taking when they were at the summit of the ridge, but trying to tune out. "I hate pictures of me."

"I know." Griff's tone wasn't unsympathetic. "But just look, okay?"

"I'm looking." His hair was messy in the picture—blown around by wind on the ridge. The blue was more than a little faded because he hadn't had time to touch it up or get to a salon, trying to move things around to accommodate this time with Griff. He'd needed the time with Griff more than he'd needed to see a stylist. Blotchy skin from the exertion of hiking and the sun. Looking fuller and pinker than usual, his lips were parted—this pic must have followed one of the spontaneous kisses Griff had doled out like candy on the hike. But his eyes were squinty—had this been an actual photoshoot, he never would have gotten away with that expression, sun be damned. His finger was crooked, probably trying to tempt Griff into a second kiss. He supposed *cheerful mess* were the words he'd use for the picture. He looked happy and playful, but not in a staged way.

"You're gorgeous to me all the time, but I love this one." Griff's voice was almost shy, and it brushed over River like a caress. "I love your hair these days—the way it almost merges with the sky on a good day. Longer suits you, makes your face look even more like a fairy king."

"A fairy king?" This was a level of fancifulness that River really needed to put a stop to, but damn if he didn't want to hear more.

"Yes." Griff nodded firmly and tugged him closer. "And the way you always look into the sun—there's something so fearless about your expression here. I love it. Not to mention, I love the way your skin gets pink when you hike—it makes me think about sex and the flush that spreads up your chest when you're really turned on."

"Sex, huh?" River could go for some of that right then, ease this too-full feeling in his chest. He wanted to be the person Griff saw, so damn bad. Be his fairy king or whatever else Griff needed. Griff loved looking at him, seeing things no one else did. Letting him look was far harder than it sounded, but River wanted to try. He flopped over onto his back. "Want to take some only-for-us sex pics?"

"No." Griff laughed harder than River had heard him and set the laptop on the nightstand. "I'm not saying never, but I've never brought the camera into the bedroom before. I'd rather simply enjoy you. Us. This."

Somehow that was the more difficult request. But River was determined to get past his hang-ups, let Griff have this. Stretching, he took a big breath, released it. "Okay. Have at me."

"Seriously?" Griff raised a single eyebrow. "I'm desperate to kiss you all over, but I don't want you lying there miserable either."

"I won't be." River hoped he wasn't lying. "I like your mouth."

"Yeah? Well, it likes you too." Griff dipped his head for a soft kiss on the mouth. "You're always so damn sweet. At first I thought it was gum or lip balm or something, but now I think it's all you."

"I think you're in a poetic mood." River tried to laugh as Griff's lips skated down his neck. He wasn't as sensitive there as Griff was, but it still felt good, and Griff seemed to instinctively know that River wasn't up for the sort of bites and sucking that worked on him, keeping it light and teasing.

"Yup." Griff's voice was muffled but cheerful as he mouthed along River's shoulder. Instead of going for his chest as River had expected, he kissed all down one arm. Biceps. Inner elbow. Forearm. Each finger. "You're so much stronger than you look, you know that?"

River got that Griff meant more than physically and that he was making some sort of point, but he couldn't bring himself to agree. Or speak at all. His throat was that tight, breath coming in little huffs. And Griff seemed to understand that too, didn't press him for a response as he continued his kisses, leaning across River to go back up the other hand and arm. Then he worked his way down River's side, and River tried hard to not dwell on whether his ribs were too visible or not visible enough—old mental games resurfacing in the tide of emotions Griff was calling forth.

The kisses along his ribs tickled, finding nerve endings he hadn't been aware of, and he shivered as Griff approached his chest.

"Can I kiss you here too?" Griff's breath was warm

across River's nipple, causing another shiver, and he nodded. The care Griff was showing him was nothing short of breath stealing. He'd never been orgasmic from his nipples or anything, even with piercings in, but Griff's gentle licks and flicks got his dick back in the game, blood rushing south as Griff took his sweet time with River's whole chest area, not only the nipples.

And when Griff's head moved lower, he was actually sort of looking forward to the contact. He had much sparser body hair than Griff and had been in the waxing habit back in his modeling days, but he still had a narrow trail of hair below his navel, and Griff licked his way down the path, all the way to the hair River tried to keep closely cropped when he didn't wax or shave it. If Griff had an opinion on River's grooming or lack thereof, he didn't show it, growling softly as he blessed River's hipbones with kisses.

"So fucking sexy. Gonna let me suck you?"

"Yeah." River exhaled. Fuck. He did want that. "Do it."

"Soon." Griff gave a dark chuckle as he proceeded to kiss River's inner thighs, scooting farther down in the bed to trail his mouth over River's knees and calves.

"Not toes." He had to draw a line somewhere.

"Oh, all right." Griff fake pouted before kissing his way back up the other leg, spending a long time on River's inner thighs, making him gasp with how good it felt. Moving so that he was between River's thighs, big shoulders spreading River's legs, he used the tip of his tongue all along the crease of River's leg. Close. So close.

"Come on. Do it." His shoulders shifted around, a strange restlessness taking hold.

"How do you feel about rimming? No-go like toes? Or can I try?" Griff punctuated his question with a gentle bite on River's leg.

"It's not like toes..." River could count on one hand with some fingers left over how many times he'd let someone do that for him, especially when not high or drunk, not that he'd tell Griff that. "Can I say stop if it's too weird?"

"Of course." Griff looked up at him, hazel eyes serious. "Always. And I'm not asking to fuck you. All I want is to make you feel good."

"You are." This time wasn't a half lie. Griff really was making him feel good. Amazing even. Cherished. Appreciated. Seen, but not in the terrible, scary way he'd feared. And he did trust Griff, trusted that he wouldn't try to turn a rim job into a license to fuck, the way some would. He'd keep his word.

And because this was Griff and apparently River had signed up for glacier-melting slow sex with him, Griff didn't go right for River's ass. Or his dick, instead laving his balls with his tongue, waiting until River was panting and rocking his hips before going lower to the sensitive skin behind his balls. It was another area River had never given much thought to, but Griff was downright enthusiastic in his exploration of the area, getting closer and closer to River's rim, but then retreating back toward his balls.

"Can I jerk off?" He didn't quite recognize his breathless voice, hadn't expected to get this into Griff's ministrations, especially not this fast. Griff's mouth was hot and generous, and the brush of his beard stubble made River tremble, little electric charges.

"No." Raising his head, Griff grinned up at him.

"That's mine. Gonna suck you, promise. Let me have my fun?"

"You're killing me."

"That's kind of the point." Without warning, Griff pushed River's legs up and back, giving himself more room and making River feel even more exposed. But right as he was about to object, Griff planted an open-mouthed kiss right on River's rim and all he could do was gasp. Yes, he was blatantly on display for Griff in this position, Griff's big hands holding his ass open, but the little jolts of panic at being this naked kept getting edged out by the deeper ebb of pleasure from Griff's mouth.

And it helped, the way Griff was so obviously into this, low growls of pleasure and satisfied rumblings as he teased River with his lips and tongue. He didn't make rimming a passing thing, a waystation on the route to other, more fun activities, something River himself had been guilty of a time or two. No, he feasted on River's ass. Maybe the literal term was tongue fucking, but that seemed too crude for River's brain, not poetic enough for what Griff was managing to do to him. Eventually River's hesitation lost out, and shutting his eyes, he sank back into the pillows and let Griff work him over, strip him bare until he was only his moans and his singing nerve endings and his rising need to come.

"Please." He wasn't usually the one begging, but here he was, desperate to get a hand on his cock. Settling for burying his fingers in Griff's hair, he writhed, seeking more. Or maybe less. Something. This was all too much, especially when Griff left his ass, moved to suck and lick River's balls, slowly working his way toward River's straining cock.

"Please. Need to come." Begging became easier the longer this onslaught went on, needy little moans and whimpers escaping his mouth as Griff finally, finally licked up River's cock. He paused to toy with the head, using his tongue to tease, until River's fingers tightened in Griff's hair. "Come on, come on."

"Need something?" Griff had the audacity, the fucking audacity, to sound all cocky and self-satisfied, like this was fun. And maybe it was for him, but for River this was a reckoning—or maybe more accurately, a reduction, him reduced to this clawing need, no more walls, no more posing or fantasies or other barriers. Just him and Griff and this thing between, this *real* thing, this *real* him here experiencing it.

And when Griff's mouth closed over his cockhead, swallowing him even as he continued to tease with his tongue, River couldn't hold back anymore, hips bucking, fucking into Griff's warm, willing mouth. Judging by Griff's muffled moans, he liked it, liked seeing River unravel like this. Ordinarily, he'd try to make the buildup last, hold back, but there was no holding back now, only a reckless, headlong tumble into pleasure. Griff ghosted a single callused fingertip across River's hole, still slick from the rimming, and that glancing contact coupled with Griff swallowing him deep had him shooting, no time even for a warning.

He supposed he yelled. He must have because his throat felt raw as Griff milked him through the aftershocks until finally he had to push Griff away.

"Too much." Yeah, he'd yelled. His raspy voice sounded like the plane scraping the gravel shore. He had a limited awareness of Griff rolling away, using one of their towels on his face, then collapsing next to River, hand already on his cock.

And the polite version of River would put a stop to that, would find some energy to return the favor, but this River was wrung out, nothing left. He licked his lips, trying to find enough saliva and brain power simply to speak, and all that came out was, "Fuck."

"Still with me?" Griff's chuckle cut past some of the cobwebs in River's brain. "God, you were so hot. Thank you. Fuck, I almost came against the bed when you shot."

Thank you. Griff was thanking *him* for one of the singular experiences of River's life? And not just best orgasm of all time but what it meant inside too—the path it had carved out, sure as ice over stone, revealing a changed self. Better. New.

He nestled into Griff's side, soaked up his warmth, the pleasantness of feeling Griff's fast-moving arm and his straining muscles. "Close?"

"Fuck, yeah. Just keep remembering the sound you made."

"I probably scared the bears away." Some higher reasoning returned, along with a little embarrassment.

"Hope so. Wanna make you scream like that over and over."

"You can. Not now because I still can't feel my toes, but sometime I think I wanna try fucking with you. Just to see. Gotta be different. Everything is with you." He was babbling, not exactly practiced sexy talk, but Griff groaned like River had bit him. Speaking of, he found the energy to lick Griff's neck, biting lightly.

"That's it. That's it. Don't stop." Griff panted, come

painting his stomach even before River could bite him a second time.

"Fuck. Fuck. Fuck." Griff fumbled for the towel again, sponging off his belly even as he kept shuddering. He pulled River tightly against him. "You're something else."

"Something good, I hope." River tried to tease, but some seriousness slipped in too.

"Best thing." Griff pressed a kiss to his temple. "Thank you."

"So you keep saying. Pretty sure I'm supposed to be the one with the manners after you went to town on me like that."

"I was just having fun." Griff managed to sound slightly surprised at this development. "And speaking of, you don't have to do anything that's not fun for you. I'm not secretly angling to fuck you. You fucking me was fun, but if fucking is more of a once-in-a-blue-moon thing for us, that's fine by me."

"Yeah." He faked a yawn. *Us.* That fantasy was back, the one where there was a them, a coupledom, a future, one where they had patterns and habits and time to explore and grow. This would probably be a good time to have a future-looking conversation, but using Griff's chest as his pillow was infinitely more attractive. Easier too. Easy to just lie here, soaking up all of Griff's warmth, pretend sleep to the point that Griff tenderly pulled the covers up around them and kissed his head again, taking care of River even now. How was River supposed to say goodbye to all of this? He simply didn't know.

Before a few weeks ago, Griffin hadn't paid much attention to the pleasure of sunrise hikes, but on River's last full day with him, he drove them north to the Cohoe Lakes area with the light only starting to change—light gray to an almost purplish before the sun washed over the area as they hiked. He'd made them mugs of coffee, and as they sat on a hilltop with a view of the early morning boaters bobbing along while sipping their coffee, he had to admit this was as close to perfect as he'd found in recent years.

River took a few photos of the small boats, but otherwise they sat in quiet contemplation. Over the past few days, they'd talked plenty—about deep stuff like their pasts, about silly stuff like movies and books, and about the sort of philosophical stuff Griffin wasn't sure he'd ever really gotten into with anyone else before. But it was these moments when neither needed to speak that Griffin truly loved—funny how silence could fill every lonely crack he hadn't realized he had.

"I should try fishing," River said at last, bumping shoulders with him.

"The better fishing is in the river close to us, especially for salmon, and if you come back I'll teach you. Never had much patience for it myself, but Indra's husband fishes often and Toby takes fishing expeditions out all the time. Come back, and I'll have him take us out." *Come back.* He said the words lightly, but they'd been on the tip of his tongue for days now.

"Griff…" River's eyes were as sad as his tone.

"Hear me out, okay? Like you said last time, I don't think either of us is ready to say goodbye for good."

"I'm not." River huffed out a breath. "But I've got a few more stops on my itinerary, then it's the movie premiere and promo surrounding that. After that it's sequestering myself in a hotel room somewhere to finish this draft and get it to my editor on time."

"So hole up here. You can write here, as long as you need." Griffin hadn't intended to make the offer, but once the words were out, they felt good and right, like the sun starting to warm the hillside. "I know my place is small and maybe it's not the privacy you need, but there are also rentals."

"You do have internet…" River's mouth twisted. "It's a tempting idea. I had some vague notion of going back east, switching out my luggage for fall and winter stuff from the storage unit near my dad's place, but there's no rule that I have to do the writing and edits on the east coast. Last book I finished mainly in a hotel room in France."

"Well, this isn't the Riviera, but you'd be welcome to come write here. I'm going out on a few more tours in the next few weeks anyway. By fall, I should be more than ready for some peace and quiet of my own."

"Maybe…" River sighed softly. "It does sound nice. And I don't want to wait all the way until mid-fall to see you again. I've got an idea of my own, but I'm not sure you'll go for it."

"Try me." Griffin's heart started to beat double time.

"I'm in British Columbia and Alberta for the next while, and I'm supposed to meet up with some friends for a birthday party in Vancouver in three weeks or so, late August. If it worked out between your work obligations, would you want to meet me in Vancouver? I thought I heard your mom say that you sometimes fly that far south for cargo contracts?"

"Yeah, we do it a couple of times a year maybe. Juneau a lot more frequently." Griffin's heart hadn't stopped hammering. "It's a little tricky going from US airspace to Canadian, gotta have the right paperwork, but we do it. Weather also plays a factor—always seems to be delays. Last few years, I let Toby or someone who wants a night out in the city take those trips."

"There's also commercial flights. It's what? A three-hour flight? That's pretty good." River's voice got more animated, clearly warming to this idea despite the ice racing through Griffin's veins. "My ticket from Seattle was on one of the deal sites and was super affordable. That might even be cheaper than fuel and other costs."

"Could be." Griffin tried to keep his voice steady, not let on how close he was to the coffee making a second appearance.

"You, me, a hotel room. Kinda like your reunion and middle fantasies, but the real thing. Could be fun. And it could tide us over until I can come write in the fall if that works out." River smiled at him encouragingly. "And I've met your family. You could meet my friends, let me show you off."

"I'm hardly the kinda guy you show off to a bunch of models." Griffin studied the dirt near his boot.

"Oh, they're not all models," River said breezily. "And they'd love you."

"Ha." Griffin wasn't buying that. "I'm gonna be honest. I haven't really been to a city other than Anchorage or Juneau since I got sober."

"Oh." River's mouth made a perfect circle as all his enthusiasm seemed to leave in a single breath, chest deflating, shoulders slumping. "The last thing I want to do is make you uncomfortable. Or jeopardize your recovery. Forget I said anything. It was a stupid idea. I'll think about coming here to write."

But he wouldn't. Something would come up, some shinier lark perhaps. Something else would grab River's attention before fall and he'd be gone and Griffin couldn't breathe, thinking about it. Because sure they could keep a friendship going with email and chat and River coming here if he had the time and inclination, but the life expectancy of such a one-sided relationship had to be around that of a flea.

"It wasn't stupid." He grabbed River's hand, squeezed it. "You make me want to try. And it's not Vegas—not sure I can ever do Vegas again. But I don't have particular memories about Vancouver, either good or bad. Maybe we could make a few decent ones."

"You'd try? For me?" River's eyes were wide, hope brimming as surely as the sun in the distance. "If it got to be too much, we could just hole up in the hotel together. Have all the sex and room service we could stand."

"I'd try for *us*." Releasing River's hand, he wrapped his arm around River and pulled him close. "I… While I'm being honest, I might as well admit that I've never felt like this before. I'm not ready to give this up, not yet. And I know it's not easy. You've got your life and I've got mine, and I'm not looking to upend mine here. My family needs me too much. But yeah, if there's a lag in the schedule, I'd like to be the kind of guy who can steal a weekend away with his…with you."

"You could say *boyfriend* and the world wouldn't end. And I've never felt like this either." River kissed his cheek. "Thank you. It means a lot, you being willing to try this. I'll do everything I can to make it comfortable for you."

"Sex and room service isn't a terrible plan B." He

tried to make a joke, but his voice still came out unsure. He was feeling his way here, heading into uncharted territory. Somehow in the past few days, he'd reached a point where he wanted River more than he wanted his quiet, careful life to stay exactly how it had been prior to River's thunderous arrival in the middle of it. He wasn't under the delusion that he could ever hope to have River long-term, but damn it, he wasn't ready to shove him away either, wasn't about to let his old fears stop him from enjoying the little time they'd get together.

Besides, maybe it would be good for him. Like doing the tour had been. River had hit the nail on the head when he'd said that Griffin had proved something to himself on the tour, shown himself that he could step outside his comfort zone. And now he'd be an even bigger help to the business as a result. Maybe this would be the same sort of deal. Prove to himself that he could leave the state, and the world wouldn't end—or at least he hoped not.

Chapter Eighteen

"So tell me again why I can't come to the airport with you?" Francesca had an excellent pout, one that made her frizzy hair bounce in the morning sun at the outside café where they were having a faux brunch of coffee and sarcasm, but River wasn't particularly moved by her plea. "I swear you're keeping this guy of yours under wraps for a reason."

"He's neither a people person nor a city person—we'll see you guys at dinner, but let us get some alone time first. He might want to nap or something."

"Or something." She rolled her eyes before slipping her dark sunglasses back on. It had been a late night of reconnecting with the other friends who had come for her birthday, most of whom would probably sleep until noon, and River was still feeling it that morning. He was looking forward to Griff's arrival for a number of reasons, but having an excuse not to go overboard partying would be nice. Francesca was a great friend, but not always the best influence, especially at one a.m. when suggesting one more club. "It's been, what? A few weeks? You must be clawing the walls. Or are you not doing the exclusive thing?"

"I suppose we are." River gave her what he knew

was a goofy grin. They'd never had a formal conversation about it, but he knew without asking that Griff would be hurt if he hooked up on one of his trips, even a casual thing, so he hadn't. Hadn't really missed it, which had surprised him. Funny how a few chats with Griff had him happier than some one-off fling. And funny how he'd thought Griff might be exactly that type of fling. But he wasn't. This thing between them had passed fling and wandered into deep, serious territory, almost without his realizing it was happening.

He liked being with Griff so much, liked who he was with him, and had been dreading parting after his second Alaska visit. When Griff had floated the idea of him coming back, he'd been relieved that he hadn't had to bring up the suggestion first, and inviting him to this weekend simply felt natural. And yeah, Griff was stepping outside his comfort zone for him in a big way, but so was River, maybe heading back to the same place for the third time in as many months and daydreaming about a fall spent with Griff and finalizing the book.

A book that was increasingly slow to cooperate, him collecting so many draft files and false starts that he felt like a cartoon of a writer surrounded by wadded-up paper and nothing to show for it. Just thinking of his deadline had him nauseated.

"Hope he's good at cyber." Francesca's hands moved restlessly, no doubt missing the lax smoking rules at her preferred European haunts. The busy downtown street right in the middle of the arts district provided excellent people watching, but her attention seemed riveted to River's love life.

"Not telling," River shot back. And actually, Griff

was surprisingly good at late-night chats and fantasy
sharing that turned into mutual pleasure sessions. His
low voice in River's ear was fast becoming his favorite way to fall asleep.

"Man, you really do have it bad. Hope you don't
crash when it ends, babe. Better start planning your
rebound spring trip now."

"Maybe I won't need one." He pushed his half-drunk
coffee away.

"Ha. I know you and no way does this last to the
holidays. You're not the relationship type. And it's not
just this nomad kick of yours—"

"It's not a kick—"

"Sweetheart, I've read the book. I know, I know.
It's therapy. But my point is that even before you took
up travel as a spiritual calling, you were high maintenance. And before you growl at me, I am too. We're
great at being fabulous, but sucky at sticking it out.
Only stating facts here."

"Yeah." Acid rose in River's throat. He didn't want
to admit she might have a point. He wasn't the relationship type, and it was probably foolish to think he
could change that. But Griff made him want things he'd
hadn't had in years, if ever. Even if the crash was coming like she warned, he wasn't pulling back, not now.

Not with Griff on his way here, taking this leap of
faith for River. But he left Francesca in a foul mood
and the crowded ride on the train to the airport didn't
help matters. Fabulous city, but the airport was a hike
from downtown. Technically, he could have let Griff
find his own way to the hotel, but he wanted to make
this as stress-free on him as possible, and if that meant
being his personal tour guide, then that's what River

was going to do. And if they had to go to that plan B where they shut themselves in the hotel room? Well, that idea was seeming better and better, especially given how pissy Francesca was being.

And soon as he caught sight of Griff walking toward the security gates where River was waiting, the idea of locking themselves away until Griff's return flight seemed like a splendid idea. After much discussion and mainly for logistical reasons, Griff had decided to fly commercial. He'd traded some flights with Toby to be able to take the days away, and Toby had needed the plane best suited to a long flight. And Griff had already been in Anchorage on the tail end of another photography tour.

That was part of the reason River hadn't wanted Francesca to come—Griff was coming off a week of being more social than he liked. River wanted to give him a little space to recharge before foisting his friends on him. And indeed Griff looked tired, deeper lines around his eyes than usual and heavier stubble. He was dressed more "city" than River had seen him, in dark jeans and a crisp white button-down shirt, no plaid in sight, but the same boots he always favored, which somehow reassured River. New setting, same Griff.

And while Vancouver travelers were probably much less likely to be shocked by two men embracing, he kept his greeting to a fast hug, not burying himself in Griff's neck like he wanted.

"Tell me you're tired and need a nap before dinner," he demanded as they made their way back to the light rail station that served downtown.

"I might need *you* before dinner." Griff winked at him, but his smile was tight. There were a ton of peo-

ple on the train platform, but it was only midday, not
rush hour. River had been in far worse crowds, but it
had probably been a while for Griff.

"I can make that happen. And I've got a happy surprise in that regard too." He led them to the far end of
the platform, away from the worst of the throng.

"Oh?" Griff stared down the track, like sheer de-
termination could make the train appear.

"I used some travel points and got an upgraded
room—shower we can both fit in easily."

"Sounds nice." Griff still sounded distracted, and
River really wished for the solitude of a hike where
he could yank him down for a kiss or a hug whenever
he felt like it.

"Listen, if the train's not your thing, we can split
a car to the airport on Sunday." They'd arranged it so
that Griff's flight back to Anchorage left a little before River's plane to Calgary. "I'm used to bumming
around various cites on public transit, but I know it's
not for everyone."

"It's fine." The train came then, and as River had
expected, seats filled fast, leaving them to stand near
each other by the doors. Which was fine by him as he
always left seats to those who might need them more,
but he worried about Griff and tried to angle himself
to buffer Griff some from the bustle around them.

"My plan is to get off at the Yaletown station, because that's close to the hotel, but if you need, we can
get off sooner, find food somewhere, maybe?"

"I'm okay." Looking braced for alien warfare to
break out any second, Griff didn't meet River's eyes.
River didn't want to touch him and make things worse,

but he prayed the next thirty minutes or so passed quickly.

To distract Griff, he brought up his least favorite subject. "There's a pizza place literally around the corner from the hotel. We could get something there, bring it up to the room."

"You're going to eat pizza?" Griff managed a raised eyebrow and a small smile, which had been River's goal.

"I'm the tour guide this weekend. You're my guest. I have an obligation to feed you foods you like."

"Oh? Is that how we're going to play it? The worldly tour guide and his backcountry bumpkin client? And they just happen to be forced to share a room?" Griff's expression loosened up further.

"We could." River took a chance and slid a little closer, lowering his voice. "Or we could just be two boyfriends who haven't seen each other in a few weeks and are about to go at it like rabbits."

"Like rabbits, huh?" Griff rubbed his chin with his free hand.

"Yup." River loved seeing him relax, even if he did tense with each stop and the people coming and going. "So the way I see it, I better keep your strength up."

"Not a bad idea. But you're eating too." Griff leveled him with a hard look. "Let me guess. You've had coffee with a side of coffee so far today?"

"Maybe." River wasn't precisely sure when he'd eaten last. Dinner, he guessed, but that had been a sushi place, and he'd just grazed off Francesca's and others' plates, hyperaware of every bite, unable to force himself to order more or let himself enjoy what little he did eat. Then there had been several clubs and some people had had fries at one of them, but fries always made him feel gross. "You want me to order online now so it's less wait time for us?"

"Yeah, something with sausage for me. Not picky." Griff peered down at River's phone. "They have a two personal pizza deal. Get yourself one of the ones stacked with veggies. Like that thing with eggplant."

"Fine, fine." River was really only doing this to distract Griff, but he ordered himself one topped with grilled zucchini and feta that he supposed he could pick at. His brain churned with familiar mental math—how many bites would it take to satisfy Griff's desire that he ate, how could he overcome already feeling uncomfortably full, how much rearranging of food rather than eating could he get away with. They exited at the busy Yaletown station, but Griff seemed more comfortable off the train even with all the foot traffic and buses and cars. Picking up their order first, they made their way to the hotel, where River already had the room and a key for Griff.

"Food second," he said as soon as the door shut. "Sex first."

"Oh no, you don't." Laughing, Griff took both boxes from him and made a show of dashing for the bed. "This smells amazing."

"Crumbs," River warned, brain still swimming with thoughts of how to get out of eating.

"Since when has that stopped you?" Griff set the food down, then sat to remove his shoes. "You okay?"

"Now that you're here? I'm great." Careful to avoid landing in the pizzas, River tackle-hugged Griff, knocking him back against the pillows. And he really was. He'd been a little...adrift the past few weeks, trying to get chapters written and experience things readers would find inspirational, and missing Griff. But now that he was here, solid and warm under River, everything was good again.

"Okay, you win." Still in a towel, Griffin flopped on the bed. "I officially love you with your piercings in. And midday sex is pretty damn good. Maybe even as good as that pizza."

"I am so much better than pizza." River landed next to him, towel falling open.

"Yeah, you are." Hell, Griffin's knees were still rubbery after River had lost interest in the pizza and flirted his way into blowing Griffin, showing off what his tongue piercing was good for, followed by a long, hot shower for two that somehow ended in a second orgasm. Griffin hadn't gone for doubles like that since he was a teen trying to break his own jerk-off record.

"Should we nap or want to play tourist?" River draped himself over Griffin.

"I'm not much of a napper." But the idea was damn tempting because he was still sort of wrung out after travel. He was never flying commercial again if he could help it—teeny seats, hordes of irritated people, and so much waiting around. And the endless stream of humanity had continued on the train, making it hard to breathe, let alone think. River had helped, talking about food and distracting him with his nearness, but he'd still been happy to reach the hotel room and close the door on the bustle of the city.

"Bet I could make you fall asleep." River kissed his neck.

"Pretty sure my dick is done for a few hours." Griffin laughed.

"Then tourist stuff? We don't have to go to any of the crowded spots, but there are some adorable galleries in this neighborhood, and I was thinking we could hit Stanley Park—it's one of my favorite urban parks—and I think a walk might be good for us both."

"I'm all in favor of a long walk if it helps you eat more at dinner. You barely had any of your pizza." He rubbed River's back, not letting him pull away. At River's sour expression, he added, "I'm not trying to control. Just worried about you."

"I'm fine. I always get like this in cities—forget to eat, get caught up in socializing with my friends. But you're here, and I'll try to eat with you."

"I don't need you eating to keep me company. I'm more concerned with whether you're okay. And you can tell me if you're not." That last part should go without saying—they'd had so many late-night soul-baring conversations in the past few weeks. Griffin had never felt so comfortable talking with another person, and he really hoped River felt the same.

"Same goes for you," River said, neatly sidestepping Griffin's inquiry. He tried again to pull away, and this time Griffin let him. Going to the dresser, River pulled out clothes—the same burgundy pants and nice shirt he'd been wearing when they met. Griffin's chest tightened. He'd been so wrong in his first assumptions, and they'd come so far since that day in such a short amount of time.

Griffin got dressed as well and tried to steel himself for being back out on the street. Late August heat notwithstanding, it wasn't terrible, a breeze coming in from the bay and clear blue skies. Around them, well-dressed office workers anxious to start their weekends a little early hustled to transit stops and filled the outdoor seating at the restaurants they passed.

"We'll use my ride share app to get to the park rather than use a bus, but let's go into a few galleries while I set up a time and pickup place." River was in full-on tour guide mode, and Griffin was content to trail along in his wake, enter a gallery in the bottom floor of a high rise. "This is one of the ones I wanted to show you."

Back when he was a teen, he'd gone with Uncle Roger to a few gallery shows in Anchorage and Seattle and Victoria, resulting in much teasing from Hank, but he'd largely enjoyed the trips. However, galleries themselves made him nervous—all the high-dollar art and pristine spaces occupied by pretty people with cultured voices able to spot him as someone who didn't belong right away. River, though, fit right in, airily greeting the gallery attendant he'd apparently met the day before.

"Wait until you see the snowscapes," he gushed as he grabbed Griffin's elbow, leading him on a circuitous route to the rear of the gallery, which was dominated by large black-and-white prints. They were pictures of the Canadian Yukon, Whitehorse and surrounding areas like the Takhini Hot Springs and the Yukon River.

"They're good." Looking around to make sure the gallery attendant wasn't hovering nearby, he lowered his voice. "Uncle Roger's work is better. The light balance in some of these feels off."

"No, *your* stuff is better," River whispered, leaning in closer. "That's what I wanted to show you. Look at the price tags. Imagine your cabin fund growing."

"Eh." Shrugging, he shuffled his feet. "I've been around Uncle Roger enough years. A lot of it is all connections, who you know. Schmoozing, that sort of thing. Roger's great at it, but me…"

"You could do it." River gave him an earnest look, probably intended to be encouraging, but it made Griffin's skin feel three sizes too small. Pressure. He didn't need this, but didn't know how to tell River that when he thought he was being helpful. River continued, enthusiasm growing even though he kept his voice low, "I know Roger's got some connections. And I do as well. If it's a matter of knowing the right people, I think we've got you covered. It's more a matter of you being willing to pursue it."

"I'm not." God, he hated disappointing River, but he had to say something to quiet the galloping in his chest.

"It would help the business." River clearly wasn't going to drop this, and he was stroking Griffin's arm like he was trying to settle a hyper dog. It wasn't working, but Griffin wasn't going to make a scene and pull away. "If you had more of a reputation of your own, people would come to see you and to do the tours with you. It would take some of the burden off Roger."

"I know." It was a thought he'd had a lot lately, and a point his mother had made too. "I just…can't. Putting myself out there… It's too much. Tours are hard enough."

"Okay." River's voice was kind, even if his subsequent sigh said he was frustrated. "I'll drop it for now. Let's look at some paintings instead."

He headed off to a nearby exhibit, one featuring impressive oil paintings of natural vistas. But Griffin lingered with the photos a little longer, trying to quiet his churning gut. *For now.* River was surely planning to return to this topic. Was Griffin being selfish, not pursuing opportunities for his photography? And was that what River needed—an urbane big-name photographer boyfriend, not some near-recluse bush pilot? Fuck. He didn't want to lose River over this.

But he also couldn't be something he wasn't. Fighting another intense wave of nausea, he followed River to the paintings.

"I don't want to fight," he mumbled.

"We're not." River tugged him closer. "Let's enjoy our afternoon together. Next stop, the park. I already used the app for a ride. You'll like that better, I promise."

"Thanks."

The drive through heavy city traffic to the park did nothing to abate his growing sense of dread. Their driver drove like he was auditioning to be a stunt driver on one of the TV shows that filmed south of here, and his chatty commentary put Griffin even more on edge, not less. The park was nothing like the wilderness Griffin was used to—all manicured trails and careful landscaping and people everywhere. It was gorgeous, no doubt, with impressive views of the bay and the city. But it wasn't the same as hiking with River back home.

For one thing, River kept checking the map on his phone, trying to find a particular beachfront trail and responding to texts from his friends about dinner. He never saw the relaxed, almost blissful look from River he'd noticed so often in Alaska. This River was agitated and distracted, walking at a pace that made it hard to appreciate the surroundings. Back home when they were alone, he wouldn't have hesitated to grab River's hand, try to center him some.

Here with all these people around, it was far harder to be what River needed. However, after the third speed-walking-while-texting interval, Griffin finally had enough. Screw it. He didn't know any of these people around them on the path, wasn't going to, and worrying what they might think was pointless. Wrapping an arm around River, he pulled him close.

"How about you put the phone away until we need to get a car to dinner?"

"Sorry." River's cheeks took on a pink stain. "Francesca and the others can't seem to make up their minds. And there was an email from my editor. And I'd wanted the trail that goes near the totem poles, but we seem to be heading in the opposite direction. And—"

"Breathe." Griffin pressed a fast kiss to his temple. "It'll all work out. I don't care where we go, as long as you're there. But be here now with me, okay?"

"I can do that. Sorry." River leaned into his embrace. "This is nice."

"It is," Griffin agreed. "How about we take that side spur ahead, just wander? I don't need a tour of landmarks."

"I know." River released a sigh bigger than the harbor they'd passed on the way to the park. "I just want everything to be *perfect* for you this weekend. I want you to have the best time."

"Hey, I got good pizza and sex." He kept his voice low. "I'm happy, okay?"

It was a tiny half-truth. Because he was happy with River, always. And with all his worries, River didn't need to know how itchy all the people around them made Griff or how his stomach refused to settle. River was trying so hard. The least he could do was the same. But not even the sternest pep talk could erase the unease that dogged his every step.

Chapter Nineteen

"You might not like dinner." River couldn't help fretting as they waited for the ride-share car near the Lagoon Drive entrance to the park. The restaurant was near all the clubs on Davie Street that Francesca and their three other mutual friends loved, about a thirty-minute walk through the city or a fast bus ride, but River was trying to minimize the stress on Griff.

"It'll be fine." Glancing around, Griffin grabbed his hand again. At a certain point, they'd flipped roles, River getting progressively more freaked out, and Griffin becoming more reassuring despite his rather obvious discomfort with the surroundings.

"It's a tapas place. I didn't want to violate your privacy and tell them why you don't drink, but I know Francesca and Luther will for sure have wine or cocktails. If that's an issue—"

"I was around some wine at meals on the tour, remember? And this last tour without you had several guests who enjoyed wine and beer as well. It's getting…well, not comfortable, but easier. Honestly, it's not that I'm tempted as much as that I hate the social pressure and expectation to partake. I don't like feeling like I'm letting people down or ruining their good time."

"I know that feeling. I hate feeling like a burden because I can't or won't eat something, so I understand a little. And I'm for sure not drinking, so you won't be alone."

"I appreciate it, mainly because I want to kiss you later, but you don't *have* to. I could deal if you had something."

"Yeah, but I don't want you to have to." On that River was rather firm. And the kissing later sounded like a good plan, one he wouldn't mind fast forwarding to. Griffin had been unexpectedly affectionate at the park, something that had warmed River's jumbled insides, calmed him down. Griffin was trying so damn hard here. The least River could do was to try to make him more comfortable.

"And tapas can be fun. Surely there will be something you like there. I'm pretty easy to please food-wise. Remember I traveled a fair bit with the air force. Reindeer sausage and moose burgers aren't the only things I can eat." Griff sounded way more concerned about what River was going to eat than the fact that there was likely to be drinking, which was both reassuring and grating.

"Yeah." The car arrived right then, which saved him further reply. River hadn't had this little appetite in months and months, not to mention the noisy controlling messages his brain kept sending him. Knowing Griff was likely to watch him eat made everything worse—it wouldn't be enough and Griff would be disappointed in him and that made him even less able to eat. And what if him not eating was a trigger for Griff?

Fuck. He wanted to make this weekend as easy on Griff as possible. Wanted him to see...

See what?

Maybe that was the problem. He was crafting pie-in-the-sky fantasies where this became a regular thing for them. River still traveling like he needed, but Griff turning up from time to time. It would be perfect. But like Francesca said, River didn't do long-term and had no business hoping for anything resembling permanency. The noise in his brain worsened, making him feel about as worthy as the gum he'd picked up on the bottom of his shoe.

"You okay?" Griff leaned in, concern apparent in his tone. "You seem kinda out of it. Do you need to cancel on your friends? Blame me if you need to, but you shouldn't go if you're feeling miserable."

God, he really did not deserve this man.

"Just a little tired and headachy." He wasn't entirely lying. His head was pounding. "I'll be fine once we're with people. I can turn it on."

"River. You don't have to do that with me, you know, right? It's okay if you've got a headache. We can go back to the hotel, I'll watch some TV on low or play on my laptop and you can sleep."

"You're the sweetest." He patted Griff's thigh out of sight of their young driver. "But we're here. And this place is apparently reservation-only and super hard to get into. Don't worry about me."

"Too late." Griff gave him a serious stare as they got out of the car. But River spotted his friends waiting, and the surge of adrenaline he'd been expecting arrived right on time.

"Birthday girl!" he called to Francesca. "You're looking fabulous at your advanced age, darling."

"Fuck off," she said with no real ire, and there were kisses all around and introductions of Griff to the crew.

"Your shoes are giving me flashbacks of that show in Paris where they had me in six-inch pumps and body glitter," he said to Francesca as they were shown to a circular red velvet booth that held all six of them snugly. He made sure Griff had the outside seat, next to him even as he continued to prattle on about modeling memories.

"You couldn't do body glitter these days." Luther, the face of a high-end men's underwear line and a regular at runway shows, had a teasing tone, but River still felt the bite of his words. "I've seen your thighs—all that mountain climbing has made you thick."

"Yeah, you've got booty for days now." Francesca laughed and patted him on the shoulder. "But it suits you. And of course, mine is worse. I'm going to need a week of double spin classes just to recover from this weekend."

And there went the rest of his appetite. Poof. Gone. But he couldn't let on, of course. Luther was Francesca's new sidekick-slash-muse, the one she'd picked up to replace River since he was gone so much. And supposedly he was one of Luther's modeling icons, which was always flattering. Not to mention Francesca was one of his oldest friends—she'd flown in from Milan for his mother's funeral, and he'd never forgotten that or the number of late-night calls she'd taken from him. They'd been teens in the modeling business together and there was no quantifying what she'd meant to him over the years.

But that notwithstanding, all the body and appearance talk that went on when he hung out with industry types was just flat-out exhausting. Francesca had clearly been to the salon while he'd been out with Griff—her hair was perfectly blown out, falling in soft sheets as she continued to go on about the new exercise regimen she was trying.

The menu featured little plates of upscale bar food—things like specialty sliders and house chips with different toppings. He let others worry about what they were getting, flipping to the drink menu, relieved to see some local sodas that looked mildly interesting.

"They have lavender soda," he said to Griff, trying to keep his voice bright.

"I'll taste it if you'll split the grilled shrimp skewer thing with me." Griff's eyes still hadn't lost their concern from earlier.

"Sure." The plates he'd seen arriving at other tables were small. It wouldn't be too hard to ensure that Griff or someone else ate his half, a game he'd played a thousand times before. Between all six of them, they seemed to order most of the tapas on the menu anyway. There would be so much food that Griff couldn't possibly keep track.

He ordered the soda, which he intended to mainly leave in front of Griff, who also ordered himself the ginger flavor and the Korean short ribs in addition to the shrimp dish. The others all had their typical cocktails, and he understood what Griff had meant earlier about it being awkward, not drinking with a group. He'd already told Francesca that Griff didn't drink and to not make a deal about it, so she didn't, but that didn't stop her from offering River a sip of her "basic bitch" martini.

"What's that we always used to say?" she laughed. "Vodka's negative calories?"

"Uh-huh." He'd always said that, back a million years ago when he'd been in the thick of the industry with her, but now that world seemed so far removed, especially from where he'd been the past few months. He'd been doing so well in fact that he'd skipped his last two therapy chat sessions, but now, a few hours back around his crowd and he was regretting that call.

"Food." Griff nudged him after their order had been delivered.

"Thanks." It took everything River had not to snap at him, and his tone still wasn't the nicest. His digestive tract felt lined with rapidly hardening concrete. The best he managed was taking a single skewer, picking at it while he tried to keep up with the conversation swirling around him.

"Are you ready for the whole movie premiere thing?" Francesca asked. "I'm flying in, of course. And so are so many of the old crowd. It'll be fabulous. Do you have your wardrobe yet?"

"For some of the engagements yeah, but I've also got an appointment with a stylist when I get to LA. They'll make me beautiful." His appetite further receded at the thought of possibly needing a size up for a tux. Objectively, that shouldn't be a bad thing. Like Francesca and Luther had said, he *had* done a ton of hiking. But his old demons didn't much care about logic.

"How about you?" Francesca leaned over to address Griff. "Are you coming to the premiere? The after-party is going to be *lit*."

"Uh…" Griff twirled his soda.

"You could." River instantly warmed to the idea. What better way to cope with his nerves than to have Griff there? His safe place, waiting for him at night, would be perfect. Griff would keep him centered, stop him from shattering into a zillion shards. "It's a ways off. You could trade with Toby again, come down for the weekend. It would be fun."

"Fun." Griff's voice sounded far away.

"Don't say no right away," he begged, keeping a teasing tone, but in reality, he was totally serious. He *needed* Griff there.

"Yeah, don't be a drag," Luther interjected. "Let River show you off. Hot mountain boyfriend. *Rawr.*"

"You guys would be so cute on the red carpet." His friend Darcy, who'd been largely silent up to this point, spoke up. "And isn't the movie studio putting you up at Four Seasons? Super swank. No one wants to miss out on that."

"Not really a Hollywood type of guy," Griff mumbled, neck and cheeks turning the same shade as the booth.

"Just think about it," River urged, not wanting to be shot down in front of his friends, but also desperately wanting Griff to say yes for what it would mean to him personally.

"Okay." Griff didn't meet his eyes and busied himself with taking more food. "Tell me again how you all met?"

It was a clear bid to change the topic, but River let him have it, launching into the story of his first gig, where he'd met Francesca. She chimed in with her own additions to the story, and there was much laughter as they hung out long enough for a second round of drinks. Griff got another ginger soda, and River tried to drink a little more of his first one. He'd be glad when they were done here and could be back in the hotel room, just the two of them. That's why he needed Griff to come to the premiere—give him an out, a reason to retreat from all the glitz and parties, and remind him who he was when he wasn't around this life.

"So where are we going next?" Luther looked to Francesca. "It's your special day. You can choose."

"Oh, you know I want to dance. Who else is in? River? I really want to see you guys dance together."

We're not a sideshow. River almost let the words escape, but called them back on a sharp intake of breath. He glanced over at Griff, not able to read his impassive stare. "Not sure…"

"Please? It's my birthday." She did her fake-pout thing, perfectly made up lips pursing.

Tugging on River's arm, Griff pulled him down so he could whisper in his ear. "You go on with your friends. I'm going to go back to the hotel room. Wake me up when you come in, even if it's late."

Fuck. If he went with Griff, he'd risk Griff thinking he didn't trust him alone in the city. Which, to be frank, River wasn't sure he did. And if he went with Griff, he'd let down Francesca, who was the whole point of the weekend what with her birthday and all. But if he didn't go with him, he'd probably be miserable worrying about him.

Some of his distress must have shown on his face because Griff patted his arm. "Hey. You okay? How's your head?"

"Your head hurts?" Francesca interrupted. "You know I've got a cure for that..."

River knew she did. She was a freaking walking pharmacy, but no way was he taking anything stronger than a Tylenol in front of Griff.

"I'm..." he started to say *fine*, then remembered what Griff had said earlier about making an excuse. "Actually, it does hurt, but I'd rather just sleep it off than take something. And Griff's not up to the whole club scene either. Would you be terribly hurt if we headed back?"

"Yes." Francesca pouted some more, then sighed. "Fine. Be that way. Luther can find some hot dude to make out with, cheer me up."

"Sorry." God, he hated letting people down. His inner critic was louder than it had been in months, his life feeling like a house of cards about to tumble down. "I'll make it up to you. Tomorrow night, okay? And coffee in the morning?"

"I'll probably sleep in." She flipped her hair. She'd be over it soon—they had too many years between them for this to break them, but she was clearly going to make River work for her good graces.

"Do you want to walk back or get a cab?" Griff asked as the group made their way to the exit. "And seriously, you don't have to leave your friends on my account. I'll just get a cab, go up to the room, and probably sleep."

"I wasn't lying about not feeling the best." He hated the defensiveness in his tone.

"Fair enough." Griff surprised him by putting an arm around him. "Let's do the cab then, save us both the walk. My foot is letting me know that I should have packed a walking stick."

"Oh, sorry. I didn't think about the park being hard on you." Great. Now he felt like a crap boyfriend on top of everything else.

"It wasn't." Something about Griff's voice said he was lying, but River didn't know how to call him on it. Instead, he stayed quiet until they were in the cab and he needed to speak to the driver to tell her which hotel.

"Is there anything from room service or a nearby store that might help you?" Griff asked him. "Toast? You didn't eat anything at dinner—"

"Told you. My head hurts."

"I get that. But food might help. Or some meds. You should have taken your friend up on her offer—"

"She wasn't offering over-the-counter stuff." God, why couldn't they be up in the room already? Then he could pounce on Griff, silence this line of inquiry with a well-placed kiss.

"Oh." Griff stayed silent the rest of the short drive. River should have been relieved, but instead he worried more. *Fuck. My. Brain.*

"Now what can we get you before we hit the room?" Griff's voice was too cheerful as they exited the cab. He was forcing it, but River couldn't blame him as he'd been doing the same thing all day.

"Nothing." He stalked to the elevators in the lobby, swiping his key card to access the upper floors. As the doors closed, leaving them alone, he turned on Griff, put a hand on his chest. "Actually…"

"Sex isn't food. Or a headache cure." Griff scrubbed at his hair.

"No kidding." Facade slipping, River gave in to the urge to roll his eyes. "But it's fun."

"That's all that really matters to you, isn't it? Having fun?" Griff's voice was impossibly sad.

"If you're not having fun, what's the point?" Old defenses stacked themselves high. Admitting how little fun he'd been having lately would be like running naked through the lobby. Not happening. And giving in, saying what he really needed was even scarier. Easier to cling to the public River, the one always up for fun who took nothing too seriously.

The elevator dinged for their floor, not that Griff seemed particularly inclined to answer. They walked to their room, not touching, two strangers again. As the door closed, River's hands shook. Fuck, he hated this. Trying to solve his mess of emotions the only way he knew how, he pushed Griff against the closet door.

"Kiss me."

"Sex is a terrible idea." Griff neatly sidestepped him, sat on the bed and removed his shoes.

"You're seriously mad at me? I came back with you!"

"And I told you that you didn't have to." Griff sounded weary, so weary. "And let's not fight. Not right now, okay?"

"No fighting. No fucking. What are we supposed to do?" River paced in front of the bed.

"Come here. Let me hold you for a while."

"So cuddling is good?" River kicked off his shoes. "How is that different than fucking?"

He hated how Griff had the ability to pry him open, peer into his most private desires, what he needed most. Because he did want nothing more than to collapse into

Griff's arms, but he wasn't sure he'd ever come back from that. He couldn't fall apart on Griff. It wasn't fair to burden him that way, but more than that, it would wreck the best thing he had going. So, no, no falling apart. Not an option.

"If you haven't figured out the difference by now, I'm not sure I can help you." Griff flopped back against the pillows. Softer now, he repeated himself, "Not sure how to help you."

"You don't need to," River lied. He stretched out next to Griff, sure that he could goad him into some makeup sex soon enough. That was all they both needed—a good orgasm to wipe the slate clean. "Let's pretend we're—"

"Let's not." Griff rolled closer and gathered River into his arms. "I'm tired. You're tired. Just lie here with me. *Be* here with me. Let me have this."

River's eyes burned like he'd stepped into a cloud of hairspray, lungs similarly filling with thick, sticky goo making breathing hard. He wasn't sure he could. It was such a simple, reasonable request, but he wasn't sure he was strong enough to grant it without losing every shred of his composure. And even if he managed to simply lie here, how could it be enough? How could *he* be enough for Griff?

Chapter Twenty

Holding River was like holding a pile of frozen lumber—
he was stiff and cold and not yielding at all to Griffin's requests. Oh, he'd gone silent and wasn't actively
arguing, but it was also damn clear that his brain was
somewhere else.

Damn it. Griffin wanted…something. He wasn't
even sure what anymore. Maybe a drink. Not like he
had in those awful weeks after Hank died and he got
his discharge and everything was a haze of drinking
and gambling. But it was there, a steady thrum, the Friday night restlessness he knew so well, the little voice
telling him how much easier he could cope with this
mess with a few shots on board, the way his hands felt
floppy and empty without a cold glass to hold, the way
his head seemed almost too clear—everything in stark
relief, including his own emotions.

It wasn't only the pretty people with their pretty
martinis and colorful cocktails that had him on edge.
He had the same awkwardness he always got these
days when others were drinking. One of River's quieter friends had spilled some of a drink with whiskey
in it, and the scent had thrown him back, made him almost feel the burn of it hitting his throat, the rush of the

subsequent buzz. So he'd focused on the food, which was sparse but tasty. Nothing like the cheap, greasy bar fare that always made him want a beer with a chaser. Taking small bites, trying to figure out what was in the sauce, making the food last were old tricks to make his hands stop clamoring so loudly for a bottle to hold.

And when that didn't completely ease the craving, the prospect of letting River down and imagining his disappointed face helped him find a little more strength to move his attention to other matters. He probably could have figured out what to do at a dance club— not dance, that was for damn sure, but he would have worked something out, maybe used his other trick where he imagined his surroundings as a giant coloring page, pretended he was shading it in section by section until the urge subsided to somewhat manageable levels.

Except even more than the availability of drinks and the surroundings, it was River who had him in dangerous waters. And for all his self-lectures and bag of tricks, he didn't know how to cope with this River who was shutting him out, little by little. A River who he didn't quite recognize. Oh, there had been flashes of the River he'd first met when the tour began—the helpful social butterfly who managed to be the life of the party—but none of the River he knew from spending time alone. The serious guy who understood Griffin like no one else did, who understood Griffin's issues because he had his own that he was honest about. The late-night talker. The vulnerable lover.

And maybe that was what he wanted. His boyfriend back. He wanted River to trust him enough to tell him what was wrong. Griffin couldn't help if River wouldn't talk, and if he wasn't talking because he was worried that telling Griffin might make him drink, then they had a real problem, one that all the cuddling in the world wouldn't solve.

Perhaps that was the real cause of his restlessness—he knew a hard conversation and difficult choices were coming, so his body was searching for old crutches to avoid the coming pain.

Trying again to find a way past River's defenses, he stroked River's side. "One thing that stuck with me from rehab was the saying 'It's okay to be not okay.'"

"Thought I was the self-help guru." River's tension only increased, body pulling away from Griffin. "And I'm f—"

"You say *fine* again and I'm going to smash something."

"But I am." River was lying through his chattering teeth, and they both knew it.

Griffin rolled so he could stare him down.

As he'd expected, River looked away, faint pink flush to his cheeks. "Or at least, I'll be okay by morning. I'd be better if you let me get you off. We could both use some fun, right?"

"I don't want fun anymore." Once he let the words out, Griffin knew he couldn't call them back. Asking River to cuddle had only delayed the inevitable. "I told you from the start—I don't do fun. And that's not what this has been to me. Maybe this is some lark for you, your annual summer fling, but it's not for me."

"It's not a fling." River sounded wounded, which made Griffin's insides do a weird wobble. Maybe there was hope. "I meant what I said at dinner—I want you to come to the premiere of the movie with me. And if you do that, I'll come back and finalize the book in Alaska. I wouldn't be making those kinds of plans if this were a *lark*."

"This isn't a…what's it called? A quid pro quo. That. This isn't trading favors. I can't come to the premiere, River. You know that."

"Is it the time off? I bet Toby would trade with you—you said he's always looking for extra shifts. Or is it the drinking thing? I'll stay right by your side—"

"I don't need you to be my keeper." Fears about why River wasn't opening up confirmed, Griffin sat up. He'd thought that River saw the best of him, the him he wanted to be, but in reality River saw him as a relapse waiting to happen. Someone who needed managing and coddling. Someone he couldn't trust. "Sure, I've got my routines that help me and I'm not looking to change them all at once—"

"Or ever." River's eyes were darts of hurt, making Griffin's chest tighten.

"That's fair. I don't want your lifestyle. I'm not looking to take it up. This trip confirmed that for me—I don't fit in anywhere other than Alaska. I don't belong out with supermodels and billionaire trust-fund babies at places you wait months for reservations at. If that's the life you want—*need*—to live, I support your choice, but I can't be part of it."

"Because it's too tempting? Help me understand here, because it sounds like you don't want to *try*."

"It's not that tempting, to be honest. But watching you like this, how you're shutting me out, trying to figure out why you're hell-bent on hurting yourself, that's…triggering. And I hate that word, but it works here. I'm stronger than I thought a few months ago, and

I've got you to thank in part for showing me that—I can be out for dinner and whatnot and I'm okay."

"Then what's the issue?" River remained on the bed, eyes closed, hand wrapped tight around a pillow.

"You. You hurting yourself, you not letting me in. I can't watch you destroy yourself. And no, I'm not going to drink tonight. Or tomorrow. But if I keep doing this…" Throat zip-tie tight, he shook his head. "… I'm just not sure. And maybe that's a risk I shouldn't take."

"So what? We're breaking up?" River finally sat up but didn't look at him. "All because you think I didn't eat enough today? Way to be a controlling dick, Griff."

"It's not about how much you ate or not—give me more credit than that. But you've been hurting all day and you won't talk to me about it."

"Nothing to talk about. You're being dramatic. Maybe you don't like who I am in the city. Maybe you don't get my sort of fun. It's not all hikes and picture taking for me."

"Is it really fun, though? Seriously. I'm not sure you had fun tonight—I didn't see you all that happy."

"I was happy." River's chin had a defiant tilt to it.

"Fair enough. You'd rather focus on having fun, not admit you're having issues. Or perhaps you're right and the issue is all with me—this is simply who you are and what works for you." He hated the thought that the person River had been in Alaska was a mirage, but he couldn't deny it was a real possibility. "And I can't do that. Can't ignore what I'm seeing with my eyes. Maybe it's fun for you, but it's not for me."

"Fine. Be that way." River sounded eerily like his wenchy best friend, pouting rather than talking. "But I think you're just scared. It's like with your photography. You're scared to take a risk. So you don't pursue it and then you can't get burned."

"If what you need is a risk-taker, some famous photographer maybe or a socialite or a world traveler, then I'm not the guy for you. I had more than my share of risk in Vegas and Reno—I'm never again gonna be the kind of guy who takes a gamble without knowing the outcome. Lesson learned and all that. I can't be any of those things you want." Driven by a rising need to escape, he quickly put his boots on.

"No, you won't try. Just say it like it is. You're scared to be with me, and you're running away."

"You're right." Griffin started shoving his belongings back in his bag. "I'm scared. I'm scared of loving you and losing you to this life. I'm scared of loving you and watching you hurt yourself. I'm scared of loving you and that not being enough." Saying that word, the l-word, letting it out after weeks of dancing around it, even in his own head, was almost enough to make him hyperventilate.

In a perfect world, River would reach for him, tell him that love was enough, admit that he was scared too, and they'd find a way to work past their fears. But as he'd expected, River stayed stony faced and quiet. This thing between them was built on sand—fantasies and mirages and fun he shouldn't have been having. Maybe River had shown him in stark relief what was missing from his life, had made him confront his own loneliness, and the way Griffin had let that concoct an attachment was on him. River had never promised him anything other than a good time. He was the one who'd tried to make their vacation fling into something it could never be, especially if River didn't trust him.

"Where are you going?" River's voice was more suspicious than emotional.

"You think I'm going to drink, don't you?" He shouldered his bag and stared River down, dared him to tell him otherwise.

"I don't want to be the one who makes you break your sobriety. Spend the night here. I'll go with you in the morning if you want to get a flight—"

"I'm a grown man. I can find my way to the airport, can find a flight back if that's what I want. I don't need you as my keeper." No, what he needed was River as his partner, his heart, his lover, but apparently he simply wasn't interested in the role. "And if I drink, that's about me and my choices, not you."

River recoiled, eyes widening as if he'd been slapped. Maybe Griffin had been harsh, but he couldn't bring himself to soften the words.

"Guess there's no reason for me to stay in anymore." River's voice was all fake cheer, which obliterated Griffin's last nerve as River put his own shoes on, scooped up his phone and wallet.

"River—"

"What's that you said about choices? If I can't worry about yours, then you can't worry about mine, and if we're breaking up anyway, what the fuck does it matter?"

"It matters to me that you stay safe."

Face softening for a split second, River sighed. "Goodbye, Griff. I want you to stay safe too. But don't worry about me. Really."

He pushed by Griffin on his way out the door, leaving Griffin too stunned to call after him, too shellshocked to do anything other than slump against the wall. His heart hammered, and his back broke out in cold sweat.

God, he hoped he hadn't driven River to do anything stupid. No matter what River said, if anything happened to him, it would be all Griffin's fault. *What have I done?*

A surprisingly chilly night greeted River, a swift breeze from the bay rushing through downtown and making him wish he'd grabbed a jacket in his hasty departure. It didn't take much effort to find where Francesca and the others were—a quick text and River was headed back to Davie Street, not even bothering with a car. In theory the thirty-minute walk should have given him time to clear his head, gather his thoughts, but in reality all it did was wind him up further. It also stoked the control demon in his brain—the rush of physical activity, the feeling of running on empty, the power he both loved and loathed.

Fuck. He still couldn't believe Griff had broken up with him. Over him not talking, of all the fucked-up things. Here he'd spent all day trying to *protect* Griff from a massive River meltdown, and then Griff wanted to get all touchy-feely about not letting him in. Well, no shit. River couldn't let him in. Couldn't break down on him. Couldn't admit he was anything less—or more— than the fun-loving tourist he presented himself as. *Professional Nomad by day, major-league fuckup by night.*

River passed the massive, circular Vancouver Public Library, which probably had at least ten copies of his book. *What a fucking joke.* It was laughable really, how he was always encouraging people to live their most authentic lives, when if people knew the real him, they'd run for the hills. The voices telling him he wasn't worthy had been deafening while Griff was talking, almost drowning out the conversation. No way could he even crack the door on what was going on in his head for Griff. Not when he was so convinced that him breaking down could lead to Griff drinking—strange city, all the temptations, impossibly emo boyfriend. It all seemed like a recipe for disaster. And yeah, Griff liked playing caretaker, but how long would that last? Especially when River revealed himself to be a hot mess beyond what Griff could deal with? So River hadn't opened up, and instead of taking the bait for easy, distracting sex, Griff had broken up with him.

River's steps sped up, taking him past all the tall buildings in the city center, past tons of other hotels bustling with guests returning from nights out. Why the fuck couldn't his life be that simple? Fuck. It had been that simple up until two months ago. Damn Griffin. He refused to believe Griff had dumped him over *not talking.* Or not eating. He'd accused Griff of it, but he didn't really believe a few skipped meals were enough to cause this sort of about-face. No, what this really was about was Griff not wanting to try to get along in River's world. He talked about River not wanting to communicate, but he hadn't been willing to admit he'd been running scared the whole time. He didn't want to sell his photographs. Didn't want to leave his town. God forbid he go to the premiere in Los Angles. And he'd said he was fine, not tempted, but he'd also obviously been rattled much of the day, not enjoying the city the way River did.

Maybe he'd simply been looking for a reason to

bail, and River just wasn't worth sticking around for. Which confirmed every single fear that had been swirling all day. Or if he was truly honest, ever since Griff had said he wanted River to come back. A flutter had started in his chest that had only become worse with time. And perhaps that was the real reason he'd bailed on his therapist. She'd remind him that he didn't have to always keep moving. But he did. Slowing down meant accepting the possibility of not being enough, of trying and still losing. And if River at his best—social, tour guide, fun—wasn't worth sticking around for, then who the hell would bother with his authentic self?

It was on that note that he finally hit Davie Street and its collection of gay-friendly nightclubs. It didn't take much effort to find the one where his friends were hanging out—big, gaudy, and loud, with several stories devoted to dancing, light shows, drinking, and being beautiful. Which Francesca, Luther, Darcy, and Pete were all fabulous at, and he found three of them sitting in a booth near one of the dance floors with a table full of empty glasses.

"Did you lose Francesca?" he asked, taking a seat next to Darcy. If ever he needed his best friend, now was the moment.

"Just getting a refill, darling. And I spotted you, so here's one for you too." Francesca tottered over on unsteady heels. Her lipstick needed touching up and her hair was starting to frizz from the hot club. "Now, tell Auntie Francesca what the mean lumbersexual did to you?"

Her voice was too chipper for this hour and her eyes were bright and glassy as she squeezed in next to him.

"Fuck. Are you high?"

"Why? You want to be?" She leaned in and brushed a vodka-scented kiss on his cheek. "It's my birthday. I'm going to have fun."

Fun. When had that become such a dirty word? Of course Francesca should have fun on her birthday. Wanting to have fun wasn't the crime Griff thought it was. Fun kept River moving, kept the negative voices at bay, let him function. Fun was awesome.

"Maybe," he hedged, not wanting to be a judgmental prick like *some* people, but also not sure getting wasted would improve his situation. He took an experimental sip of the drink Francesca handed him. Very heavy on the vodka, light on the fruit juice, and all the negative-calorie jokes he'd made to his friends at his lowest came back to him. Back when he'd shared an apartment in New York, they'd had a fridge with four vodka brands in the freezer and nothing else.

"We broke up," he admitted to the table at large, but mainly Francesca, who was distracted, watching Luther head to the dance floor with some dreadlock-rocking younger guy.

"Inevitable." Her eyes were still on the guys.

"You think?" He took another bracing sip of the drink. "We had a good thing going. But he said I shut him out. Didn't *talk* enough."

"Who needs talking?" Finally looking his way, she rolled her eyes. "Just fuck him silly."

"I tried."

"Then it's his loss." She gave him a fast hug.

"I guess." River wasn't so sure that it was all Griff's fault.

"You're going to LA soon. Maybe you can bang the actor who plays you in the movie. That would be a kick. And someone in entertainment would be good for you, get you back to where you belong."

"I don't wanna fuck an actor." The drink burned less going down now and made it easier to get the words out. *Where you belong.* Did he belong here in this world? He'd spent a lot of years believing he belonged nowhere, making that part of his personality, his brand so to speak—belong nowhere, fit in everywhere. Having a place in the universe had seemed limiting. And scary. Having a place meant it could be ripped away, one tragedy or fuckup away from being out in the cold, missing what had once been. And missing was the *worst.* Better to not have tried.

"I don't belong anywhere." He'd meant the words to come out arch and superior, but instead some sadness crept in. Fuck.

"Of course you do. You were one of the hottest names in modeling and everyone *loved* you. I still don't get why you ran away from that." She waved her hand dismissively. "But whatever. You're Mr. Famous Author now. There's no one to say that book three can't be you bumming around Europe with Luther and me. I miss you."

"I didn't run away." River slumped back against the bench.

Her answering laugh was not unkind. "Of course you did. And I understand. Hospitalization is no joke. You weren't in a good place. I supported you taking a break, some time away. But you're healthy now, right?"

"Right." The word came out all weak, but Francesca didn't seem to notice. She was supposed to be his best friend, the person who at one time had known him better than anyone, but lately she seemed wrapped in her own world, a world he simply didn't recognize anymore.

"Then come hang with me in Milan after the premiere. I'll introduce you to some new people. Who knows, maybe you'll even pick up a few gigs again."

Oh God, just the thought of that had the drink burning a hole in the pit of his stomach. "I've got a book to finalize."

"You can write anywhere." She wasn't wrong, but all of a sudden, River wanted the plan of writing near Griff. Which was stupid and why making plans was a bad idea—he'd gotten his hopes up and now anything else was going to feel like settling. He groaned and she leaned in, pressed a hand to his head. "You sure you don't want something for your head?"

"I'm sure." Actually, he wasn't sure of anything anymore. "I need to get out of here."

"Out of the club?" She gave him another awkward one-arm hug. "I'm sure the others will be ready to go soon."

"No. Out of here. Out of the country. The continent maybe." The flutter in his chest was now a full-fledged dragon beating its mighty wings.

"Don't you have deadlines? What's your next stop anyway?"

"Fuck deadlines."

"That's what I always say too." She pushed his glass closer to him. "Why don't you let me get you a refill and you can decide where you're running to this time?"

"Not running." He tossed back the rest of the drink. But he was lying and he knew it. He was running because it was the only thing he knew how to do, the only thing that might quiet the dragon in his chest.

Chapter Twenty-One

Griffin wasn't sure how long he sat on the hotel room carpet, reeling, knowing he should run after River but unable to make his limbs move. And really, what would be the point? River seemed determined to self-destruct, and Griffin couldn't be there for the fallout. He didn't need to be in this city either. He needed to be home, back to his routines, his quiet life, the things that kept him safe, kept his priorities in check. He'd been wrong to think he could have this thing with River, wrong to think this weekend was something he could handle.

The walls of the hotel room seemed to inch closer and closer to him, boxing him in. *Time to go.* He couldn't stay here any longer, staring at the bed where they'd been so happy only a few hours ago, swearing that he could still smell River. Picking up his bag, he headed for the elevators. It was late, but there were still people everywhere—crowding the lobby bar, on the sidewalks heading into clubs, in cars clogging the streets.

"Can I help you, sir?" Oops. He'd lingered outside the hotel's doors a few moments too long, and now the doorman was looking at him with concern. "You need a cab?"

"Uh…" That would be the smart thing, wouldn't it? But he hesitated, listening to the clink of glasses from the nearby patio bar. Cab would be the right thing, but the easy thing was a whole different story.

"Going to the airport? I'm looking to share a car." A petite redhead, few years older than Griffin, with a large wheeled suitcase spoke up. "I've got a red-eye to Tokyo. Don't know what I was thinking, agreeing to a late-night flight."

"Yeah, airport." He shook himself out of his indecision. Airport. Home. It was what he needed. He summoned up what he hoped was a grateful smile for the woman who'd been the push he needed. The doorman flagged them a black Town Car driven by an older woman with a no-nonsense demeanor.

"I'll let you have the back seat to yourself," he told the other woman, moving to the front passenger door.

"No, don't. I'm a nervous flier and I need some distracting conversation."

Griffin couldn't very well turn that down, so he took a seat in the back next to her. "Gotta warn you, though, I'm not much on conversation."

"Oh, I can probably talk enough for both of us." She gave a little laugh as they headed south toward the bridge that connected downtown with the rest of Vancouver proper. See? Griffin still had his sense of direction. He could have made it back on the train, no issues. And as his chatty cab mate launched into a story about why her Calgary-based company was sending her to Tokyo he was kind of regretting not doing that.

"What about you?" She finally paused for breath as they passed a pub with a full patio. "Late night flight too?"

"Not sure." Griffin wasn't sure why his hands clenched, only relaxing once the light changed and they passed the pub. "Gonna have to see what's available, if they'll let me change my ticket, I guess. God, I hate flying commercial."

"A pilot?" Her eyes twinkled. "Let me guess, the Yukon?"

"Alaska." Apparently it was obvious that he didn't belong in the city, that he was from the north. *Never should have come.*

"Oooh, sexy. Is it true they still don't have many women up there?"

That made Griffin laugh despite himself. "My mom and sisters would take issue with that."

"But no Mrs. Pilot?"

"No. And no offense, but I just broke up with my boyfriend tonight. Not really looking for...anything."

"Oh." Her mouth made a perfect circle. "I'm so sorry. You want to talk about it?"

"Nope." Not now, maybe not ever.

"Well, if he cheated, he's an idiot."

"No one cheated." God, why couldn't the airport be closer? "More of a...communication thing."

That sounded so lame, even to his ears. What if he was doing what River had accused him of—running away because he was scared? What if he'd been too hard on River for his refusal to talk to or lean on him? Fuck. He didn't know anything anymore.

"Those can be a bitch." She tapped her fingers against the doorframe, and Griffin counted the minutes until they'd be at the airport. "My late husband and I used to have the worst fights over silly stuff. I get it."

Even in his haze, Griffin picked up on the word *late*. "I'm sorry for your loss."

"Eh. It's been three years, you know? And I'll never regret the fifteen years we had together. But I sold our house, took this job with its insane amount of travel. I keep busy."

"Travel can be good for that." He tried to sound sympathetic while his mind raced. Wasn't that what River was doing? Keeping busy, outrunning both his grief over his mother and his eating disorder. And who was Griffin to judge him for that? God knew Griffin had enough off-the-wall coping mechanisms of his own. But even if he understood where River was coming from, there still wasn't any future for them. Griffin coped by staying put. River coped by moving around. He'd tried to compromise, coming here this weekend, and see how that had gone. No, compromise just wasn't in the cards for them.

"It can," she agreed. "It doesn't make up for an empty bed, though. No matter what city I'm in, I still wake up surprised to be alone in bed."

"Yeah." That was probably going to be Griffin the rest of his damn life. He'd had River in his bed, in his life, and now it felt as if someone had switched his life from color to black-and-white, like he was going to spend forever missing something he'd only had the barest glimpse of.

Their driver expertly navigated the airport traffic as they approached the terminal, heading first to the sign for the international airline the woman had mentioned using, and she started gathering her things.

"And on that depressing thought, I'm going to need

a drink before my flight if I can find anything open. Join me?"

Griffin gulped. Fuck. He was tempted. And not by his fellow traveler—she was nice enough and he wasn't so oblivious that he'd missed her flirting. He wasn't remotely interested in flirting back. However, he could almost taste the whiskey already, ashy and harsh with that mellow finish he still craved even now. Neat, no ice to temper the burn, double to get him where he wanted to go that much faster.

"Come on, what would it hurt? Have a drink with me, then sort out your ticket."

Everything. It would hurt everything. Fuck this city. Fuck this night. Fuck River. It took everything he had to grind out, "I can't."

"Oh, well, can't blame me trying." She gave him a crooked smile before tipping the driver and exiting the car, driver following her to unload her suitcase.

"US departures or you need a different destination?" The driver, who had otherwise been quiet up until this point, addressed him as she climbed back behind the wheel. She had a way of talking that reminded Griffin of his mom.

Fuck, what did he need? To go back to the hotel? Try to catch River? The idea of requesting a ride to a bar, that pub they'd passed maybe, also flitted through his brain, seductive as silk, caressing his every wounded nerve ending. And something of his dilemma must have shown in his face because the driver turned around in her seat, softening her tone.

"Thought so." She nodded matter-of-factly. "You need to find a meeting? I've got an app on my phone. No charge for the ride or the pickup after."

"Thanks, but I don't do meetings." He gave her the same line he used on his mom. "I'm okay."

"Really?" There was an edge to her tone that cut through all his bravado and denials, exposed every weak and hurting part of his soul.

God, he ached. And not just for a drink. For River. For himself. For screwing up the good thing they'd had going. For not being the person River needed or deserved. For everything he'd let himself start to want and everything he'd let go of tonight. He hadn't been this miserable since Hank, and the urge to run from the pain was almost overwhelming. He was a wreck, and he was restless, a terrible combination.

You're scared. River's voice echoed in his head. *Running away.* Fuck. He was, wasn't he? Maybe they both were. Trying to outrace hurt. And how the fuck could he get mad at River for not accepting help when he couldn't do the same?

"No, no, I'm not okay." His voice sounded like it came from the bottom of the bay, but he got the words out, and relief hit him in a cleansing wave. *It's okay to be not okay.* And maybe he couldn't help River, couldn't save him, but he could save himself. And that would have to be a start. No way could he figure out what to do about River if he didn't do this, right here, right now.

Blinking against the harsh morning light, River exited the train and walked briskly toward the international departures terminal. Vancouver International Airport was predictably busy for a Saturday morning. He hadn't done a "browse the deals page and go where the cursor clicks" trip in forever. Too long really. He needed this random adventure even if it would push up close to the premiere and push back his writing plans. But like Francesca said, he could write anywhere. Including—he had to look down at his phone to verify—Punta Cana. It was still this hemisphere, but he hadn't been to the Dominican Republic before, and an island sounded great right about now, even if it was hurricane season. He'd found a steal of a deal, and he'd roll with it.

He'd managed to slug back some coffee and over-the-counter painkillers to combat a wicked hangover from hanging out with his friends far too late. He'd crashed in Francesca's room, sleeping on a chaise before returning to his own room only long enough to collect his luggage. And what clothing and supplies he had weren't entirely suitable for a tropical island this time of year, but he wasn't worried about that. Rolling on.

Walking through the terminal, he checked his phone while the PA system blared. He hadn't heard from Griff—not even an "I'm back home" text or anything like that. And definitely not an "I'm sorry" either. Even a "let's be friends" text would let him know that Griff was alive and okay. But nothing. And he wasn't going to be the first to text. If he was the one to apologize, then he might have to actually start talking, explaining stuff, and he was still convinced that was a bad idea. He couldn't dump on Griff. Besides, like he'd told both Griff and his friends last night, he was fine.

He caught a glimpse of himself in a mirrored piece of wall. Okay, sure, he looked a little pale. He supposed an uncharitable person might say gaunt. And his clothes were yesterday's and he had zero fucks to give about that. But otherwise? Fine. A little anxiety was nothing exploring a new place wouldn't cure. New place. New people. New River.

And if it didn't make it into the book, that was fine too. He had enough material now, he was pretty sure. And even if he didn't, he'd wing it, hit a few places while finalizing the book if it ran short. Honestly, he was less worried about page count and more about wisdom. How the fuck was he supposed to tell people to go find themselves and love themselves when he was no longer sure who exactly he was, and was pretty sure he didn't love the current version of himself either? He had fan mail from all over the world, people telling him how he'd broadened their horizons, made them travel with a fresh point of view. He'd be letting them down if this latest book didn't deliver.

Or if they knew what a big fraud you are... His negative voices were even louder than the PA system that morning. Fraud. Impostor. Hack. Loser. It was damn hard to keep up his usual pleasantness with security personnel and the clerk at the newsstand who recognized him from his book, which sure enough was sold there. He signed a copy for the clerk, managed what he hoped was a smile, and tried not to snap when the girl asked for a picture.

Finally, he collapsed into an empty seat near his gate. Across from him was another gate filled with people bound for Mexico, and judging by the colorful attire and excited groups, many were bound for a cruise.

"Mom!" A young woman came racing toward one of the groups, a family by the looks of it—older adults, a middle-aged couple with kids, and a few young adults. Three generations, if he wasn't mistaken.

"Bunny!" The older woman's face transformed, eyes

wide, mouth slack, pure joy radiating from her as she caught the younger woman up in a tight hug.

River's sinuses burned, and he felt a little guilty, watching their reunion. Everyone in the group had to have a turn hugging the newcomer. *Family.* It was everywhere he looked—kids playing in the open space near the windows that overlooked the tarmac, parents and teens in clumps of seats around the gates. Nearer to the ticket counter, a couple in matching *Just Married* T-shirts sat holding hands. A grandmother type paced with a fussy baby, humming a soft tune. A mom played cards with two school-aged kids.

God, I miss that. He didn't like to let himself dwell on missing his mom, on missing what he'd once had. Being around Griff's family had started this strange wistfulness in him, made him miss his distant siblings, wish things were different. Hell, he even missed his dad, or at least who he'd been when his mother was alive. He wanted what Griff had—a group of people to belong to, to care about, to be lifted up by. True, he had his friends, but last night had been the latest unsatisfying evening in a string of them. He didn't belong in Francesca and Luther's world, not anymore. It was a big reason why he'd…

Run away.

Fuck. Francesca was right. It was what he did. He ran away. He'd run away from his family after his mom died. From his dad after the Marisa fiasco. From his modeling contacts after almost dying. From his friends when that part of his existence kept pulling him down. Hell, he was running away now, away from the fight with Griff, away from his ill-fitting friendships, away from himself. Yes. That was it. He was running away from the book he was less and less sure about. Away from the fact that he couldn't remember his last full meal. Away from this self-loathing and negative talk. Away from how damn much losing Griff hurt.

But his bones ached with the knowledge that it wouldn't be enough. It didn't matter where he went in the world, he was going to miss Griff. And all these years of running and he *still* missed his mom. Across from him, the big family had welcomed a few others to their group, but Bunny and her mom clung to each other like they hadn't seen each other in years.

Who would you be if you stopped running? He wasn't sure he was ready to find out, but he couldn't stop himself from pulling out his phone with shaking fingers, dialing a little-used number.

"Hello, Dad?"

Chapter Twenty-Two

"You don't have to go with me." River stared at the soup in front of him rather than the man at the stove. Unfamiliar kitchen, its layout all wrong from the one he'd spent years in. But there were hints. Same silver clock on the wall even if the paint color was a garish ruby. Same art deco painting opposite the dining area with its new, much smaller set. Same giant mugs that served as soup bowls, some of the few kitchen items that hadn't been replaced.

"No, I don't." His father finished serving himself and came to sit next to River at the breakfast bar. Old kitchen hadn't had one of those. "But I took the day off, and that way I'll be around if…needed."

"I don't think Jennifer's going to admit me or anything." He took a small sip of the soup. Tomato. From a box. But made by someone who seemed to care more than River had given him credit for, meeting River's plane himself and clearing his calendar so that he could take River to see his counselor and doctor. He'd talked to Jennifer on the phone, and she'd insisted that he also have a full physical with his GP and some blood work too.

While you're in town, she'd said, like it was something River did all the time. Like he was *supposed* to be here, not Punta Cana, not his planned itinerary. Like he popped in on his dad and Marisa unannounced like this frequently. Like he was here for pleasure and not because he'd hit a new low. He didn't even remember much of the flight to New Jersey, fitfully dozing and second-guessing himself the whole way.

"I'm off to school pickup. First week back to school here so we're still getting in a routine." Marisa came into the kitchen, pale blond hair caught up in a low twist that complemented her designer jeans and layered top. She'd been giving River a wide berth, and even now addressed his dad, not him. She wasn't mean about it—if anything she seemed a little afraid of him, hanging back, trying to let him have his dad to himself by occupying the kids. "Do you need anything from the store?"

"River?" His dad turned to him, expectant look on his face. "Any preferences for dinner?"

"Nah." Not wanting to be a total dick, River had gone back to the newsstand at the Vancouver airport, picked up two small bears, which he'd handed out to the kids, slightly ashamed that it was the first souvenir from his travels that he'd given them. It said something about him that he knew little more than their names, and it made his back tighten and stomach clench. He didn't even know what they liked or even what grades they were in now. He'd peeked in their rooms—one had a space theme while the other had dinosaurs. "Whatever the kids want is fine."

Marisa gave him a tight, tentative smile. "Thank you. Good luck this afternoon."

Maybe he'd feel up to talking to the kids after his

appointment. Play a game with them or something. It was a bit mind-boggling to think of them as old enough for school and board games and such. Griff had said that his family played games all the time during the long winters as kids. River and his older sisters never had, preferring movies and TV and an endless string of after-school activities. But maybe these two were different. And since he was in town, it wouldn't kill him to make the effort.

"Shall we head out?" his dad asked a while after Marisa left, putting their lunch dishes in the dishwasher. His smile was too bright, but River forced himself to try to return it.

"Sure."

The SUV was new too, and River was silent as his dad navigated the unfamiliar high-end subdivision to get back to the main road.

"Do you need to visit your storage unit after your appointment?" They turned past the elementary school River had gone to. The PTA had named a tree in the courtyard after his mother for all her years as president. He'd never seen it. But maybe this week he'd tag along to the kids' drop-off or pickup, take a picture of it, send it to…

Griff. Fuck. How did he keep forgetting that they weren't speaking and that he couldn't send a text or an email?

"River?" his dad prompted.

"Sorry." He blinked, trying to get more alert. "No, I don't need anything from it today."

It was the smallest size unit the place offered, a collection of neatly labeled plastic totes with clothing organized by season, a few boxes of books, and a box or two of keepsakes from his childhood and modeling days. An even smaller box lived back in the guest room at his dad's with valuables he hadn't trusted to storage. No furniture because he'd always shared a place back when he'd been based out of NYC, and it had been easiest to simply let his former roommates keep the few items he'd acquired. So that was it, the sum total of his worldly possessions in one box, a suitcase, and a glorified closet with a lock.

Griff's cabin might be small, but it was full of personal touches—the quilts his sisters had made, the bulging bookshelves with well-loved keepers, the neat little kitchen. He'd known it was Griff's place the moment he'd stepped inside. And someday Griff was going to get his dream cabin with its bigger bathroom and a kitchen worthy of his cooking efforts. Walls to hang his photographs. That too would be his, would have his stamp on it. What would it be like to have a place like that? Where would he even start? He wasn't the decorating type. Hell, he couldn't even stick to a hair color longer than six months. Who would trust him to pick out bedding and dishes?

"You okay? You seem a million miles away."

"More like five thousand," he said without thinking.

"Pardon?" His dad blinked as they stopped for a red light.

"I met someone in Alaska." He'd been planning to save that for Jennifer, let her prod him into revealing what he'd been up to, not even sure he could get the story out for her in a single session.

"Is that a good thing or a bad thing?" Drumming his fingers on the steering wheel, his dad glanced over at him, concern in his eyes.

"Good. The best." He licked his lips. Again the answer had simply sprung forth. "And the worst."

"Ah. So it's like that." He turned past a grocery store River didn't remember being there and a gas station where a diner had once been. This town had marched right on by without him, growing and changing. Just like his dad and the half-siblings he barely knew. River had thought that perhaps coming here would shake something loose, give him a sense of home and place and purpose. Like Alaska was for Griff. But instead, all he saw was more evidence of change, more proof that he didn't belong here.

"It's gorgeous there. Alaska, I mean. Summer in Denali reminded me of Camp Flint Rock. You might like it there."

"Good old Camp Flint Rock." His dad had been a camper there once upon a time too. Despite his hectic schedule, he was an outdoorsy guy, taking River on his first hikes, something River liked to forget when the memories grew too sharp to handle. "You going to give us a reason to visit? Marisa likes skiing."

River's teeth grated so hard he'd be surprised if his father didn't hear it.

"I'm sorry. I know she's a sore subject. I was just trying to make light, say we'd come see you if you decide to go pan for gold or whatever they do there."

"She's not a sore subject. Not anymore at least." Heart heavy, River looked out at the highway taking them to the medical complex where Jennifer and his doctor were based. "It's been years now. I should be over it."

"But you're not." His dad's voice was gentle. "And

that's okay. I know there's not much I can say that will make it better for you."

"Are you happy?" His voice had more edge than it needed, surprising him with how much the reply mattered to him.

"Yes, yes I am." Eyes distant, his dad sighed. "I know that's probably not what you want to hear. But it's true, Marisa and the kids make me very happy. I like our neighborhood, the community center there, the friends we've made. I like seeing your sisters and their kids from time to time. And I miss you, more than you'll probably ever know. But yes, I'm happy."

"I'm glad." River's voice sounded like it came from beneath the Holland Tunnel. What would it be like to be happy like that? To make his peace with the past? Embrace the future the way his dad had with Marisa? It took him a second to realize that it wasn't anger making his hands fist. It was envy. He was jealous. Jealous that his dad had found a way to move on while he'd been mired in grief for years. Jealous that his dad really did seem happy.

"I don't want to forget her," he whispered. "Her voice keeps fading. I keep a few video clips on my laptop, but they don't sound like her. And her smell. That lily-based perfume that they don't sell anymore. And nothing tastes like her cooking either. I never asked her for a recipe. Not a single one. I doubt Willow or Jade have any either."

"They were on her laptop." His dad's voice was quiet as he took the medical center exit. "Organized in her bookmarks folder. I saved them all. Rigatoni and holiday cookies and minestrone soup. All that. Willow's still doing the vegan thing and Jade doesn't cook, but I saved them. Would you like me to print them for you? We could put them in a book."

"Yeah." River scarcely trusted himself to nod. "I've never cooked, not really, but my…Alaska guy cooks. He might like the soup."

There was an alternate reality where they were still friends, where Griff would make him the soup on his little stove and River would get to eat it in his dining nook, and River wanted that so badly even his fingers and toes ached.

"I bet he would." His dad didn't sound the least shocked that River's someone was male. "And I saved a few other things you might want. Playlists she used on the treadmill. A few essays she wrote for a parenting blog. Paper journals. Willow got her jewelry and Jade took the holiday dishes, but I always thought you might want the paper stuff."

"I do." His heart sped up, a harsh *thumpa-thumpa-thumpa* that rattled his ribs. He lacked the words to tell his dad what it meant that he'd saved something.

"Tell you what, after your appointment, let's go through all of that together." A muscle twitched in his dad's jaw as he parked the SUV. Maybe he knew without River having to say a word.

"I'd like that." Inside, big hunks of ice broke loose, a summer thaw cracking him open.

"Do you…" His dad paused, breath whooshing out. "Want me to come in with you?"

"Yeah." His nod shocked him, made him a little dizzy. He had been fully intending go in alone, cope with his latest screwup on his own, find his way back from the bottom, just like he always did. But maybe it meant something that he was here and not on an island somewhere. What he'd been doing the past few years had stopped working. Maybe doing his usual wasn't what was needed. Maybe he didn't have to be alone.

And it wasn't an answer to the Griff-size hole in his heart, but it was something, something he could build on.

Griffin leveled the plane out on his approach to the lake. *Home again.* He'd made a cargo run north, his first long flight since…

No. Not thinking about River. The long hours in the sky had been far too much time alone with his thoughts as it was. He didn't need a fresh wave of sorrow. No, he needed to land this plane safely, get to his cabin, take the longest shower his hot water tank would allow, and then get on with his night plans. Which did not include stewing.

After he docked the plane, he made his way to the office. It was late, but his mom would be still working. And waiting for him, not that she'd admit that. And sure enough, he found her hunched over her desktop in her office, printouts surrounding her on the desk. The office was small but familiar with maps on the wall that had been there since his childhood and photographs of all the family on the desk. A white board next to the door showed plans for the day, and she'd already updated it for tomorrow.

"Griff." Her wide smile warmed him, reminded him what he was fighting for each day. Her love for him had never wavered, and he wasn't going to let her down. "I've got a roast in the slow cooker at home. You want to stop by for some?"

"Thanks, but I've got—" he rubbed his neck and

looked at his feet "—a meeting. Was going to shower and head down."

"That's wonderful." Coming around the desk, she patted his arm. "I'm proud of you, you know."

"Thanks." Her praise made him twitchy, like a sand-paper jacket he couldn't wait to shed. He'd told her a very limited version of what happened in Vancouver, and he supposed he was damn lucky that she still trusted him to fly, even knowing that he'd faltered.

"You make any friends at the meetings yet?" Her tone was casual, but there was an undercurrent of parental nosiness there along with a subtle "are you moving on yet?" message.

"Not really." He hated to disappoint her, but the important thing was that he was going, right? He wasn't there to make friends, and it wasn't like he was going to replace River anyway. He'd been a once-in-a-lifetime shooting star in Griff's life, not a role easily filled.

"Griff…" His mother's tone was wary, and his back tightened automatically. "I made the roast hoping to talk to you tonight. Not about work stuff. Something personal."

"I don't want to date anyone." He could smell a setup about to happen, and he was putting a stop to that idea right then.

But she only laughed, leaning back against the desk. "Not anything about you. Me."

"You what?" He blinked.

"I want to date."

Griffin swallowed hard and looked, really looked, at his fiercely independent mother, the one who'd raised them all on her own, who'd made this company a success, who kept them all in line, who'd fought tooth and nail to bring him back to the fold, to get him help. River's face flashed before his eyes again too—he could still hear River's pain with his father remarrying what felt like far too soon. But Griffin had the opposite problem—after thirty years, he had a very hard time imagining his mother with any romantic inclinations whatsoever.

"Please tell me it's not Ted." He liked the yacht owner just fine but wasn't sure he wanted him in the family so to speak.

"It's not Ted." A slow, secret smile teased at her lips. "Maybe…once upon a time. But that ship quite literally sailed. It's someone else. Someone you know."

"Ernie at the gas station?" He racked his brain trying to think of single men—or heck, women—around his mother's age nearby.

"No." She gave a near-comical shudder. "Not Ernie. It's… Well, I'm just going to say it. It's Roger."

"Uncle Roger?" Griffin sagged into a nearby office chair. "You've got to be kidding? You guys have known each other… What? Fifty years? More? What's changed?"

"Since school, yes." Her smile faded a little. "I knew him and your father both, but somehow it was always Brian… You know how these things go. Brian and I were the couple, and Roger had his own life. Then Brian died, and a part of me did too. And Roger's career took off, but he was always so helpful with the family and the business. There was a time, you were a young teen maybe, and he sort of hinted, and I thought about it, but I simply didn't want to rock the boat. We worked together. We were family. Why add a romance that would probably fizzle out?"

"Why indeed? You sound like me." Griffin stretched his suddenly too-tight neck. Why try? Why pursue something with an expiration date? "All relationships are doomed, right?"

"Except for the ones that aren't." Her tone was chiding, like Griffin's sarcasm wasn't as welcome as he'd thought. "The lucky ones make it. The ones who put in the work, maybe. Who knows?"

"I sure don't," Griffin admitted.

"None of us do." She reached over and squeezed Griffin's hand. "But anyway, Roger's fall and recuperation up at the house dredged up some old feelings, and we've decided to pursue this thing."

"Pursue? What does that mean exactly?"

"Griff." She raised an eyebrow at him. "Do I really have to spell it out for you? If you must know, he's asked me to get married. The holidays maybe."

"Married?" Griffin's jaw dropped to land somewhere near the box of copy paper on the floor. "That's a little sudden, isn't it?"

"Fifty years. You said so yourself. He doesn't want to wait too long. Says we're both too old for that. Says there's no certainties in life. But I haven't said yes yet. I said we'd start with some dating. And maybe he's not so fast to return to his place. Tell you kids. Take it day by day."

"That sounds smart." He rubbed his jaw. "You don't want to rush things."

"We're not rushing—we're discovering what's been right in front of our eyes before it's too late. He says it's always been me. I'm not sure I believe *that*. But he's an old romantic who doesn't want to let me slip away. He said last night that sometimes you simply know that you've found your one, but timing tripped us up. And my hesitation did the rest. For decades."

Too late. Was it too late for him and River? *You simply know.* And he did, all the way down to his cracked and scarred soul. There wouldn't ever be another River in Griffin's life.

If his mom and Uncle Roger could wait fifty-odd years for their chance, could do the work his mother alluded to, maybe he could find similar courage. Before it was too late.

Chapter Twenty-Three

"Your food should be here soon." River's dad came into the bedroom of the suite the movie studio had booked for them. "The clothes look nice."

River's stylist had left after delivering clothes for his next few obligations including the premiere. They'd spread them out on the bed, grouping each outfit with accessories down to the socks and shoes.

"Thanks. Not so sure about how the hair turned out…" He'd been to the salon earlier in the morning, getting color and a cut. He'd left the top longer and more tousled while getting the sides and back trimmed up. As for color, he'd brought a picture in of the sky in Denali, and the colorist had mixed a custom light blue shade with purple undertones.

"It looks fine. It's been so long since I saw your hair without some sort of color that I'm not sure I'd recognize you without it," his dad teased.

"Good. Maybe I'm done with being recognized." This was probably his last color indulgence for a while if his other plans came to fruition. He wanted to just say fuck it and go back to something in the brown family, but the publicist for the studio had insisted that his colorful hair was one of his hallmarks.

Fine. He'd deal with this last obligation, then he'd be free again, free to be the self he needed to be. The self he was slowly trying to heal. The old River would have never dreamed of having his dad out here for the premiere and press junket, but when he'd volunteered to take the week off and come along for moral support, the new River had admitted that might help him to better stick to the program his therapist and doctor had written out for him.

A knock sounded at the door, and his father headed back to the living area. "I'll get it."

River stayed behind, not in any hurry to eat, even though he'd agreed to try before their next engagement. But then he heard a familiar rumbly voice and his name. *No way.* Not daring to hope, he hurried out of the bedroom.

"River?" his father called. "I think it's for you."

It was entirely possibly he was having some sort of out-of-body hallucination because Griff stood there in the doorway. He looked like River remembered, like his favorite pictures of him, plaid shirt with rolled-up sleeves, faded jeans, scruffy jaw. Way too Alaska for Hollywood, but one of the most welcome sights River could summon up.

"Griff? What are you doing here?" He had to blink several times, making sure he was awake.

"I…uh…I'm not sure." Griff's eyes darted to River's father. "I wanted to talk, but maybe this is a bad time."

"This is my dad," River said before Griff could jump to any conclusions. "And you can talk."

He hoped he didn't sound *too* ominous, but that was probably a losing battle, given the jumbled mess of emotions coursing through his veins. He motioned for Griff to come into the suite.

"I'll give you guys a moment," River's dad said right as the food arrived. Total three-ring circus with his dad accepting the room service tray and Griff shrinking back against the wall.

"I should go." Griff's strained face made him look ready to bolt any second.

"Stay. You can keep me company while I eat. I've got a press engagement later, but I'm supposed to eat first. Dad ate earlier while I was dealing with my stylist."

"And Dad's going to go return some work calls." River's dad gave them both an encouraging look. He'd heard enough about Griff the past few weeks, and he had to be curious, but it was nice of him to offer them privacy for…whatever this was.

"You came." River's tone came out more mournfully than he'd intended as he took a seat on the couch, near the coffee table with the tray of food. He motioned for Griff to take the nearby chair.

"Yeah. That's bad?" Griff's voice was tentative.

"Only because I was coming to *you*. I was. I've got a ticket and everything. But I wanted to… Never mind. It's stupid."

"No, what? Wanted what?"

"I wanted to have my shit more together when I saw you next. I had a whole plan, but now you're here. And I think I'm glad—don't you dare leave—but I'm kind of a mess still. This premiere week stuff is hard. That's why my dad is here."

"I figured it wasn't going to be an easy week on you. I'm glad your dad came." Griff leaned forward, elbows resting on his knees. "That's sorta why I came. And you should go ahead and eat your food."

"I will." His voice was too sharp, but he went ahead and removed one of the food covers and ripped off a piece of toast. "You were worried about me?"

River wasn't sure how he felt about that. Defensive maybe, old habits dying hard and all that. He didn't *want* to be worried over. He took a bite of bread that tasted like clay and stared Griff down, daring him to pity River.

"That. And I missed you." Griff gave him a crooked smile.

"You couldn't text? Call?" Of course, he could have done any of those things himself and hadn't, fear holding him back. Easier to focus on his plans than deal with the very real possibility that Griff wouldn't pick up his phone.

"Thought you might be more likely to talk to me in person. And like I said, I wondered if maybe you could use a friend this week. Despite everything, I still want to be your friend."

"Friends don't give up so easily. Friends don't go weeks without a word." He wasn't being that reasonable given his own actions, but he couldn't seem to modulate his pissy tone.

"Fair enough." Griff held up his hands. "You know how you said you had a plan? How you wanted to be more together when we talked? Maybe I had some of that going on too. I wasn't ready. I needed to work some on me first, get my head on straight."

"Yeah." River sighed, some of his anger receding. "I get that. But you're not the only one who worried. I didn't even know if you got home safe."

"I did." Griff's grimace said there was maybe a story there. "And I didn't drink if that's what you were thinking."

"That's good. I'm sorry I made it seem like I didn't trust you."

"Yeah, that stung. A lot. But maybe I didn't fully trust myself either. My sobriety was more…fragile than I wanted to admit. I went to a meeting there, then caught a flight home. Went to a lot more meetings once I was back."

"I thought you were against meetings and therapy?"

"I was. I didn't want to admit that I might need help. But then I realized that I was doing exactly what I accused you of—trying to go it alone, not reaching out for help, not admitting when I wasn't okay, pretending that I had it all together when inside I was a mess."

"You were right. I was doing that." Not able to meet Griff's gaze, River studied his hands, twisting his fingers. "And I'm sorry. That's what I was going to tell you when I finally saw you again. That you were right. I wasn't okay. And I'm still not, but I'm working on it."

"Me too." Griff moved his hand like he was going to pat River then seemed to think better of the gesture. River summoned some courage and reached out, meeting him halfway, fingers brushing. It was the barest of contact, but it made River's feet curl against the carpeting.

"I was going to run away after our fight." He hadn't been planning on admitting this, but the words tumbled out anyway. "I was going to go to this resort in the Dominican Republic that I picked at random. But I…I've run so much, you know? Years of running. I was so tired, Griff."

"So what did you do?" Griff's voice was wary, as if he was bracing for the worst. Maybe River wasn't the only one with trust issues.

"I went home. Sort of."

"You went back to Jersey? To your family?"

"Yeah. Guess I figured that I had tried everything else. And I was just so tired of pretending I was okay. I couldn't do it anymore."

"You didn't have to pretend with me." There was a world of hurt in Griff's words.

"I know. And I wasn't pretending when I visited you. Promise. But once I was back on my own, the pretending and doubts and negative self-talk became second nature again, and I couldn't shut it off, even when it meant losing you."

"I could have been a lot more understanding. It wasn't fair of me to try to force you to talk to me, let me help. I should have known better than to think I could save you from yourself."

"But you did help me." River grabbed his hand in earnest now. "Every hike. Every sunrise. All the time we spent together—it was all one step closer to healing for me. And yes, I pushed you away in Vancouver. That's on me, not you."

"It's not all you. I did some pushing too." Griff squeezed him back.

"Healing isn't linear and it's scary shit. I think I was terrified of what I was feeling, of what it meant, letting you closer and closer. I was so afraid that me breaking down would mean bad things for you. And us. I just couldn't let you see me losing my shit. And then it was too late."

"I was scared too," Griff whispered, voice rough.

"And it shouldn't have been too late. I shouldn't have ended things, at least not like that. That was my own fear talking."

At least not like that. River didn't like the sound of that, didn't like the implication that maybe they should have ended some other way.

"River?" his dad called from the bedroom door. "You've got that interview soon. You should probably get changed. Did you eat?"

"Sort of." He broke off another piece of toast. "And yeah, I'll get dressed. Just a second."

"I'll leave." Griff stood. "I probably shouldn't have unloaded all this on you right now."

"You're not leaving." River leveled him with a hard stare. "You came all this way for a reason, right?"

"Well, yeah." Griff still didn't sit back down. "But I kept you from eating and now you've got a thing..."

"You can come. You can keep Dad company while they film the segment. It shouldn't take terribly long. And then I'll eat more afterward. A late dinner with you maybe?"

"I could do that," Griff said slowly. "If you're sure that me being here isn't making things worse for you."

"I'm not entirely sure *what* I'm feeling, honestly. But I don't want you to leave."

"Okay." Griff nodded, sitting back down in the chair. "I'll stay."

Relief mingled with a lot of other emotions River couldn't name churned in his insides, making him feel like he was back on Ted's yacht, unable to get his bearings. Unfortunately, there weren't special motion sickness bracelets to help cope with his feelings about

Griff. He didn't know what happened next, only that they weren't done. Not yet.

Griffin still wasn't sure exactly what he was doing in LA, a feeling that worsened while he waited for River to get changed for his interview. He'd been acting on instinct, he supposed, but instinct was still nerve-racking as all hell. After his talk with his mother and realizing that he didn't want to let River get away, going after him had seemed like a decent plan. Wasn't like River was likely to turn up on his doorstep. Except River had said he had a plan, that *he* had planned on coming to Griffin.

Which should have calmed Griffin down, but River was still impossible to read—he seemed to alternate irritation at Griffin's presence with happiness with hurt that he didn't seem ready to let go of. And that hurt was understandable—they'd both said a lot of things, both had weeks to nurse their pain, and it made sense that River wouldn't be ready to forgive and forget so fast. Made sense, but still wasn't easy.

And judging from the stony looks River's father kept giving him, he knew something about their breakup and was equally unwilling to let Griffin off the hook. Griffin tried to take some solace in his presence, though—if River could make peace with his father, move beyond years of discord, maybe that meant there was hope for him and Griffin.

"Okay. I'm ready." River emerged from the bedroom in a navy jacket over a coordinating silky T-shirt and light gray pants. The outfit brought out the blue in both his hair and eyes, and somehow managed to make him look older, more confident. Out of Griffin's league.

"The studio sent a car. They just buzzed my phone to let me know they were downstairs."

Griffin didn't give in to the urge to ask River again if he was sure he wanted him along, but he certainly felt as unnecessary as snowshoes in July as they made their way downstairs. At the car, River's father deftly slid in next to the driver, leaving Griffin next to River in the back seat, not that resuming their previous conversation seemed like a good idea. That sort of soul-baring, emotionally exhausting talk would have to wait for a better time.

Timing. It was entirely possible that Griffin's sense of timing sucked, but after seeing his mother delay something that now felt inevitable for decades, he'd been impatient. Yet now that he was here, he could exhale somewhat, try to cultivate patience. River needed to do this interview and then he needed to eat without distractions. All the questions bouncing around Griffin's brain could take a number.

Instead, he tried to make small talk, something he sucked at, asking about the press tour and premiere, which was scheduled for the next day.

"Tomorrow's going to be crazy. Friends flying in from all over, pre-party *and* after-party. The movie's getting good buzz, which the studio is happy about, but I'll be glad when this is over."

"I bet." Griffin refrained from offering advice or reminding River that he didn't owe anyone anything and could do as little as he wanted. The firm set of River's sculpted jaw said that such opinions wouldn't be welcome. "When does it calm down for you?"

"The wide release starts Thursday, so there's some press obligations through the weekend, but then it slows. Dad's going back on Sunday. And I told you I had a plan. I have a ticket for Monday."

"You really were coming." There was so much else Griffin wanted to say, but couldn't, not right here, not with them entering a vast gated lot of Hollywood studios and movie sets. They were headed for a taping of a well-known late-night TV show. River, the director, and the Hollywood star who played River were all on the show. River never got a chance to reply what with everyone piling out of the car.

The driver, who was also apparently some sort of assistant with the movie studio, led them through a maze of hallways to a room where Griffin found a patch of wall to hold up while River was surrounded by people vying for his attention—a production assistant for the talk show, makeup people, entourages for the director and the actor, who in Griffin's opinion looked very little like River. Sure he was tallish and slim and apparently had dyed his hair for the part, although it was back to a bleach blond now, but he had too many muscles, too much tan, too little depth to his eyes. He also had a Southern accent and nothing in common with River's melodic east coast tones. A very touchy-feely girlfriend hung on his arm, and she said something that made the real River give a tight laugh.

There were ample snacks in the room, but Griffin knew River would likely ignore the food, much as he'd barely picked at the tray earlier. He'd spent a lot of time the last few weeks trying to understand River's issues and to come to terms with the fact that there was likely little Griffin could do to make things better for him. This wasn't something he could "fix" through sheer force of will for River any more than River could be responsible for Griffin's sobriety.

"He'll be okay." Holding a can of sparkling water, River's dad came to stand next to Griffin. "These things exhaust him in a way they never used to, but he's been holding up all right. You can stop glaring at the movie studio people."

"Sorry." Griffin hadn't even been aware he'd been frowning. But it was true that even knowing that he couldn't save River from his demons, he still wanted to wrap him up, protect him from stressful situations. And the stiff way River held himself, the tension around his eyes and mouth, the fakeness of his laugh, all showed he was stressed. "Did he even consider not doing the publicity stuff?"

"Yeah." River's dad sighed and took a long drink of his soda. "He did. But he also didn't want to break his obligations to the studio. And as much as he's a force of nature, he's also private. I don't think he wanted word to get out about what he's been going through."

"Yeah." Some of Griffin's guilt over knowing he was part of that turmoil seeped into his voice. "Probably doesn't help that the movie made him out to be some sort of foodie." He'd heard enough complaints about that from River before they'd broken up.

"It's almost as bad as them adding a romance to the end. River doesn't usually do romance." The man gave Griffin a wry look that was hard to decipher but there was a warning there too.

"For what it's worth, neither do I. River's the first person I've had...serious feelings for in half a decade or more. And I don't think I owe you an explanation, but I'm not out to hurt him again. I want to make things right."

"See that you do. He's…fragile. Easily bruised, maybe."

"I think he's stronger than people assume. Maybe even stronger than he knows." Griffin felt compelled to defend him.

"We're on in five." A production assistant herded River and the other two guests out to make their way to the stage while a large screen flipped on in the room so they'd be able to watch the recording.

And like his dad had predicted, River did well, turning his sparkle on, much as he had in Vancouver with his friends. His only stumble was when the host asked him about the next book, and River visibly paled before recovering to say airily, "No spoilers."

Finally they were done, and Griffin truly was hungry and ready for a late supper. He wanted to give River a hug, hold him close. Not because River needed propping up but because Griffin needed it too, needed that contact. But they weren't quite to that level of familiarity again yet.

"Takeout?" River's dad suggested. "I've got an app, and I could have something waiting for us back at the hotel."

"Griff probably needs meat." River managed a small smile. "Get some sort of beefy Chinese food for you guys, and I'll have hot and sour soup and maybe an egg roll."

"Excellent." They hashed out an order as they made their way through traffic back to the hotel, and the delivery person arrived shortly after they were back in the suite. River's dad scooped up the kung pao chicken and a container of rice.

"I'll take mine in the other bedroom, give you guys some privacy. I need to call Marisa anyway."

Judging by River's pursed mouth, Marisa was the stepmother, and Griffin couldn't resist asking about it as soon as his dad was gone.

"How'd that go? Seeing her and the kids, I mean. It couldn't have been easy." Griffin helped himself to some of the beef with broccoli. They were sitting next to each other on the couch this time, and he tried to take that as a positive sign.

"Eh." River shrugged as he unwrapped a soupspoon. "They're nice kids. Played a bunch of rounds of that board game you tried to teach me. I still lost. And Marisa's okay. She made an effort, so I guess I'm trying to do the same. I'm trying to not be the sort of person who holds a ten-year grudge, you know?"

"Yeah. Grudges aren't very helpful." He tried to imply with his tone that he meant any lingering grudges between them, too. "Including ones against yourself. That's something I'm working on at least."

"My counselor is big on forgiving yourself. I'm not the best at that." River took a small sip of the soup.

"Me either."

"I get so angry that I have limitations." River set his spoon down and looked away. "It's not fair. I hate it. I think that's part of why I run away so much—maybe I'm running from myself."

"I get that. I get angry too," Griffin admitted as he passed River an egg roll. "Because you're right, it's not fair. It's not fair that certain things still trigger me, and I get you feeling like that too. But don't be so hard on yourself. It's not all about you running away—you've gotten a lot out of travel. It's part of who you are, and I'm not looking to change that and don't think you should either."

"Thanks. I do like traveling. And you're right, it has helped me. It gave me back my life in a lot of ways. But I also used it as a crutch, a way to avoid facing my emotions. And I want—*need*—to work on that."

"I hear you. Maybe for you it was running away, but for me it was staying in place, hiding away from the world. You weren't wrong when you said that I was scared to take risks. I was. And I'm going to work on that as well. I'm not going to lie and say it's easy, but you make me want to take risks again. Good ones, ones where the payoff might just be worth it."

"Like coming here?" River took a thoughtful nibble of the egg roll.

"Yeah." Griffin nodded, his own appetite receding under the enormity of what he'd done. "Like coming here, asking for a second chance."

"You said you were scared to love me." Looking right at Griff, River's mouth set in a thin line and he decidedly did not mention the second chance bit.

"I was. But that doesn't mean I didn't already love you. I was trying to keep myself from hurt, but it was too late. I'd already fallen for you."

"If you loved me, that wasn't the best way to show it, even if you were scared. Because now, I'm scared—worried that your feelings might be conditional. I can try to talk more, but I can't promise that I'm not going to slip up. And the last thing I want is to trigger you."

"You won't. That was wrong to pin on you. It's on me how I react, and I reacted badly in Vancouver, no

two ways about it. And what I feel for you isn't conditional. We're both going to screw up from time to time,
I'm sure. And we both have things we're working on,
but I still want to try."

"You said all I cared about was having fun. And that
you weren't the guy for me. It might have been your
fears driving you, but that *hurt*."

"I know." Griffin slumped back against the couch.
"That wasn't fair of me. I really was afraid that you
needed something I simply couldn't give. But you'd
also proved to me over our time together that you were
far more than only a party boy. Maybe I was missing
the guy you'd been in Alaska, but instead of saying
that, I lashed out."

"I didn't need some fantasy guy. I thought you knew
me better than that. I just needed you."

"And I did a shitty job of being there for you. I
know." Griffin scrubbed at his hair, making the already unruly mop even more so.

"Maybe you needed to be there for yourself more."
River's voice was thin and filled with a sadness that
almost broke Griffin's heart all over again.

"See, that's exactly it. I'm not sure that ending
things with you was what was best for me. Or necessary. I think I was too tangled up in my fears and feelings to make that call. And now that I've had some time
to think, I really do want to try again. You do bring
something to my life, something that I think I need."

River was silent a very long time, and finally Griffin had to prod him. "Can we do that? Try?"

"Damn it, Griff." River let out a shaky laugh. "I was
going to come to you, convince *you* that we needed a
second chance, get you to take a risk on us. I've got

a lot to apologize for too—I really did shut you out. And I've spent weeks trying to find the right words for that, and now you've spoiled my big move. Now I'm all twisted up. I'm not sure what I want anymore."

"Do you want me to go back home? Wait for you to show up next week? I can do that." His heart started crashing into his ribs, like a boat that had lost its moorings.

"No." River scooted closer. "But I also want to be fair to you. The next few days are going to be chaotic and exhausting. You don't have to stay just because I want you to. I'll still come to you next week."

"I can't stay all the way until next week—I only switched a couple of days with Clancy and Toby. But I can stay until the day after tomorrow, be here for you however you need for the premiere. Then, yeah, I'll wait for you to come back." He had to swallow hard, trying to calm his clattering chest. Trust. He'd trust that River would come back, that the timing would work out for their second chance.

"Will you stay here tonight?" River bit his lower lip, which made Griffin wrap his arms around him. "I mean, I'm not sure if I'm down for sex with my dad in the next room, but…"

"If you want me here, then I'm here. And what? You're not up for a real-life version of the stay-quiet game?" Griffin laughed and held River close, trying to soak in his nearness. "I'm kidding. I don't need sex tonight. Just you is plenty."

"Thanks." River pressed a soft kiss to his lips. Not a sexual thing as much as comfort thing, something they both desperately needed as they made their way forward, tried to figure out how to have a future together. But as they kissed, Griffin was determined that they would get that future, would find a way to support each other, to have the sort of relationship River deserved. And okay, he deserved it too. He was working on believing that, but they both deserved happiness, and he wanted to make that happen.

Chapter Twenty-Four

Something warm and hard pressed into River's back. Something that smelled delicious and made him stretch like a cat to further burrow into the warm bulk. Something that made him reconsider his "no sex where my dad can hear" policy. He'd slept better than he had in weeks, even if the most he and Griff had gotten up to was some lingering kisses before sleep. He liked that though, liked that they didn't *need* sex—it felt cozy, like they were a long-time couple, not one newly re-united.

But now he was hard and it had been weeks and he really wanted Griff, wanted to push aside some of the longing and loneliness and wallow in the hope that they'd both get a chance to make things right.

"Maybe I *can* be quiet," he whispered, bumping his ass into Griff's morning wood.

"No, you can't." Griff kissed his neck. "And I'm not sure I can look your dad in the eyes if either of us fails at that game."

"It'll be okay." He turned in Griff's arms so that he could give him a soft kiss. "I'm sure he figured out that you're not sleeping on the floor in here."

Griff groaned and pulled him in closer so that their

pajama-bottom-covered erections rubbed together. "Maybe…"

"That's what I'm talking about." River met his mouth for a longer, more searching kiss, one where he reacquainted himself with Griff's taste and preferences, remembering how Griff liked things just this side of rough.

But right as Griff worked a hand under River's waistband, his phone trilled on the nightstand with a message.

"Fuck." Having a feeling who it was, River reluctantly pulled away and reached for it.

"More like no fuck." Griff flopped over onto his back and put an arm over his face.

"Yup. Like I was hoping, my stylist thinks they have a tux for you. They're bringing some options by soon."

"You sure you want me at the premiere?" Griff's mouth twisted. "I'd be okay waiting around here for you to come back if you don't want to be seen with a scruffy mountain man."

"Don't be silly. You're hot as fuck. But it's your call. Whatever you need. If you're asking me, however, yes, I want you there. Just seeing you there will help ground me." Admitting that was hard, but asking for what he really needed was getting easier each time he tried it.

"Okay. No crazy colors on the tux, and I don't need to be in pictures, but I'm happy to be there for your big night." Griff sat up, which River supposed marked the end of trying to sneak in some sex. "And I'll let you know if the party stuff gets to be too much for me. I'm trying to do better about figuring what my limitations are before I smack into them."

"I would be *thrilled* to have a reason to leave early."

River dropped a kiss on Griff's bare shoulder. "Seriously."

"But your friends—"

"Are toxic," River finished for him. "I knew that before Vancouver, but I kept trying to have them in small doses. Moderation. But moderation doesn't really work for me when it comes to body image stuff. I'm always going to love Francesca and the rest of that crew, but trying to fit into their world isn't something I want to do anymore. The price is too high."

"That sounds smart." Griff sounded like he was choosing his words carefully, which River appreciated. He knew Griff wasn't a fan of his friends, but his restraint in not piling on River's critique of them showed a maturity River wanted to emulate.

"So we'll make an appearance at the events tonight, but I had already decided to do the bare minimum socializing before you showed up."

"Unlike me, you're a people person." Griff pulled him in for a one-armed hug. "I would never want to stand in the way of you having friends."

"I get that. But maybe I just need some better ones. New ones." River licked his lips. He wasn't quite ready to tell Griff *all* his plans yet. Simply him being here was new and terrifying and wonderful all at once. Planning for the future was beyond his present capabilities.

"Well, you could always go to Kansas City, see Melanie and Dan," Griff joked.

"Or I could do my plan, come to you next week."

"I'd like that." Griff's eyes went serious. "Stay as long as you want too. No rush."

River swallowed hard. Maybe it would be okay to mention—

"River? Your stylist is here." His dad sounded far more chipper than the hour called for. "And there's coffee and food."

They both quickly put on clothes and went to deal with the stylist, a striking person named Kini with long black hair and far better winged eyeliner than River could ever manage this early in the day. They had proved to be a miracle worker, producing three tuxes for Griff to choose from. Griff, of course, went with the plainest, blackest, most sedate of the bunch—a classic cut suit with a straight black tie.

"I look like a hit man infiltrating a fancy event," Griff groused.

"Sexy bad guy is not a terrible look at all." Kini offered an encouraging smile. "Now you go get back into your comfortable clothes, and I'll make the few alterations myself and have it back to you by this afternoon."

"Thanks." River waited for Griff to be back in his usual wardrobe before thinking about coffee and food. He knew the longer in the day he waited to eat, the harder it would be, so he forced himself to have toast and eggs along with the coffee and to enjoy feeding his leftovers to Griff, who ate like he hadn't polished off a mountain of Chinese food the night before.

"Dad gave me some of my mom's recipes," he told Griff. "There's a soup thing that uses the slow cooker that I remember her making some on school nights."

"Send it to me. I'll make sure I've got ingredients for when you visit."

Making plans for the visit helped to center him some, helped quiet his nerves, so while they lingered over their coffee he indulged in discussing logistics until his interview with a print publication. Then the day was a whirl of friends arriving, interviews, getting dressed and heading to the pre-red-carpet party near the theater.

"You look amazing," Griff said on their way. "Is that okay to say? Because I love that color of gray on you."

"Thanks." River felt his cheeks heat, like he was some teen who'd never had a compliment before. It was a nice tux, light gray with a modern cut and blue tie that matched his hair. He leaned in to whisper in Griff's ear, "You can take it off later."

Griff sputtered, turning an adorable shade of pink before whispering back, "Thin walls, remember? It'll keep."

Trying to devise a way to have silent sex later was an excellent distraction for how completely overwhelming the evening was—the crush of people, all the famous friends and movie studio people, his agent and his editor, both of whom discreetly inquired about his deadline, making his neck sweat. The focus on looks and gossip—who was wearing what, who had brought someone new, who had a new deal—was exhausting. As was worrying about whether Griff was okay. But he was trying to do a better job than he had in Vancouver of letting Griff worry about himself and trusting that he'd be okay with the constant parade of cocktails around them and the unfamiliar social situation.

And he was. Not the life of the party or anything, but he'd found a corner where he was talking with the stunt man boyfriend of one of the actresses and seemed happy enough with his soda while continuing to send River reassuring looks.

Finally, it was time for the premiere, red carpet and all. Neither Griff nor his dad wanted to walk the red carpet, so they'd meet him inside instead. It felt like running a gauntlet, all the cameras and people and questions being lobbed at him. He knew he screwed up more than one answer and his hands were clammy by the time he reached Griff in the lobby.

"Your dad ducked into the men's room. You holding up okay?" Griff wrapped an arm around him as they made their way into the theater.

River three weeks ago would have lied and said yes, yes he was fine. But if nothing else, Griff deserved his honesty. If this thing between them was going to work, he had to trust Griff to see him at his less-than-perfect and ideal.

"No. I think I'm about to crack into a zillion pieces. This all feels surreal—like someone else wrote this book and got the movie deal."

"Well, you did. And it's an awesome book. Read it on the plane on the way down."

"Really?"

"It's a good book." And somehow Griff's simple praise was worth a hundred decent reviews. The knot in River's chest loosened a little. "You deserve this success. And it's okay to feel…whatever you're feeling. I'll help you put yourself back together afterward."

"I'm a mess." River sagged against his shoulder as they took their seats.

"Yeah, but you're *my* mess. Nowhere I'd rather be right now, promise."

That helped too, knowing that Griff wanted to be here, that River wasn't scaring him away. And it helped too that he didn't try to hand-wave River's issues away—telling him that he was fine or other platitudes. That he understood River wasn't okay and wasn't rushing to "fix" him made River want to hug him and not let go, made him a safer place for River to have his meltdown or whatever the heck was going on with his emotions.

"I might cry," he warned.

"I brought tissues, and unlike this suit, I'm washable." Griff gave him a fast kiss on the head. "And for what it's worth, I'd probably be emotional in your shoes too. It's a big deal, putting something you love out there."

"Thanks. I feel like I don't deserve you," he admitted.

"Welcome to my head. All the time. Part of what took me so long to come after you was feeling like you were too good for me, like you deserved something different in a person, something more than I could provide."

"Oh, Griff. All I need is *you*." Weirdly, it helped, knowing that Griff had all the same doubts and fears as he did.

"And if I ever do anything big like this, you can repay the favor, okay? I sent some stuff to a contact of Uncle Roger's last week. It's not a Hollywood premiere, but just a show in Anchorage would be a huge deal for me."

"Are you doing it for me?" He wasn't sure he liked that idea. "I mean it. I need you—not a famous photographer boyfriend or whatever else you're thinking."

"I'm doing it for me. Because it's time. Because it would help the family, help the business, help the cabin fund. And because kinda like with coming after you, I'll never know unless I try. And when I thought about the risks of coming to talk with you, sending a few photographs to a gallery owner didn't seem like such a big deal."

River had a few ideas of his own about the cabin fund, but now wasn't the time to share those, not with his dad joining them and the show about to start. But as Griff took his hand and the opening score started to play, he had fresh faith in the future. His chest felt inadequate to hold all the hope surging through him. *I'll never know unless I try,* Griff had said. And maybe that applied to them as well. They wouldn't know what they could be, how good this thing between them could grow, if they never tried. And right then, he wanted to try with his whole being.

"If you keep watching your phone, you're going to end up with engine grease in weird places," Toby teased as they did maintenance on one of the planes. It was a slow day, which meant plenty of time to check his phone for signs of River's progress.

"I'm not nervous," Griffin said, pocketing the phone.

"Yeah, you are. And it's cute. But I'm surprised you didn't go fly to get him yourself. I thought supermodels were all about letting others ferry them around. Are you sure he even has a driver's license?"

"He's not a supermodel anymore. He's a writer." Griffin wasn't sure whether the distinction mattered or not—he was simply River, each part of him significant and making up the whole like the components of an engine. "And in any event, yeah, apparently he can drive. He wanted to rent a car since there's no snow yet and the weather's not terrible and didn't want to be dependent on my truck."

"Griff, I say this with love, but maybe he fears for his safety in that rattletrap of yours."

"Truck might be old, but it runs." Griffin glared at him.

"Like you." Toby was younger than Griff, but not that much, and Griffin only grunted in response to his teasing, which seemed to only encourage Toby more. "You never know, if he needs a younger model…"

"He doesn't." Griff had always sort of envied Toby's approach to hookups—he'd never tried to hide that he went for tourists of all genders, but he also never went for seconds either. And no way was he getting any part of River.

He got why River wanted to make his own way here, not be dependent on him flying or driving him around. The cynical part of Griffin knew it was a good exit strategy—if things didn't work out with them, River could simply leave. But the more hopeful part said that Griffin had told River to stay as long as he wanted, and River was just being practical about wanting some independence if he was staying for more than just a weekend.

God, Griffin hoped he was staying for more than simply a weekend.

Finally, his phone buzzed with a message right as they finished their work for the morning. *About thirty minutes away. Will let myself in.*

"Go. Take a long lunch. Or a half day," Toby urged. "You're not scheduled for any flights, and I can finish the rest of what needs doing around here."

"Well…" Griffin didn't like taking off early, and he had left the cabin unlocked for River, but the temptation to rush home was strong. It had only been a few days, but it felt like far longer, and things still seemed tentative, like they were feeling their way forward. Their few phone conversations had been nice, but Griffin would feel better once they were face-to-face again.

"Go." Toby made a shooing motion with his hand. Not needing to be told a third time, Griffin headed for the truck and made it home just as River pulled in next to his truck in a small SUV. He'd obviously listened to Griffin about getting something with good tires for the wet weather they'd been having in the lead-up to the start of winter.

"You're here," Griffin said stupidly, relief taking him by surprise, hitting him square in the chest. He'd known River was coming, but hadn't really let himself fully admit the depth of his wanting until right that moment.

"I am." River stood before him, eyes uncertain. He was wearing his unicorn sweatshirt and a pair of faded jeans, but something about him seemed older than usual. "Do I have to kiss you out here, or are you going to ask me in?"

The joking loosened some of the tension in Griffin's back. It was the same River. In his time in LA, he'd come to see that it wasn't that River was two different people, one city and one Alaska, as he'd feared, but rather that River was made up of infinite sides, some of which got muted in one place or the other, but all of which made him tick. However, he'd be lying if he didn't admit that he'd been looking forward to seeing the parts he liked best about River bloom again.

"Come here," he commanded, opening his arms. They'd kissed in LA, of course. A fair amount actually. But this felt different, and it wasn't just the relative privacy. River was *here*. Griffin's whole body thrilled to that fact. This was more than just a mad dash by Griffin to try to make things right. This was a real, true second chance, time to sort out what and who they were.

He tried to put all that into his kiss—his gratitude that River was there, his hopes for the future, even the fears he was still struggling with. And maybe River got that message because he kissed Griffin back like he'd been lost at sea for months, as if he were cramming everything he had into the kiss. He hauled River closer, almost lifting him off his feet.

"Don't you dare try carrying me. Caveman." Laughing, River pulled away and darted the few remaining steps to Griffin's cabin. Giving in to unfamiliar playful urges, he chased after River, racing him into the cabin, gently tackling him to the bed.

"Finally. I've got you right where I want you." He kept his voice light, but there was a seriousness there too because he meant it. This was right where they were both supposed to be.

"Good." River ended on a chuckle as Griffin buried his face in his neck. "What are you doing?"

"You smell good." Griffin wasn't going to apologize for trying to get as much River as possible.

"So does your place."

"Soup for your lunch in the slow cooker. *Later*." He licked River's ear for emphasis.

"Thought you had a thing against nooners." River's fingers had already found Griffin's shirt buttons.

"Not today." For River, he'd break an awful lot of his self-imposed rules. "Missed you too much."

"Missed you too." River yanked him down for another long kiss before continuing, "Not being able to get you naked in LA sucked."

"Feel free to make up for lost time now." Griffin rolled to his back so that River could more easily continue unbuttoning him. "And I understood. You had enough to deal with."

River had been far too exhausted after the premiere stuff to even think about sex, even if they hadn't had his dad in the next room, and Griff had been happy to simply hold him until he'd fallen asleep. He'd held him all the way until he'd had to leave, feeling like he was leaving a piece of his beating heart behind. And now he had it back and he could do more than hold on and he was almost giddy.

Leaning down, River bit at Griffin's neck before tugging his shirt open. He made a frustrated noise. "An undershirt? Really?"

"Hey, it's chilly in the hangar this time of year." Griffin sat up long enough to lose both shirts as River pulled off his own shirt.

"Guess I shouldn't ask how it is in January. I'll be unwrapping you like a mummy."

Swallowing hard, Griffin stared at him, trying to figure out if he was serious—that there was a chance he'd be around in the deep of winter—or if he was simply teasing.

"You could find out," he said gruffly.

"I could." River straddled him in an easy movement. *Please. Please do.* There was a limit to how much Griffin was prepared to beg, but he was sure all his hopes and wants were visible in his eyes. *Stay. Stay forever.* The words wouldn't come, but the emotions… God, the emotions were right there.

"I've had a fantasy all week." River licked his lips as he peered down at Griffin, a blue-haired siren.

"Anything," Griffin said and meant it.

"I keep thinking I've had enough first-time role-play for a while. You've given me a taste for middles. But then I realized that this is kind of both—a first time and a middle. Everything feels fresh again, both like we've never done this and like we never stopped."

"Yeah." Running his hands down River's lean sides, he reveled in his warmth and nearness.

"And I keep spinning this fantasy where we're back together—"

"We are," Griffin growled.

"Yes." River gave him an angelic smile before continuing. "We are. And we spend forever kissing and touching."

"Come back down here and I'll show you forever."

That got a happy sigh from River but didn't get Griffin another kiss yet. "You're sweet. So sweet. Let me finish my fantasy?"

"I love it already." Palming River's ass, he rocked his hips upward so River could feel exactly how hard he was.

"I think you'll love how it ends even more. I keep thinking about that time when I told you I wanted you to fuck me someday. I want to ride you. That's what I want." River danced his fingers down Griffin's chest, over his stomach, down his denim-covered erection.

Griffin's breath caught, not entirely sure how to reply.

"Come on, Griff. Don't you want to fuck me?"

Chapter Twenty-Five

Griffin's heart shook right along with his hands as he searched for words.

"You don't have to," Griffin felt honor-bound to protest. "I know that's not your usual thing, and fuck, keep that touching up and I'll come in my jeans. I'm good with whatever you want."

"I want this. Partly because everything is different and new with you and I want to see if this is too. And partly because I said 'someday' and then there were no more somedays and I missed everything we'd never do as much as all the things we had. And partly because I got off to this idea three times the last week." He laughed as if that had surprised himself too, and maybe it had.

"Okay. But if you hate it—or hell, mildly dislike— we stop. Because I've had fantasies the last week too, and in all of them you're coming like a geyser. Loudly."

"Oh, Griff. I..." Face turning soft and warm, he drifted off before pressing a soft kiss to Griffin's lips, but Griffin knew what he wanted to say because the words were right there in his own throat too. This wasn't about sex or negotiating how they were going to get off. Under all the teasing and the fantasies, this was a reunion. A reclaiming. A reckoning even. There had been something between them, right from the start. Something big and scary and special.

It was there in every kiss, every touch, every word they left unsaid. Griffin gave himself up to the kiss, to being what River wanted and needed in that moment. He let River set the pace, have his fantasy of endless kisses and slow explorations. And it wasn't any sort of sacrifice. Lying back, being at River's whims freed him from his own head, took away the guesswork that had always been Griffin's least favorite part of sex.

Waiting to find out what River was in the mood for was like unwrapping a stack of presents, each one better than the last. After spending a long time stretched out on top of Griffin, kissing, River slid down, biting and licking Griffin's neck, getting more aggressive.

"Fuck. I missed that," Griffin groaned, stroking River's back.

"Missed you too. And the way I can almost get you off entirely from neck kissing." River smiled up at him, all sun after weeks of rain, and Griffin's heart caught all over again. Resuming his explorations, River seemed determined to drive Griffin out of his mind.

"Think it's not 'almost.'" Giving a pained laugh, he clutched at River. "Keep that up and I'm going to make a mess."

"Love that. But...not today." Eyes sparkling like a genie about to grant wishes, River sat up. "I've waited too long to have my way with you. Lose the pants."

He moved off Griffin long enough to shed his own jeans and riffle through Griffin's nightstand, tossing a condom and lube on the bed while Griffin scrambled out of his pants.

"Eager?" River pushed him back down on his back, straddled his waist again. "I like that."

"Come up here. Want to taste you, get you close."

"Oh, reducing you to putty turns me on plenty, trust me." River palmed Griffin's erection, apparently in no hurry to grant Griffin's request. "And this is my show, right?"

There was the barest hint of uncertainty in his voice, a vulnerability that touched Griffin on a deep and primal level and made him look River deep in the eyes, not joking when he said, "Always. Whatever you need."

"You. I need you." River's voice dropped to a whisper.

"You've got me." Rather than reaching for River, he laced his hands behind his head and rolled his spine, trying to show River that the control was all his.

"Fuck, you're sexy like that." River gave him a slow smile before he rolled a condom on Griff's cock. He had to count backward from one hundred to keep from coming when he smoothed on the lube, but he kept his hands where they were.

And his reward was getting to watch River's face as he slicked up his fingers and reached behind him. He was far more limber than Griffin, twisting like an X-rated yoga pose as he exhaled slowly.

"That's…yeah…" River moaned softly, almost as if the sound surprised him. "Fuck… Mmm…"

"God, I could come just watching you." Griffin's cock throbbed. Not asking to see or to help was killing Griffin in the best way.

"Better not." River gave him a stern stare. Shifting position slightly, he gripped Griffin's cock, lowering himself down with a slow exhale. His face was a mask of concentration, a mental photograph Griffin was never forgetting. "Little…more… Yeah…"

The narration was going to do Griffin in even more than the tight pressure against his cockhead. His thighs tensed with the need to thrust up, but he kept his hips pinned to the mattress, letting River control this.

"There…just…wait… Oh…" River's head fell back, exposing the long, graceful neck that had enchanted millions and that only Griffin got to see like this, tense, flushed with passion. His torso rippled, and he took a little more of Griffin's cock. Rocking back and forth, each shallow slide was easier than the last, but still Griffin didn't thrust.

"Can I touch your cock?" he asked, desperate to make River feel even a tenth as good as this was for him.

"Nuh-uh." Eyes tightly closed, River moaned low. "Let me…"

"Whatever. Whatever you need," Griffin promised.

"Yeah…" Hands moving to Griffin's chest, River dug his fingertips into Griffin's skin, a sharp edge that Griffin's dick apparently liked a great deal. He wasn't fully inside River, but his balls tightened and he had to break out the math tricks again to keep his orgasm at bay.

"Fuck." Riding a razor thin edge of not coming, he couldn't stop his needy moans from escaping. "Please."

"You wanna come? Gonna beg me?" Opening his eyes, River smiled, a cat who had his mouse exactly where he wanted it.

"Please." If it was begging he wanted, then it was begging he'd get. And with each moan, each plea, River slid a little further down. "Want you to go first."

"After," River said firmly. And okay, if that was what he truly wanted, Griffin wasn't in a position to argue. His body was all-in on giving River whatever he wanted.

"Close. Faster. Please." It wasn't going to take much—the tight heat clenching his dick was so damn good that even River's subtle rocking was almost enough friction. And when he smiled down at Griffin before speeding up, Griffin's heart was so full, it might burst even before he came. He was beyond caring—if this was how he went, so be it. What a way to go out.

Instead of fighting his too-big feelings about the moment, about this man, he gave in completely, let them swamp him.

"Need this. God. Love this." *Love you.* He didn't add that last one to his babbling, but oh, how he felt it.

"Come," River commanded, and Griffin was powerless to deny him. Climaxing without thrusting his hips, without grabbing River, without taking over, was a new thing for him. Somehow the holding back made the sensations that much more intense, centered everything first on his cock, then his abs and thighs, orgasm spreading out, a wave hitting the shore. Or maybe a glacier breaking free—the last of the ice he'd surrounded his heart with gone, leaving behind tender feelings that overwhelmed him even more than the orgasm.

"*Yes.*" River kept up his motion, riding Griffin through the climax, moaning along with him.

"Too much." Griffin meant the emotions as much as the physical sensations. But when River swung off him, he felt the loss of his presence immediately. River settled in with his head on Griffin's shoulder, one leg tossed over Griffin's as he reached for his own cock.

"Fuck. That was sexy." River was breathing hard, fist already moving fast.

"Let me." Finally stretching his arms out, Griffin brushed his hand out of the way, took over the stroke.

"Not gonna...take much..." River arched his back, as if he was seeking more of the contact, so Griffin gave it to him, tightening his grip. "Fuck. What a power trip."

"Yeah? You liked that?" Griffin pressed a kiss to his head.

"Mildly..." River gave a strained laugh. "Come on, come on. Faster."

"Want you to come." Griffin rolled slightly so that they could kiss properly. River met him with a desperate hunger, moaning and whimpering against Griffin's mouth as his hips bucked in time with Griffin's strokes. And then he was coming, coating Griffin's hand with it, and collapsing against Griffin.

"Oh hell." River yawned. "Too...sleepy..."

"You nap." Griffin took care of the condom and used a washcloth from the nightstand to clean them both up as good as he could. "Sleep. Then shower. Then I'll feed you."

"Stay." River yanked Griffin down next to him. "Don't get up."

"I won't." Griffin doubted he could sleep, but holding River was hardly a hardship, and he was more than happy to lie here, drifting on good feelings. There was nowhere he'd rather be than right here, right now. And he'd do whatever it took to make sure he got to stay in this happy cocoon. He had River, had a second chance, and he wasn't letting go.

* * *

"I could get used to this sort of service," River joked, but really he'd been in four-star spas and felt less pampered. Hair still damp from the shower, he was propped up against pillows on Griff's bed, tray of food in front of him, Griff sprawled next to him.

"Good." Griff gave him a goofy smile before returning to his own bowl of soup.

He supposed some might find Griff's caretaking to be too much hovering, but far from feeling smothered, he felt...*loved*. Oh, neither of them had said the words, but they'd hung between them all afternoon, there from that first kiss when River arrived, through the sex, all the way to this soup that Griff had made from one of River's mom's recipes. He was loved and he loved in return, and what had once seemed impossible and scary now just seemed cozy. Perfect even.

Like the sex had been. He'd started it as an experiment, a curiosity about what it would feel like with Griff, and ended up stripped down to his core, discovering far more about himself, about Griff, about *them* than he'd bargained for. He'd been fucked before, but this was nothing like that—part of it was how Griff had let him have total control, made him feel powerful and strong, and part of it was simply how he felt about Griff, which in turn made him feel differently about the act.

He doubted fucking was likely to become a huge part of their repertoire so to speak, but it had been... cathartic was probably the best word. Healing. And how lovely was it that they *could* have a repertoire, that they could look forward to a future with both routine and once-in-a-while sex.

"Do you work tomorrow?" he asked Griff, trying to keep his voice light.

"Yeah. Flight to Anchorage. You've got writing to do while I'm gone, right?"

"Yeah." River couldn't help his sigh. Even if the words were finally flowing, he still had a lot of catching up to do to make his deadlines. "I do."

"If you make me a list, I can get whatever you'd like for dinner while I'm there. You want to try another of the recipes?"

"Soup came out fabulous." Even if he was slightly impatient to execute one of his plans, he loved how simple and domestic this was, plotting meals and plans for the day. "Yeah, we can try something else, something simple that I won't burn if I help."

"Glad you like the soup. I made enough for dinner too." Griff laughed. "I'd say I'm a bad host, but I did get cupcakes as well."

"Hey, my mom's cooking *and* cake?" River did a pretend stern look. "Did you forget to tell me something? Is this is our last meal?"

"No, it's the *first* meal." Griff's look was decidedly tender. "At least I hope. You didn't tell me how long you think finalizing the book will take?"

River let out a groan. "I'm rewriting whole chunks of it. It's got a new title and everything."

"Oh? *Further Adventures of a Professional Nomad* didn't stick?"

"Nah. *Professional Nomad* will be followed by *Amateur Human* and it's still my North American adventures as planned, but the focus is more...personal. More honest."

"I'm sure your fans will love it no matter what." Griff's tone was cautious. "Am I in it?"

"Only if you want to be, but it would help if you said it was okay to do some mention of us. I'll let you read it first." He was proud of himself, doing two hard things back-to-back, asking Griff for permission to put him in the book, something he'd been stressing about for days, and offering to let someone read his rough draft, something he rarely did. But the more he'd thought about it, the more Griff and Alaska were at the center—the *heart*—of his more recent journey, the one that had brought him full circle to a place where he could contemplate having a home again. Realizing that the book needed to be less about finding adventure and more about finding himself, learning to stay put when it mattered most, had made all the difference and now even with all the rewriting that loomed, he was excited and energized.

"I want you to write the best you can for *you*. And if that means we're in it, then so be it. I'm sure we can find a way to keep certain things private."

"That sounds perfect." River liked the sound of that *we*, the idea that they'd work together to find some balance between Griff's private nature and River's need to explore everything that had changed for him. "But it's going to take some work to get the book ready. You're likely to get sick of me before I'm done."

"Not likely." Griff patted River's thigh. "I meant it when I said stay as long as you want. How long did you get the car rental for?"

"Uh." River gulped. He couldn't lie to a direct question. "I didn't. I bought it. Dad helped me figure out how to do it from LA. It worked out to a far better deal than paying the equivalent of a mortgage for a month's rental."

He knew he sounded a little defensive, but this had been a huge decision for him, and he wasn't sure what he'd do if Griff reacted badly.

"You bought a car? But isn't that the sort of commitment you hate? Didn't you tell me everything you own fits in a few boxes?"

"Yes, well, now it can fit in my car. And now I really can stay as long as I—*we*—want. As long as you'll have me, that is."

"Of course I'll have you." Griff moved the tray out of the way so that he could pull River snugly against him. "Don't be silly. But I don't want to tie you to this area, make you change your lifestyle. I like you exactly how you are. You don't have to prove anything to me by making it through an Alaskan winter or something like that."

"But how else will I get to unwrap you in January?" Fake pouting was easier than admitting how very much this meant to him. But Griff deserved his truth as well. "And I know. I know you don't want to change me. That's what makes it easier to admit that I do want a change. For me."

"As long as it's for *you*." Griff kissed his neck.

"It is. I thought going back to Jersey would be going home, but it wasn't. I'm glad I reconnected with my dad, but it wasn't a homecoming. All it did was make me miss here more. I'm not saying it's *home*, not yet, but I think it could be, and I want to stay long enough to find out." Getting all that out made his pulse race and he had to look away, wipe his sweaty palms on the blanket.

"Hey." Turning River's face back toward him, Griff looked him deep in the eyes. "I want that too. It's funny. I've lived most of my life here, but it feels like I've been waiting for home too—a place to call my own. I thought maybe the military would give me that, but it didn't. And coming back here gave me my life back, but it wasn't quite home."

"It wasn't?" he whispered. Griff was so firmly tied to this area, it was hard not to see it as his home.

"No. It wasn't until I met you that I realized that maybe it wasn't a place I was wanting all along but a person. Someone to call my own. If home can be a person, then you're mine."

"Really?"

"Really." Giving River a soft kiss, Griff held him close for a long moment before gently pulling away. "Can I show you something?"

"Yeah." River's head swam, ears ringing like he'd taken a fall. And maybe he had. Down the rabbit hole to where this was really happening, where this was his life, his future.

Rushing over to the bookcase, Griff returned with one of his sketchbooks—not one of the coloring books, but a blank pages book with simple blue binding. "This is silly—"

"No, it isn't." River knew instinctively that whatever it was, it was far from silly.

"I was playing around the other night, and I drew this." He opened to a set of pages in the middle of the book.

"It's your cabin." River liked the simple brown wood exterior a lot, liked how Griff had done both a front and side view, and then there was a floor plan followed by interior sketches.

"See? It's a little bigger than I was originally thinking." Griff's neck had flushed red, and his voice was strained. "Here's the master bedroom, with its own little porch, and a bathroom with a giant shower, as per request."

"I love it." River traced a finger over the sketch of the bathroom, trying to will it into existence. "And is that a hot tub on the porch?"

"Yeah. And see this one? This one is the upstairs loft." Griff pointed at another sketch. "I've got another room to be my computer room with photography stuff for me, but this is something I just added. See, there's a desk in front of a window and a chaise in the corner and bookshelves…"

"I see." It was entirely possible that River was going to expire from the sheer force of want.

"I thought maybe it would make a good spot to write." Griff's voice was shy, uncertain. "Not that you can't write anywhere—"

"I could write there," River said slowly, testing the words out. "I think I really could."

"Yeah?" Griff's eyes reflected back every ounce of hope surging through River. "I mean, this is still a ways off. Not next week or anything. But maybe, if I sell some photos, do a few more photography tours next summer…"

"I want to help." He'd come here to say exactly that, had hatched the plan back in Jersey, had wanted to tell Griff when he'd appeared in LA, but making himself speak was hard. That was why he'd been antsy about Griff's plans for tomorrow—he was eager to drive around, see potential places. But wanting was far easier than saying. "I've got money. And I haven't paid rent in years. I've been thinking about this a lot, and I'd like... I want to invest in your cabin plans."

"Really?" Griff's expression was impossible to read—slack mouth, open eyes, strong jaw. "Like... a partnership? Like you want to go in with me on the land?"

"Exactly. A partnership is a good way to put it. But more than that... Griff, I want to make your dreams come true. You've let me have dreams again for the first time in forever, have plans and not be scared by them. And I want to make your dreams—this dream—come true."

"You already have." Griff's voice was rough. "You've made dreams I didn't even know I had come true just by being here with me, giving us a chance. You're the dream, not the cabin."

"Yeah, but you gotta admit, that shower would be sweet..." River couldn't help teasing, even as his sinuses burned and he had to blink hard.

"It would, but only if you're in it." Grabbing River's hand, Griff brought it to his lips, pressed a kiss to the palm. "I mean that. And the dream works if you're there part-time. I've been thinking about that, too. If you need to travel, have adventures, I get that. I'll be right here for you when you make it back."

"I think being here together will be its own adventure." River stroked Griff's scruffy jaw. "A new chapter for me, very literally. And I think there are a lot of adventures we can have in this region—camping, hiking, exploring. But I get what you're saying. If I travel, having a place to come back to…that'll be brand-new. Its own kind of adventure."

"It will. I want all that." Griff leaned in for a fast kiss. "And I'm not ruling out occasionally going with you—you and the last few months have proved to me that I'm stronger than I thought, that it's not this place or this routine that keeps me on a sober path, but *me*. My choices. My actions. And I might never like cities, but I'm not afraid anymore, and that's a big deal to me."

"To me too." River sagged against Griff. "I was so afraid of stopping, of who I'd be if I stayed in one place. And now… Now, I want to see. I mean I'm pretty sure I'll still be a mess part of the time—"

"We both will. And that's okay." Griff held him close, as if he got that River was about to shake apart from all this emotion.

"Maybe it's not that we're perfect for each other. But that we're imperfect—this is a place where I don't have to be perfect. And you don't either. And we don't have to be perfect together."

"Exactly. I don't want just one part of you. I want it all. The good, the messy, the hidden—all of it. I want *you*."

"I want you too." River gave in to the urge to kiss him then, because the alternative was the tears that kept threatening to escape. And that would be okay. He trusted Griff enough to trust him with his tears now, but he didn't want to cry right then.

He wanted to celebrate, to take joy in what they were building here together, the possibility of what they could become over time. In who he'd be when he let himself have this. And as they kissed, he knew, deep inside, that he'd like that self, that rather than strangling him like he'd always feared, roots would make him stronger. Maybe it was only by putting down some roots that he'd truly bloom, and, he couldn't wait to find out.

Chapter Twenty-Six

Five months later

Griffin tugged at his tie, already ready to lose it.

"It was a lovely wedding." River put the same lilt on *lovely* that he always did, and suddenly Griffin's collar was tight for a whole different reason. "Did you get the pictures you wanted?"

"Some. It's not like there's a shortage of photographers here." He had to laugh because there had been enough flashbulbs for one of River's glitzy Hollywood parties even though they were at a rustic inn on Kachemak Bay with only a few dozen people in attendance, most of whom he was related to in one way or another.

And all of whom he'd escaped, finding this quiet balcony overlooking the main reception below them, letting him collect his thoughts. The party was barely organized chaos—all the nieces and nephews racing around in fancy clothes and his coworkers jostling and joking alongside his siblings and their spouses. He'd needed a minute after he'd finished getting pictures of the cake cutting. Not that he'd minded River finding him terribly much. He'd brought a slice of cake and two forks and made himself all cozy on the little couch next to Griffin.

"No one's going to care if you take it off. You did your best man duties." River reached over and tugged Griffin's tie loose. "I still can't believe your mother decided on a Valentine's Day wedding."

"Oh, I'm pretty sure Uncle Roger did some fancy persuading on that one after he didn't get the Christmas wedding he'd been angling for." But somehow he had gotten a Christmas Eve engagement out of Griffin's mother, which had been followed by epic negotiations leading them here to this moment fifty years in the making.

Below them, Griffin's mother laughed and picked up one of the smaller kids. Her long hair was elegantly wound around her head and studded with hothouse flowers Griffin had picked up himself in Anchorage the day before. She wore a pale gray dress that matched the silver strands in her hair and a pink sash that matched the blush in her cheeks anytime Roger looked her direction. Griffin had never seen her more radiant or beautiful than when she said her vows.

"Some things are worth waiting for." River bumped shoulders, smiling up at him. "Like spring."

"It's coming." Griffin had to laugh because as he'd predicted, River had been over the novelty of an Alaskan winter sometime in January and they still had a minimum of another two months to go.

"I'm not pining for a tropical island," River assured him. "Or okay, not *much.* I'm just impatient for the ground breaking. Now that the papers are all signed, I just want them to get started."

"Me too." After much searching, they'd finally settled on a parcel of land, almost five acres, with a creek running through it, a nice natural rise with a view of the inlet, and a long winding drive that further separated the land from its nearest neighbors. "I almost want to frame the plans the architect sent over last week."

"I can't believe she captured so much of your drawings." River beamed. He'd been in his element all weekend, helping with all the little details like the tin plane centerpieces and feeding off the parties and celebrations. But still taking time for quiet moments with Griffin, like this here. Griffin liked to think of himself as kind of a human charging station for River, a place where he went to get his energy back up and to get centered.

"Even the shower." Griffin winked meaningfully at him.

"And the writing nook. Not that I'm ever writing again." River sighed dramatically.

"You'll write again. You're just burnt out from edits." Griffin wrapped an arm around him. After much revision and back-and-forth with his editor, *Amateur Human* had a final draft and publication date. The media tour loomed large in Griffin's mind because he couldn't completely shut off worry about how River would cope, but he knew the house plans would be a good distraction for him, and he planned to pepper him with pictures and updates. "You already sold the next book to your editor. And spent the advance. You'll write."

"Yeah. Eventually." River's editor had fallen in love with *Novice Homesteader,* River's idea for a book chronicling the house build and other Alaskan adven-

tures. And seeing as how they'd pooled their savings
for buying the land and securing the construction loan,
Griffin was rather invested in keeping his writer writing.

"Speaking of burnout, I got you a present."

"A present?" River's eyes went wide.

"It is Valentine's Day," Griffin reminded him, fishing in his pocket for the folded paper he'd put there.
"Sorry there's no card."

"It's okay. My present for you is in the nightstand.
Not wrapped." River waggled his eyebrows.

"I can't wait to see." A happy shiver raced up his
spine as he handed River the paper. Whatever it was, it
would be fun. And yes, he could have fun these days.
Lots of it in fact. He'd gone from being afraid of fun,
of what it meant, to embracing it with River. Because
life with him wasn't all seriousness. It couldn't be.
They needed the fun parts too, both in bed and out of
it. He'd discovered the unique pleasure of giving River
impromptu hikes and snow machine treks and learned
what it meant to accept fun back.

"Tickets to Tucson?" River turned the paper around,
almost as if he expected the letters to rearrange themselves on him.

"You've had enough snow. You deserve a little sun
break, and it's sort of a working trip for me." Neck
heating, he looked down at his polished boots.

"It is?" River blinked.

"One of the buyers from the Anchorage show has a
vacation home in Arizona. Snowbird retirees and all
that. He put me in contact with a gallery owner friend
there. They offered to show some of my photographs,
but they want do a little reception thing." He couldn't

keep the nerves out of his voice. "So, you get a short vacation and getaway from the snow, and I get you when I freak out about the show."

"You'll do fine. The Anchorage show went great and so will this one." River kissed his cheek. He wasn't wrong—most of Griffin's pieces had sold out the night of the opening, and thanks to Roger's contacts, he had shows later in the spring in Seattle and Vancouver. "And thank you. A trip does sound good. Maybe we can even do a spa day…"

"*You* can do a spa day. Get a massage. Do your hair a fun color for spring or something." River had gone back to light brown for the winter, but Griffin found that he kind of missed the various shades of blue.

"I might. But you should come too."

"Maybe you can talk me into a haircut before the show," he allowed.

"And let me pick the clothes at least?"

"What? I can't wear plaid in the desert?" He pretended to shudder.

"No." River kissed his neck, biting lightly right below Griffin's collar. "And now I'm feeling bad. You got me a whole trip and my present is much sillier."

"I love silly. And you." He meant both things— River had made him rediscover the parts of him that liked fun and silly teasing and little games. And he did love River, with everything he had. Sometimes he thought about Hank, about the years he'd spent pining. And that had been love of a kind too, but it was nothing compared to what he felt for River, what they'd built together in just a few short months. He'd never fully understood what a difference having feelings returned would make.

"Love you too." River had a tendency to whisper the words, which Griffin kind of liked—it was as if the words were still new and special to him too. Like he didn't want to say it too loudly and risk scaring them away. Which wasn't going to happen. Griffin wasn't going anywhere.

"How much longer until we can escape do you think?"

"Eager much for my surprise?" River met him in a quick, light kiss.

"Eager for *you*." Not letting River get away, Griffin deepened the kiss. Let the party swirl around below them, happy voices echoing. Let himself escape into the special space they made for each other, the place that only existed when they were together like this. River had given him so much that he'd thought he'd left behind forever—fun, adventure, silliness, companionship, caring, love. Griffin might be the pilot, but River was the one who had taught him to fly on wings he hadn't even realized he possessed. And now he couldn't wait to see where those wings carried them next.

* * * * *

To find out more about Annabeth Albert's upcoming releases, contests, and free bonus reads, please sign up for her newsletter here or eepurl.com/Nb9yv.

Acknowledgments

A huge thank-you to my agent, Deidre Knight, who believed in this project from my first excited ramblings and to Carina Press for giving it a splendid home. I love my whole Carina Press team, especially my editor, Deb Nemeth, who always manages to find the right way to make me dig deeper, polish harder, and search out the core of the story. I appreciate her so much. And the rest of the team is pretty darn awesome too—thank you to the art department for my fabulous covers and the hardworking PR team as well as all those behind the scenes and in management.

This book couldn't exist without my amazing writer friends. I am so grateful to Camp NaNoWriMo's July efforts as my cabin sustained me with their love, support, and enthusiasm. Erin McLellan and Karen Kiely provided me with amazing Alaska resources and invaluable beta feedback. Edie Danford, Karen Stivali, and a very special anon reader also provided fabulous beta assistance. Wendy Qualls is my plotting buddy, and Layla Reyne keeps me sane with writing sprints and friendship. To all my writing friends, thank you so much for being there. I cannot name you all, but you enrich my life so much. Thank you for the gift of your time, wisdom, and friendship.

I also have the best readers in the world. My reader's group, Annabeth's Angels on Facebook, provides joy for my life in ways I never could have imagined. Thank you to all my readers, all around the world. Every mention, share, like, retweet, word of mouth, purchase, note, and other support means the world to me. Thank you to my readers for taking a chance on this new series and new adventure with me!

Finally, thank you to my friends and family who love me and stand by me no matter what. I'm only able to do this because of you.

*Coming soon from Carina Press and
Annabeth Albert:*

*After a freewheeling bush pilot with a family
counting on him finds himself at the mercy of the
silver fox corporate lawyer he's stranded with,
neither expects the sparks that fly. But for their
fledgling passion to have any sort of future, each
will need more than near-death realizations to forge
a path forward.*

Read on for a preview of
Arctic Wild,
*book two in Annabeth Albert's new
Frozen Hearts series.*

Chapter One

"What do you mean she's not coming?" Reuben tried to catch his breath after the long dash from the security checkpoint to the gate for his flight. While waiting for Craig to explain this turn of events, he slipped off his suit jacket. He wouldn't ordinarily wear a suit for a long day of travel, but after an early morning meeting ran late he'd had no time to change.

"She just called. Someone leaked the Henderson Motors buyout news, so now they're having to work double time to both get the deal done and find the source of the leak. Heads are going to roll, and she's on the warpath. You know Leticia. Damn it." Craig looked both impressed by his spouse's reputation and ready to kick something. "And now I've taken a week off to spend time with my wife—no offense, Rube—and she's going to be in meetings while I'm four time zones away with no cell coverage. Fuck this. Last three vacations we've planned have all either been canceled or turned into working trips."

"I know." Reuben wasn't sure what else to say. This whole trip had been Craig's idea. Ever since another partner at Reuben's law firm had returned from seeing his adult kid in Alaska, Craig had been full steam

ahead on the idea of going on an Arctic wilderness adventure and had settled on Reuben's impending birthday as an excuse to drag him along. The argument
that Reuben and Leticia worked too hard at their law
firm was an old one, and Craig had made a passionate
case for the trip. He'd also lobbied for Reuben bringing someone along, but that plan had fallen through
when Dan broke up with Reuben around Passover. Still
smarting from that dismissal, Reuben had no desire
to bring someone just for the sake of not being a third
wheel. And zero time to date. That too.

"I seriously don't know what to do anymore. We
never see each other, and when I do see her, she's
shackled to her cell or laptop." Craig rocked back and
forth on the balls of his feet. "My marriage is crum-
bling, and hell if I know how to save it."

Reuben was the absolute last person to hand out relationship advice, but he tried for a sympathetic tone.
"Do you want to just forget the whole thing?"

"You'd love that, wouldn't you?" Craig's eye roll
was worthy of Reuben's teen daughter, not a forty-
something corporate event planner. Unlike Reuben, he
was dressed more casually in a pullover and khakis and
his rumpled hair suggested he'd spent more time that
morning worrying about his wife than his appearance.
"More time to work for you. But, no, much as I want
to run after my wife, we can't completely cancel. This
is the family company that Vale kid's boyfriend works
for. They're counting on our business, and it would be
beyond rude if all three of us back out. And it's your
birthday in two days. Come on, Rube, you seriously
want to turn what…forty-eight this year in an office
with a stack of papers in front of you?"

"Eh. It's just another day." Reuben shrugged. And really, it was. He wasn't a big sentimental guy. Amelia, his daughter, had made noises about skipping her end-of-the-year eighth grade field trip to spend the day with him, but he'd insisted she go with her class. It was simply another number on the calendar for him, but Craig loved making productions about holidays. And unlike Reuben, Craig was obsessed with how close to fifty they both were now, something Reuben really tried not to stop and think about. "And I'm not saying to cancel for *me*. You're going to be miserable. If you stay, at least you can try to see Leticia when she's free, maybe go out to dinner, catch a show with your time off. Staycation or whatever. Try to talk to her, maybe."

"You're not wrong." Craig slumped against a nearby concrete column. "I really do want to save this thing before it's too late. But I know you. If I say I'm not going, you're going to back out as well. And then you'll be at your desk on your birthday."

"Priority boarding for flight 435 to Seattle-Tacoma should begin shortly," a female flight attendant announced over the loudspeaker. Fuck. Not much time to argue with Craig, who was clearly spoiling for a fight.

"Let me worry about my birthday. If I say I'll go ahead and go, would that help?"

"You'd really do that? Go to Alaska without either of us?"

"Is it really that big of a deal?" Reuben didn't like Craig's implication that he'd be helpless on his own. "Sure, it's a long flight, but I did Brisbane and Tokyo last year, Jakarta the year before. Did Europe with Natalie back when we were together, more than once. It's not like I'm a stranger to travel. And there's a guide, right?"

"Yeah, but this is roughing it. Bush planes and national parks."

"Which you were all for a few weeks ago," Reuben reminded him.

"Yeah, I was. And I'm still pissed to have to miss it. Damn Henderson news. So you'll do it?" Craig didn't bother to disguise his skeptical once-over, eyes traveling over Reuben's suit and his leather carry-on.

True, Reuben wasn't exactly dressed for Alaska, but he drew himself up to his full height and gave his friend his best hard stare, the one that usually sent first-year associates scurrying for their desks. "Sure."

Now going felt almost like a point of pride. If Craig really thought he wasn't up to the task or would chicken out, something ridiculous, he'd forgotten who Reuben was. One of the most sought-after corporate lawyers in the tristate region, a fixer with a reputation he'd honed for twenty-five years now. Partner in a large firm with an impeccable reputation for getting the job done. He didn't shy away from challenges. Sure, he'd rather do almost anything other than fly to Anchorage today, but he was perfectly capable of going, making Vale happy—which might give him an ally in the current management drama at the firm—and proving Craig wrong at the same time. Win-win.

"Okay. *Okay.* Thank you." Craig smiled for the first time since Reuben had shown up, but it was a tentative grin with none of his usual confidence.

Reuben clapped him on the shoulder. "I'll handle this. You handle your relationship. I've got faith you guys can get through this." He tried to put conviction behind his words. Granted, his own relationships seldom survived his career, but he did believe Craig and Leticia were good for each other. If anyone could make the never-ending work and life balance thing work, it would be them.

"Yeah. And who knows, maybe this will be good for you. A nice escape on your own. Tell me you're not bringing work."

"Just for the flight," Reuben lied. He figured with a string of boring nights ahead of him, he could get through a backlog of document reading as long as he had power. But Craig would scoff at that plan.

"Socialize. Chat up the guide. Hike. Enjoy yourself."

"Now boarding for our first class and priority members for Flight 435 service to Seattle-Tacoma."

"That would be me," Reuben said, mainly to avoid more life advice from Craig. "Take care of Leticia."

"Okay, will do. I'll message the guide, tell him it'll only be you."

"You do that." Reuben forced himself to smile and not grimace at the sudden realization that he and this tourist guide were about to be stuck with each other, like it or not. Probably some grizzled old mountain man pilot, older than Reuben, like those guys on the reality show Dan had made him watch an episode or two of. Maybe he'd be the strong but silent—please God *silent*—type and leave Reuben to his reading in peace. Yes. That would be perfect. If the guide kept to himself and didn't expect much out of him, maybe this whole thing wouldn't be so terrible.

"So, the bear is like *right* there, staring us down, near the doors to the plane, and we need to take off soon to get the folks back in time for their flights home. And what you think we did next?" Toby deliberately widened his eyes and leaned forward, enjoying how the two other patrons at the hotel bar did the same thing.

He hadn't yet figured out whether the two young out-of-towners were brother and sister, friends, or a couple, but he did love a captive audience, and they were an excellent distraction while he waited for this week's client to show. Client, singular, because apparently one of the other two was some high-powered super attorney who'd bailed on the Alaska vacation at the last possible minute. And knowing how lawyers loved to nickel and dime people, he had no doubt the missing two would suggest that a refund was in order. A personalized private bush plane tour wasn't cheap, and Toby had been counting on his percentage of the take from three tourists, not one. One who was late at that.

"Drink?" The bartender asked a well-dressed man walking up to the bar area right as Toby was about to continue his story. Given that the dude certainly looked like he could afford Toby's services even as his pricey duds hardly looked ready for the back country, Toby got off his stool and moved away from the eager duo.

"Not yet. I'm meeting someone." The guy had an East Coast accent with a tone that said he was used to being listened to. He looked around, distracted, eyes scanning right past Toby. *Typical.* Thousand-dollar suit and not the sense of a reindeer.

"Mr. Graham?" Toby stuck out a hand. He was wearing an official Barrett Tours polo—new this season because his boss was never going to stop dreaming up expansion plans—and clean jeans but he still felt decidedly unkempt next to this guy's smooth elegance. He supposed some people would call the guy a silver fox—older, distinguished face, well-trimmed facial scruff and full head of silver-tinged hair—but silver *bear* might be more accurate, given his height, broad shoulders, and overall bulk. Older didn't usually do it for Toby, but he had to admit the guy was hot in that aging-movie-star, rich-dude sort of way. "I'm Tobias Kooly, your guide. Glad you made it."

"Call me Reuben, please." He shook Toby's hand— nice firm grip, large hand, the sort of confidence Toby associated with a guy who got things done. "This is supposed to be a vacation—I can be Mr. Graham back in the office. And since it's just us, we might as well be informal."

"You've got it. My friends mainly call me Toby. And speaking of friends, I'm sorry yours couldn't make it. Man, passing on a vacation to stay in the office. Can't imagine doing that. But lawyers, right?"

Reuben did a slow blink, the sort of thing that immediately told Toby he'd screwed up. "I'm a lawyer too. And yes, these things happen. Way too often, actually. Millions—possibly billions—are on the line in the deal Leticia stayed behind for."

"Oh, sorry." Fuck it. He didn't usually suffer from foot-in-mouth disease, but he'd clearly gone for the wrong tone here. Not the start he wanted. "Didn't mean to be flip. And I thought my boss said you were an events planner."

"No, that's Leticia's husband." Reuben's sigh made Toby feel like he hadn't done a good enough job listening to Annie's run-down of the clients. "And good that you mentioned *boss* as I suppose you have some paperwork for me? Waivers and such? We might as well get that over with."

"I do." Toby grabbed his folder off the bar. The guy sounded like Toby was offering a colonoscopy, not a week of fun, which meant Toby was going to have to work harder than usual to make a good impression. "But you're probably starving. Let's grab a table. It's dinnertime here, but you're a bunch of hours ahead. We usually tell people to come a day or so early to get acclimated to the time change."

"We didn't have that kind of time." Reuben followed Toby to a nearby table, but cast a glance over his shoulder at the other tourists. "You don't need to finish up with your...friends?"

Damn it. Not that Toby had been doing anything wrong, having a soda to kill time and getting a little bit of flirt on, but Reuben made him feel like he'd been goofing off on the clock.

"Nah. Let's get you some food." He did spare a smile and a little wave for the other tourists though, just to prove he wasn't a total ass, raising his voice to say, "Sorry. Business calls." The duo waved back and returned to their drinks.

Reuben had the sort of distant but respectful manner with the server that Toby had come to expect from rich people, fussing over the wine list but not dipping into rude territory. Toby stuck with his soda and ordered the burger he always got when meeting clients at the hotel. He could expense his food, but he tried not to take advantage of that. He'd leave the steak and garlic mashed potatoes to Reuben, who also ordered a red wine with a name Toby wasn't even going to try to pronounce.

"Thanks for suggesting food." Reuben cut his meat into small, precise bites. "The options on the plane were decidedly lacking."

"Your friends did tell you that most of the meals on the trip are fairly rustic, right?" Toby didn't want him getting his expectations up that all meals would be this nice. "It's all small local lodges and simple but hearty meals. Some of the lodges have wine or beer, but the selection is usually limited."

"I'll be fine." Reuben waved Toby's concern away. "I grew up in Brooklyn on very basic fare. I'm not a picky eater."

"Good." Toby pulled out the paperwork Annie had sent, glancing down at the itinerary before handing it to Reuben. "I'm planning to stick mainly to what we worked out for the three of you, but you can tell me if you don't want to do something, and we can change it up."

"Excellent. I'm sure Craig and your boss came up with a good plan, but I don't mind more downtime. I brought plenty to keep me busy."

"I can't guarantee Wi-Fi at most of the stops." This wouldn't be Toby's first corporate client who couldn't disconnect from work, and explaining the limited cell and internet service was never fun.

"I expected that. I preloaded plenty of reading on my laptop, which has a long battery life."

"That should be okay. Most places have electricity." Personally, Toby couldn't see the value of bringing a stack of work on a once-in-a-lifetime vacation. And why look at a laptop instead of the scenery? But he nodded anyway. He knew better than to argue with a client. If Reuben wanted to work the trip away, so be it. "We leave first thing in the morning—it's an early start, which is why we usually meet up the night before. But you did have a long trip in. Do you want me to try to push the flight plan back?"

"Don't be ridiculous." Reuben's stare had a hard edge to it, a man who would not stand for coddling, which Toby could respect. The look also made his insides heat, an unexpected spark of arousal—commanding didn't usually turn his crank, but as he was in the midst of something of a dry spell, he supposed even hot, older, presumably straight silver bears could get his motor humming.

"Sorry." He looked away, not wanting to reveal his line of thinking—this was not a guy who would take kindly to being Toby's eye candy for the week.

"I'm used to long days. As long as there's coffee, I'll be perfectly fine."

"There will be time to grab coffee before we head to the seaplane," Toby assured him.

Dinner almost finished, Reuben took a long sip of his wine. "Now, about that paperwork? I really should think about checking my email."

The man had to be exhausted and in dire need of sleep, but Toby had a feeling this guy would never admit such mundane needs. So Toby focused on getting him to sign the necessary waivers. Exactly like every other lawyer Toby had ever met, Reuben took his sweet time reading the waivers, frown lines deepening with each page until finally he let out a mighty *harrumph.*

"Not your doing, but your boss needs better boilerplate." Reuben shook his head.

"I can't take you up in the plane unless you sign." Toby had been down this road before with clients who wanted to cross out sections or write in others. Someone please save him from the rich and picky.

"Fine. Guess I'm putting my life in your hands." Reuben signed, and Toby's insides did a weird shimmy, like maybe he didn't want that responsibility, didn't want the possibility of letting this man down.

"Thank you." Toby took cell pictures of the signed documents for Annie and also returned them to his folder so she'd have a hard copy for her records.

"So…" Reuben sat back in his chair, not in the apparent hurry to get up to his room that Toby would have figured. "How does the story end? What did you do to the bear?"

Damn it all to hell. Reuben *had* heard that part of Toby's story. And ordinarily, it wouldn't be that big of a deal and he'd give Reuben the same dramatic ending he'd been planning for the young tourists, but there was something about this guy that simply kept him from lying or showboating. It wasn't the suit or the expensive shoes and haircut—Toby had told tales for many a rich client before. Maybe it was Reuben's intense stare— the one that said he was listening, really listening and didn't want to be disappointed. Or the set of his jaw, like he'd recognize a lie for what it was and judge it accordingly. Whatever it was, for a change, Toby didn't feel comfortable with his usual bragging.

"Not a thing," he admitted, truth spilling out. "Made the tourists wait behind me, and we gave the bear space, let him lumber away. You don't mess with bears. We were late taking off, but I made up time in the air, and they still caught their flight home."

And they'd tipped well, happy to have such an exciting adventure and close call with nature that they

could tell their friends about. Boring, predictable ending, but when it came down to it, Toby would rather
keep the clients alive rather than have a moment of
glory. Of course, he was damn good at editing in those
moments of heroism when picking people up or when
a group needed a good story. But Reuben didn't need
to know *all* his tricks.

"I see." As it was, Reuben raised a manicured eyebrow, narrowed eyes saying that he knew Toby had
been planning a different ending for his audience earlier, but he didn't call him on it, continuing with a more
casual tone. "I'm good with letting the wildlife have
its space. Not big on animals."

"All animals? No pets?"

"No." He shrugged, showing off his broad shoulders
and the way the expensive suit fabric clung to them.
"Never had the time or the inclination, really."

"That's too bad." Toby had a sudden vision of Reuben with a big old mutt of a dog, tracking mud all over
everything. Yup. That image just didn't fit this cultured
man at all. And why that made Toby a little sad, he
couldn't quite pinpoint. Reuben didn't have a wedding
ring on, and the idea of going home alone to a quiet
house every night simply didn't sit well. Toby needed
some chaos to feel truly at home himself.

"I really should get to checking my messages, see
what can't wait." Reuben stood, and after making arrangements to meet at the front desk in the morning,
Toby let him head to his room under the email pretense.
Honestly, though, he hoped the guy slept. Tomorrow
was going to be a long day, and a grumpy, tired lawyer who already kept looking like he'd rather be anywhere else was only going to make Toby's job that

much harder. And without the other two paying clients, Toby really did need to score that tip at the end, try to offset the possible loss in income if Annie ended up giving a refund to Reuben's friends. It might be a long week, but one way or another, Toby was going to win Reuben over, get him to enjoy himself. He'd tackled far bigger challenges than one prickly lawyer.

* * * * *

Don't miss
Arctic Wild *by Annabeth Albert,*
coming June 2019 wherever
Carina Press ebooks are sold.
www.CarinaPress.com

About the Author

Annabeth Albert grew up sneaking romance novels under the bedcovers. Now, she devours all subgenres of romance out in the open—no flashlights required! When she's not adding to her keeper shelf, she's a multi-published Pacific Northwest romance writer. The #OutOfUniform series joins her critically acclaimed and fan-favorite LGBTQ romance #Gaymers, #PortlandHeat and #PerfectHarmony series. To find out what she's working on next and other fun extras, check out her website: *www.annabethalbert.com* or connect with Annabeth on Twitter, Facebook, Instagram, and Spotify! Also, be sure to sign up for her newsletter for free ficlets, bonus reads, and contests. The fan group, Annabeth's Angels, on Facebook is also a great place for bonus content and exclusive contests.

Emotionally complex, sexy, and funny stories are her favorites both to read and to write. Annabeth loves finding happy endings for a variety of pairings and particularly loves uncovering unique main characters. In her personal life, she works a rewarding day job and wrangles two active children.

Newsletter: *http://eepurl.com/Nb9yv*

Fan group: *https://www.facebook.com/groups/annabethsangels/*